Praise for *New Yor*

BRENDA JOYCE's

Masters of Time series

"For intense emotions, power-packed writing, alpha males and building sexual tension, Joyce is unrivaled. In the second installment of the Masters of Time she lures us into the seductive world of good and evil as the brotherhood of the Masters fights demonic powers. She grabs and holds you a willing captive from the opening until the very end."
—*Romantic Times BOOKreviews* on *Dark Rival*

"Her world of Healers and Masters is rich and the plot well-handled.... The supporting characters are excellent, the sex scenes are plentiful...and the plot thick, making this sophomore series entry a fine entertainment, sure to gratify fans of the bestselling kickoff."
—*Publishers Weekly* on *Dark Rival*

"Bestselling author Joyce kicks off her Masters of Time series with a master's skill, instantly elevating her to the top ranks of the ever-growing list of paranormal romance authors. Steeped in action and sensuality, populated by sexy warriors and strong women, graced with lush details and a captivating story...superlative."
—*Publishers Weekly,* starred review, on *Dark Seduction*

"A powerfully emotional, ingenious novel about a world peopled with characters that completely capture your imagination. The pages sing with excitement, drama and passion. Joyce sets the standard for otherworldly lovers."
—*Romantic Times BOOKreviews* on *Dark Seduction*

Also by *New York Times* bestselling author

BRENDA JOYCE

The Masters of Time series

Dark Rival

Dark Seduction

The de Warenne Dynasty

A Dangerous Love

The Perfect Bride

A Lady at Last

The Stolen Bride

The Masquerade

The Prize

Watch for the upcoming Masters of Time novels

Dark Victory

March 2009

Dark Lover

September 2009

DARK EMBRACE

ISBN-13: 978-0-373-77334-3
ISBN-10: 0-373-77334-X

DARK EMBRACE

This edition published by arrangement with Harlequin Books S.A.

www.HQNBooks.com

Printed in U.S.A.

This one's for all of you who have supported
my new series, The Masters of Time,
with so much incredible enthusiasm!
Thank you!

Once again I must give my sincere thanks to
Laurel Letherby, without whom I'd be lost
in every possible way. I also want to thank my editor
Miranda Stecyk for her phenomenal editing—especially
her line editing, which is the best I've ever had.
Please, keep on cutting!

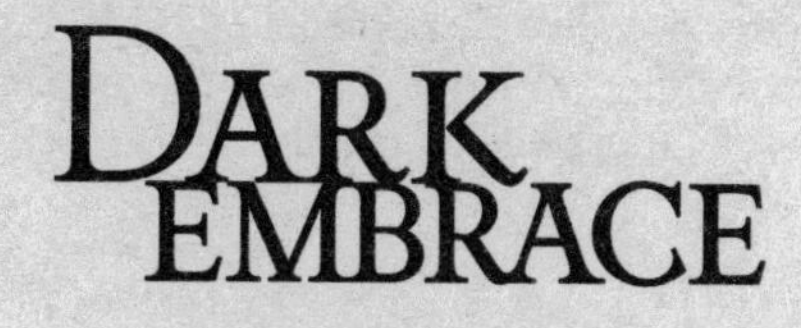

PROLOGUE

Loch Awe, Scotland, 1436

"A HIGHLANDER WITH NO CLAN, no father but Satan's spawn and ye still war for land? 'Tis not the land ye need, Lismore," Argyll spat. "Ye need a father and a soul."

Aidan of Awe trembled with rage, the glen behind him filled with the dead and the dying. His Campbell rival sawed on his steed's reins and smiled savagely, clearly aware he had delivered the final blow that day, and galloped off toward his departing army.

Aidan breathed hard, blue eyes flashing. His breath was warm in the cold winter air, hanging there like the smoke from the camp's fires. He could not know if Argyll had chosen his words with care or not. It was not a secret that he was a bastard, born in rape and shame. Still, when his father was alive, he had been the king's favorite and the Defender of the Realm. Aidan realized he could turn over Argyll's meaning a hundred times and never decide if the man knew the entire black truth about the Earl of Moray. But in these dark and bloody times, only the most foolish of men would be oblivious to the war between good and evil that raged across the world, and the Campbell was no fool. Perhaps he knew of the matters secretly spoken of betwixt the Masters and the gods.

He turned now to stare at the last of the warring men, his leine soaking wet and clinging to his muscular body. His men were all Highlanders and they'd fought mostly on foot, with long and broad swords, with daggers and pikes. They were dirty, tired, bloody—and loyal to him. Men had died for him that day. The snow was red with their blood—and that of the Campbells.

Aidan took up his stallion's reins. His men were returning from the glen, trudging tiredly toward him, their larger weapons heaved over shoulders, the wounded being helped by their comrades. Still, every man smiled and nodded at him as they passed. He spoke or nodded to each in turn, to let each man know he was grateful for their arms and valor.

Tents were raised and cook fires started. Aidan handed his stallion off to a young, hopeful Highland lad, when he felt a frisson of alarm. The emotion came from afar, but the vibration went entirely through him.

In that instant, he knew that the fear he sensed came from his son, who was safely at home.

Or so he had thought.

With his seven senses, he pinpointed Ian. His son remained at Castle Awe, where he had left him.

He did not hesitate. He vanished into time.

It took a very brief moment to be flung through time and space back to Castle Awe. The leap ripped him through the forest, pine branches tearing at him, and then past the rock-strewn, snow-tipped mountaintops, through white stars and bright suns, with such terrible gut-wrenching force and speed that he wanted to scream. The velocity threatened to rip him from limb to limb, and shred him into tiny pieces of hair and skin. But he had been leaping time for years, ever since being chosen, and he had learned how to endure the torment. Now his only thought was that evil was hunting his son, and his determination overshadowed the pain.

He landed in his own north tower, going down to all fours so hard it was as if his wrists and knees had shattered. The chamber was spinning with dizzying speed while he urgently tried to become oriented.

The room had not ceased turning when he felt a huge evil presence approaching, a power so great and so dark that he dreaded looking up.

With the evil, there was Ian's fear and rage.

He raised his head, in growing horror.

A huge man stood in his chamber doorway, holding Aidan's young, struggling son.

His father was not dead. Moray had returned.

Aidan leapt to his feet, eyes wide with shock, as the terrible comprehension sank in.

The Earl of Moray smiled at him, very much alive, white teeth flashing. "Hallo a Aidan."

Aidan's gaze slammed to his son. Ian did not resemble his mother, who had died in childbirth. He looked exactly like his father: fair in complexion, with vivid blue eyes, perfect and beautiful features and dark hair. It took him one moment to comprehend that Ian wasn't hurt—yet. Then Aidan looked at the man who had alternately seduced, raped and tortured his mother—the deamhan who had spent a thousand years stalking innocent men, women and children all over the world.

Clad as a courtier, in long velvet robes of crimson and gold, he was blond, blue-eyed and handsome. He did not look a day older than forty years. "I decided it was time to meet my grandson," Moray murmured in flawless English.

Aidan trembled. Nine years ago, his father had been vanquished at Tor in the Orkney Islands. His half brother, Malcolm, and Malcolm's wife Claire had beheaded Moray in a great battle, but only with the help of a goddess. Evil could not live without a flesh-and-blood body, although it was rumored that the greatest demonic energy was immortal. Aidan had never really believed his father gone; he had secretly expected him to return one day. *He had been right.*

"Yes, I am alive," Moray said softly, their gazes locking. "Did you really think I could be destroyed?"

Aidan breathed hard, preparing for a terrible battle. He would die to save his son from whatever Moray intended. "Release Ian. Whatever ye wish, I'll do it."

"But you know what I want, my son. I want you."

Of course he did; nothing had changed. Moray wished to turn him into his greatest deamhan, a nearly immortal soldier of destruction and death.

"I'll do as ye wish," Aidan lied. As he spoke, he blasted Moray with his god-given power.

But his father's teeth flashed in a delighted smile and he blocked the surge of energy easily. Then silver blazed from Moray's hands like lightning, and Aidan was flung across the chamber into the far wall. The impact took his breath away, but he remained on his feet.

A dagger appeared in Moray's hand, and he sliced through Ian's ear.

Aidan shouted as blood gushed all over his son's pale leine. "Cease," Aidan roared. "I'll do as ye wish!"

Ian choked on pain, holding his head. Moray grinned at him and pushed the piece of ear across the floor with the pointy tip of his shoe. "Do you wish to keep it?"

Aidan trembled in rage.

"Obey me and he will not suffer," Moray added softly.

"Let me stop the bleeding." Aidan had healing powers. He started forward for the piece of ear. He would put it back together, make it mend.

Moray held Ian harder, causing the boy to grunt. "Not until you prove yourself to me."

Aidan halted. "I'll heal him first."

"You dare to barter with me?"

In that instant, Aidan knew that unless help arrived in the form of other Masters, they would battle to the death.

"No aid comes," Moray said with a laugh. "I have blocked your thoughts. No one knows what you suffer now."

He believed him. "Tell me what I must do to free an' heal my son."

"Father, no," Ian cried, his blue eyes wide.

"Be quiet," Aidan said firmly, meeting his gaze.

Ian nodded, mouth pursed, near tears.

"The village below Awe. Destroy it."

Aidan went still.

Moray stared at him, smiling.

Aidan became aware of his heart pounding, slow and sure, sick with dread. He knew every inhabitant of that village. The villagers traded and bartered with the castle, with him, on a daily basis. They depended on him for their livelihoods and their lives. The castle defended the village from all attacks, and Awe was sustained by their services and goods. Most importantly, he was sworn before every god on earth to protect the Innocent.

He could not destroy an entire village of men, women and children.

Moray took the dagger and laid it against Ian's throat. Blood oozed and Ian cried out, blanching.

Aidan leapt unto time.

He landed in the castle's great hall moments earlier. The huge room spinning with shocking speed, he saw Ian there, calmly conversing with his steward. On his hands and knees, he tried to fight for his power and choke out words. "Ian. Son!" He would somehow prevent this, undo it. The rules were very clear—no Master could go back in time to change the past. But he would change the past now!

Neither his son nor the steward heard him.

Shocked, Aidan got up. "Ian, come here," he began, but Ian didn't hear him this time, either. His son walked from the hall, heading up the stairs.

They couldn't see him or hear him.

Something had happened to his powers.

He refused to believe it. He ran after Ian, rushing up the narrow, winding stairs. The moment he reached the upper landing, he saw Moray materialize in the upper corridor, surprising his son. Like Ian, Moray could not see him. Aidan tried to blast Moray with power, but nothing came from his hand or his mind. Furious, desperate, as he saw Moray move to seize Ian, Aidan tried to blast him again, but with the same results. "Ian," he screamed in near panic. "Run!"

But Ian did not hear him, and Moray caught the little boy in his powerful embrace. Ian began struggling, and Aidan almost wept as Moray started toward the north tower, dragging the nine-year-old with him.

Aidan ran after them. He launched himself at Moray, intending to assault him as an ordinary human might—but an invisible wall came between them, sending him reeling backward across the corridor.

Were the gods interfering? He was incredulous.

He cried out in fury and saw himself landing in the tower on his hands and knees. There were other rules. A Master must never encounter himself in either the past or the future. The rule was not explained. Afraid to move, he watched his younger self look up in horror.

"Hallo a Aidan," his father said to the man he had been a mere moment ago. "I decided it was time to meet my grandson."

Was this why a Master must never encounter himself in another time? Because he would lose his powers? For he could only stand there and helplessly watch as the drama unfolded—the very drama he had just lived through!

"Yes, I am alive," Moray said softly. "Did you really think I could be destroyed?"

"Release Ian," his younger self said. "Whatever ye wish, I'll do it."

"But you know what I want, my son. I want you."

Aidan watched as his other self tried to blast Moray—and as Moray's own power sent Aidan flying across the tower and into the far wall. He breathed hard, tensing, knowing what was to come. Before Moray lifted his dagger, he launched himself at him again.

Aidan crashed into the invisible wall and bounced off it, choking on rage and anguish. The dagger sliced off the lower lobe of Ian's ear. Ian choked on a scream, and Aidan heard his other self roar in rage—as he did.

And as the other Aidan tried to barter with his demonic father to heal his son, a huge force began dragging him inexorably toward the trio. Aidan tried to halt, but he simply couldn't. He was rapidly being swept toward his younger self.

Aidan braced for an impact, uncertain of what to

expect when his body came into contact with his younger self.

"The village below Awe. Destroy it."

But there was no impact. Briefly there was an odd, sickening sensation, and then he was staring at Moray and Moray was staring back at him. He was no longer a spectator to the terrible drama. He had gone back in time to prevent this moment—to change it—but now he was facing Moray. He had come full circle to the precise moment when he had leapt.

He could not destroy an entire village of men, women and children.

Moray took the dagger and laid it against Ian's throat. Blood oozed, and Ian cried out, blanching.

Aidan's mind raced and he shielded his thoughts so Moray could not lurk. He did not have the power to change this moment.

He was sick now, sick in his soul. "Release my son and I will destroy the village," he said tersely.

"Papa, no!" Ian cried.

Aidan didn't look at him.

Moray grinned. "You will have the boy when you have proven you are *my* son."

"Papa," Ian panted in protest.

Aidan looked at him and wanted to cry. "I willna be long."

"I'll die for them!" Ian cried, struggling furiously now.

Moray jerked him, his expression one of anger and disgust. "He will be useless to me," he spat.

"You won't need him. You will have me," Aidan said, meaning it. He left the tower, feeling as if his soul had already left his body. His movements felt mechanical, except for the wild pounding of his heart and the lurching of his stomach. For the first time in his life, he felt raw fear.

He went swiftly downstairs, awaking the five armed men who slept in the hall. They fell silently into step beside him.

Outside, the moon was full, the sky a deathly black, stars glittering obscenely. He roused another two dozen men. As their mounts were saddled, the men gathered torches. One of the men came up to him, his face set and grim. "What passes, Aidan?"

He looked at Angus, refusing to answer. A steed was brought forward and he vaulted into the saddle, signaling his men to follow.

The troops rode through the gatehouse and over the icy bridge that spanned gleaming waters. When they reached the village on the loch's shores, Aidan pulled up. He did not look at Angus as he spoke. "Burn it. Leave no one—not even a dog—alive."

He did not have to look at Angus to feel the man's absolute shock.

He stared ahead at the village, not bothering to repeat himself.

A moment later, his men were galloping through the thatched cottages, torching the straw roofs, which instantly became infernos. Men, women and children fled their burning homes, crying in fright, and his men chased them down, one after one, swiftly ending each life with one thrust of a blade. Screams of terror filled the night. Aidan sat his restless mount, not allowing it to move. He knew his face was wet, but he refused to wipe the tears. He kept Ian's image close in his mind until the night was silent, except for the hissing of flames and a single woman's sobs.

Her weeping abruptly ended.

His men filed past him, no one looking at him now.

When he was alone, he choked and slid from the mount. He began vomiting helplessly and uncontrollably in the snow.

When he was done, he stayed there, breathing hard. The screams echoed in his mind. He kept reminding himself that at least he had saved Ian. And he knew he would never forget what he had just witnessed, what he had just done.

He heard a movement behind him.

Aidan slowly got up and turned.

A woman stood by some trees, weeping soundlessly, clutching the hand of a small, terrified child. She was staring at him. His heart lurched in absolute dread. He unsheathed his sword and started toward them.

She didn't run. She hugged her child and shrank against the huge fir tree, eyes wide. "Why, my lord? *Why?*"

The hilt of his sword was sticky in his hand. He meant to raise it. He said hoarsely, "Run. Run now."

She and the child fled into the woods.

He tossed the sword at the ground and leaned his face on his arms, against the tree. *Ian...he had to free Ian from Moray.*

And then he felt the shocking, evil presence behind him. Tensing, Aidan whirled. Moray stood there, Ian in his grasp. He saw the blade Moray held flash silver.

"Give me my son!"

Ian made an odd, strangled sound.

Horrified, Aidan saw the dagger embedded in Ian's chest. "No!"

Moray smiled—and Ian's eyes rolled back in his head lifelessly. Aidan screamed, rushing forward as Ian became limp. But when he reached them, they were gone.

For one instant, Aidan stood in shock and disbelief. *Moray had murdered Ian.*

Anguish began, and with it, more rage than he had ever felt. He howled, holding his head, and furiously, he leapt back in time. *He would not let Ian die.*

He returned to that moment at Awe when he had found Ian in the great hall with his steward, but once again he had no power, and no one could see or hear him. He tried to assault Moray, but an invisible wall came between them and the past repeated itself, exactly. This time, he was a sick spectator as his younger self sat on his steed and watched his men destroying an entire innocent village.

And this time, when he saw himself discover the woman and child, he rushed forward. "Do it," he shouted at his younger self. "You must do it!'

But the man he had been a moment ago did not lift his sword. "Run. Run now!"

The woman and child fled into the forest. He watched as his younger self turned to face Moray, who held Ian tightly to his chest.

And that huge, unnatural force began pulling him inexorably toward the trio. Aidan screamed in warning at Ian, at himself, but no one heard him. He saw the silver dagger flash.

The anguish was even greater now, but so was the rage.

He fell to his knees, howling and maddened, and then he leapt back in time again.

And again.

And again.

And each and every time, it was the same. An entire village destroyed by his command, one small woman and child fleeing and Moray still murdering Ian before his very eyes, only to vanish with his dead child.

And finally he gave up.

He roared and roared, blinded by the grief. He cursed evil; he cursed the gods. He was below Awe's curtain walls, although he did not recall returning from the village. And then, finally, the tower roof above his head collapsed. The entire wing of the castle started to crumble. He wept, openly and brokenly, as the stone walls rained down upon him. And when he was buried beneath his own castle walls, he became still and silent.

Aidan waited to die.

CHAPTER ONE

The Present
September 2008, New York City

THE ROAR OF HUMAN PAIN AWOKE HER.

Brianna Rose sat bolt upright, awoken from a deep sleep, horrified by the sound. It was filled with rage and anguish and disbelief. And then the pain cut through her.

She doubled over in her bed, clutching herself as if someone had actually slid a butcher's knife through her chest. For one moment, she could not breathe. She had never experienced that kind of anguish in her twenty-six years. Panting hard, she prayed for the pain to end. Then, suddenly, it did.

But as the torment vanished abruptly, a man's handsome image flared in her mind.

A new, terrible tension began. Carefully, Brie sat upright, shaken and stunned. Her loft was silent, except for the sounds of the cars and cabs driving by outside on the street, and the accompaniment of blaring horns. She trembled, glancing at her bedside clock. It was ten after one in the morning. What had just happened?

All the Rose women were empathic to one degree or another. Their empathy was supposed to be a gift, but too often it was a curse, like now. She had been consumed with another human being's pain. Something terrible had just happened, and she could not shake the dark, handsome image she'd just seen from her mind.

Brie trembled, tossing aside the covers. Was Aidan in trouble?

She became very still, her mouth dry, her heart thundering. She'd met him exactly a year ago, perhaps for two whole minutes. Her best friend, Allie, had been missing for weeks and she'd returned briefly to New York—from the Middle Ages—with Aidan's help.

He was the most beautiful man she had ever seen. Allie had explained about the secret Brotherhood and the men belonging to it, men who called themselves the Masters of Time. All were sworn before God to defend mankind from the evil in the night. Brie hadn't been surprised—there had been rumors of such warriors for as long as she could remember. In fact, like Allie, she and her cousins, Tabby and Sam, had been thrilled that the whispers were reality.

Brianna had no personal delusions. He was absolutely unforgettable, but she knew a man like that would never look at a woman like her twice—or think about her twice, either. She didn't blame him. She didn't even mind.

She was really good at wearing baggy clothes to hide her curves, and she never wore her contacts. Her eyeglasses were downright ugly. She knew that if she had her dark hair cut and styled properly, if she dressed fashionably and wore makeup, she'd probably look exactly like her mother, Anna Rose.

Brie had no desire to resemble her beautiful, passionate and rebellious mother in any way. Anna had been that rare Rose woman who had not been handed down any gifts. She had been destructive, not constructive; her touch and beauty damaged instead of helped others. In the end, she had hurt those she loved the most, and she had destroyed not only her own family, but herself. Brie didn't want to recall finding her mother dead on the kitchen floor, shot by her jealous boyfriend, with her father weeping over Anna's body. Being a retiring nerd was way better than following in Anna's footsteps.

But Brie had other gifts, making her a lot less nerdy than she appeared. She had been gifted with the Sight. It was the greatest gift a Rose woman could have, handed down from grandmother to grandchild. Brie had been terrified of her visions at first, but Grandma Sarah had explained that the Sight was a precious gift, one meant to be cherished. It was a great resource, meant to help people, which the Rose women were destined to do—and had been doing for hundreds of years. Grandma Sarah had taught her almost everything she knew about good, evil and life.

By now Brie was almost accustomed to the wiles of Fate. Life wasn't easy and it wasn't fair, and the good died young every single day. She didn't blame Anna for her uncontrollable passions. She knew Anna hadn't been able to help herself. She'd resented her sisters for having their gifts and their lives, and her own simple marriage hadn't been enough for her. She'd been an unhappy woman. She had been selfish, but not cruel—and certainly not evil. She hadn't deserved an early death.

It was all ancient history. Dad had remarried—the best thing that ever could have happened to him. Anna was dead and buried, but not forgotten. Brie was determined to be as solid, dependable and trustworthy as her mother was not. Her life was helping others, giving selflessly—perhaps to make up for all the hurt Anna had inflicted. She was thrilled to be employed by the Center for Demonic Activity, a secret government agency dedicated to the war on evil. There, she fought dark forces throughout the ages from the basement, at a computer.

Her cousins claimed she was doing her best to hide from men. They were right. The last thing she wanted was for a man to notice her. She would probably die a virgin, and it didn't matter.

Aidan hadn't noticed her, she was certain, but she had taken one look at him and had fallen hard. She was hopelessly infatuated. She thought about him every day, dreamed about him at night and had even spent hours on the Web, reading about the medieval Highlands. The Rose women came from the northern Highlands originally, so she'd always been fascinated with Scotland's history, but now she foolishly hoped to learn more about him. When he'd brought Allie back to the city from 1430, he'd appeared to be about twenty-five years old. Allie had returned to her lover, Black Royce, at Carrick Castle in Morvern. Brie wished she'd asked her friend about Aidan, but their visit had been too brief. So she kept returning to Carrick's history, yearning for a mention of a man named Aidan, but that was like looking for a needle in a haystack. Still, there were many references to the powerful Earl of Morvern and his fair Lady of Carrick. Brie was thrilled. Even across time, she knew Allie and Royce were fulfilling their destinies together.

She would probably never learn anything about Aidan, and she was sensible enough to realize it, but that didn't stop her crush. A fantasy was harmless. She hadn't even tried to talk herself out of it. If she was going to fall head over heels in love and never act on it, why not do so with someone absolutely unattainable? Aidan, a medieval Highlander with the power to time travel and a mandate to protect Innocence, was a really, really safe bet.

Brie was feeling sick now. It was one thing to have visions and empathy, but she had just *heard* Aidan roaring in anguish, as if he'd been in the same room with her. How close by was he?

What had happened to him?

Afraid he was in the city, and hurt, Brie got up. She was clad in a simple pink tank top and briefs. It was Indian summer, and even at night it was warm and humid. She hurried across her large, shadowy loft, hitting lights as she went. She'd half expected Aidan to be present, maybe unconscious in the shadows and sprawled out on her floor, but the loft was empty.

At her front door, which was triple locked and had multiple alarms, she peered through the peephole into the hall. It was lit and empty, too.

Her loft was thoroughly fortified with Tabby's spells and prayers and Brie wore a Celtic cross that she never took off. A small page from the Book handed down through generations of Rose women was also framed and nailed to her door to keep evil out. But Brie said a silent prayer to the long-ago gods, anyway.

She could feel evil, very close by, drifting about the streets, preying upon anyone foolish enough to defy Bloomberg's voluntary curfew. But she didn't want to think about the city's problems now. She had to somehow find Aidan and make sure he was okay. Maybe Tabby and Sam could make heads or tails out of this. The other person who would probably have a clue was her boss, Nick Forrester, but she was hesitant to call him. She kept a very low profile at CDA. He knew nothing about her gifts—or her cousins and their extracurricular activities.

Brie grabbed the phone as she went to her computer and began logging onto HCU's immense database. The Historical Crimes Unit was a part of CDA. She spent her days—and even her nights—looking through two centuries of case files, searching for historic coincidences. Her job was to find matches between their current targets and demons operating in the past. It was amazing how many demons terrorizing the country today came from past centuries.

Because searching for coincidences involved comparisons with active cases, she had access to current criminal investigations, including federal, state and local NYPD records. Multitasking, Brie began to search for the most recent reported criminal activities as she dialed her cousins' number. She pictured Aidan lying hurt on a dark, slick city street, but she knew it was only her imagination responding to her worst fears.

Tabby answered, sounding as if she'd been deeply asleep. She'd divorced well over a year ago. It had taken her a long time to recover from her husband's infidelity, and she had just begun dating again. But she was very conservative, and Brie had expected her to be alone and asleep.

"I really need your help," Brie said swiftly.

"Brie, what is it?" Tabby was instantly awake.

"Aidan is in trouble—and I think he's nearby."

Tabby paused and Brie felt her trying to recall just who Aidan was. "You don't mean the Highlander who brought Allie back last year?"

"I do," Brie whispered.

"Can this wait until morning?" Tabby asked.

It wasn't safe for anyone to tool around the city after dark. "I don't think so," Brie said grimly. "It wasn't a vision, Tabby. I felt his pain. He's in trouble—right now."

Tabby was silent, and Brie heard Sam in the background, asking what was wrong. The sisters shared a loft just a few blocks away. "We'll be right over," Tabby said.

Brie hung up, slipped on her jeans and sat down to seriously go over the cases she'd pulled. She was immersed in files when the doorbell rang twenty minutes later. She'd found nothing, and she supposed that was a relief. What she didn't want to find was a dead victim with Aidan's description. For all she knew, though, he was immortal. She hoped so.

Maybe the worst was over, she thought as she went to let the girls in. Maybe he'd gone back in time, where he belonged.

Tabby entered first, a willowy blonde in slacks and a silk tank top who always looked as if she were on her way to or from the country club. No one would ever guess from looking at her that Tabby was an earth mother. Sam followed, shockingly gorgeous even with her short-cropped platinum hair—but then, she had a Lara Croft from *Tomb Raider* body. Brie admired her immensely because she was so fearless and so open about her sexuality. She happened to know that Sam's messenger bag was loaded with weapons, and she carried a stiletto strapped to her thigh beneath the denim miniskirt she wore. On anybody else it might be corny, but on Sam it was darned serious.

Tabby took one look at Brie and rushed to hug her. "You are so worried!"

Sam closed and locked the door. "Did you find anything?" she asked, nodding at the computer.

"He's probably gone back to his time," Brie said. She wet her lips, aware of an absurd disappointment.

"Don't look so happy about it," Sam said wryly, striding across the loft to the computer and peering at the screen. "I don't think a man like that is easily hurt."

"I think he was tortured. I have never felt so much pain," Brie said.

Sam didn't look up from the screen, scrolling through files she had no right to view.

Tabby put her arm around Brie. "You're so pale. Are you all right?"

"I'll survive," Brie said, forcing a smile.

"Are you sure it was Aidan?" Tabby asked, rather unnecessarily, as Sam sat down at the desk. Tabby glanced at the poster from the movie *The Highlander*, which Brie had framed and hung on her living-room wall, her amber gaze narrowing.

"One hundred percent. I saw him as clear as day. It wasn't a vision, but it wasn't my imagination, either. I can't empathize across time. I certainly can't hear someone cry out from far away. He was here, close by. He was hurt. Really, really hurt." Brie trembled, feeling sick again.

"If he's hurt and in the city, we'll find him," Sam said firmly.

Brie felt reassured. Sam always got what she wanted.

"When did you put that poster up?" Tabby asked.

Brie blinked at her. "I don't remember," she lied, flushing.

Tabby stared. Then she moved toward the living area. "Well, this looks to be an all-nighter," she said cheerfully. "It's almost three in the morning, and I don't think any of us will make it back to bed." She began laying out her mother's crystals on the coffee table.

And the roar of anguish began again, deafening Brie. She gasped, stunned by the bellow of rage. Her hands flew automatically to her ears. His pain sent her down to the floor, where she doubled over, crushed by it, consumed by it…imprisoned by it. This time, the sensation was unbearable.

Oh my God, what's happening to Aidan? Is he being tortured?

"Brie!" Tabby screamed.

Vaguely, she was aware of Tabby holding her, but it didn't matter.

Brie knew they were ripping his heart out now. They were ripping *her* heart out. She wept in Tabby's arms, her world spinning with shocking force and then going black.

Aidan, she somehow thought. He was dying from the torture, and she was dying, too.

NICK FORRESTER sat at his computer in his night-darkened living room, clad only in his jeans. He'd completely forgotten about the leggy blonde who lay asleep in his bed. In fact, he couldn't recall her name. He'd picked her up outside the Korean grocery, and maybe he hadn't ever known the name. It was late, but he didn't need more than a few hours of sleep—especially not after a long round of sex, which he found energizing. Sex always empowered him.

He was working again. The "witch" burnings in the city were on the rise. His latest intelligence debriefing had indicated that Bloomberg was seriously considering calling in the National Guard, and he thought it was about time. Pleasure crimes still dominated the murder rate, but those random demonic acts were almost unpreventable—like suicide bombers. The "witch" burnings were another matter. He knew in his gut that the gang leader of these medieval crimes was a great demon from the past. His gut was always dead-on.

Now he was immersed in medieval history, looking for any references to such burnings in past times. HCU had software to look for coincidental data, but he didn't trust the damn programs and he never would. The program wasn't that sophisticated, only matching words and phrases. A single isolated burning of a heretic, a traitor or a witch didn't interest him, nor did the burning of a thirteenth-century peasant's home or a baron's castle. He was looking for a series of the violent crimes, probably committed by a group of adolescents but run by a single, very clever entity.

His cell buzzed.

Nick picked up at the first ring. A woman he did not know spoke. "Brie Rose needs medical attention, ASAP!"

"Who the hell is this?" he demanded, alert but annoyed at her commanding tone. He was wary, too. She could be a crank or even something else.

"Her cousin Sam Rose, and if you don't want her going to Emergency, you need to send your people in. Hurry—she may be dying." The phone went dead.

Nick was already speed-dialing his own medevac people while pulling up Brie Rose's file on his HCU screen. In thirty seconds, he had sent his medical team to her loft and was pulling on a T-shirt, seizing his Beretta, car keys and shoes. He ignored the sleeping blonde as he left his condo, stepping into his shoes in the elevator. A minute later he was peeling out of the building's underground garage in his black Expedition; eight minutes later he was leaping out of the vehicle, an ambulance marked Cornell Presbyterian already in front of Brie's building. The ambulance belonged to CDA, and was deliberately mismarked.

He went up with the paramedics, growing aware of Brie's struggle. He could feel her fighting for her life, and her fear of dying. Alarmed, he searched the perimeter but did not sense evil nearby. He couldn't discern what had put her on the brink of death.

A beautiful blonde who looked like a rock star met him at the door. He felt her power and instantly knew she was a vigilante warrior. Glancing past her, he saw Brie, unconscious on the floor, in another beautiful woman's arms. That one had power, too, but it was not that of a Slayer's. He didn't have time to try to identify it.

Although he knew the gossips nailed him as cold and uncaring, it wasn't true. He'd hand-selected every single employee at HCU and considered them all his personal responsibility, especially mousy Brie. He was even a bit fond of her—and not because she was brilliant. He felt sorry for her. She was a recluse, with no life outside of work. He had sensed her powers before he'd hired her. It had taken him a moment to decide what they were but he could read minds whenever he chose and he was fairly conscienceless about it if it was in the line of duty. He didn't expect her to come clean. He knew that her unusual perceptions were often used on the cases he sent to her and that worked fine for him.

As the medics went to take her vitals, he said grimly, "What happened?"

The woman holding Brie in her arms looked up at him. He felt his interest quicken. She was elegance and beauty personified. She said hoarsely, "She's empathic, and someone we know was being tortured. She felt everything they did to him. She's hurt."

"No kidding." He was wary. These women were outsiders. How much did they know? And vigilantes always messed up his investigations. He looked at his watch. It was 3:24 a.m. "When did it start?"

"Eight minutes ago," the blonde with the body said. From her voice, he knew she was Sam Rose.

"Frank?" he asked.

"Her pulse is weak and her blood pressure is low," the medic said, administering oxygen.

Brie's eyes fluttered. Nick knelt beside her, smiling. "Hey, kiddo. We'll take care of you. Tell me about your friend."

She gasped weakly, "I think they're slowly killing him, Nick." Tears fell. "Please help him. He's one of us."

He stared at her, lurking. His eyes widened; Brie had met one of the Highland warriors? He was her *friend?* His agents had been hoping to bring in a Master for a long, long time.

"She had an episode earlier," Sam said tersely. "That was when she called us."

Nick absorbed that. "What do you know about the Highlander?"

Sam Rose was good, he had to hand it to her. Her

eyes didn't even widen, not a drop. "I'm worried," she said. "If this person is being tortured, Brie might go through this again when they start in on him."

"She won't make it," the other blonde cried. "I've never seen her like this."

"Take her to Five," Nick said. Because the agency was covert, CDA had its own medical facilities known simply a Five. But as Brie was loaded onto a stretcher, he pulled Frank aside. "Can an extreme empathic reaction kill her?"

"I don't know."

"Is it a safer bet to keep her sedated until we can remove the source of the empathic reaction?" When Frank nodded, Nick said, "Do it."

The *Town & Country* blonde said, "I'm staying with her."

Nick seized her shoulder, staring as coldly as he could. It wasn't hard to do; he was getting pissed. How much did these women know?

"Lady, you are not cleared to stay with her. You and your friend are coming with me, now, to my office."

She stared at him, close to tears. "After we tell you what we know, I beg you to let me stay with her."

"I'll think about it." He looked at the warrior, Sam; and because he didn't like the look in her eyes, he read her mind. "You're coming with me, but I'll put all my agents in the field. If your *friend* is in the city, we'll find him."

Sam stared at him, clearly unhappy with his decision. He was aware she wanted to hunt. "Yeah, well, I hope you find him alive," she mocked.

BRIE STRUGGLED TO SWIM THROUGH the thick, heavy darkness. She heard voices, but they seemed impossibly far away; still, she wanted to reach them. Some of the darkness shifted…lifted. Her mind flickered. She needed to think. There was something happening, something she had to do. She didn't know where she was, but she sensed Tabby and Sam were nearby, and there was relief in the comprehension.

"Brie? It's me, Tabby. Can you hear me?"

Tabby sounded closer now. Why was she so heavy, so groggy? Brie fought to swim to her cousin. Light began shining against her closed lids, and she somehow opened her eyes. Instantly, she blinked against the sterile white light of an office or a hospital room.

Tabby held her hand. "Welcome back."

Brie met her concerned amber eyes. Without her glasses, she couldn't see farther than her hand, but she didn't have to see Tabby clearly to know it was her. Her mind remained sluggish, but she knew there was something urgent she had to remember. And suddenly she gripped Tabby's hand hard in return. "Aidan!" There was total recall now. "Did you find him?" As she spoke, she saw the blur that was Sam, standing next to Tabby. Dear God, her boss was behind them. He was entirely out of focus, but it didn't matter, she still felt his hard, unwavering stare.

"No, we didn't." Tabby slipped her eyeglasses on for her. "Is that better?"

So much fear for him began. Without a doubt, Brie knew that he was being tortured by great evil. He could still be alive and in torment—or he could be dead.

"How do you feel?" Nick asked.

Brie was almost afraid to look at him now that she could see. He was a macho-looking man of about thirty—muscular, tall and really good-looking;

women were always trying to pick him up. Nick was a cool player, but he was all work and no play when it came to HCU.

"Am I drugged?" She finally looked at him, and sure enough, he had that steely, take-no-prisoners look in his eyes.

"Pretty heavily, but we're taking you down so we can chat." Nick smiled, as if encouraging her to be candid, but that smile never reached his blue eyes.

"It's been twenty-four hours, Brie," Tabby said softly, squeezing her hand. Her gaze was filled with worry.

Brie stared at her, almost reading her mind. Now she remembered fighting the pain, in this very room. "He's still being tortured," she gasped.

"Every other time we brought you down, within an hour or so you started having extreme empathic reactions to your friend," Nick said flatly.

Brie blinked at him. He'd stressed the word "friend." How much had she said? Nick was pissed; she could feel it, even as messed up as she was.

"Maybe you can tell Nick something to help his people find Aidan," Tabby murmured.

"It's hard to think," she whispered. Had Tabby told Nick about the Masters of Time? As groggy as she was, she was certain Nick wouldn't be surprised that the rumors floating around the agency about a race of evil-fighting warriors were true. Sometimes Nick seemed to know *everything.*

Nick said to the physician, "Take her down a bit more."

As the sedation was further decreased, Brie recognized that she was ill with exhaustion. She felt nauseous, and she began to realize how utterly sore her body was. Every muscle throbbed, as if she was the one who'd been mercilessly tortured. But her mind leapt to life as the sedation was reduced. What had they done to him? Was he alive? "How can I help?" she asked Nick, trembling.

He dismissed the doctor and turned to Tabby and Sam. "Goodbye, ladies."

Tabby was alarmed. "I can't leave her."

Nick gestured toward the door. "You can, and you will. It will only be for a few moments."

Brie didn't want to be alone with him and she knew Tabby knew it. Sam gave Nick a cool glance. "Don't bully her," she said.

When they were gone, he said, "I need you to come clean, kid. If you want to help your friend, you need to clarify exactly who we're looking for."

Brie wished she could think more clearly. "His name is Aidan—and he's not from our century." She stopped. "He's from the past, Nick."

He leaned close, his face expressionless. "When did you meet the Highlander, Brie?"

He was really mad. "I met him a year ago," Brie breathed, hoping she was doing the right thing by telling Nick the truth. Their eyes locked. "You're not surprised."

Nick folded his muscular arms across his chest. "Tell me more about him."

Brie tried to think clearly. The Brotherhood was secret—Allie had stressed that—but so was CDA and every unit within. "When I met him, he'd come from 1430, from Carrick Castle," she said. "He has powers, Nick—special powers, just like the demons do."

Nick searched her gaze and Brie had the uncanny

feeling he was searching her mind. He said softly, "Does the name Aidan of Awe ring any bells?"

Oddly, the name resonated with her.

"Take her up," Nick snapped.

Brie felt the last bit of fogginess dissipate. Nick became completely clear, his eyes blue steel. He knew all about the Masters, she realized.

"Yeah," he said, "and I've wanted to bring one in for a long, long time."

But he hadn't even finished when she heard Aidan.

His roar of pain was filled with despair and protest.

This time, it was the roar of grief.

Brie went still.

He's lost everything. Before she could assimilate that, a huge weight fell on her, crushing her. She cried out in alarm and fear as more stones fell, rapidly burying her in darkness.

Brie wanted to panic and scream; she wanted to fight the rocks, try to push up against them. But instead she lay very still, absolutely calm, aware that she was entombed.

"Brie, what is it?" she heard Tabby cry from far away.

Brie's eyes widened. She was looking up at black stone; it was as if she was buried alive. She tried to move her arms, her legs, but stone pressed in on her from all sides.

Aidan had been buried alive.

And he was utterly calm, utterly resigned, a man without hope.

She reached out to him.

She felt him start.

She tried to focus entirely upon him. He was physically trapped, unmoving. Like her, he had no difficulty breathing. He was staring at the blackness. She felt him more acutely now. The stones were painful, their weight crushing, but he didn't care. They weren't crushing him to death. It was the heartache that was killing him.

And she felt his acceptance of death.

He was waiting to die.

"Brie, honey, it's okay. You're here with us, on Five."

Aidan, Brie tried. *You can't die!*

If she had reached him, he was now gone. He had slipped so far away that she couldn't feel anything at all.

"Can you hear me?" Nick asked, sounding far away.

She could, but she couldn't answer Nick now. Aidan had powers. He could break free of the rocks and stone if he wanted to. If she had reached him a moment ago, surely she could find him again. She was almost certain he had felt her, or heard her. She strained for him, calling his name. *Aidan, break free of the stone.* She waited for him to respond. A long time seemed to elapse, and he never moved, never answered.

She couldn't stand this. *Don't die!*

Nick was speaking to her again.

"Brie, it's Nick. We've given you Ativan. It's an antianxiety med, and you should be feeling pretty good right now. You're at CDA on Five and we're taking care of you. You're having an empathic reaction again. Look at me."

Brie felt her body soften. She looked at Nick. His handsome face and sexy body formed before her, coming gradually into focus. Someone had put her eyeglasses on, she recalled inanely, and she smiled.

"Good. To find the Highlander, we need you. Where is he?"

She could see Aidan so clearly now, in his grave beneath the rubble, a red castle soaring above a loch. Brie said, "There's a castle on a lake. He's in Scotland…and he's in the past." She was so surprised by her response that she faltered, but she knew she'd sensed the truth.

"Are you certain?" Nick asked. "Are you certain he's not in the city?"

"Yes." Brie had never been more certain of anything. She had been wrong earlier. He hadn't been close by. She'd try to figure that out later, she thought. "We can't let him die."

Nick turned away and said, "Her Encounter last year should have been reported. Now that I know what you two ladies are up to, any Encounters or Sightings come right to me. Failure to do so is against the law."

"I'm not aware of any such laws," Sam said bluntly.

"It's against Nick's law," Nick said swiftly. "And you really don't want to break Nick's law."

Brie was floating, feeling really wonderful now, as if she'd had three or four glasses of champagne. Sam sat down and smiled at her. "Your boss is such a jerk."

"Yeah, he is," Brie agreed, aware that Nick had walked out. No, he'd stalked out, like a hunting tiger.

Sam leaned close and whispered, "I'm calling in every favor I have. If he's here, someone's seen him. You just rest."

"He isn't here. He's far away." Her happiness was gone. "I don't want him to die. I love him, Sam."

Sam's blue eyes went wide. "Brie, I know you're high right now, but if it's Fate, you know we can't change it."

"It can't be his time," Brie whispered. She wasn't

sure what happened next, but Sam was gone, and it was only her and Tabby, who sat by her bed, holding her hand. Then Brie blinked curiously. A little boy was standing at the foot of her bed, clad in a white hospital gown that was oddly belted. He started speaking urgently to her. His blue eyes were so familiar, as if she knew him, but she didn't think she did. Brie realized she was too high to hear a word. He seemed frightened. She knew he wanted to tell her something important, and she turned to Tabby. "What is he saying?"

Tabby was surprised. "Who are you talking about?"

Brie looked at the foot of her bed, but the little boy was gone. "I guess it doesn't matter," she said.

She must have been dreaming.

CHAPTER TWO

Castle Awe, Scotland—November 1502

SEX NO LONGER MATTERED TO HIM.

Like the best wine drunk far too often, it could not be appreciated. Pleasure escaped him now.

But he moved harder, faster, into the woman, not seeking release, even though a release was inevitable. Instead, he used her for his own ends, taking power, euphoric, until she lay unmoving and silent beneath him.

Aidan held himself over the woman, breathing hard. He had experienced the powerful ecstasy of *La Puissance* thousands of times, a climax that combined raging power with sexual release. When he had first begun to hunt Moray after Ian's murder, he'd taken power to assure himself of victory over the deamhan he was now sworn to kill. But Moray had vanished in time, fleeing him. And Aidan had needed more power to chase him.

Power was addictive. He lusted for it now. Unfortunately, the lust for power was terribly arousing. Otherwise he would not even bother with the sexual act.

Still consumed with a sense of invincibility, he moved away from the woman. He stood and leaned against the wall, arching back, savagely relishing the power coursing through his muscles. It even throbbed in his bones.

No one could defeat him now—not man, not beast, not deamhan and not even a god. Not even his demonic father. His father had returned to murder Ian, when a beheading would destroy most deamhanain. There were Masters who believed Moray immortal. Others said he had returned with otherworldly help. Aidan had dared to demand answers upon Iona. MacNeil had told him Moray's return was written, but that no deamhan was immortal, no matter how it might appear.

Ian's image seared his mind, as hot as a firebrand. He welcomed the pain.

"Is she alive?" The other woman gasped, kneeling half-naked beside the Innocent.

He barely glanced at the lush redhead, who was flushed with her own pleasure. He'd left the Innocent alive, although barely. "Aye. Tend her."

Anna Marie took the limp woman in her arms, but she was staring at him with glittering eyes. Most women feared his desire. Having lurked in her mind on several occasions, he knew that she both feared and desired his passion—all of it. Now, she said, "Do you want me again?"

He'd found her in Paris in the mid-eighteenth century. She was the courtesan of a prince. She enjoyed hours in his bed and understood his need to take far more than pleasure from her and others, even simultaneously. Her presence was convenient, especially because he never slept and there was one certain way for him to pass the long, dark hours of the night.

He hadn't slept in sixty-six years.

Sleeping only brought nightmares.

He bared his teeth at her. What she did not understand was that he looked at her with absolute indifference, and felt nothing when their bodies were joined except for the lust for power and revenge. He would avenge Ian, even if it took an eternity to do so.

"Nay." Naked, his body still hard and huge, he stalked from the chamber, and as he did so, he heard her moan.

He didn't care. He didn't need her or the other one now. He had enough power to destroy his father—if he could find him. For Moray had vanished into time sixty-six years ago, and Aidan had been hunting him ever since.

It was time to hunt now.

A pair of chambermaids was hurrying down the hall. A glance at the single, barred window at the hall's east end showed him that the sun was high. He'd been with the women since the previous day at dusk. The maids looked at him and froze in their tracks, terrified and mesmerized at once. Ignoring them, he was about to enter the east tower room when he felt a huge power approaching, fierce and determined and white.

He roiled with anger, instantly aware of the intruder's identity. He turned to face his half brother, Malcolm, the man who had unearthed him from Awe's rubble instead of allowing him to die.

He would never forgive him for it.

Malcolm of Dunroch came up the stairs at the hall's far end, a large, powerful man in a leine and dark-green-and-black plaid, wearing both long and short swords, his muddy boots indicating a long, hard ride. Dirt flecked his bare thighs. His face was flushed with anger. "Ye canna march on Inverness with the rebels," he said harshly, striding up the hall. He gave Aidan's naked body a quick, dismissive glance.

"Do ye nay march on Inverness with Donald Dubh an' Lachlan Maclean, yer cousin?" he mocked, knowing Malcolm was too busy saving Innocence to bother with political intrigues. Politics didn't interest him, either, but feeding and horsing his four thousand men did.

And destroying the Campbell was something he could still do for his son.

Malcolm's face hardened. "Ye'll hang with the traitors when they're defeated," he said tersely, legs braced as if to bar his way.

"Good," Aidan said softly, meaning it. He wasn't afraid of death. He looked forward to it—as long as Ian was avenged first.

Malcolm seized his arm. "'Twas not yer fault. Ye have yer destiny to return to, Aidan."

"Yer nay welcome here. Get out," Aidan roared, shrugging him off. He whirled, entering the tower room and slamming the door closed behind him.

His damned brother was wrong. He had failed to keep his son safe. He had saved hundreds of Innocents, but not his own son; he would never forgive himself for it. He steeled himself against the anguish, but too late.

From the door's other side, he heard Malcolm's every silent thought. *I willna let ye die an' I willna give up on ye. Nor will I be leavin' Awe soon.*

Furious with his brother, hating him for refusing to lose faith, Aidan threw the bolt down on the door. Inside it was dark and cold. No fire burned in the stone hearth and every small arrow slit had long since been nailed closed with shutters, so the darkness was complete.

Eventually Malcolm would leave. He always did, as there was always a deamhan to vanquish, an Innocent to save. Malcolm served the gods as if his vows were his life, with his wife at his side. But Malcolm was not a deamhan's son. He was the son of the great Master, Brogan Mor, and a Master himself—as well as the laird of the Macleans of south Mull and Coll. They had nothing in common.

Malcolm had been raised at Dunroch by his father and then, after Brogan Mor's death in battle, by his uncle, Black Royce, to be chief of Clan Gillean. Aidan had been sent as an infant into a nobleman's foster care, for his mother had retired to an abbey to spend the rest of her life there. Malcolm had often gone to visit Lady Margaret at the abbey, ever the dutiful son. His calls had been welcome. Aidan had met his mother but once, when he was a Master, and she had not been able to look at him. He had quickly left her to her prayers and repentance.

He had grown up an outsider; his brother had been the next great laird, a Master whose vows were his life.

Aidan had forsaken his vows the day of Ian's murder.

If Moray's return was fated, the gods, apparently, had written his son's death, as well. He hated the gods passionately and he cursed them now—as he did every single day of his life.

He felt Malcolm leaving the hall, going below, and his mind began to ease. His senses intensified impossibly. Tonight, he thought, he would find and destroy Moray.

Tonight, he would tear Moray's throat out with his teeth. Then he would feed his heart to the wolves.

And he gave into the wolf, a savage and ruthless beast he could barely control, an animal intent on mayhem and death. He lifted his face toward the moon and howled. Outside, he felt the pack gathering and begin to howl in return, lusting for blood and death. He quieted, leaving the wolves to their eerie, savage chorus. He was ready now.

He walked to the center of the circular room and sank to the floor, where he sat cross-legged on the cold, hard stone.

More than six decades had passed since his son's murder. His demonic father could be in any time, in any place. Moray clearly thought himself the victor in their privy war, but he was wrong. Their war would never end, not until one or both of them was vanquished. He didn't care which it was—as long as Moray went to the fires of hell with him.

He began sifting through the sands of time, in the future and the past, through deserts and mountains, villages and cities, searching for Moray's evil power.

Hours passed. He strained through time, evil everywhere, a long, painstaking process. The moon rose. He did not need to see it to know. The hairs on his nape prickled, like hackles rising. But the blackest power he was hunting eluded him.

He could not give up. He growled in frustration.

And through the hours of the day and then the night, Innocence wept for salvation. He heard every single cry for aid, for his senses were not just attuned to evil but to its helpless prey. Men, women and children begged him to rescue them from destruction and death.

He would not recall the last time he had protected Innocence. It was before his son had died.

He ignored their cries now.

He did not care who died.

TABBY UNLOCKED THE DOOR FOR HER, giving her a smile. "Isn't it great to be home?" she asked.

Brie didn't smile back. She stepped into her loft, wearing the clothes Tabby had brought her—an oversized sweatshirt embroidered with a blue-and-gold dragon and her comfy loose-fit jeans. She was more worried than ever about Aidan. She'd spent another full day at Five, under close observation, and she was champing at the bit. She had been taken off all sedation and the antianxiety medication, so once again she could think clearly. Aidan was no longer being tortured, and he was no longer crushed by stone. She couldn't feel anything from him at all.

God, was he even alive?

She was adept at blocking out human emotion, for it was a necessity in order to get through each and every day. But she hadn't been able to block his torment at all. His emotions had consumed her as no one's ever had before, even across centuries. What, exactly, did the fact that she felt him so powerfully across time mean?

Everything was meant to be, and every Rose woman knew it.

Brie shivered as Tabby's cell phone rang. Brie shut and locked the door, going to her work station on the far side of the loft. She sat down at her PC, which remained in sleep mode. *He could not be dead.*

Tabby came over. "That was Sam. She's talked to every contact and snitch she knows. It looks like you're right. He's not here."

Brie whirled her chair to face her. "How could I empathize across time?"

Tabby clasped her shoulder, their gazes locking.

"You must really love him, Brie. It's the only explanation I can think of."

Her heart lurched. Her crush had been so safe and silly, until now. Loving him was terrifying, because he would never love her back—even if their paths crossed. "It's just a crush," Brie whispered, turning back to her PC. She was praying that there was another reason for her amazing empathy.

But now she stared at her computer's wallpaper, the ruins of a castle on Loch Awe. Nick had asked her if the name Aidan of Awe was familiar. Her heart thundered. It felt so right. She'd put up the wallpaper after meeting Aidan…and there was no such thing as coincidence.

This past year she had been tempted to go through HCU's immense historical database, looking for a mention of him, but it was against the rules to use the system for personal projects and she hadn't done so. She hit a button and CDA's site filled her screen. She began to log on, a process that required three passwords. She had something to go on now. And what did Nick know about Aidan, exactly?

If HCU had anything on him, by now, Nick was on it.

Brie was still amazed that she hadn't been fired.

"What are you going to do?" Tabby asked. "He's not here, Brie, and we can't time-travel."

Brie bit her lip and punched in a search for Aidan of Awe. As the search began, she shifted restlessly, and then she cried out, getting a hit.

Tabby peered over her shoulder.

The message on her screen was glaring. *Aidan of Awe—Level Four—Access Denied.*

"There's a file on him?" Tabby exclaimed.

"I'm only Level Three," Brie cried in frustration.

"Maybe that's not our Aidan," Tabby tried.

Brie stared at the flashing message. "It's him. I *know* it. Damn Nick," she cried.

Tabby started. "Brie, you're exhausted. You absorbed so much pain, you need to rest. Leave the search to Forrester. He's certainly on this."

"I can't," Brie said. She was afraid to ask Nick what was in that file—he was so intimidating—but she had to try.

"Can I make you something to eat?" Tabby asked.

Brie didn't care, even though Tabby was a great cook. As Tabby went into her kitchen, separated from the loft only by the kitchen counter, she went to her favorite online research library. She had part of his name to go on now. As she went to her medieval-Scotland virtual bookshelf, she dialed Nick. It went right to voicemail.

Brie pulled the first of two hundred and thirteen volumes, and as she typed in the words *Aidan of Awe* in the search box, she said, "Nick, it's Brie. Please call me at home. Thanks."

Her search yielded zero results, and she pulled the next volume and repeated the search. On her fourth search, a sudden nausea began, and Brie cried out. The floor tilted wildly, accompanied by a terrible feeling of dread.

And the vision began.

She gripped the arms of the desk chair tightly, no longer aware of her surroundings, entirely focused on what she was meant to see. Aidan was lying on his back. He was bare-legged, wearing high boots and clad in a leine and black cloak, the latter pinned to one shoulder and belted. His hands were folded atop the belt, which held two huge swords. The image sharpened. He was asleep, his eyes closed, his face relaxed, at peace. The necklace he wore became apparent, as if her mind's eye had zoomed in on it. A fang, capped with gold, lay against the hollow of his collarbone.

He turned into stone, becoming an effigy atop a tomb.

She sprang to her feet, crying out.

Tabby was hovering over her. "What did you see?"

Brie hardly heard her. She could not have seen what she had! Her premonitions were never wrong. She looked at Tabby, aghast. "I saw him in stone effigy, atop a medieval tomb."

Tabby took her hand. "Brie, he's from the fifteenth century," she said carefully.

"So what? Allie is still alive, isn't she? And he was alive the other day!" she cried. And her grandmother's ring began pinching her.

Brie had been wearing Sarah's garnet ring since she was thirteen. Sarah had always claimed it would protect her and enhance her gifts. She twisted it nervously, aware of desperation surging. Tabby said, "Honey, he *is* alive, somewhere, farther in the past. But we can't time-travel like they do."

Brie stared at her. She wanted him to be alive right then and there. "My visions are a tool. They're meant to help others. Why did I have that vision?" she cried.

"I don't know. Brie, would you please rest? And eat?" Tabby returned to the kitchen, then set a sizzling plate before her. Brie had been hungry earlier; now, she had no appetite.

"I'm going to go," Tabby said. "I haven't been home in three days. The neighbor's been taking care of the cats and the plants. And I really need a shower."

Brie stood to hug her. Tabby looked as if she was

on her way to take tea at Buckingham Palace. "I'm fine. Thank you for everything."

When Tabby was gone, Brie—almost desperate—went on to her next search, and the words *Aidan of Awe* produced a result. She froze in sheer disbelief. Then, her heart leaping painfully in her chest, she hit the enter key. She quickly skimmed down the first page and began to read.

In December 1436, Aidan, the Wolf of Awe, a Highlander with no clan, sacked the stronghold of the Earl of Moray at Elgin, leaving no one alive.

She breathed hard and read the rest of the page.

However, Moray escaped the Wolf's wrath intact, to take up his position at court as Defender of the Realm for King James, the same position he had enjoyed ten years earlier. But when James was murdered at Perth the following February, Moray, who was known to be at court, vanished, never to be heard from again. Quite possibly, Moray was slain with his king. The Wolf of Awe proceeded to spend the next nineteen years ruthlessly destroying the families and holdings of Moray's three powerful sons, the earls of Feith, Balkirk and Dunveld. Retribution came from Argyll, and in 1458 Castle Awe was burned to the ground. Although the Wolf spent twenty years rebuilding his stronghold, he forfeited his other holdings, his title and earldom (Lismore) to King James II. He remained universally distrusted and feared until his demise. In

> 1502, after his mercenary role in the MacDonald uprising, he was accused of treason by the Royal Lieutenant of the North, the powerful Frasier chief. Badly wounded from an escape attempt, he was publicly hanged at Urquhart.

Brie couldn't see the page, for her vision suddenly blurred. The terrible Wolf of Awe could not be her Aidan. Her Aidan was a Master of Time, sworn to protect Innocence through the ages, a mighty hero defending mankind from evil, upholding God. And Aidan could not hang. He would simply vanish into the future or the past.

Except he had been badly hurt.

She started to cry, but wiped the tears away. She read the next sentences.

> His tomb had been carefully restored at the ruins of Castle Awe on Loch Awe. To this day, it remains a popular tourist attraction.

She was so upset she was shaking. She looked at the plate Tabby had set down before her and wanted to wretch. Picking the plate up, she carried it to the kitchen, set it down and leaned hard on the counter. What did all of this mean?

If she went to Loch Awe now, would she find the tomb and effigy she'd seen in her vision?

The Wolf of Awe had been *hanged.* He was cruel, mercenary. Surely he was not the same man.

But in her vision of him, she had seen her Aidan before he'd turned into stone. He'd worn a wolf's fang.

Good humans were possessed every single day and then they committed unspeakably evil acts.

Brie moaned. Had Aidan become the Wolf of Awe? Was it somehow possible?

Her head exploded with pain. Brie stepped behind the counter into her kitchen, opening the refrigerator to chug a glass of wine. She was shaking like a leaf. *What had happened to him?*

Brie slammed the refrigerator door closed. She had to know what was in that Level Four file. She grabbed her purse and keys and stormed from the loft. If Nick wasn't at his office, she'd wait.

HE FELT THE MOON SETTING for the third time.

Aidan slowly came back to the tower room, a dark despair clawing at him. This hunt had lasted three days and he had not found anything.

He blinked and adjusted his eyes to the dark, shuttered room. As the swirling black evil and the cries of innocence faded, he became aware of his body and his power. All sense of euphoric invincibility was gone. Most of what he had taken three nights ago was gone. The power in his body was hardly ordinary; it was that of the son of one of the greatest deamhanain ever known to Alba. He was arrogant enough to think he might, even without the extra life coursing through him, be capable of defeating a lesser god.

Still he was tired. His body and his mind begged him for rest, but it was time to think of other, worldly matters. He commanded an army of four thousand men—some soulless humans, others fierce Highlanders. He usually sold his army's services to the highest bidders, and had done so for the past sixty-six years.

He didn't care about the land, the mortal power—although he needed the gold to maintain his army, but he took vast pleasure in every single battle. If he could not engage Moray, he would go to war and relish destroying his other enemies, one by one.

The MacDonalds were marching on Inverness, a royal garrison, and he was joining the rebels, as Malcolm had said. He had personally helped Donald Dubh, their imprisoned leader, escape from Innischonnail, where the Campbell had imprisoned him. Argyll had been infuriated. Had Ian lived, he would have been pleased and proud.

A cry of alarm filled the tower.

Aidan was on his feet, bewildered, unbelieving.

He had met her once in the future, perhaps seventy years ago, and had not thought of her since then. Now he recalled a small woman with white powers, dressed in shapeless garments and ugly spectacles.

Why had he just heard Brianna Rose cry out in alarm? How had he just seen her frightened face so clearly? He had ceased hunting evil through time.

No other cries resounded, but he could feel darkness now, encircling her.

Tension riddled his body. He did not protect Innocence; he used it ruthlessly for his own means, for the attainment of power. He did not want to know what was happening to her. He simply did not care about other people's problems.

She screamed.

It was a scream of fear and pain; he knew she'd been wounded.

He did not think. He leapt.

STILL DEVASTATED BY THE IDEA that Aidan had become the Wolf of Awe, Brie hurried down the block. Dusk was approaching and she knew she had better not be caught outside. The city wasn't safe after dark and although the mayor's curfew was voluntary, very few of the city's denizens disobeyed it. Every shop on the street had already closed, except for the grocery store on the corner, and they were pulling their blinds.

She started to run. She couldn't recall ever being this upset, not even when Allie had vanished into time last year. But she had known that Allie's journey to the past was her Fate, she'd even seen the golden Highlander coming for her. This was entirely different.

The Book, handed down from generation to generation of Rose women, was very clear on the matter of Fate. It could never be defied by a mortal. Only the gods could rewrite it—and they never entirely did.

But sometimes events happened that were not in The Game Plan and the Gods corrected things when they went awry. Eventually, what was meant to be would happen.

Brie prayed that the historian she'd read had gotten all his facts wrong, or that her vision was wrong. She began to think that maybe she'd better go to Scotland and check out the tomb there, but she was really afraid of what she'd find. And why was her grandmother's ring bothering her? It had always fit perfectly, but now it was pinching her.

Brie stared at the ring. "This is meant to happen, isn't it?" she murmured.

Her grandmother had passed away a decade ago, at the ripe old age of 102. She'd been in full possession of her faculties right up until she'd taken her last breath.

When she passed away in her sleep, Brie had somehow known her time had come and spent the night at her grandmother's Bedford, New York, house. Sarah Rose had died smiling, and Brie often felt her presence.

She felt her now. "I mean, I could have felt all that pain and anguish last year or the year before—but I felt it now, for a reason. He needs me. I'm supposed to help him." She thought about her crush. Had she become infatuated with him so she could help him? "Why else would I feel him so strongly?"

She felt her grandmother's benevolence. If Sarah approved, Brie was on the right path, she thought. That only made her more determined to get into that Level Four file.

A shadow fell across the pavement directly in front of her.

Her heart seemed to stop with alarm. In a moment the sun would be vanishing beneath the horizon and the city would be lost in the gloom of the night. She'd never make it all the way to CDA.

A teenage boy stood in front of her, smiling maliciously.

He was pale, pimply and wore a long black cloak, marking him as a member of gangs who reputedly burned "witches" at the stake.

Brie breathed. "Get lost!" she cried, even though she was terrified. "It's light out!"

"Not for much longer." He snickered.

She tensed as three more teenage boys barred her way, all of them ghostly white, their lips nearly purple, wearing the same long black cloaks, as if they'd come from the Dark Ages.

She knew all about the ongoing investigation into these gang members at CDA. The "sub-demons," or subs, as they were often called, were human, with normal DNA and very real identities. They were missing boys and girls, belonging to distraught family members, but, robbed of their souls, they were pure evil.

Brie whirled to run, and faced two more leering teens in black hoods and cloaks. She was in big trouble. She prayed that Tabby and Sam would sense it and come to her rescue. And simultaneously, she thought about Aidan. It was instinct. If he was near, he had the power to save her.

"She's fat and ugly," one boy said. "Let's find someone else."

Brie didn't want to die, but she didn't want anyone else to die, either. She glanced back over her shoulder at the setting sun and cried out. The sky was mauve now, the sun out of sight. In another moment or so, dusk would become night and she would be killed.

Brie tried to run.

They let her. She ran as hard and fast as she could, across the empty street, aware of them laughing with malicious glee. Hope began when she didn't hear their footsteps behind her. She was going to make it. She didn't know why they'd let her go and she didn't care.

Suddenly three different boys appeared in front of her and barred her way, grinning. She tripped, crashing into them, but was seized from behind and pulled ruthlessly up against a lean and young male body. *They had only let her go to torture her.*

She fought wildly, writhing, her mind exploding into shards of terror. Her captor jerked on her so hard that something inside her snapped. Brie screamed in pain and fear.

The boy holding her laughed. The pimply-faced blond boy held a knife and he hooked it into her jeans, jamming it through the denim. She felt blinded by her terror. The steel met the sensitive flesh of her belly. He said, "Witch. You're a real one, ain't you? You reek of witchcraft!"

"No!" Brie begged. But she didn't dare struggle now.

The boy glanced past her. His face paled and his eyes widened with alarm.

A low, long, very menacing growl sounded.

It was otherworldly.

Shaking, Brie looked behind her.

A huge wolf with blazing blue eyes crouched behind her and the boy, his hackles raised. Wolves did not exist in New York City. This one was oversized, demonic. Brie felt his huge black power.

And in that split second of utter comprehension, before it leapt, she met eyes that were human.

The Wolf of Awe had heard her.

The wolf snarled and leapt—at *her.*

She screamed, glimpsing enraged blue eyes, expecting the beast to land on her, dragging her down and mauling her to death. As her heart burst in terror, the beast somehow twisted and landed only on her captor, and she spun aside.

The wolf ripped the sub's throat out and then, with a bestial roar, turned to one of the other boys.

They had guns and they started firing at the wolf as it drove another teen to the ground, savagely ripping him apart the way dogs shred stuffed toys. Brie was frozen in horror, but only for a single breath. She turned to run.

But as she did, the wolf raised his head, bleeding from its shoulder and its chest. It looked right at Brie with its eerily human eyes. Brie backed up, terrified. It leapt at one of the other boys and she did not think twice. As the sub-demon screamed, she fled.

She ran up the block as hard and as fast as she could, acutely aware of the snarling wolf behind her on the city street, making sounds she wished she could not hear. She somehow unlocked the front door of her building and ran inside. She didn't even think to lock that door or use the elevator. She ran up the three flights of stairs to her loft and somehow unlocked her door, her hand shaking as if with Parkinson's disease. Slamming the door closed, she speed-dialed Nick. Tears blinding her, she spoke before he could even answer.

"I think he's here. He's shot. He needs medical help, Nick!" She wept into the phone.

"Don't fucking move," Nick said, and the line went dead.

She dropped the phone, images of the vicious wolf as it destroyed the boys filling her mind. Subs or not, they were human. Sometimes, souls could be reclaimed when evil was exorcized.

Instead of calling Tabby and Sam, she silently begged them to hurry to her. And then she went still, paralyzed.

A huge power filled her loft behind her.

Brie began to shake uncontrollably. Slowly, she turned.

Aidan of Awe stood there.

CHAPTER THREE

HE WAS A MAN, NOT A WOLF, and he was bleeding from his gunshot wounds. His blue eyes blazed with rage and fury.

Brie cried out, pressing her back into her door. This man bore no resemblance to the Master she'd met last year and she couldn't breathe, choking on fear. She looked from his beautiful, furious and ravaged face to his bloody body, utterly naked, and then at the gold chain he wore, the fang hanging on it. She inhaled. He was all hard, rippling muscle and his entire body throbbed with tension.

She tore her gaze upward. "You're alive," she gasped. "You're hurt!"

His blue eyes were livid. "*Never* summon me again."

His anger enveloped her. It was terrifying, for there was so much hatred in it. Brie shuddered. The power of his hatred made her begin to feel sick. She tried to shake her head. She hadn't summoned him!

He was the Wolf of Awe.

What had happened to him?

The Wolf wanted blood and death. Brie felt the bloodlust. And she had seen the evil.

Her mind was reeling. "You've been shot." She realized she was whispering. "Let me help you...Aidan."

He snarled at her. "Come closer an' see how ye can really help me, Brianna."

He remembered her.

His mouth curled unpleasantly.

She exhaled harshly. She didn't move, not convinced that he wouldn't turn into that wolf and rip her to death. But he had saved her from the gang. If he was going to hurt her, wouldn't he have done so already?

Her temples pounded with the pain of having taken in so much of his rage and hatred. Feeling faint, perhaps from uncertainty, she met his glittering blue gaze. His hard stare was cold, menacing. *How could a man change so much in a single year?*

She was terrified of him, but she was supposed to help him, wasn't she? "You're bleeding," she whispered. "You could bleed to death."

He barked at her, a dark, bitter laugh. "I willna die. Not yet."

She tried to feel past the hatred and anger, the lust for more blood, but if he was weakened or in pain, it eluded her. He was probably too full of adrenaline just then.

She pushed the fear aside. She would not risk him bleeding to death. She turned and opened the linen closet, not far from the kitchen. She took several towels out and faced him. His gaze moved from the towels in her hands to her face.

The distance of a small kitchenette separated them. She started forward slowly, in case he tried to seize her, or worse, turned into the Wolf and leapt at her.

"Dinna!"

She faltered by the kitchen counter. "Here." She held out the largest towel.

He looked even angrier.

Brie tossed it at him.

She thought he meant to catch it. Instead, he batted it away with one hand. Her gaze dropped of its own accord and she knew she flushed. "You need clothes—and medical attention," she whispered, dragging her eyes upward. Their gazes locked.

"I need power," he said dangerously.

Demons lusted for power. All evil did. Brie felt tears of fear and despair well. She somehow shook her head. "No." That Wolf had been evil. That Wolf had destroyed those teenagers. How could this be *her* Aidan?

He suddenly turned and picked up the towel, his every movement filled with raw fury. He wrapped it around his waist. When he looked at her with his blazing eyes, he said, "They were lost."

She trembled. He had just read her thoughts. "You don't know that their souls couldn't be reclaimed."

He snarled at her.

"Are they all dead?"

"Every last one," he said savagely, as if triumphant.

She wiped at her tears.

"Ye cry for the deamhan boys?"

She was crying for him. "No. I'm sorry. You saved me, and I'm judging you."

It was a moment before he spoke. "I hardly saved ye, Brianna," he said, so softly that her heart skipped.

Brie found her gaze fixed on his. Her tension changed. Desire charged through her body in response to his blatantly seductive tone.

He knew. He smiled. "Ye ran. I hunted ye here," he said as softly.

He spoke as if he meant to take her to bed, not maul her to pieces. She became still, her body tight now, quivering, while fear surged. She began shaking her head. She wouldn't believe it. She would never believe him capable of hurting *her.*

She prayed that he had not fallen so far into black evil that he could do such a thing.

But, dear God, she was standing face-to-face with the man she had just spent the past year dreaming of.

Brie wet her lips and backed up.

His lust escalated dangerously, changing. It overshadowed the anger, the hatred. The need to draw blood vanished. She began to feel dizzy, hollow and faint. Her heart was pounding so hard, it hurt. His gaze was on her face now, and the tension that throbbed between them seemed so charged, Brie thought the air might blaze.

Brie closed her eyes. So much emotion and tension were swirling in the room, she was becoming confused. She had to keep a grip on her mind. She couldn't desire him now! He was simply too dangerous.

She fought for control, and when she opened her eyes, he looked oddly satisfied, as if he sensed her internal struggles. "Aidan, please sit down." She swallowed, knowing she'd sounded like Tabby with her first-graders. "I can stop the bleeding until the medics get here." Keeping up the pretense, she nodded toward the sofa.

He laughed at her. "Dinna speak as if I'm a small boy. Three bullets can't kill the son of a deamhan."

She went rigid. *He could not be the son of a demon.* Was this a bad, bad joke?

"Aye," he said, growling. "The greatest deamhan to ever walk Alba spawned me."

More tears rose. How could this be happening? "You're a Master!"

"Damn the gods," he roared.

She cringed, shocked. "They'll hear you!"

"I dinna care!"

Brie did not move, searching his furious gaze. *He hated the gods.* She trembled, afraid for him.

His blue eyes changed, becoming brilliant now, blinding. "Ah, Brianna," he murmured. "Ye care so much."

His lust for power and sex made her reel. Her body fired on every possible cylinder, but she was also sickened in her heart. The rage and hatred, the lust, the frenzy of it all was too much for her to bear. "What happened to you?"

"Come here," he said softly.

She tensed, instantly aware of what he intended.

"Ye want to come to me, Brianna."

She did. She wanted nothing more, and suddenly she wasn't sure why she was hesitating.

He started.

Brie thought his surprise was a response to her hesitation until her front door blew open and Nick stood there with his gun drawn.

Brie came out of her trance. Before she could scream at Nick, Aidan seized her, his strength shocking, fury blazing through him into her. Brie gasped as he pulled her up against his rigid body, her back to his chest.

Instead of feeling terror, a shocking sense of familiarity struck her.

When he spoke to Nick, his breath feathered the side of her neck and ear, leaving her breathless. "Do ye really wish to see if ye can murder me…afore I murder her?" Aidan taunted.

Brie clung to his strong forearm, which was locked beneath her breasts. His arm hurt her ribs terribly, reminding her that the sub might have bruised or fractured one of them. It was a welcome distraction from her conflicted senses, because she was acutely aware of his heart pounding slow and thick against her shoulder blades. Worse, he was only wearing her towel. There was no mistaking what was pulsing against her hip.

But, blended with the sexual desire she felt from him, there was murderous intention.

He seemed to hate Nick.

"Brie, don't move," Nick ordered calmly, his blue eyes the coldest she had ever seen.

"Nick, he saved me. Don't kill him!" she cried, terrified for them both.

Aidan jerked on her, clearly wanting her silent. "Ye seem fond o' yer little woman," he said to Nick mockingly. "Mayhap she should have summoned ye to her side, instead o' me."

"Let her go. She's an Innocent. You and I, we need to talk, calmly and reasonably, Aidan."

Aidan's answer was immediate. Brie cried out as Nick was blasted with blazing, visibly silver energy. Nick was pushed back against the wall as if by a huge gale.

She felt Aidan's focus shift entirely to Nick. "Well, well," he said softly, with great relish.

She was surprised. Demons could hurl their power so strongly that they'd send ordinary humans across entire football fields. Had Aidan withheld his power with Nick?

She knew what he meant to do before he hurled another kinetic blast at her boss. "Don't," she began, but it was too late.

The silver lightning blazed into Nick. To Brie's shock, Nick seemed to absorb the impact this time, reeling but remaining upright. He pointed the .45 at them and said dangerously, "I'm trying really hard not to blow your brains out. Oh, and I'm a dead shot."

Brie gasped, "Aidan, we're all on the same side. Please, don't do this."

Aidan nuzzled her cheek, which made her body explode with urgency. "I'm enjoyin' myself too much to cease now," he murmured.

Brie felt her body scream for his in spite of the terrible crisis. She somehow looked at Nick. "He is good, not evil, Nick. Don't shoot."

"He's turned, Brie. He turned a long time ago. If you can't feel the black power in this room, it's because you've been brainwashed."

Brie shook her head desperately. "No."

Nick said, "Let her go, Aidan, and I'll let you go."

Brie knew it was a lie. So did Aidan, because he laughed. "Ye forget, *Nick,* I can leap away whenever I choose. Ye canna stop me. I stay here to war with ye because it pleasures me." More silver energy blazed.

Nick grunted, going down to his knees, but he somehow kept the gun in his hand.

And Tabby and Sam appeared on the threshold of the loft, both of them breathless. As they halted, Sam's favorite weapon appeared in her hand, a steel Frisbee with a dozen knifelike teeth. She could sever a man's head from his body with it—a great way to bring even the purest demons down. But she said, in disbelief, "Aidan?"

"Sam, he saved me. Don't hurt him," Brie cried.

Aidan jerked her closer to his hard body. "Be quiet."

Nick was back on his feet now. "How good are you with that thing?" he asked Sam.

"Good, but I won't risk hurting Brie, too," Sam said, never taking her gaze from Brie and Aidan.

Tabby, who was amazing in crises, now sank to her knees and started chanting a spell. The Book of Roses had been translated long ago from Gaelic to English, but her spells were always spoken in the language of their foremothers, which gave her magic all the power the Ancients would allow.

Aidan's body filled with a new tension. Brie glanced up, and for the first time saw wariness reflected in his eyes.

He didn't fear Nick or Sam and their weapons, but he feared Tabby's magic. Brie instantly guessed her cousin's intentions. Aidan could not be restrained with ropes, shackles or steel bars. Tabby intended to bind him with a spell, making him an impotent, virtual prisoner.

Aidan snarled and his grasp on her tightened.

"Don't," Nick snapped.

It was too late. Brie gasped as the force began. They whirled through the room, through the loft's walls, through the building, across the city skyline. And then, as they were hurled with the speed of light through the atmosphere, past suns and stars, she screamed, the velocity ripping her body to shreds.

He did not make a sound.

HE HELD HER TIGHTLY, his senses furiously ablaze as never before. He was acutely aware of the woman in his arms—the Innocent he had leapt through time to rescue. As they landed, he instinctively shifted his body to break her fall. He did not know why he did so. He shouldn't care if she was hurt.

She screamed from the impact anyway.

He welcomed the pain of landing on the stone floor.

He had leapt time, against his own will, to protect her from evil. He had just served the gods.

His rage increased.

They had landed in the tower room, which remained in absolute darkness. She wept in his arms now, sobbing from the torment of the leap through so many centuries, her body atop his. He was acutely aware of her torment.

He did not want her in his arms. He did not want to feel her pain or be aware of her body. He *hated* her hair in his face. And he hated her for what she had done to him.

When he had forsaken the gods, he'd done so by spilling his own blood all over Iona's holiest shrine, where the Brotherhood lived. His defiance was written in blood and death, and not just his own. He'd poured the blood from the Innocent at Elgin all over the shrine, too.

"Ye canna walk away from yer vows."

Aidan knelt in the blood of his victims, breathing hard. "Get away," he warned the greatest Master of them all—MacNeil, the Abbot of Iona.

MacNeil came closer. "Yer in grief. I'm sorry, Aidan, sorry fer what was done."

"What was done?" He leapt to his feet, enraged. "Do ye speak of my son's murder at my own father's hands? Did ye see the murder in yer precious crystal? Did ye ken Moray would come an' steal his life from me?"

Tall, muscular and golden, MacNeil looked at Aidan with compassion. "I canna see all, Aidan. Ye must let Ian go, lad."

"I will never let him go!" he shouted.

"His death was written," MacNeil began, clasping his shoulder grimly. "In time, ye'll ken the truth."

Aidan wrenched away from the man who had chosen him. "Written? Is that why the gods wouldna let me leap to save him? Did they block my powers so my boy would die?"

MacNeil did not answer. It was answer enough.

"Aidan?" Brianna breathed.

He jerked, shocked that such a painful memory would dare to claim him again. He had just served the damned gods, he thought, as if Ian hadn't been taken from him.

"Aidan?"

He turned to stare into a pair of beautiful green eyes, framed with lush, dark lashes. He felt her heart now, beating against his, and he was so aware of her it was almost as if he'd never held a woman before. A vaguely familiar tension began as he stared at her, along with a flutter of anticipation. It had been so long that he could barely recognize the sensation, and he was confused.

Did he desire her *sexually?*

His hands were on her waist. Beneath the baggy garments, her waist was small, with no flesh to spare. Their gazes held, hers wide, and he moved his hands up her rib cage, beneath her clothes, until her heavy breasts bumped them.

She gasped.

His manhood surged between them, against her belly. His mouth felt dry. He was tempted to touch her breasts.

His blood coursed even faster now. What was he doing? Although he had been shot three times and the leap was weakening, he had the ability to heal unnaturally and quickly. In a short time, his wounds would be gone. But her power could restore him instantly. Holding her, he could almost taste her power. He could take her now; she deserved such abuse for daring to interfere in his life.

He was indifferent to sexual pleasure, indifferent to a woman's face, her hair, her eyes. He desired no one. He lived with lust; it was entirely different. Power served him so well.

He didn't want to be aware of the feeling of her body against his.

He should never have taken her with him.

If he took her power now, she wouldn't look at him with any faith or hope at all. In fact, she'd be incapable of doing very much of anything for days afterward, until her body had recovered from his rampage. That knowledge served him well, because he hated hearing her thoughts; he hated her wondering about what had happened; he hated her compassion and pity—just as he hated her.

He reached for the snap on her jeans and bent her mind to his.

She moaned, long and low, eyes closing.

The sound was familiar. All women instantly succumbed. Suddenly he was even more furious—with her, with himself, with the gods, the deamhanain—with everyone. He pulled her down angrily and moved over her, and she looked up at him, her eyes glazed with the desire he had deliberately instilled in her.

Now she would not pity him or believe in him, or anything else. She would be his sexual slave until he released her from the enchantment.

Moments ago, at her home in the future, she had

desired him—and he hadn't enchanted her. But she had loved him for a long time....

He didn't want her love, either!

For one moment he stared at her face.

She was everything he was not, everything he had once been.

He cried out, cursing, and leapt to his feet. He breathed hard. "Return to yer senses." He whirled and strode from the tower, slamming the door so hard behind him that the wood splintered, the panels shearing apart.

His mind spun incoherently as he rushed down the corridor. When he opened his chamber door, Anna Marie sat up in the bed, clad only in a silk chemise.

"Get out," he roared at her.

Her eyes widened in shock.

He decided he would murder her on the spot if she didn't leave immediately. She understood and paled, slipping from the bed. Circling him, she fled.

He slammed the chamber door closed and the stone walls reverberated.

Then he leaned against the wall, and for the first time in decades, he succumbed to a moment of utter confusion.

What had just happened to him?

Why hadn't he taken her, using her for the power he needed and craved, as he did them all?

Deep inside his body, something flickered, and he feared it was his soul.

His answer to the unfamiliar, unwanted feeling was instantaneous. He took a crooked chair and threw it at the wall, breaking it in pieces. A memory came swiftly, one long forgotten. Once, before his son's murder, his home had been filled with beautiful furnishings and treasures collected from all over the world, from many different times. His brother Malcolm had broken a Louis XIV chair in a fit of rage over the woman who was now his wife, Claire.

Aidan clutched his temples. He did not want to remember having once had a home filled with beauty. After Awe had been burned to the ground in 1458, he had never considered refurbishing it with any luxury.

Very deliberately, he shut his mind down. The past was finished. He would never enjoy such a home again, nor did he care to. As for the woman in the tower, he did not know what had just happened, but it did not matter. He'd lost his soul long ago and that was exactly what he wanted.

The woman, Brianna, had to go back to where she had come from as soon as she was strong enough to withstand another leap. She had brought forth memories he had no wish to entertain, and he did not like the fact that he had hesitated to satisfy his lust for power and life. He was a half deamhan. He decided that if she came close another time, he'd make certain she feared him as much as the rest of Alba. The next time, he would take her. Maybe he'd go so far as to take pleasure in her death.

The idea was disturbing.

BRIE SAT UP IN THE COLD DARKNESS, stunned.

Aidan had just slammed from the room. She couldn't breathe, but not because every movement caused her ribs to really hurt.

Aidan had just mesmerized her the way the demons did.

There was no doubt. Her body had been on fire a moment ago and she had lost her ability to think. She had been frantic for their union. But he had walked away, and the spell was broken.

She hugged herself, trying not to panic, her teeth chattering from the cold. He hadn't seduced her against her will, and she tried to reassure herself. But he was the son of a demon—he had told her so. She hadn't wanted to believe it, but she was starting to now.

How far had the Wolf gone?

How could the son of a demon ever have been a Master?

"He's turned, Brie. If you can't feel the black power in this room, he's brainwashed you."

Images of the Wolf viciously mauling those boys to death filled her.

But he hadn't hurt her—yet. He had saved her, even if he'd viciously destroyed the subs, even if he was so angry it was terrifying.

Demons did not save Innocence. They ruthlessly destroyed it. He wasn't as evil as Nick claimed. He had a conscience. Didn't he?

She was not reassured. They'd obviously leapt through time, and she had a pretty good idea of where they might be. Her heart hammered uneasily. He'd taken her hostage, or prisoner, or something. She was in over her head.

And where were her eyeglasses?

Her panic was complete. If she'd lost her glasses, she was almost as blind as a bat. If she couldn't see, how was she going to protect herself? The room was pitch-black and she groped the floor carefully, immediately realizing they'd landed on rough, uneven stone.

If she wasn't in a castle chamber, she didn't know where she was.

She had to find calm—no easy task when the son of a demon had just abducted her for no apparent reason. She did not know his motives and couldn't even guess them. Brie tried deep, slow breathing, ignoring the pain in her rib cage. She reminded herself that she was here because of her sudden empathy across time for Aidan. He had rescued her from evil and brought her to the past. There was a reason for it all.

Brie shuddered. He bore little resemblance to the man she'd been infatuated with for the past year. He was frightening in every possible way—his anger, his sexuality, his hatred. His face might be as beautiful as ever, but his eyes were so flat, without light—almost like the eyes of demons, except that their eyes were black and soulless and Aidan's remained sharply blue.

If he had a conscience, could he be redeemed?

Brie sat up straighter, wincing against the pain. Aidan did not appear to be redeemable. Surely she was not his salvation!

Shocked that she would even think such a thing, Brie managed to get to her feet, holding the aching side of her ribs. She leaned against the cold stone wall, certain he'd gone out of the room. She didn't know what she was going to do when she found the door and stepped out of it.

She prayed that she would step out into a bright New York City summer day.

She was pretty sure Hudson Street was not outside that door.

She started forward, staying close to the wall, until it turned at a right angle. She followed the wall until her hands slid over a coarse wooden door, with some of the panels splintered off the frame. She fumbled for a doorknob or latch. When she found it, she hesitated. Once she walked through that door, there was no turning back.

Aidan was outside that door, somewhere.

Brie opened it, revealing a shadowy hall. The corridor was a blur, but there was no mistaking the flickering lights on the walls. The hallway was lit with candles in sconces. She was definitely in a castle in the past.

It crossed her mind that, if that historian had his facts right, it was before December 1502, because Aidan clearly hadn't been hanged yet.

She turned and saw an open embrasure. Outside, the night was blue-black. She inhaled, and the air was scented with pine and the sea. Brie walked over to the loophole. Ebony water gleamed below, and the distant shores were pale with snow.

She'd been transported to the Highlands. The last time she'd smelled such invigorating air had been on a summer vacation spent trekking across the northern half of Scotland. In spite of her trepidation, some excitement began. The Highlands would always be home to a Rose woman.

It was freezing cold out—and inside the castle, too. She shivered, wishing she had a coat.

A door farther down the hall opened. Brie instantly felt Adam's hot, hard power. It didn't feel evil—but it didn't feel white, either. She jerked back against the wall, wishing she could vanish into the stone. Even though she couldn't see clearly, she knew it was Aidan stepping out from the chamber.

He turned toward her and stared.

Her mouth went unbearably dry. Why had he taken her back in time with him? What did he want? What was her purpose?

He started toward her. She didn't have to make out his features to know that he was unsmiling. She realized he'd put some kind of wall up. His anger felt distant, not as violent or threatening. His shocking sexual urges were gone, along with the bloodlust. She was only slightly relieved.

As he came closer, she realized he was clad as a medieval Highlander in a belted tunic, a long and short sword, his legs pale and bare over knee-high boots. In fact, he was dressed just like her vision of him in effigy, except she couldn't see if he wore the fang necklace.

She tensed as he paused before her. It was a moment before he spoke. "I'll have a chamber readied fer ye." His tone was carefully neutral.

She was relieved he was exercising self-control over his emotions. "Where am I?"

"Yer at my home, Castle Awe. I'll have ye sent back to yer time when yer stronger," he said brusquely.

His gaze was so hard and unwavering, she flushed. Maybe it was better that she couldn't see his expression, because even blurred, his regard was unnerving. She felt almost as if she'd been trapped in a cage with a wild animal and that she didn't dare move, for fear of provoking him.

But with the two of them alone in the hall, it was impossible not to recall being in his arms. Even shielded, his power was so male and sexual that her pulse raced. She would always find him terribly, unbearably attractive, she thought.

What she hadn't felt earlier, though, was his magnetic pull. A force pulsed between them, urging her toward him. She probably hadn't noticed it before because of her empathy. His turbulent emotions had been an overwhelming distraction, but his magnetism was shockingly strong now.

She would ignore his pull. "Are you okay?" she asked carefully. She couldn't discern any bandages beneath the tunic.

His gaze narrowed. "Ye ask after my welfare?"

She wet her lips. "You're the one who got shot." Because of her, she thought.

His anger roiled, pushing at her. "I'm almost healed." He was harsh.

So he had an extraordinary recuperative power, she thought. That was not demonic, either. Demons didn't heal, not even themselves—they destroyed.

"A maid will show ye to yer chamber. Ye can stay there." He whirled, striding down the corridor.

She had no intention of remaining in the hall, alone in the dark of the night—especially with her impaired vision. He had started down a dark hole that was obviously a spiral staircase. "Wait, please," she cried, rushing after him.

He began to vanish down the spiraling steps, as if he hadn't heard her. He was obviously ignoring her.

Brie rushed forward, pain erupting from her ribs. Her depth perception gone, she tripped and went flying down the stairs.

She landed hard. After the agony of their journey through time and her bruised or fractured ribs, it hurt impossibly and she cried out, tears finally filling her eyes. For one moment, as his hands instantly closed on her arms, she felt dizzy and faint. And then she felt only his large hands and the strength coming from them.

His grasp was *reassuring,* she managed to think. But that was impossible, because of what he had become.

"Will ye nay watch where ye go?" he demanded with heat. "Do ye have two left feet?"

Her ribs throbbed and she looked up into his vivid blue eyes. His mouth was inches from hers. She was almost in his arms, so close she could see him perfectly. What was she going to do with her attraction to him?

His eyes changed, smoldering.

"I can hardly see at all. I need my eyeglasses," she managed. Had he just looked at her mouth?

"Yer hurt," he said flatly, his gaze on hers. "The possessed boys hurt ye."

She nodded, biting her lip, wanting, absurdly, to apologize for being a klutz. Even more absurdly, she wanted to move closer to him. He simply didn't feel that dangerous now. She felt like putting his hand on her throbbing ribs, as if his touch would soothe them. And she felt like touching his perfect face. The urge to reach out to him was so strong, she began to lift her hand.

He became very still, his face hardening, his eyes brilliant now. Abruptly, he put his arm around her and hefted her to her feet, then pushed her away, against the wall.

His anger spewed, filling her. She began to feel sick, his emotions too much to bear. "Stop," she begged. "What is wrong?"

"Ye stay far from me," he warned. "I dinna wish to have ye here. I dinna wish fer ye to have any cares fer me an' I dinna wish to converse! Do ye ken?"

She gasped. "You brought me here! I wasn't given a say in the matter."

His mouth curled unpleasantly. "Yer friend Nick needed a reminder. He canna triumph over me."

Their gazes were locked, his blue eyes ablaze. "Is that why I'm here?" Brie didn't believe it.

He stared, his eyes harder now. "Ye summoned me against my will. I dinna care fer any summons, ever. And I dinna like yer man, Nick."

Brie stared back, perturbed. "I do not have the power to summon anyone. You heard me, and you rescued me," she said slowly. "For all that anger, you did the right thing. Oh…and Nick is not my man. He's my boss."

"I dinna care," he snarled. His sudden anger shifted, a mask settling over his features. "Claire's below. She'll heal yer ribs." He turned to go.

He knew she was hurt, and somehow, he knew exactly where. "Aidan, wait."

He faced her. "Will ye ever cease yer talk?"

She took a breath. "You saved me from the subs. I haven't said thank you. Thank you, Aidan," she added firmly, and she smiled hesitantly at him.

His eyes widened. Angered all over again, he whirled and started down the stairs.

He was a powder keg, she thought, and it took only a word or a look to set him off. She started after him, but didn't dare rush. There was more light on the landing below, and she saw his shape far ahead, vanishing into another room. A moment later she paused on the threshold of the great hall.

Although she couldn't make out details, it was a huge, high-ceilinged room. One wall contained a massive fireplace, where a large fire blazed. Two chairs were before it, and a long table was in the hall's center, with benches on either side. The room was large, yet the furnishings were so spare.

Aidan sat at the head of the trestle table and was pulling a trencher forward. Brie smelled roasted game and ale.

She hesitated. He wasn't alone.

A small boy of nine or ten stood beside him. He was dressed like Aidan, in a knee-length tunic and a plaid, and he had dark hair and blue eyes. Brie almost thought she knew him, but that was impossible.

The boy looked at him pleadingly, but Aidan only drank from a heavy cup. Brie sensed the child was really distressed.

Brie tensed. It was one thing to be rude to her; it was another to ignore an unhappy child.

Brie was so upset it took her a moment to speak. Maybe she could help the child, if Aidan would not. "Hello," she said, smiling brightly even though it was forced. "Do you speak English? Can I help you?" she asked, kneeling so they were eye to eye.

Aidan choked on his wine. His brilliant gaze had widened with shock.

Brie ignored him. The boy was now facing her. He was so familiar, yet she knew she couldn't have met him. "I'm Brie," she said softly. "What's your name?"

The child seemed bewildered.

Brie's concern escalated. "Are you okay? Where's your mother?" she asked, realizing he might not speak English.

Aidan shot to his feet with a roar. "What ploy is this?"

Brie leapt back. So much pain went through her that she was blinded by it. The pain came from him, not her ribs.

Aidan seized her arm, shouting at her. "Who do ye speak with?"

Brie fought the pain flooding her. That terrible knife was in her heart again, and with it there was so much despair. Her vision cleared, and she looked at the boy. He started speaking to her. She did not hear a word.

Her heart slammed as a vague memory tried to surface.

Aidan seized her shoulders now, hurting her. "Who do ye see?" he roared at her.

Had she seen this boy on Five? Brie looked at the frightened, expectant child, then at Aidan. "Oh my God. You don't see him?"

Aidan turned white. "Nay, I see no one!"

CHAPTER FOUR

BRIE GASPED. SHE COULD SEE THIS CHILD as clear as day, as if she had perfect vision. But the boy was invisible to Aidan. She was facing a child's lost soul. "It's a little boy," she whispered, her gaze locked with Aidan's.

Aidan's pain struck her so hard that it sent her to her knees.

"Where is he?" he cried in anguish. "Why do *ye* see him? Do ye see him still? I canna see him!"

On her knees, Brie held her chest, fighting the pain, fighting to breathe. She looked up at Aidan, past the waiting ghost, but couldn't speak. No one could live with such torment, she thought. She felt tears start to trickle down her face. "He's…here…beside you!"

Aidan moaned. Then, pulling her to her feet, he demanded, "What does he want?"

"I don't know…what he wants," she gasped, his grief hitting her in brutal wave after brutal wave. "I can't…this hurts too much….please, stop!"

Aidan stared desperately at her, his fingers digging into her arms.

"Stop," she wept. "I can feel everything you're feeling…you have to stop!"

The little boy began fading. He was talking swiftly now, but not making a sound.

"Wait! Don't go!" Brie cried.

It was too late. The little boy had vanished.

"Did he leave?" Aidan asked, ravaged.

Brie nodded. He was clamping down on his pain. It took her another moment before she could speak. She was left with a dull, throbbing heartache. "Who is he?"

Aidan released her. "My son." His eyes mirroring the terrible torment he was shielding from her, he strode from the room.

Aidan was haunted by his child.

Brie collapsed onto the bench, her head on her arms on the table, overcome by what had just happened. Aidan's soul was tormented. He was grieving for his dead child. No one should ever have to go through the ordeal of losing a child. Was this how he had lost his faith and his way?

Her grandmother's ring suddenly began pinching her finger. Brie was certain Grandma Sarah had something she wished to say. But Brie was so upset she couldn't sense whatever it was.

Aidan hadn't been able to see his child, but he'd known right away who she'd spoken to. Had Aidan seen his son's ghost before? Why was she the one who could see his son today?

But then, why was she so shockingly and painfully empathic toward Aidan, even across time?

Somehow it was all connected, she thought, and that included her being in the past at Castle Awe, where his little son's ghost was.

Suddenly, a wolf's mournful howl sounded.

Brie sat up, every hair on her body standing on end. The lonely howl was endless, a sound of impossible anguish and deep, dark despair. The grief and hopelessness slowly crept into her, filling her, until she felt as if she was lost in an endless black maze with no possible way out, an eternity of despair ahead.

Just as the howl seemed to have finally faded, it started again, and the long, lonely cry resounded. She stood and walked slowly to the great hall's threshold. Even if she had considered cutting and running earlier—not that she could simply leave Awe—she would never do so now.

This man needed healing, she thought, trembling. And he also needed a friend.

It might not be the best idea to have so much compassion flooding her now, and offering him friendship might be dangerous, but she couldn't stop her feelings—nor did she want to.

Grandma Sarah's ring eased on her finger.

The windows in the corridor outside were small, and she was drawn to the closest one. Through the bars, she looked into an outer ward and at the castle's soaring curtain walls. A full moon was hanging overhead, burning a fiery orange. A red moon rising was the harbinger of great evil, but this was a glimpse of the moon as she had never before seen it. She did not know what the fiery moon meant.

Footsteps sounded, and Brie started as great, white power touched her. A couple turned the corner. The man was a drop-dead gorgeous Highlander, clad exactly like Aidan except for the color of his plaid. It took her a moment to look at the woman at his side. She was very attractive and very tall, with auburn hair. She wore a long leine, a belted plaid and a shortsword—and then Brie saw blue jeans beneath her tunic.

Brie's surprise vanished. Allie had gone back in

time last year, and she had just time-traveled, too. The odds were that they weren't the only ones who'd found a way to journey through the ages, and the auburn-haired woman walking toward her was proof.

The strange woman hurried to her. "You're hurt!"

"I was attacked—in New York City," she said unsteadily, her eyes glued to the woman's face. She had an American accent and wore her hair in a very all-American ponytail.

The woman wasn't surprised by Brie's statement. "I'm Claire, and this is my husband, Malcolm of Dunroch." Claire laid her hand directly on Brie's bruised ribs, which made Brie wince. "Let me heal you."

Brie nodded, biting her lip as warmth flowed into her from Claire's hands. She saw that Malcolm stood by one of the barred windows, his expression grim as he gazed out into the night. She didn't have to be telepathic to know that he was listening for the Wolf, waiting for it to howl again. Its reverberating cries had faded. Brie was certain that there would not be any more anguished howls. "It's Aidan," she said softly.

Malcolm turned toward her and their gazes met. "Aye." He added, "I am Aidan's half brother."

Brie was more than surprised, she was relieved and thrilled. Aidan had a family in his corner.

Claire removed her hand. "I'm not a great healer, but that should be better. How do you feel?"

Brie took a breath, and no pain resulted. "Wow. Way better. Thank you. I'm Brie," she added.

Claire stared intently. "Did Aidan do that to you?"

"No!" Claire was Aidan's sister-in-law, and even *she* thought Aidan capable of hurting her. Unnerved, Brie said grimly, "A gang of boys attacked me, not Aidan."

Malcolm suddenly strode to them. "I'll take ye back to yer time, lass. 'Tis nay safe fer ye at Awe."

Brie tensed. In the past moments, it had become very clear that she could not go anywhere—not when Aidan was in such torment. "I don't think he'll hurt me," she said firmly. Their eyes met and held. Malcolm's gaze was frankly searching. She refused to blush, not wanting him to suspect she had inappropriate feelings for his brother. "If he wanted to hurt me, he had a dozen chances to do so."

Malcolm and Claire exchanged looks, which did not escape Brie. Malcolm said, "I have chosen to keep faith, but I dinna trust him very well. I dinna think yer safe here. He uses women at will. Why take the risk, Lady Brie?"

Brie lifted her chin, her heart pounding. Malcolm was wrong. Aidan could have used her in the tower, and he hadn't. "If you're telling me that Aidan commits crimes of pleasure, I do not believe it."

Malcolm flushed. "I willna believe it, either," he said. "But it's best fer ye to leave Awe."

He wasn't certain just how demonic Aidan had become. Her heart hurt her now. "He needs his friends," she said unsteadily. "He needs me," she added. And she felt color finally creeping into her cheeks.

Malcolm stared at her, as did his wife. "My brother needs no one, an' he'll be the first to tell ye so. He has no friends, nary one. Ye dinna ken him well, lass."

Brie shook her head, upset. "No one can live alone. Everyone needs friends."

"Aidan lost his soul decades ago," Claire said softly. "He has become a dark and dangerous man. He is not the stuff of romantic dreams. I hope you can see that. I hope you aren't interested in him."

"I'm a Rose," Brie said, hoping to hide her feelings, which were clearly somewhat obvious. "Rose women are gifted, and we're meant to use our gifts to help those in need. I have the Sight and I'm a strong empath. I met Aidan a year ago, briefly, and never expected to see him again. But recently I have been consumed with his pain and torment, and it's unlike any empathy I've ever had before. I've been brought here for a reason, Claire."

"An' what reason do ye think yer here for?" Malcolm asked bluntly.

Brie hesitated. "He saved me," she told them. "The subs would have murdered me and he *saved* me. Maybe it's my turn to help him."

Claire gasped, "He hasn't rescued an Innocent since his son was murdered."

Brie breathed hard, anguished for Aidan and his child all over again. "Was it a demon?"

"It was his father," Claire said.

"Oh, God," Brie whispered, aghast. "What he has suffered! No wonder he has become so dark!"

Claire grasped her arm. "Brie, you are too involved!"

"How can I not be involved? He needs me—he needs us," she added quickly, flushing. "We have to help him."

"Help him how?" Claire cried. "Help him find himself? He is ruthless, Brie."

Brie hugged herself. "If he was as ruthless as you say, I wouldn't be standing here."

Claire was pale. "Are you really thinking of befriending him? To what end? To guide him back to his vows? He isn't the same man, and I don't think he'll ever be that man again. He'll destroy you."

Malcolm took her elbow. "She cares fer him, Claire."

"Obviously!" Claire cried.

Brie realized there was no point in trying to hide her feelings. "I can't walk away from him—not when he is in such torment. I can't walk away from his son's ghost, either."

"If there is a ghost," Claire said.

Brie jerked. "Why would you say that?"

"Because Aidan is the only one who has seen Ian."

Brie was stunned. "I can see him."

Claire's eyes widened and she exchanged a sharp look with Malcolm.

"The gods have a reason fer all they do—when they bother with us," he finally said.

"Maybe you are right, and there's a reason you are here," Claire said to Brie. She shook her head. "Aren't you afraid of him? We fear him. *Everyone* fears him. He *should* be feared."

Brie did fear him. He made her uncomfortable, and he was so unpredictable. She was terrified of the Wolf. But she didn't think he would hurt her. She'd meant what she'd said earlier. He'd had many chances to do so. "He still has a conscience."

Malcolm started. "Ye have faith. I am pleased."

Claire spoke grimly. "Befriend him—save him if you can—but do not trust him," she warned.

Brie knew it was really good advice. And the truth was, she didn't quite trust him, so Claire's advice would be easy to follow.

Malcolm spoke. "I still fear fer ye, lass. In good conscience, I canna leave an' Innocent in this place with my brother. Would ye care to come to Dunroch with us? Ye can save him in bits an' pieces, from a safe distance."

Brie wasn't going anywhere. "I appreciate your

concern, but I'll stay here." She couldn't befriend Aidan if she was at Dunroch. She stared at the handsome couple. "Do you guys know Black Royce and the lady of Carrick?"

Malcolm smiled. "Royce is my uncle, lass, and we ken them well."

Brie felt so much relief. She desperately needed backup, and Allie was the best backup there was. "Are they far from here?"

"By horse, Carrick is a two- or three-day ride, depending on the time of year," Claire said, grinning. "I should have known you and Allie were friends. I'll let her know that you're at Awe."

"Thank you," Brie said. She wasn't as alone as she'd been an hour ago, and now, understanding more of what had happened to Aidan, her purpose was becoming clearer. "I have one more question. What is today's date?"

"'Tis November 18th," Malcolm said. "November the 18th, in the year 1502."

Brie froze in horror.

HE LAY IN THE COLD, WET EARTH, panting hard, uncontrollably, his head on his paws. Overhead, the moon was huge and bright. *Brianna could see his son.*

He'd howled his anguish until he could not howl anymore. *Why could she see Ian when no one else could, except for him?*

The pack of wolves that had gathered, heeding his despair, ringed him in the glade where he lay unmoving, overcome with torment. The females wanted him; the males would die for him, and they would remain there until he changed forms, protecting him. He made no move to do so. In that moment, he did not ever want to go back to Castle Awe.

Why had Ian gone to her today, instead of to him?

And why could she see him so clearly, for long moments, when he was cursed with a brief glimpse?

A wolf could not weep. A wolf could not moan. He rose up on his haunches, and this time when he howled, the sound reverberated through the forests and to the mountain peaks. The pack took up his cries.

His son had been haunting him since the day he had been murdered. It did not matter whether he was at Awe, at Dunroch, at court or in battle, whether in the future or the past—the moment came unfailingly every single day. He might be turning the corner of a corridor, leaving the great hall or exiting a stairwell. He could be hunting a stag, or in the bow of a galley. But from the corner of his eye, suddenly and with no warning, he would glimpse his small son.

And for one heart-stopping instant he would come face-to-face with Ian, who would stand there looking at him, so very frightened, and then vanish.

There had been 14,093 such moments in the past sixty-six years.

But today, Ian had gone to Brianna.

What did it mean?

No one had ever glimpsed the small ghost except for Aidan. He knew that his servants thought him mad, as did Malcolm and most of Alba. And now *she* had seen Ian, too.

Not a single day passed in which he did not yearn for and anticipate that momentary sight of the only person he still loved.

Not a single day went by in which he didn't dread the sight of his dead son.

Because that single glimpse wasn't enough. That

single glimpse was torture. It was so obvious that Ian wished to speak with him—but the moment he tried to do so, Ian would vanish.

The howls faded. The pack was restless, sensing his intent. Aidan stood, hackles raised, the pack gathering. Her image was engraved on his mind. He did not want her at Awe—he did not want her in his life—but he would never let her go now.

He bounded into the woods, the pack following, to take out his fury on the innocent beasts of the wood.

"HAVE YE SETTLED HER FER THE NIGHT?" Malcolm asked with a smile. As concerned as he was for his brother, the sight of his wife always made his heart leap and his body stir.

Claire closed the chamber door behind her. "Yes. She's so exhausted, she passed out the moment her head hit the pillow. Malcolm, I'm worried about her."

Malcolm went to her, pulling her into his arms, wanting to pleasure her a hundred times before the sun rose but knowing their passion had to wait. "Claire, I can send her back against her wishes."

"I know, but she's so determined, Malcolm. She is not what I would have expected, not for Aidan."

He looked into his wife's beautiful eyes. "Yer a warrior, Lady Allie is a healer an' Lady Tabitha has great spells. But can I remind ye that when we first met, ye had no clear power? An' when Lady Tabitha first arrived at Blayde, her spells often failed. Only Lady Allie had great powers when she came to the past."

Claire bit her lip. "She's a computer geek, Malcolm. She told me so. She works for CDA, but in the basement. She does *research.* She isn't a warrior, a healer or a witch. If Aidan chooses, he will destroy her. She is no match for him. He's probably already seduced her and used her."

"She has gifts, Claire," Malcolm reminded her gently, "and a powerful faith."

"Yes, she has a deep faith in Aidan, Malcolm. The kind of faith I had in you, the kind of faith Allie had in Royce, the kind of faith Tabby had in Guy. She is in love with him, even if she doesn't know it."

"An' ye dinna think she can survive her love—an' his hate?"

"I am afraid for her. I want to protect her for the journey she seems intent to start upon," Claire cried.

"So ye wish fer me to send her back?" he asked, bemused. He knew his wife so well now, and he knew her answer.

Claire hesitated. If she had learned one thing, it was that love could heal anyone and that Fate was the strangest of bedfellows. She had been in over her head with Malcolm, but the impossible had happened—their love had triumphed against all odds.

Reading her mind as he always did, Malcolm said, "She's a pretty lass, Claire. Mayhap she's meant to bring my brother back. She thinks so. That kind o' faith will serve her well."

Claire breathed, aware that the wrong decision could mean Brie's death. "Let's give her a few days," she said. "Let's give Aidan a few days."

BRIE WASN'T SURE WHAT AWOKE HER, but suddenly she was staring at a night-darkened ceiling, aware that she was not alone.

Claire had shown her to a small chamber on an

upper floor. She and Claire had begun a conversation about the Brotherhood, and Claire had started to tell her about three holy books and a shrine, but Brie had been too tired—and too upset about the date of her arrival in the past—to listen. Then she had seen the bed and stumbled toward it, falling into it without even removing her Sketchers. Brie knew she'd passed out the moment her head had hit the pillow.

Now Brie slowly sat up, trying to adjust her rotten vision to the darkness. A small fire remained, dancing in the hearth. She blinked, tension arising. There was a shadow at the foot of her bed.

She felt so much male power, neither black nor white.

She breathed nervously. "Aidan?"

The shadow did not move or speak.

Brie knew it was Aidan, but he emanated no emotion at all, just heat. She tried to stay calm, but it was impossible. "Is everything all right?"

Suddenly he walked to the fireplace and began throwing more wood into it. The fire blazed, illuminating him as he turned back to her. "Dinna fear me," he said harshly. Across the small chamber, their gazes locked. "I willna hurt ye."

Brie did not move. There was only his presence and his power and her acute senses and gifts. In the vacuum of the night, she knew he meant his every word.

She stared toward his blurry shape and he stared back. She thought about the fact that it was November 1502, and he would hang by the end of the year—if history was right. She thought about the fact that a long time ago—she did not know how long—his own father had murdered his child. She thought about the fact that he had once been a man who smiled easily and defended Innocence. He was grieving now, furious, and he was being haunted by his own dead child.

He hadn't answered her. She didn't know why he had come to her room, but she knew she wasn't in any jeopardy. Compassion swelled. He had spent the night mourning his son. She would never forget the sound of the Wolf howling at the orange moon.

"Are you all right?" she asked again softly.

He remained facing her, too far away for her to see his features or expression. "Aye."

She needed to see his face. She wanted to know what he was feeling and thinking, without having to experience it as an empath. On the other hand, she hesitated, because it was the middle of the night, and they were alone in her bedchamber. She pulled the covers up higher. "Aidan, I met Malcolm and Claire."

His answer was to take the room's single chair and move it closer to the bed. He didn't sit down. "I wish to speak with ye, Brianna."

She wasn't surprised. His emotions were blocked, so they might have a normal conversation. She was almost thrilled. "I guess it must be pretty urgent."

"'Twill be dawn shortly. Please come an' sit."

Brie realized the sky was softening with gray and violet light; dawn was creeping across the Highland horizon. She hesitated, hoping he wanted to talk about his son. Then she slid from the bed, fully dressed. She pushed her heavy hair behind her ears as she went to the chair. His hands were on the chair's back. Her body seemed to hum as she sat. She hadn't mistaken his magnetism. This close, his power seemed to vibrate toward her, and vice versa.

He released the chair, and she felt his hands brush against her hair as he did so.

She reminded herself that now was not the best time to feel any attraction. She closed her eyes. She had to stay neutral and ignore his heat and pull, his masculinity and looks. She wanted to save him. She wanted them to be friends. That took precedence over everything else.

Besides, anything else wasn't an option.

When she opened her eyes he was staring, only steps away. She could see him so clearly. His vivid gaze was on hers, serious and searching. But the moment she looked into his eyes, his lashes lowered. He had no intention of allowing her to see into his eyes—or his soul.

But he seemed almost himself now. He could have been that long-ago Master, a man dedicated to the gods and sworn to defend mankind. Yet she knew he had taken a long, dark journey away from that man.

She wasn't sure what had happened after he'd ceased howling tragically. It might be better that she didn't know. "I heard the Wolf earlier. Why do you do it?"

His mouth curved mirthlessly. "Because I can."

"Do you do it often?"

To her surprise, his gaze dropped to her mouth. "Often enough," he finally said.

She hugged herself, becoming uneasy. Had he just looked at her with sexual interest? Had he done so earlier that night? "I don't like the Wolf."

He shrugged.

"Beasts are prey or predator," Brie said carefully. "We both know the Wolf is a predator." He looked at her. "And animals do not have a conscience."

"Yer meaning?" he asked, rather coolly.

"How convenient that Wolf is for you."

His face tightened. "Aye, the Wolf serves me well."

"But the Wolf has a conscience, after all, just as you do. I saw it."

His shoulders lifted, stiffened. "Dinna challenge me."

Brie hadn't meant to provoke him. "I'm not! I was thinking aloud, trying to understand you. I'm sorry."

"Ye dinna need to comprehend me, Brianna. Dinna even try." His eyes flashed with anger.

She had raised a sore subject. She did not want to make him mad. "I am sorry about your son," she said, meaning it with all of her heart. "I am so sorry. What happened is so terrible—tragic and unfair."

He was so still he could have been carved from stone. Then she saw his chest rising and falling beneath the vee neckline of the leine. She could see the fang necklace he wore.

He folded his bulging arms across his chest. "Ye saw Ian," he said bluntly, "when no one has ever seen him, except fer me."

So Aidan could see Ian, too, although apparently not all of the time. She nodded, trying to search his gaze, but he wouldn't let her. "Malcolm and Claire told me what happened. How long has he been haunting you?"

His face tightened. "He was murdered sixty-six years ago next month."

Brie was shocked. Aidan had been haunted for a human lifetime!

"What did he wish o' ye?"

"I don't know," she said truthfully. "He was trying to speak, but I couldn't hear him." She stopped. The little boy had been afraid and desperate, and telling Aidan that would only cause more anguish.

Aidan flushed with anger. "I can hear yer every thought," he warned. "He was afraid."

Oh, God, he *was* telepathic. "Yes, he seemed very afraid." And suddenly a wave of grief hit her, very much the way an ocean wave might.

"Why did he come to ye, instead of me?" he cried. "He's been tryin' to speak to me fer all these years! What does he want to say?'

His desperation added to the flood tide of anguish. It was hard to speak. "I don't…know."

Suddenly the anguish and desperation vanished, tamped down in his soul. Brie breathed, shaking like a leaf. She had to monitor her thoughts, so as not to hurt him. "The other day, I felt your suffering, across time. There was so much pain and anguish, I thought you were being tortured. There was rage, and then, at the end, there was grief, and it was the worst emotion of all—like now. You weren't being tortured, were you? It was about Ian."

"Moray took my son from me." He breathed hard. "I stood there, helpless, while he was murdered! I tried to stop Ian's murder by going back in time. I tried again an' again…. I failed."

Aidan had witnessed his son's death many times, and she had felt his pain as he relived the murder.

Her head ached now. "Did the demon bury you alive?" she asked carefully.

Aidan turned away. "I brought my own walls down."

Brie wanted to reach out but didn't dare. "So you were buried alive and you waited to die."

He faced her. "'Twas sixty-six years ago. Now I live for my revenge."

His savage, ruthless bloodlust overwhelmed her,

frightening her. But she didn't blame him—she couldn't. She couldn't help thinking about how his poor son's soul was suffering, caught between this world and the next one. Ian did not deserve his fate, just as his father did not.

Aidan had heard her silent thoughts. He met her gaze, his mask briefly cracking apart. She saw a man near tears—she felt that oceanic wave of grief again.

Brie stood and grasped his arms, shocked by the steel-hard muscles there. "We'll figure this out together."

His rage erupted. He pulled away. "There is no *we,* Brianna. Ye dinna blame me fer wantin' revenge. I'll tell ye who to blame. Blame the gods! Damn every single one o' them!"

His anger sent her backward across the room. "You don't mean that!"

"Oh, aye, I mean it," he snarled at her. "My son was innocent, more innocent than anyone. I took vows to serve Innocence, yet my son was taken from me. It was written?" he roared. "Well, I have written the fate o' the gods, but they're cowards, because they willna come to earth to fight me."

He was challenging the gods. No mortal could win and neither could a demon, nor the son of one. "Please take back your words," she whispered, terrified for him. "Before they hear you—before they accept!"

"I hope they can hear me!" He paused at the fireplace, leaning against the stone, his back to her, trembling.

She wanted to comfort him; she didn't dare. She wanted to beg him to take back his words; he would refuse again or start another tirade. She wanted to run from the rage, which was making her sick; she couldn't leave him now. So she simply stood there, looking at the most beautiful man in the world—and the most tortured one.

A long moment passed as he fought his rage. Then he looked at her. "Ye'll be stayin' close to me now."

Brie tensed, uncertain of his meaning and wary of his intentions.

He turned and strode to the door, where he paused. "Tomorrow we leave Awe."

"Where are we going?" she asked nervously.

A cool smile formed. "We go to war."

CHAPTER FIVE

BRIE STIFFENED, certain she had misheard him. "What?"

"We ride within the hour," Aidan said. "We march on Inverness."

Brie was stunned. Her mind raced. This was the year of his execution, and it was already late November. He was hanged for treason! She was filled with dread. "Are you riding with the MacDonalds?" she managed.

His gaze narrowed. "Ye ken our wars?"

Oh, God, Brie thought. "Aidan, treason is an offense punishable by hanging."

"I dinna care much for the Earl o' Argyll," he said with a ruthless look. "Yes, I ride with MacDonald. I've promised him four thousand men. We fight for the Lordship o' the Isles."

"And which side is the Royal Lieutenant of the North on? He's a Frasier, isn't he?" Brie demanded, thinking about the text she'd read. "You ride against the Crown. They will hang you for treason!"

His eyes widened.

Brie turned away from him, shaken to the core of her being. She had gone back in time to a point frighteningly close to Aidan's execution. She wasn't meant to stop Ian's murder, but she was surely meant to stop Aidan's hanging...wasn't she? For there was no point in redeeming a man slated for death.

Before she could think further, he had her face in his hand. He'd tilted her chin up so that their eyes locked. "Ye can tell me about my hanging later." And he strode from her bedchamber.

Brie stared after him until he was gone from her sight. Then she held her head, her temples throbbing.

He was taking her with him. She was going to march on Inverness with four thousand rebel Highlanders?

She had to stop him from going to war or, failing that, prevent his imminent execution. He was in so much pain. He needed healing and his son needed peace. If he could let go of his grief, maybe he could heal and find his way back to his faith.

My god, Brie thought, her headache increasing. She was only one shy and modest techno geek, and not a very brave one—at least, not until recently. What were the gods—and Grandma—thinking? What was *she* thinking?

A maid appeared, hesitating on the threshold of her room, interrupting her rampaging thoughts. She held a pile of clothing in her arms. "My lady? His lordship wishes fer ye to clothe yerself. 'Tis cold by day and colder by night," she added with a smile.

Brie started. Aidan was thoughtful enough to send her warmer clothes? The maid laid a pile on her bed, and Brie saw a long linen tunic, a black plaid, a belt and fur-lined boots. Then she saw the pince-nez on top of the plaid. She rushed to it. "A pair of medieval eyeglasses!"

"His lordship took them from his steward," the maid offered.

A pair of thick lenses was connected by a simple

wire, with no earpieces. Brie didn't care. She put them on her nose and was thrilled when the maid's features became clear, right down to the freckles on her nose. She might not have twenty-twenty vision, but she could see.

Aidan had gotten eyeglasses for her.

It felt like the kindest thing anyone had ever done for her.

She turned, and really looked out the window.

A loch was beyond, as if the castle floated upon it, and the rising sun had stained the water peach and gold. Silver swans drifted in the ethereal morning light, as did a flock of ducks. The shores beyond were covered with snow, but thick, emerald-green woods emerged from them. Beyond the forests, mountain peaks were shrouded in the morning mist, white with snowcaps. For one moment, Awe felt magical.

But it wasn't magical—it was medieval, and she was about to go to war. The maid had left. She removed her sweatshirt and put the tunic on over her T-shirt and jeans. She threw her sweatshirt back on, kicking off her sneakers and stepping into the high, furry boots. The plaid was huge—the size of a queen-size blanket—so she draped it over both shoulders like a cape. She added the belt, hoping to hold it in place, and was relieved when she became slightly warmer.

Had Aidan meant to be kind, or were the gestures been simply practical ones?

Uncertain, Brie left the bedroom. Ahead was the west tower. It was an open, circular room with no walls separating it from the hall she was crossing. That meant that it had been built for defensive, military purposes. The windows were glassless and of various sizes. The tall, skinny loopholes were for artillery. Others were for bowmen, and the widest was for bombards and mortars. Brie started to become aware of a seething mass of savage and masculine humanity close by.

Dread arose in her, and she ran to the closest loophole.

The bailey below was a sea of men and animals.

Her heart lurched. There had to be hundreds of men below. Armor glinted in the morning light. Interspersed amongst the knights and chargers were the standards of their bearers, waving above them in vivid colors. She could make out the Highlanders, too, in their pale leines and colorful plaids.

Her pulse had soared to a dangerously high point. She felt so much savagery below. She glanced across the bridge spanning the loch and squinted. She couldn't see well, but the bridge was shimmering, undulating, as if it were alive.

"He has four thousand men," Claire said from behind her.

Brie whirled. "Is that bridge filled with men?"

"And their mounts, and even some pack animals. The army was here when we arrived yesterday, and it backs up to the village on the eastern shore."

She couldn't breathe. She was really going to war with a medieval army.

"Are you okay? You're as pale as a ghost."

That was a bad choice of words, Brie thought. "I've always secretly wanted to live out *Braveheart*."

"He and Malcolm have argued about his taking you with him, but he is determined." Claire was grim.

Brie stared back as grimly. "Are there really four thousand knights and Highlanders out there? How many men do the bad guys have?"

"I don't know," Claire said. "But now that you can

see Ian, Aidan won't let you out of his sight. He'll keep you safe."

Of course, Brie thought. He was taking her with him because she could see his son's ghost, and not for any other reason. It crossed her mind that she'd rather be important to him in a far different manner, but she shoved that treacherous thought aside. "Can he be talked out of this war? I'm pretty sure the rebels will lose."

"They do," Claire said. "I already did some research on the Internet."

Brie stared at her.

Claire grinned. "I have a few tricks up my sleeve." She sobered. "I learned long ago to accept the power of the Ancients. They brought me to Malcolm. I am what I am and who I am because it was written. Feel free to try to convince him to back out. He will or he won't. If this is what the Ancients have decreed, then it will pass."

Brie already knew all this. If Claire knew about the hanging, she wasn't giving an inch.

"By the way, Allie knows you're here. I sent her a message, special delivery."

"Did she reply?"

"Not yet. Royce is still furious with Aidan for something he did about fifty years ago, so it might take her a bit to get in touch with you, as long as you're hanging with him."

Brie decided she didn't want to know what Aidan had done to anger Royce and Allie.

"I just want you to know that I'm on your side, and so is Malcolm," Claire said. "Can you promise to be careful? And by that I mean I'm more worried about Aidan than I am about the royal armies and the Campbells."

"We actually had a civil conversation earlier," Brie said. She almost told Claire that Aidan had been thoughtful enough to find her the pince-nez.

Claire hesitated. "Women in love don't think straight. You need to be *really* careful. Just think things through before you make any life-altering decisions," she said.

"I think my life has already been altered and it's out of my hands. Can I assume that Aidan is a good soldier and he knows what he's doing?" She had *Braveheart* battle-scene images flashing through her mind now. They were bloody, filled with gore and tragic. She shivered.

"He's a hell of a soldier. Not too many noblemen command four thousand men. He's been a mercenary for a long time and he knows what he's doing. You'll be safe behind the battle lines." Claire suddenly hugged her. "You look so worried, as if you're on the way to the guillotine."

"I am worried. There's so much going on. I really didn't need a treasonous war right now. My plate is kind of full." *Overflowing, actually,* she added silently.

"Rebellions like this one are pretty ordinary in the Highlands. Don't brood over the fact that it's an act of treason. Look, Malcolm and I remain neutral in these wars, because our vows come first, but if you need us, summon him. He'll be listening."

Before Brie could thank her, Aidan's huge, hot power swirled into the tower room. It was like a cyclone of testosterone. Flinching, she turned to face him.

"We ride now," he told her, eyes ablaze with what looked like savage excitement. Did he *want* to go to war?

"Guard her with your life," Claire said to him. "And I mean it."

He gave her a cool look. "Mind yer affairs, an' have

Malcolm mind his. She's my concern now." He nodded imperiously at Brie.

Nervous energy consumed her. She walked over to him, and his gaze locked with hers. "I am seconding the motion," she said softly. She really wanted to get through this war in one solid piece—if she couldn't deter him from it.

His lashes lowered. "Ye'll live to see the morrow," he said. "Even if I dinna."

NICK STARED OUT OF HIS THIRD-STORY window at the city sidewalk below. It was half past eight in the morning, another warm and bright Indian summer day, and the pedestrians hurrying to work on Hudson Street were in short sleeves and tank tops, the men carrying suit jackets over their arms. Traffic was heavy, mostly yellow cabs and dark Towne cars. He really didn't notice any of it. Twenty-four hours had elapsed since Brie had been abducted by Aidan of Awe.

A sharp knock sounded on his open office door. He knew who it was before he turned.

His latest HCU recruit, Kit Mars, grimaced at him, and he gestured her inside. Interestingly, she was distantly related to Brie Rose. He'd recruited Kit out of Vice at the NYPD, not just because she was damned good at her job—and like Brie, had no life but her job. He'd been after her because she'd watched her twin sister die in a pleasure crime when she was eighteen, not far from the Wailing Wall in Jerusalem. She had motivation, and lots of it.

Kit came inside, a folder in her hand. She was a very attractive, slender woman with fair skin and dark hair, which she wore in a blunt, no-nonsense cut. Nick had never seen her wear a stitch of makeup, or anything other than a black top and black pants or jeans. He approved. Kit was hot on the war against evil, and she was ambitious. If she stayed away from a personal life, she was going places.

And she didn't have a clue that she had an ancestor in common with the Rose women.

"This is a compilation of the field data you asked for, going back to the moment Brie first began empathizing with Aidan of Awe," she said seriously.

"You've got nothing," Nick said, reading her mind. He had no patience left.

A flicker of worry crossed Kit's face. "We've got zip, Nick. I'm sorry. I'll keep trying."

"Let's change the drill. Run program 6C and start expanding the quads. We have every available agent in the field. If they're still in the city, we will find them." He was filled with tension, but working hard to control it. Brie was his agent, his responsibility, and by now, she could be very dead.

Aidan of Awe might have belonged to the unnamed Brotherhood once upon a time, but he reeked of evil now. Worse, it was highly likely that he'd taken her through time. If that was the case, she could be anywhere, in any time.

There was nothing worse than losing an agent in the past. He'd mourned every agent who'd died in the line of duty, but an agent lost in time was even worse. He wouldn't let it happen to Brie Rose.

Big Mama was running full-time. She was the agency's supercomputer, and she was analyzing more than three thousand historical case files, a quarter of which were so highly classified only three people, himself included, had access. Maybe, just maybe, once upon a time, someone had seen her, and it was in a report. One mention and he'd know where to look for her.

Kit left, and his beautiful secretary poked her head in. She looked like a human version of Barbie. Beyond her stunning, blond good looks, she was the best assistant he'd ever had. She was cleared to Level Five and was one of the other two people with access to HCU's most classified data. He'd known Jan—and trusted her—for a really long time.

He crooked his finger and she came in, wearing a very revealing jersey dress. She was holding a folder, which he hoped was what he was waiting for. Closing the door, she said, "You said you wanted this fast, and I worked as quickly as I could. According to our original file, he was first sighted by our people around 1425 or so—maybe a few years earlier. I assume you know that history records his execution by hanging in December of 1502, which is when his stronghold, Castle Awe, was seized by the Earl of Argyll."

He knew all that. It was in the original file.

"He pops up a lot in this century, Nick, but always before he was turned. There are sightings of him in Rome, Milan, Paris and Dubai after the millennium. I'm pretty certain the man sighted by our agents those eleven times was still on our side."

"The bastard who took Brie is evil," Nick said flatly. Why were there so many sightings of the good Aidan, and none of the bad? "How many case files have you gone over?"

"Sorry, hon, only eighty-eight. There's 535 Level Five classifieds left. He was hanged in 1502, and that man was turned. If so, the man who took Brie came from a period roughly between 1425 and 1502." She grimaced. "I know that's a big chunk of time. I think I can narrow it down a hair. His ruthless destruction of anyone and everything in his path began in late 1436." She added apologetically, "That's a sixty-six year window."

"You forgot to mention he could have come from 1500 and vanished into 1700—or any damned time he chose."

"Don't I know better than anybody?" Jan asked softly. "Let's hope someone spots her somewhere, in some time."

He drummed his fingers on the table. "I'm running out of time. Brie is not a field agent. She isn't tough. She hasn't had any PES training—or any survival training, period. That empathy could kill her…if he doesn't do it first."

Only field agents took Past Era Survival courses. Nick decided that policy was changing.

"I know. I'll get back to the fivers." Jan stared closely. "Are you really okay?"

Jan knew more about him than anyone. He instantly closed off to her. This was not the time to revisit *his* past. In fact, his life was a closed book, and he intended to keep it that way.

She retreated. "When you need a shoulder, let me know. Hey, Nick? Sometimes even macho men cry." She shrugged. "Her cousin is waiting outside. Said *you* called *her*."

He glared at her. Jan had come to his family's funeral, all those years ago—the last time he'd ever shed tears. "Send her in. I want another report at 5 p.m. After that, I'm taking matters into my own hands."

Jan appeared worried. "Nick, for God's sake, don't do anything foolish. That last sortie did not go well."

Nick waved her out.

Sam strode into his office, her blue eyes sparking with anger. "Great job, Forrester. It's been twenty-four hours, and my cousin is still in the hands of a Master gone bad."

"Sit down," he said, annoyed.

Sam sat and deliberately flashed her tanned thighs at him, crossing her legs. She wore a short denim skirt, a muscle tank and leather jacket and biker boots. It was impossible not to look at those sculpted legs and she knew it. She carried a large purse that he already knew contained weapons, because he'd watched her coming through that security earlier. Every video camera in the building had a feed into his computer. He'd especially liked how cool she'd been when his security team had frisked her, removing the stiletto from her thigh.

"I'm really worried," Sam said tersely. "And Tabby is out of her mind with fear."

He took his own seat behind his desk. "Want a job?"

She gave him a look. "Not if you're my boss."

"Thanks, Rose. There are laws against the way you play at night."

"Nick's laws?"

He raised his brows, exasperated. She'd be a pain to control. "You know damn well the Clinton-Feingold Anti-Vigilante Act was passed in 2001, making your extracurricular activities a felony."

She leaned toward him and he saw the black lace of her bra. "Arrest me."

"What's with the attitude?"

She was filled with fear for Brie, the anxiety making her sick and desperate. He softened. This woman would never admit to fear and never cave to it. He wanted her, bad, but not for himself. He liked his women soft, easy and not all that bright. He wanted her at HCU.

"I can't stand this. Why am I here? We both know I'm too independent and outspoken to work for you."

"I guess Brie's mentioned I'm a royal pain in the ass?"

Sam finally smiled. It made her shockingly beautiful. "Yeah, she did."

He leaned forward. "How long do you think our little friend can last while in Aidan of Awe's control?"

Sam's smile vanished. "She's a Rose. Rose women handle the worst tragedies."

"How long do you think she'll last in the medieval world, if he's taken her back there?"

"She'll rise to the occasion, but damn it, we have to find her!" Sam cried.

He slid a folder over his desk toward her. When Sam reached for it, he laid his hand on the file, preventing her from taking it. "In or out?"

She met his gaze. "What's that?"

"Level Five case files."

Her eyes widened. "Brie is only Level Three and she's been here three years!"

He sent her a charming smile, one that always instantly disarmed women. "If you come in, you're going right to the top."

She wet her lips.

He had her, he thought, satisfied. "That's usually for my eyes only. Now it can be for your eyes, too."

"I'm in," Sam said hoarsely.

He released the file and she flipped it open. He sat back in his chair, arms folded, waiting, as she began skimming the pages. Within two minutes, her eyes widened, and she froze. Then, slowly, she looked up at him. "Holy shit," she said.

He grinned.

"In 1888, a CDA agent named John Duke filed a report about a demon slaying. A demon *he* slayed… in 1602."

"Welcome to CDA," Nick said. "Oh, and Sam? You might want to catch up on your history of the Highlands."

AWE WAS A FOUR-WALLED CASTLE, with corner and middle towers and a gatehouse with two flanking towers. Beyond that there was an outer ward that was almost a separate garrison, and the bridge that led to Loch Awe's shores. Brie was acutely aware of Aidan as they walked through the inner ward toward the gatehouse. Although he was controlling his emotions, she could feel his warrior power seething. It felt very raw, very brutal and very barbaric. He seemed to be heating up over the prospect of battle, and she wasn't sure what to make of that. It was a reminder that, good or bad, he was still a medieval man with a medieval agenda.

She couldn't help wondering how many would die before this rebellion was through. Scotland's history was particularly bloody and tragic and she was starting to appreciate how civilized the modern world was. "Has it ever occurred to anyone, perhaps even the MacDonald, to negotiate for what he wants?"

Aidan glanced at her. "In the Highlands, politics an' war are one an' the same."

"I'll bet," she said.

She saw that the tunnel within the gatehouse had two portcullises, both of which were raised. It wasn't unusual. An intruder getting past the first set of iron bars would be quickly trapped between it and the second gate once it was closed. She looked up as they entered the tunnel and, sure enough, saw the murder holes above her head. The intruder would be doused with burning liquid or burning arrows. Oil wouldn't be used, because it was too expensive.

There was no escaping the violent nature of this world, she thought in dismay. She looked down as they hurried toward the first raised portcullis. They were walking over a trapdoor. "What's below?" she asked warily.

"A pallet of daggers," he said, not breaking stride.

"Have you ever been besieged?" she asked thickly, every hair on her body raised. She was thinking about what happened to invaders when the trapdoors opened beneath their feet. Being caught up in the medieval world made it impossible to ignore how cruel and savage its people were.

"Aye, when Argyll burned Awe to the ground."

Brie gasped. "Is that why you're riding with MacDonald against Argyll?"

He smiled at her with relish. "Yer a clever lass, Brianna. I even helped Donald Dubh escape. He was Argyll's prisoner," he laughed.

Brie halted. "This is a blood feud! You don't care who is Lord of the Isles, you just want to fight Argyll!"

He halted, facing her, his eyes hard and cold. "I like war."

She trembled. "Why? Because it's easier to fight than to grieve?"

He flushed and, eyes blazing, strode past her.

Brie ran after him, wishing she hadn't said what she had. But her instincts had been right. A modern man would get past his grief by indulging in work, sports, an affair. Aidan was choosing war.

Somber, she followed him out of the gatehouse and into the shadows cast by the flanking towers, coming face-to-face with his army of Highlanders and knights.

Her heart stopped. It was one thing to look down on the sea of soldiers and beasts from the tower, with everyone somewhat out of focus; it was another to be so suddenly in their midst. Every instinct she had fired in alarm. Every educated person knew the dangers of a crowd, and this barbaric mass of humanity was a maddened, war-hungry mob. She had her defenses up, but with so many men present, it was impossible to block the soldiers out entirely. Their savagery and bloodlust overwhelmed and sickened her now. So much evil was present in the army of madmen, and that was the most frightening thing of all.

Brie turned away as a red-haired Highlander thrust his dagger into a knight's leg, the knight instantly cleaving him with his spiked club. She didn't want to see what would happen next.

Darker shadows fell over her. Trembling, Brie looked up. Four knights had ridden over to her, and evil surrounded her now. Their visors were up and they looked down at her, leering. Their eyes were dark and soulless and glittering madly.

These men were possessed.

Aidan suddenly appeared at her side, and then he stepped between her and the four knights. "Come closer an' die."

The knights whirled their mounts, spurring them away and back into the mob of men.

Her stomach roiled. She was not relieved. "How many of your men are demonic? How many are possessed?"

He instinctively clasped her elbow, steadying her. "More than half are possessed, or are lesser deamhanain," he said calmly. "The rest just like murder an' rape an' being paid fer it."

She clung to his hand in disbelief, looking into his brilliant blue eyes, sick to her stomach. "You do not let them rape," she said furiously, refusing to believe it. "You do not let them murder the Innocent!"

His face hardened. "I have four thousand men. Ye think I can control every one? Ye think I even wish to do so? They need compensation fer their labors!" he snapped.

Brie shook her head, aghast. "Ever since you rescued me, I have refused to believe you are evil. You saved me. You have a conscience. I have seen it!"

"My men rape when it pleases them to do so," he shouted at her. "I grow tired of ye lookin' at me with so much damned faith!"

"I am not wrong about you," she insisted.

He leaned close, his anger exploding. The wave of rage would have flung her backward, off her feet, if he hadn't been gripping her. "I *am* evil. I gave up my soul long ago and I have no use for it now. I dinna want or care fer yer faith! Find someone else to save."

"Then why did you save me?" she cried.

"I dinna ken why I saved ye in New York City," he said harshly. "But now, I save ye only so ye can speak with my son."

"And when I finish being useful to you, then what? Will you murder and rape me, too?"

His face hardened impossibly. "Ye tempt me,

Brianna. I wouldn't mind succumbing to my lust and usin' yer pretty body."

She gasped.

"So I suggest ye keep yer mouth closed an' dinna interfere now—not with my plans, not with this war. If yer fortunate, if ye do as I wish, I'll send ye back to yer time when I'm done with ye—*intact,*" he snarled.

Oh my God, she thought, her cheeks on fire. He had read her mind and knew she was the modern world's only twenty-six-year-old virgin.

His eyes widened.

So did Brie's. "Are you reading my mind?"

A slight pink flush seemed to mar his high cheeks. "Ye think so loudly."

She turned away, mortified. He hadn't known—she'd misunderstood his choice of words—but he knew the humiliating truth now. She wanted to vanish into the dirt. Better yet, she wanted to find herself in her loft in the present, realizing that this was an insane and not-very-pleasant dream.

His grasp on her seemed to tighten. Then he spoke with care. "I gave ye my word. I said I wouldna hurt ye. I meant it. Just keep yer distance from me."

She pulled away from his hard hands. "I need a weapon," she said tersely, not looking at him. Did he think her an absolute nerd? Did it matter? She *was* a nerd, and he was no prize. "I cannot manage without a means of defending myself."

She could barely believe what she was saying, or that she meant it. At home she carried pepper spray and a gun, but she'd never used the gun except at a firing range. If she had the weapon now, though, she'd use it.

He tilted up her chin, forcing their gazes to collide.

"Ye can have as many weapons as ye wish." He dropped his hand to reach into his boot, and handed her a small dagger. "Take this fer now, but ye willna need it."

Brie clutched the dagger. As small as it was, it still did not fit comfortably in her hand. But then she hated weapons, and doubted any weapon would feel right.

"Ye'll live to go home, Brianna. Dinna think so much."

She looked up at him. His harsh tone had softened ever so slightly. Was he trying to reassure her? His gaze was odd, searching.

He stepped away from her, breaking the moment. "Can ye ride?"

When he wasn't angry, he reminded her terribly of the old Aidan. She wet her lips, acutely aware of him now. Somehow, the seething army had vanished into an indistinct and jumbled background, as if it were just the two of them standing there. His power tugged inexorably at her. "Not really."

He had seized a pair of reins from a young page, and led a gray horse forward, not looking at Brie. She wondered if he was aware of that magnetism, too. "She's docile. Ye'll ride with me at the start."

"I haven't been on a horse since I was five, and then it was a very small pony in a very small riding ring." She focused on the horse. It was *huge.* But she wasn't going to tell him she was afraid of riding because the pony had bolted and she'd fallen off and broken her arm.

He studied her and said, "Get on. I'll lead ye, or Will can."

"Great." She smiled brightly at him.

He handed the reins to Will. Before Brie could

blink, Aidan had seized her waist and was lifting her abruptly and setting her down on the saddle. The gray horse snorted, shaking its head, moving restlessly. Brie seized the saddle, her heart thundering.

Aidan palmed her knee while jerking on the bridle. “If ye relax yer legs, ye’ll be fine.”

Brie met his gaze as his hand enveloped her knee. It was a simple, offhand gesture, but his hand was warm and strong, even through her jeans. He was grim and unbearably gorgeous. She’d probably never have his hand on her leg again. Her body warmed and she thought about his hand sliding upward. Being around him was not easy.

He dropped his hand and leapt onto a big, magnificent black charger. Brie stared, breathless. The animal was as beautiful an example of its species as its master, and it suited Aidan perfectly. The stallion was explosive and hot, as if it knew they were going to war and it wanted to go immediately. It pranced and reared, kicking out at the closest horses. All of them dodged to get out of its way. Aidan simply sat on the beast, as if allowing it a moment of mischief. Then he laid his hand on the stallion’s huge shoulder, and it went still.

Brie looked at man and stallion—a magnificent pairing—her heart racing. He had enchanted the stallion, she thought, certain he was still speaking to the black horse, in some language only the two of them shared. She would never tire of watching him, she thought. Then, clearly aware of her watching him, he looked up at her from beneath his thick lashes.

His eyes were hot and bright.

She inhaled. She’d never received that look before, but she knew what it meant. It was sexy and promising and so impossible; it was the look a man gave to a woman when he wanted her.

Suddenly Aidan whirled the black, unsheathing his sword and riding into the fray of knights and Highlanders.

Brie stared after him, her pulse explosive, her heart filled with yearning.

The stallion reared, screaming, pawing the air. *"A Dhomhnaill!"* Aidan shouted, raising his sword high.

His warrior power abruptly, intensely filled the ward, almost knocking her off the mare. Swept by so much force, Brie held on to the saddle horn, overwhelmed by the power and excitement, by adrenaline and bloodlust.

Four thousand men, within Awe and on the loch's shores, responded. *"A Dhomhnaill!"*

His frenzy—and the frenzy of his four thousand men—consumed her. Brie did not move, clutching the saddle. *"A Dhomhnaill,"* she whispered into the echoing roar, aware of having no will of her own now. He had mesmerized everyone, and she was no exception. Her mind was consumed.

And once more, the black took to the air. Aidan's sword bit the sun. *"A' Madadh-allaidh à Aiwe!"*

"A' Madadh-allaidh à Aiwe!" the men roared.

The castle walls visibly shook.

And this time, the war cry echoed for long moments, filling the ward, the castle, and cloaking the loch, where the water churned and the ducks took flight. It filled the woods, where the pines danced and wolves suddenly howled. Even the mountains shuddered.

Brie stared at Aidan, who was in a savage euphoria. So was she.

His men roared again. Brie understood the war cry: *For the Wolf of Awe!*

His blazing eyes swung to hers. He spurred the stallion to her. “We’re ready,” he said, reaching for her reins.

“A’ Madadh-allaidh à Aiwe,” Brie whispered.

CHAPTER SIX

"CAN YE WALK?" Aidan asked her.

Her mare came to stand beside his stallion. Brie was sore, exhausted, chilled to the bone and incapable of even smiling at him. But now she glimpsed the field below the ridge where they sat astride their horses. The sun was setting, fingers of bloodred staining the deepening sky and the snowy glen, and a sea of tents, cook fires and men filled the horizon. She couldn't recall ever seeing such a welcome sight. "Thank God," she murmured, shivering.

They had been riding all day. Aidan hadn't said a word to her since leaving Awe, and for most of the day he'd left her with Will and the four huge giants, who were her bodyguards. Twice Aidan had returned to her side, and she knew it was only to see if she was in one piece. He had kept a tight rein on his emotions and she felt nothing from him when he came by. Considering she'd been so swept up in the war frenzy that dawn, she was relieved.

She'd managed okay. The mare was pretty mellow, and Brie decided she even liked her. At noon—or when she assumed it was noon—Aidan had returned to hand her a half loaf of absolutely delicious bread, stuffed with a meat she couldn't identify. Before she could say thank you, he'd galloped off.

It had been the best sandwich of her life. Clearly, the Earl of Sandwich had not invented the meal.

Now Aidan urged the stallion down the ridge, leading Brie's mare. They were stopping for the night, and Brie couldn't wait to get off the horse and collapse in front of a warm fire. Why anyone liked riding horses was beyond Brie's comprehension. If only there was such a thing as a medieval Jacuzzi. She'd settle for a natural hot spring.

Aidan halted before a large black tent with red and silver trim, which was flying a red flag with a snarling black wolf's head set against a large gold Celtic cross. Brie stared in shock, forgetting all about her aching muscles and blisters.

Aidan leapt from the stallion. As he handed the reins to Will, his hand moved over the horse's neck in a gesture of affection. "I'll help ye down."

"What is that?" Brie gasped, nodding at the pennant.

"My standard," he said.

Demons feared crosses and all holy objects. They lost all their power when on holy ground or within a holy place. No demon would bear such a standard—at the least, it would be weakening. "That's a cross," she said.

"I've had the standard fer decades," he said abruptly. "It brings fear into the minds and hearts of my enemies. Do ye wish to stay on the mare all night? It can be arranged."

She stared into his simmering blue eyes, aware that he was becoming angry because she was raising a subject he did not wish to discuss. He blamed the gods for Ian's fate, and he'd walked away from them. He acted as if he hated them, but did he really? She wasn't buying, not for a New York minute, that he used the old standard solely for its effect on his enemies.

Was he clinging to a sliver of his previous life? Subconsciously, was he clinging to faith?

"To answer your question, I think I'm crippled for life. And no, I do not want to sit up here all night. I wouldn't mind never getting on a horse again."

His face tightened as he held up his hand. The moment Brie put her hand in his, she felt his heat, his virility. His gaze lifted, his blue eyes searing and bold.

How could he not feel the pull between them, too? she wondered. She reminded herself that he had the ability to make every woman want him. But he didn't need to use his powers of sexual enchantment, because most women would look at him and drool. She knew she had better remind herself that this was very one-sided. His interest in her was her connection to his son, period.

But what, exactly, would their sleeping arrangements be?

He clasped her waist and a moment later she was standing on the ground. As he released her, Brie winced. Her legs were done. She'd probably be lame for life. "Ow," she finally said, looking up at him. "And I do mean ow."

For an instant Brie thought he might smile, but his face remained set in stone. "After a good night o' sleep, ye'll be fine fer the march tomorrow."

She doubted it.

"But if yer too sore, ye can ride in a weapons cart."

Great, Brie thought. She'd seen the carts pulling early medieval cannons—both the smaller mortars and the larger bombards. Those vehicles looked even more uncomfortable than the back of a good-gaited horse.

"Will, help Lady Brianna into the tent an' settle her fer the night."

Brie had the feeling she'd been dismissed. As far as she could see, there was only one black tent flying Aidan's flag. If she slept there, where was he sleeping? She had a huge reason to be concerned—in fact, she had about four thousand of them. "Aidan, I can't sleep alone."

He had been about to walk away. He paused, slowly looking at her.

She flushed. "Demons are everywhere. My being alone in that tent is not a good idea."

"I hardly said ye'd sleep alone." Galloping hoofbeats sounded, and he turned.

Brie looked past him. A rider streaked toward them from the north, where Inverness lay. Aidan strode forward as horse and rider halted, the bay coated in sweat and lather. The rider, Brie saw, was a young Highland man. Obviously an emergency was at hand.

She prayed the march would be called off. That would solve the matter of his hanging, at least for now.

A flurry of Gaelic followed.

"What are they saying?" Brie asked Will, who was waiting patiently for her.

"Royal armies are on the road ahead, coming south, hoping to cut us off," Will told her, apparently unperturbed.

Brie did not like the sound of that. "Cut us off from what? Will there be fighting?"

"We're to tryst with the MacDonald an' Maclean armies, closer to Inverness. But the Frasier has his men between them an' us. Come into the tent, my lady.

Ye'll be warmer inside. An' dinna think o' the battle on the morrow. Ye'll be well-guarded."

"Tomorrow!" Brie cried, utterly aghast. Aidan would go to war *tomorrow* and commit treason. There would be no taking it back!

She turned and saw Aidan stalking off into the camp, various men following him. She got it. They were the leaders of the lesser ranks and he was having a war council.

How on earth was she going to stop him from going to war? Will lifted the heavy canvas flap. Brie stepped inside and was instantly distracted.

The interior was spacious and well-furnished. She was surprised by the sight of a small bed on a low wood frame, the bedposts beautifully carved. A portable desk consisting of a slab of attractively carved wood on two plain stands was present, as was a chair with a leather seat and back and a beautiful, iron-banded wood chest. A Persian rug was on the dirt floor. "This is how Aidan goes to war?"

"Aye. 'Twill take months to besiege Inverness," Will responded.

Brie slowly faced him, acutely aware of the single bed behind her. Aidan had made it clear that he and she were sharing the tent. One of them would probably sleep on the floor.

It shouldn't be a big deal, but it was. "There's only one bed."

Will grinned at her. "Then yer fortunate, my lady. His prowess is well known."

Brie tried not to look at the bed. Every inch of her was firing up, when she knew nothing was going to happen. Except…he'd given her that male look twice today. Sex was probably no big deal for him. What would she do if he made a pass at her?

Her heart thundered. She'd accept. She wouldn't even think twice about it. She recalled Claire's warnings and dismissed them. Aidan wouldn't hurt her. He wouldn't use her—not demonically. She was sure of it. And only a fool would refuse a man like that.

Will glanced at her. "O' course, we have hundreds of women to choose from. He may be well occupied until late in the night."

"Of course," she murmured. A medieval army would have a population of camp followers, especially for a long siege. They weren't going to share the bed, or the tent. He'd probably have Will sleep inside with her, to guard her. She was dismayed, absurdly. She should be relieved.

Brie sat down on the bed and realized she was ready to collapse. She wasn't just physically exhausted, but mentally, too. She needed to think, to figure out how to convince Aidan to retreat from this war. But just then, she was too tired.

The tent flap opened and Aidan stepped inside. He gave Will a look, which sent the young man out. Brie stood as he walked to the desk, not looking at her. The spacious tent suddenly felt really small. She was acutely aware of the bed behind her, and the fact that they were alone.

"Will says you'll fight the royal armies tomorrow."

He poured a glass of wine. "Aye."

She trembled. "I made the decision to trust you. You have to trust *me* now."

He turned and stared for a long moment. "Why should I trust ye, Brianna?"

"I have your best interests at heart."

He laughed without mirth. "Aye, ye plot to change my life, against my wishes."

Brie tensed. He was right. "You're so caught up in your grief, you can't think straight."

He tossed back some wine and said, "Dinna dare speak down to me."

She trembled. "I am not patronizing you."

He drank more wine, then refilled his cup and another one.

"Aidan, you have lost your way. I want to help you find it again."

"I beg to differ with ye," he said coldly. He thrust a cup at her. "I dinna lose my way—I found it. I like the darkness."

"No one likes the dark. That's like saying you'd rather be alone and unloved than surrounded by friends and family, beloved by all." She clutched the cup to her chest.

His anger crashed against her. "I like the darkness," he said flatly. "I like being alone…an' I dinna yearn fer love."

She wasn't going to win this argument—not just then, Brie thought.

"But we both ken *ye* yearn fer love, Brianna. Ye yearn fer *my* love," he mocked.

She was finally angry, and hurt. "Not fair. You can't keep reading my mind whenever you choose! And I am not so foolish as to want you to love me!" But her heart ached even more now.

He faced her, arms folded, his expression one of smug male skepticism. "But ye've loved me since we first met."

She felt crimson. "It was a crush. Women have

crushes all the time. A crush isn't love. It's harmless, like a dream."

His mouth curled. "Like a virgin's dreams?"

Brie almost gasped. *He knew.* He knew she dreamed and fantasized about him sexually. "I have been nothing but kind to you," she said hoarsely. "Do you want to humiliate me? Because I am humiliated now!"

His mouth firmed and their gazes clashed. "Ye need a real man, not foolish dreams."

Brie went still.

"Why are ye a virgin still?"

She was aghast. "That's a very private matter."

"Is it? 'Cause ye think about sex all the time."

She knew she was even redder than before. "I don't want a relationship." In case he misunderstood, she continued. "My mother was a very wild woman. She had many lovers, but she didn't have any gifts. I don't want to be like her. I am really busy using my gifts to help others." She glared. "Like I am trying to help you now."

His gaze was narrow and unwavering upon her. "So ye want to be ugly."

She breathed hard. "I am not interested in flaunting my body, my hair or anything else!"

He made a harsh sound. "Ye can hide all ye want, but ye have pretty eyes an' nice hair. Only a blind man wouldna notice."

Brie was certain she'd mistaken his meaning. "You think I'm pretty?"

His mouth curved. "Brianna, I think yer pretty, but it doesna matter. In the dark o' night, I never look at a woman's face. I only use her body."

Brie turned her back on him, shaken. She took a deep breath and said, "I don't believe you."

He laughed at her.

She dared to face him, and watched him drinking his wine. Suddenly she believed him. He really didn't care who he was with—it was about sex, only sex. It wasn't about attraction or anything else.

Her grandmother's ring began pinching, hard.

Brie imagined her, and Grandma Sarah wasn't smiling now. She was stern, as if telling Brie to get focused and remember why she was in the past. She didn't want to think about her grandmother now. This was too important. "Don't you miss holding someone in the middle of the night—someone you love?"

He whirled, spilling his wine. "Are ye mad?"

Brie shook her head. "I'm sad."

He stared, and his anger burst forth. "No one holds ye in the middle of the night, Brianna!"

"But I have a life, with family and friends who love me, and I love them."

"Good! When ye go home, ye can share a joyous, lovin' reunion!"

Grandma's ring hurt her finger now. Brie looked at it, and it almost looked as though the garnet was glowing. "What do you want?" she muttered. Then, realizing she'd spoken aloud, she noticed Aidan watching her with interest.

"My grandmother guides me from the dead," she said shortly.

He shook his head and walked out of the tent.

Brie tried to take the ring off, just to relieve her finger for a moment, but she couldn't. She sighed and sat down. Tears filled her eyes, only partly from exhaustion. She'd been brought back to the year of his hanging, and the reason was obvious. She was in the Highlands to save his life, both figuratively and literally. Less obvious was the possibility of redeeming him.

Maybe she was mad, she thought, to even think of guiding Aidan back to the gods. She couldn't help pushing him and testing him, she realized. If he was as evil as he said, their debate would have amused him instead of angering him.

Everything angered him.

And why not? He'd lost his son. The gods could have intervened, but it had been Fate. It was tragic and unfair, and to make matters worse, his son had been haunting him for sixty-six years. She'd be angry, too.

Her infatuation had to go. It was in the way. She hadn't gone back in time for a fling—or a life-altering romance.

But she was still feeling hurt. At least they were having a dialogue, she thought. Brie walked over to the tent flap and lifted it. Aidan was standing outside, right there, and he glanced at her. She shivered and pulled her wool plaid more tightly round her. "It's cold. Come back inside." She was going to stop him from fighting Frasier tomorrow.

He slowly smiled. "So ye can seduce me away from my plans?"

"I couldn't seduce a randy freshman on spring break," she said. "I could never seduce you."

He walked past her, back into the tent. "I won't hang, Brianna. Not anytime soon."

She tensed. "That's not what history says."

He shrugged.

"Aidan, if you fight tomorrow, you are committing treason, and you will hang. Frasier will make certain of it."

His gaze changed and became searching.

"Can you please postpone the battle? Please?" she pleaded.

He shook his head. "I dinna mind dyin'. But I willna die until I have avenged my son. So ye need not fear my hangin' anytime soon."

"Do you want to die?" she cried. "Are you in so much pain that you seek escape in death?"

He jerked angrily. "Ye ask too many privy questions! I am tired of yer insolence, yer pryin'. I am tired of ye, Brianna!"

Somehow she shook her head and stood her ground. "You can read my every thought, and you are ruthless in doing so. Unfortunately, I don't have that power. It's okay for you to read my mind and uncover my secrets, but I can't ask a few personal questions?"

His eyes were wide. "The little woman has nails," he said softly. "But ye need claws, Brianna, if ye think to go up against me."

"I don't want to fight with you," she said tersely.

"O' course not. Ye want to heal me, redeem me—and share my bed." His eyes flashed.

She trembled. "Does being cruel please you?"

"Aye, it pleases me greatly!" he snapped.

Ian stepped between them.

Brie gasped.

Aidan's eyes widened. *He had seen Ian, too.* And then he cried out in savage frustration. "Nay! Come back, Ian! Come back!"

But Ian was still standing there, looking back and forth between them. Brie couldn't understand why Aidan could no longer see him. The small ghost turned and began talking rapidly to his father. She could not hear a word he said.

Aidan's face had become a reflection of raw, ravaged grief. He looked years older. "Is he still here?" he cried frantically.

She took his hand. "He's still here. He's speaking to you, but I can't hear him."

Suddenly tears welled in Aidan's eyes. "Talk to him," he begged her. "Please, talk to him." And a tear slipped free and started a slow track down his cheek.

She had never seen a grown man cry, much less a man like this one. His grief was mushrooming in the tent like a nuclear cloud. It swept through her with stunning force. It crushed her from above, from the sides. She had to fight to stand upright, to breathe. *Aidan did not deserve this.* "Ian," she gasped. "Can you hear me?"

The boy faced her and spoke.

"If you can hear me, nod," she whispered. Aidan's pain was so strong and consuming that she felt faint. If he didn't control himself, she was going to pass out.

Ian nodded at her, his eyes wide, as if he was listening carefully.

"What's happening?" Aidan demanded, wiping his face with his forearm. "Tell me about my son!"

"He can hear me," she cried, meeting his stunned eyes. "Aidan, you're hurting me." She had been forced to her knees.

Aidan covered his heart with his hand, but Brie was aware of the pain racking it, and it felt like it was about to explode. But as he battled himself, she felt the terrible anguish begin to dull. The sensation was like drowning and then finally breaking through the surface for air. She gulped oxygen.

When he pushed the grief further away, she stood up. "Ian, are you here to speak with your father?"

Ian nodded and waited expectantly for her.

Aidan cried, "Tell him how much I love him! Tell him I will find and kill Moray to pay fer what he did! Tell him I hunt the deamhan bastard every single day!"

Brie glanced at Aidan and then back at Ian. "Your father loves you," she said softly. She knelt closer to the little ghost. "Are you here to ask him to release you to the afterlife?"

Ian shook his head.

Brie was shocked.

"What did he say?" Aidan demanded, even paler than his son.

"He said no," Brie said slowly, still stunned. Why wouldn't the little boy wish to leave this realm? He'd been dead for almost seventy years. "Ian," she began, but the little boy began frantically shaking his head. He pointed at her.

"What do you want to say to me? Do you want to tell me something?" she cried.

He nodded. He pointed at Aidan now.

"And you want to speak to your father, too?"

Ian nodded, then burst into tears of frustration. And he started fading.

"Don't go," Brie screamed, but it was too late.

And Aidan knew, because he turned away from her, his body convulsing with his grief.

Released, his anguish erupted into the tent, lancing through her. She staggered under the repeated blows, then fell under the crushing weight. His pain kept pouring down on her. On her hands and knees, hurting so badly she wanted to die, she somehow looked up. This was how Aidan felt, she managed to think.

Aidan wept silently by the tent's closed flap door.

She knew he wouldn't want her comfort. She didn't care. She somehow stood and staggered to him, fighting her way through the hot waves of anguish. Brie managed to lay her hand on his back.

He roared incoherently at her and wrenched away from her, shoving through the tent flap. Brie didn't hesitate. He needed her now, as never before, and she ran after him. It was like slogging upstream through a high, racing river.

He moved faster, leaving her behind, climbing the hill toward the ridge above. His pain was dulling. She panted, lungs bursting, legs hurting. The force of his grief had lessened, and she could run more easily now.

He halted on top of the ridge, silhouetted in anguish and misery against the violet sky. Brie froze, seeing the waves of pain emanating so clearly from him. A few stars began to emerge in the growing darkness.

The waves visibly receded until he stood there alone, as mystical as an old god or a mythical hero. Brie took a deep breath, needing the air, and she started to trek up the ridge slowly. When she reached him, she put her arms around him and gently embraced him from behind.

He stiffened.

"You need comfort," she whispered unsteadily. She laid her cheek on his trembling back. "Let me comfort you."

He turned. Suddenly she was in his arms, his hands hurting her shoulders. "Well," he snarled, "ye can comfort me the way the camp whores do."

"I will comfort you as a *friend.*"

"I dinna have friends," he shouted at her, shaking her.

"You are so wrong. You have *me.*" Her own tears finally gathered.

His eyes widened. "Dinna weep fer me!"

He still gripped her, but she lifted her hand and laid it on his rough cheek. "There is *hope.* I began a communication with Ian. It may take some time, but we will find out what he wants, and then we can release him."

"I canna release him," Aidan cried.

His tears were falling again, over her hand, and his rising grief filled her, too. She caught his beautiful face in her hands. "Let me help you. We can find a way to release Ian together."

He seized her wrists so hard that she tensed in alarm. "How can ye help me? Yer a virgin," he mocked cruelly.

She understood his fury, his need to lash out. "It's okay."

"I like courtesans and whores," he hissed.

"I am not leaving you like this. In fact, I am not leaving you anytime soon." She stroked his jaw.

He threw her hands aside. "Dinna touch me! Dinna come close. I dinna want yer friendship an I dinna want yer warm little body in my bed. I want power. I want blood," he shouted at her. "I want my deamhan father's head!"

Brie cringed, Aidan's wrath filling the night, filling her. It was so savage. "I know you do. I want revenge, too."

"Ye ken nothin'! I want my son!"

"I know!" she cried, seizing his hands. His pain-filled, blue gaze met hers. "Aidan, Ian is dead. You have to let him go."

"He's my child! How can I let him go?" he cried, and tears streaked down his face.

"You can…and you will," she whispered.

He jerked away from her hands. "I canna leave my son!"

"Then you are selfish," she said. "Can't you see that your poor son wants peace, and until you give up, let go and stop this vengeance, he will never be at peace?"

His eyes were huge. "Damn ye, Brianna!"

Aidan strode toward the forest. She watched him until he vanished into the darkness there. Hadn't Grandma always said that the truth hurt the most of all? She tripped, stumbling down the hill, crying now. She hadn't meant to be cruel, but she had spoken the truth. If Aidan could only see what he had to do, then he could find peace, too.

And maybe he'd recover his soul, at last.

CHAPTER SEVEN

FROM THE EDGE OF THE FOREST, Aidan stared down the ridge, watching her stumbling to his tent. When she was safely inside, the handful of men he'd chosen to protect her clearly at their posts, he stared blindly into the night.

There was hope?

If he dared believe that she might truly speak with Ian and then she failed, he might finally die from the pain. It had been eating him alive for sixty-six years, and he knew he could not withstand it for much longer.

But he did secretly hope she might succeed, otherwise she wouldn't be in his tent.

No matter what she said, though, she was not a friend.

He had no friends, not one—not even Malcolm. The Masters feared him; Malcolm feared him—and no one trusted him. Except, of course, Brianna.

The deamhanain also mistrusted and feared him. They knew the truth. They knew he was evil—but not as evil as them. They knew he turned away from mayhem, ignoring it instead of causing it. They knew he lusted for power and took it, yet they knew he left the Innocent alive, not dead. He was the son of a deamhan, but they knew he was neither a man, a Master nor a deamhan, but some strange beast in their midst.

I am your friend.

Why did she wish to be the friend of a half deamhan, half beast?

She was a fool. He could understand her loving him from first sight; many ladies had loved him instantly when he had been a very different man. But she was a fool to love him now. She was a fool to have trusted him before he had decided that she served him well alive. She was a fool to be determined to save him from hanging, and put her own life at risk in the Highland wars. And to even think to redeem him? That was madness.

He had no interest in salvation. He had meant it when he had told her he'd found his way, not lost it. His standard meant *nothing*. Saving her from the gang in New York also meant nothing. He must have sensed that she would soon be useful to him. As for the fact that he was soon going to hang, she had to be wrong. He would never embrace death unless he had avenged Ian first.

Moray had vanished in time, but he would not die without taking his demonic father with him.

And he would not die until he knew what Ian wished to say to him.

Suddenly the grief he kept shackled in his chest rose up, consuming him as it had earlier. He cradled his face in his hands. The urge to weep came again. He hadn't cried over Ian's death, not till that day. Aidan could not understand why his grief had finally boiled over. Of course, it was somehow her fault.

She had disturbed his life the moment he had first heard her cries for help and rescued her from evil. She continued to disturb him with her faith, her plots, her plans. He had almost found comfort in her touch a moment ago, when he must *never* find comfort with her. He had to avenge Ian's murder. He must never forgive the gods for what they had taken from him. If he did, he might walk away from his vengeance.

And now Brianna wanted him to let Ian go? How could he even think of doing such a thing?

He trembled. His mind felt crushed, as if weighted down by huge stones. He could not tolerate fatigue. Tomorrow was war. He had to ignore the urge to lie down and rest; he would not sleep. He couldn't imagine the nightmares sleep would bring.

He didn't have to look at his tent to sense her. He was attuned to her all the time now, so if danger came, he could protect her. She was soundly asleep.

What woman of her age was a virgin?

He realized he was staring at the black shadow of his tent. He could pretend otherwise, but he did want her and he had from the moment he'd first seen her. He was aware of her in a way he hadn't been aware of any woman, in all the years since his son's murder. He was afraid of what it might mean.

He must never go to her for pleasure and he must never find comfort in her arms.

A wolf howled. In sheer frustration, he felt like answering the call, but he didn't move. A memory assailed him.

He smiled down at his beautiful Irish mistress, holding her in his arms after lovemaking. She smiled back at him, whispering how much she loved him. He loved her, too, a little, and he moved away from her to give her a gift.

She'd wept over the simple gold necklace.

He'd held her and caressed her, put the necklace on for her, fed her sweets. When they were joined again, they were both smiling and laughing until the earth shattered....

Aidan cried out, enraged. What kind of foul play was this? Why was he thinking of Catriona, who had been dead for a long time? He wasn't that man anymore—a man who could harbor genuine affection for another, a man who could smile and laugh, a man who enjoyed watching a woman open a gift, a man who was pleased by her pleasure!

I love you.... Catriona's voice washed over him, even though he had no wish to revisit the past. And he saw them together, two lovers in the midst of so much simple, mortal pleasure, alive with happiness.

Her eyes darkened, turned green. A silly pince-nez sat on the tiny bridge of her nose, amidst three freckles. I'm your friend, *Brianna whispered, touching his cheek, as he slid deep and hot into her. She was smiling, her eyes aglow with love.*

And the pleasure was stunning, but not as stunning as his need.

Aidan stood stiffly, unmoving. He was in disbelief. *What was happening to him?*

He was dreaming of taking Brianna to bed for sexual pleasure. He needed power, not pleasure, and he did not want a friend! He did not want to ever see her looking at him that way, with her warm body beneath his, joined with his. But his body was recalling pleasure for the first time in decades: simple, mortal, sexual pleasure; pleasure for the sake of pleasure and nothing else.

He did not like this!

He started down the hill. Tomorrow he was going to war, and tonight he would take power with a dozen different, faceless women. He would wallow in the power, relish it, embrace it. Evil lusted for power, and so did he.

But she wasn't sleeping soundly now. She was dreaming.

Every Master and deamhan knew that dreams were reality, but of a different realm, one transcending the physical and earthly plane where mortals were bound until death.

That was why dreams were so often vivid. For they were real—mortals simply didn't know it.

But the dream world was governed by a whimsical goddess, and the rules were as insubstantial as the realm. Every dream could be unwritten or rewritten an infinite number of times, an infinite number of ways. In dreams, Fate was constantly erased, eroded, changed. In dreams there was right and wrong—and then there was no right, and no wrong, because the next dream would be different. And in a dream, no one could die.

In her dreams, he could not hurt her, and if he did, tomorrow it could be rewritten.

He tensed, refusing to lurk now. The whores' camp was very close to the southern wood. But although he was determined to ignore Brianna, he faltered. She dreamed of him all the time, and her thoughts had told him her dreams were very sexual and erotic. He wished he hadn't ever heard her thinking about her active fantasy life.

His heart was racing now.

His loins were hot and thick.

He glanced at his tent and his mind slipped helplessly into hers.

But the dream was an innocent one. She was with her lady friends.

He was almost disappointed that she was dreaming about the women and not him, but it was better this way. He made up his mind and started to walk away, but as he did, he listened closely to her. She was so happy and so well-loved. And then she looked at him and smiled. *"Aidan."*

In her dream she stood on the threshold of a room, starkly and lushly naked. There was no mistaking what she wanted—and what would happen next.

He knew he must turn his mind away from hers. He knew he must continue on to the whores' camp.

He knew that whatever happened next, it could be rewritten on the morrow.

Ablaze, he stepped into her dream.

I AM SHAMELESS, BRIE THOUGHT, slowly crossing her loft. Her body was hot and alive, and she felt as beautiful as a seductress. She felt her hips swing as she went to him; she felt her hair tangling over her breasts. Aidan stood in the doorway, unmoving. His blue eyes were blazing with heat and desire, their brilliance almost blinding.

She could barely breathe, and her mouth was dry. She knew she was dreaming; she couldn't possibly be in New York City with him, like this, but it didn't diminish her excitement. "I am so glad to see you," she whispered. "I have missed you."

He started. His face set, he said, "Hallo, a Bhrianna," and his smoldering gaze slid down her naked body.

She went still. No one had ever looked at her in such a bold, hot way—no, Aidan had looked at her that way. He had looked at her that way when she was not dreaming, at Awe—she was almost certain. And no one had ever desired her this way before. Vaguely, she wondered at her empathy. Why was she feeling him in a dream?

His gaze had become an erotic caress. Her skin tingled beneath it, swelling. Distracted, she gasped, "I really need you."

His mouth shifted but didn't curve. "Aye." He reached for her.

His hands closed on her, and his grasp was stunningly real—too real. Her body fired, and the heat in his eyes thrilled her. "You want me," she managed. But she was confused.

"Aye, in yer dreams," he said tersely.

Something was awry. Brie inhaled. Their gazes held. "This *is* a dream, isn't it?"

"Does it matter?" He pulled her closer and she gasped. He reached for his sword belt, and suddenly all of his clothes vanished, even his boots. Brie looked at his hard, sculpted body. She looked at his perfect, tight face and his huge arousal. She wet her lips, her pulse so rapid now she started feeling faint.

He clasped her shoulders, breathing hard. His tension was so high it had become painful. "I am going to take power, Brianna, but I won't hurt ye," he said harshly.

He was going to take power, not make love to her? That was all wrong. In her dreams, he made love to her, and laughter followed in the aftermath of their passion. In her dreams, she felt her desire, not his. "I'm becoming nervous," she whispered.

His eyes darkened, and he pulled her close against his hard, quivering body. "Dinna fear me now," he whispered.

Brie gasped. The contact between their skin was electric, shocking, exciting—and real. Her confusion increased. Was she dreaming or not?

His face impossibly set now, he pushed her hair back over her shoulders, and suddenly his hands slid down her back. She shivered in pleasure and lifted her eyes to his. He was staring at her mouth with a raw hunger. Then he met her gaze.

"What's wrong? Why aren't you kissing me? Why do I keep feeling you?"

He shook his head, and slid his hand quickly over her breast. She gasped in more pleasure, but he abruptly lifted her in his arms and was carrying her to her bed. Why wasn't he caressing her and kissing her? she wondered, finally becoming alarmed.

He laid her on the bed, panting. Sweat beaded his temples. His hand slid into her hair, anchoring her head. "Ye canna control yer dreams," he said. Softly, he added, "Ye canna control me."

"Something is wrong," she breathed, but she no longer cared. Tears came. "I'm hurting and hot. Hurry."

His gaze slid down her body. Brie realized he was fighting himself, but she didn't know why. Then he reached down and slid his hand over the slick depths of her womanhood. She arched against him, throbbing softly.

But he didn't caress her.

She arched again and somehow looked at him. "Please."

His blinding gaze lifted to hers. He was trembling; he shook his head. "If I make love to ye, I am doomed."

Brie jerked to sit up. *This was not a dream.*

He stood, magnificently aroused, his entire body

taut. He shook his head and started to back away, but his gaze kept moving back down her body as if he had never seen a naked woman before.

Brie leapt to her feet and took his face in her hands. "I love you. It's only a dream. Let me make love to you."

He started shaking his head in negation, but his gaze was fixed on hers—hot, hard and anguished. He was distressed. She felt that now, too.

"You're the one who's afraid," she whispered. She tried to smile, and ran her thumb over his jaw. To her shock, he gasped, his eyes flying in confusion to hers.

She drew back, releasing his face. "What is it?"

He breathed hard, panting. "Dinna touch me, Brianna," he said.

And she felt him clearly. *He was afraid of her touch—and desperate for her to touch him, too.*

Of course he was. Had any woman touched him with true love and affection in sixty-six years? Brie cupped his jaw and stroked her thumb along the hard ridge there. He cried out, but instead of pulling away, his thick, dark lashes fanned out.

His desire stabbed through her. Inhaling, Brie covered the slab of one pectoral muscle with her other hand. She ran her hand across his spectacular chest. He moaned, arching back. His desperation consumed her, thick with explosive heat and desire. This man was starving for love and affection, she thought.

"God," he whispered.

Brie trembled, aching impossibly now, and stood on tiptoe, kissing each nipple slowly in turn. He cried out, jerking back. "Cease."

Their gazes clashed, his wide with alarm.

He was going to vanish into reality. Instantly she put

her arms around him and held him, hard, letting her love cloak them both.

He did not vanish. His desire soared.

"It's all right," she whispered.

His pleasure spiraled wildly as she held him. She thought she might shatter soon, but she stepped back, caught his hand and kissed it with the love consuming her. Then she brought it to her breast.

His eyes held hers, shimmering oddly.

"It's all right," she said again, meaning it.

His hand closed slowly, tentatively, on her breast. Then his palm scraped her hard nipple and swept up over her shoulder. "I must go." He turned to leave, and he was massively aroused.

She caught his hand, aware that his tension was about to break.

He slowly faced her.

Brie took his face in her hands again, heard him gasp, "No," and ignored him. She pressed her mouth to his.

He went still, lips closed, as she began kissing him with all the love in her heart. His mouth softened. She licked the seam of his lips and kissed him again, and he finally opened for her.

Brie kissed him deeply, and Aidan moaned long and low, tragically. It was the sound of a man who had been lost and alone for a lifetime.

Suddenly his hands caught her shoulders and he claimed the kiss, deep and wet, openmouthed and frantic.

He kissed her as if he had never kissed a woman before, and he cried out.

Brie felt him come to that mighty precipice just as he turned away from her. She wrapped her arms around him from behind, aware of him battling the explosive pressure. She couldn't stand it, either, she thought. Then he gasped, seizing her hands and clenching them tightly against his abdomen. And he exploded.

Brie felt as if she was soaring through the stars, stunned and holding him tightly. She whirled, shocked by such empathy, as he gasped again and again until he finally calmed and sagged in her arms. Breathing hard, her body still on fire, she felt his body become still.

He had not been able to withstand her touch, not when it was infused with her love.

He was suddenly facing her, flushing. "'Tis but a dream."

And she sensed what he intended. "Don't leave me now, like this."

His hard blue gaze held hers. "I am sorry." He vanished.

Brie cried out furiously, in dismay. And instead of the pale walls of her loft, she stared into the dark shadows of the night.

Her pulse was pounding, and she was feverishly hot and aching everywhere. Owls hooted. The wind sighed. Brie realized she lay in a small bed beneath heavy wool blankets and a fur. She blinked. She had been dreaming.

It had been so real.

It had been so strange.

In that instant she recalled every moment of the dream encounter. Uncomfortable and alarmed, she sat up abruptly, glancing toward the open tent flap.

Aidan was silhouetted in the shadows. It was obvious he was staring at her.

Had that been a dream or not? "Aidan?" she whispered roughly.

He turned and walked away.

She leapt up and ran after him. He had paused by a small fire, and he turned to watch her approach. Across the darkness, their eyes met.

Brie slowed. She should be furious at him for watching her while she slept and for watching her while she had a very private dream. *If* he had been watching her dream. Because the dream remained incredibly vivid and terribly strange. He hadn't made love to her, but she had made love to him, in a way. He had been *desperate* for her touch and her love.

She knew damn well that dreams often held secrets that were meant to be revealed or were harbingers of the truth. When had he last been loved, really loved, by any woman?

"Ye willna recall the dream in the morning," he said harshly.

"Don't you dare enchant me," Brie cried furiously.

"Go back to sleep." He walked away.

Brie turned back to the tent and was suddenly confused. What was she doing, wandering about the Highland camp in the middle of the night? Had she just spoken to Aidan, and if so, about what?

Had she been dreaming?

THEIR ARMIES MET AT FIRST LIGHT. It was midday now. Initially both bowmen and artillery had fired upon their opposing foot soldiers, mowing down the marching front ranks as the two armies inexorably approached one another. But the fighting had become vicious at last, and it was the kind of fighting Highlanders lived for: hand-to-hand and sword-to-sword combat.

The sun was high, and it beat the bloody earth.

Vultures soared. Wolves waited. Dead archers and gunners, Highlanders, slain knights and their chargers littered the fields. Only a few dozen men remained, all locked in mortal combat. Aidan finished a royal soldier, welding his sword right through the man's armor. As the man went down, Aidan turned.

The flame-haired warrior coming at him was a giant with an ax and sword, and a mace and spiked ball. The rival was a head taller than Aidan and his black eyes were soulless, which savagely pleased Aidan. He wasn't ready to retire from the field—oh, no.

Aidan laughed at the warrior, lifting his broadsword.

The giant grinned back and began twirling the ball on the chain.

Aidan lifted his double-edged broadsword higher as the giant said softly, "Mayhap you should have taken power last night, instead of pleasure from a virgin in her dreams."

Aidan froze as the spiked ball spun at him. And his sword gave way, for his arm could not break the surprising velocity of the blow. He gasped as the skin was flayed from wrist to elbow, but he somehow kept a grasp on the huge sword. *Who was this?*

The ball swung back at his chest.

Too late, Aidan roared, putting his entire might against it, using the sword again. The ball struck hard on the blade and skidded across it, digging into flesh and bone before bouncing away. The pain surprised Aidan and brought him to his knees.

"If you prefer virgins, my son, it can be arranged."

Aidan looked up at the giant, and there was no mistaking his eyes. No longer black, they were blue. *They were his father's eyes.*

Aidan lurched upward as the giant swung his mace at his head.

He caught the blow with his shoulder this time, grunting. *The giant had his father's strength because Moray had possessed him—as no deamhan had ever possessed a human before.*

There was no time to understand how the giant could look at him with Moray's cold eyes. And before Aidan could defend the next blow, the spiked ball ripped across his chest.

Almost blinded by the pain, he finally struck at the giant, cutting a swath from his throat to his navel.

The huge monster towered there, reeling as if in a wind. "Ian lives," the giant said softly, and he viciously struck the mace at Aidan's knees.

His kneecaps seemed to shatter as he went down hard on his chest and face.

The giant said again, "Hallo, a Aidan," and there was no mistaking his father's voice now.

There was no mistaking his father's mocking laughter, either.

On the ground, Aidan roared in fury and swung his broadsword across the giant's ankles, severing his feet from his legs.

The giant grunted, staring down at Aidan in surprise, and then began to topple over.

Aidan dropped his broadsword, his short sword and his dagger in his hands. He stabbed his dagger into the giant's heart, but his father laughed at him again. The sound did not come from the giant, and Aidan realized his father's power was independent of this body. He drew his shortsword across the giant's neck, panting. And he stood staggering over the body, watching the giant's head rolling across the rocky ground.

More laughter sounded, but from above.

Aidan stiffened, still reeling. His knees seemed useless, and he had to fight to stand. He looked toward the cruel, taunting laughter, and saw a black energy spiraling into the sky. Aidan had just beheaded an inconsequential being—and his father's power remained intact.

Moray had returned. But what was he, now?

BRIE PACED OUTSIDE OF AIDAN'S TENT. It was growing dark. Most of the men had returned from the battlefield after noon, all bloodied, many wounded, but the majority of them pleased, clearly having enjoyed a bloody battle to the death.

Where was Aidan?

She had been vomiting all afternoon. The brutality of the battle, the cruelty and death, swirled over her, through her, making her dizzy and faint. So much violence was on the plain below that she couldn't block it out, nor could she isolate what was happening to Aidan. Her empathy was a curse she might not survive. She thought she had felt every blow delivered that day.

God, where was he?

She began to shake with the depth of her fear for him. It would be dusk soon. She had expected some kind of brief engagement, but the sound of medieval artillery—the explosions made by mortars, the clash of swords, the screams of horses—had awoken her at dawn.

Now the camp was raucous, the men celebrating. Fires were roaring, instruments like flutes and fiddles were playing. Women laughed, the men were drunk and loud and some were actually fornicating out in the open with the camp women, who seemed to be enjoying it.

Brie ran up to almost every soldier who passed, begging for word on Aidan. Every reply was the same. "He still fights, lady."

But she knew the battle was over, because she couldn't hear swords clashing, or gunfire, or cannons. And suddenly she couldn't stand upright.

Brie collapsed, screaming, the skin on her arm burning as if it had been torn off. And then another terrible lash seemed to flay her chest and belly, leaving it raw and burning, as if on fire. She clutched her abdomen. Looking down she expected to see blood, but nothing was there except the tunic she'd belted over her modern clothes.

Aidan was injured.

And then her knees seemed to break into a million pieces. She went down, moaning in agony. Suddenly Will was beside her. "Lady? What passes? Is it poison?" he cried.

She was briefly blinded by the pain. After all she had withstood that day, she was incapable of movement, incapable of making a sound. Brie stared up at Will. Aidan had just been terribly wounded. Her vision blurred with tears.

"Dinna move," Will said.

Brie closed her eyes, finally breathing. She did not know how long she lay there, but at some point she opened her eyes, meeting a blue-black night sky that was winking with stars. The moon was nearly full tonight, and it was starkly white. The torment was fading.

Will sat beside her and cried, "Thank Jesus."

Brie sat up, aching in every fiber of her being. *What had happened to him?* "Is Aidan back?"

Will's face tightened.

Brie covered her face with her hands—and then she heard hoofbeats.

Will stood, surprised. "'Tis the black stud. He bears our master!"

Brie staggered upright and saw the black stallion cantering toward them, Aidan astride. She cried out, rushing forward, overcome with relief.

But her relief was short-lived. The horse halted, and Aidan stared down at her. She took one look at his blood-soaked tunic, then at his crimson left arm, and became faint. "Can you get down?" How utterly calm she sounded.

"Aye." He slid from the horse as if he had a sprained ankle, nothing more.

She now saw his swollen, black-and-purple knees. "Oh, God," she gasped.

"I'm fine," he said. He handed Will the horse and strode to the tent, not even limping. The flap closed behind him.

She had witnessed an expression on his hard, grim face that she had never seen before—one of vast concern.

Brie hurried into the tent just as Aidan tossed his bloody leine to the floor, standing only in his boots. "Get Will. I want my boots off," he said tersely.

Brie looked at his raw torso and his left arm. "Sit down." She whirled and left the tent to find Aidan's page. "Will, bring water and soap, and whiskey or wine and anything else to clean his wounds." Did they even have whiskey in the sixteenth century?

Will nodded and ran off.

Brie returned to the tent and saw Aidan standing there, unaware of her, lost in thought. She had been right. Something terrible had happened. She went to him and touched his arm, about to help him sit. As she did, a memory swished through her.

Her hand on Aidan's jaw, his thick, dark lashes fanned out, a harsh cry, simmering desire.

She was confused. Aidan suddenly looked into her eyes. She focused. "Let me clean you off."

He sat. If it hurt to do so, he didn't make a sound. "Can ye get my boots off?" he asked very quietly.

She hated his calm demeanor! Now she prayed he'd erupt into rage. She took a boot and pulled it off, but not without a huge effort. She looked past his groin at his raw body. "How much does that hurt?"

"It doesna hurt."

She reached for the other boot and yanked it off after a few moments of tugging. He was covering his pain. "What happened?"

"Doesna matter." He lay on his back on the bed.

He was really hurt, and blocking it from her, she thought. She had never seen him appear tired, let alone lie down. The tent flap moved behind her and she was relieved to see Will with a bowl of water, soap and linens. "Thank you," she said.

Aidan slowly sat up. "Will can attend me. Leave."

"Like hell," Brie cried softly. She already had the basin and linen and soap. His face hardened, but she ignored it, gently going for his raw chest. His body tightened as she tried to wash it, but he didn't make a sound.

She knew it hurt. She slowly and methodically washed the area. Suddenly she heard Will snicker. Brie glanced at him and he shrugged. "The Wolf will live," he said, and walked out.

Brie turned back and realized why Will was so

amused. “How can you be aroused now?” Clearly he was shielding himself from her, because she couldn’t feel the desire, just as she couldn’t feel his pain.

His eyes blazed. “I want ye to leave—now.”

She went still.

“I need power,” he said softly. “I can heal myself, mayhap because I was a Master once an’ the gods are confused, but I’ll heal quicker if I take power.”

And she understood why he was aroused. “You would never hurt me—you swore that you wouldn’t.”

He breathed hard. “I am hurt as I haven’t been hurt in my entire life, an’ I am tired, very tired…. Ye need to leave.”

He dropped the block on his emotions. Thick lust swirled and filled her. It was hot and ravenous, dark and predatory, indifferent to everything but itself and intent on self-gratification. But with it, she felt desire.

She tensed, aware of the incredible difference between his passions. “I will never believe that you commit pleasure crimes.” Was she deluding herself? She’d felt this lust before, when they’d first met after her rescue from the gang. “Hold still,” she said, and she poured what looked like scotch over his raw torso. The lust was making her ill, but the desire made her heart race.

He grunted. “Are ye jealous of the women I’ll take to my bed tonight?”

Oh, that hurt. She did not look up, trembling. “You have this huge reputation as a great lover, and I don’t think that would be the case if you left your lovers dead.” She seized his left hand and started washing his raw arm with water, swiftly this time because she was so upset.

I am going to take power, Brianna, but I willna hurt ye.

She stiffened as his words washed through her mind. She looked up. He was staring at her.

"I don't believe it," she whispered.

"I leave the women *alive,*" he said harshly.

It was so hard to grapple with what he was telling her. Yet that lust for power was unmistakable.

"Ah, ye've finally lost yer faith. Do ye fear me now, too?" He shrugged her off. "Dinna touch me."

She backed away. He met her stare. "No, Aidan," she finally said. "I don't fear you. And I guess I was right—you haven't left a trail of dead Innocents in your wake." But she was terse. He was the son of a demon. Demons lusted for power and took it at will. Demons destroyed. But he hadn't used her, taken power from her or destroyed her. And while history accused him of many bloody deeds, he was admitting to leaving his lovers alive.

Dinna touch me.

Brie tensed, suddenly recalling her hands on his hard chest, his trembling, taut body, his spiking desire and hers. "What happened in that dream?"

Aidan looked at her with surprise. "Ye can fight my powers o' enchantment?"

"You came to me to take power," she said slowly, struggling to remember. "But you didn't, did you?"

He stood, reaching behind him without turning, taking a plaid and wrapping it around his waist. "Yer a fierce, annoyin' woman," he said, eyes hard. But his gaze moved to her mouth.

It was déjà vu. He had looked at her mouth with so much hunger…but he hadn't kissed her. She had kissed him—and then he had kissed her back. "You kissed me."

"Ye recall the dream?" He was disbelieving.

"Just bits and pieces of it." She shook. "Oh my God. That kiss—it was *huge*." Her eyes widened as she recalled the explosion of passion. "It was desire, not lust! Did we make love?"

"Yer still a virgin," he snapped, his anger blazing. "It was a damned dream!" He reached for a bottle of wine sitting on the portable desk and popped the cork with his fingers.

Bracing against the anger, Brie whispered, "Then why are you so upset?"

His mouth curled. "I'm hardly distraught over a dream. I haven't thought about it, not until now."

He was lying. She felt the lie quivering between them, just the way she felt the desire cowering behind the lust for power. "Take the spell off me."

He looked coolly at her. "So ye can relive the dream?"

"*You* came to *me* in a dream," she whispered. Her heart lurched. What had happened?

His eyes widened. Then, savagely, he replied, "I came to use ye, Brianna, but ye refuse to ken the truth."

She hugged herself. "No. Because I recall that kiss, and it was filled with passion."

"I need power," Aidan said, his gaze brilliant with sudden fury. "I want power. I went to ye to take power!" He whirled. "Ye want sex? Ye want pleasure? Find a lover, but it won't be me."

His fury caused Brie to collapse on the bed. She looked up at him. He was livid, but the memories started rushing over her, through her. "Making love won't doom you, Aidan. It will heal you."

"Ye canna heal me, Brianna. I willna allow it." His teeth bared, he stormed from the tent.

CHAPTER EIGHT

AIDAN STRODE AWAY FROM HIS TENT, furious with Brianna. The moment he'd closed the flap behind him, he started to limp. Pain stabbed through his knees and throbbed within him. He hadn't exaggerated. He was injured as he hadn't been injured since he'd been chosen by the Brotherhood. That giant had been dangerously powerful—and he knew its power had somehow been enhanced by Moray. He had just barely escaped with his own life.

But he hadn't destroyed the evil consuming the giant.

Head down, knees aching, his chest and arm still on fire, Aidan suddenly felt a huge and familiar white power barring his way. He halted, looking up, dismayed.

MacNeil stood before him, his green eyes dark, his expression grim.

A new, terrible tension assailed Aidan. "O' course. How foolish o' me not to ken ye'd be here." MacNeil had the Sight, although he conveniently claimed he could only see when the gods allowed it. He had either seen Moray's return or he had sensed it.

"Let me heal ye, lad," the tall, golden man said softly.

"Fuck off," Aidan snarled. "I'll take power from the whores."

"Yer in pain. 'Tis clear Moray has spent the sixty-six years growin' his evil powers. Yer fortunate to live this day." MacNeil swept his hand out, and white rain shimmered over Aidan.

He would never forgive MacNeil for callously accepting Ian's death, and for knowing of it without warning him. He would never forgive MacNeil for choosing the gods over his son. Even though the healing shower instantly began to soothe his injuries, Aidan flung his power furiously at MacNeil. The golden Master blocked the silver wave easily and it veered off into the woods. Trunks cracked apart and the trees slammed to the ground, which briefly shook.

"Do ye feel better?" MacNeil asked.

"I will hate ye till I die," Aidan snapped, breathing hard. "Did ye come to hear me beg fer help? Because I will never do so!"

MacNeil laid his hand on Aidan's arm. A wonderful warmth swept through Aidan's entire body, and he knew he was healed from the day's terrible battle. "I would never expect ye to beg fer anything from anyone, Aidan. But ye need me an' ye need the Brotherhood."

Aidan shrugged away. "So ye'll battle with a half deamhan?" he laughed.

"To vanquish Moray? Aye, I'll command the brethren to aid ye. I already have."

"I dinna want or need yer help," Aidan said, but he began to seriously recall the events of that day. He did not know the extent of Moray's powers and he did not know if he had enough power, on his own, to destroy him once and for all.

"Ye've seen his newest power of possession." MacNeil spoke quietly.

"Aye." Aidan finally gave in. He needed information, so he would tolerate the abbot. "Can he emerge as anyone, at any time?"

"Aye, but 'tis easier fer him to possess the weak an' the evil."

Aidan turned away. One of Brianna's demonic bodyguards could turn the corner, and it could be Moray. He faced the golden Master tersely. "He's disguised his evil well. He used to bring a great chill with him. I used to feel his black power long before I faced it. I dinna feel any chill or his particular power today."

"He has been carefully sowing his powers all these years. He's learned to hide until he wishes otherwise. He managed to find a part of the Duisean," MacNeil said, "and I think he has it hidden in yer lady's time."

Aidan went still. The Duisean was the Book of Power, stolen from its holy shrine hundreds of years ago. The Brotherhood had been searching for it for centuries. "So he used the book to come back from Malcolm's vanquishing," he said slowly.

"His return was written," MacNeil said flatly. "I dinna ken if he had the pages of the Duisean then."

"Like my son's death?" Aidan cried, trembling.

"I am not a god, and I do not debate their Wisdom and writings with them," MacNeil said, laying his hand on Aidan's shoulder another time.

Aidan wrenched away. Ian's death had been written. Hadn't it?

Ian lives.

His heart filled with a savage, unbearable pain. He had been doing his best to avoid recollection of those terrible, cruel words until now. It was not true. It could not be true. Moray wished to torment him to his death this time.

"I remain sorry fer yer loss," MacNeil said gravely.

Aidan shook with despair. "He told me Ian lives."

"He plays ye, lad."

Aidan trembled, staring. If Ian was alive, he could not be a ghost. Ghosts came from the dead. There was no hope. He did not want to ever have hope again.

"He distracted ye today. He'll do so again. He's played ye yer entire life, cat an' mouse. He hunts ye now."

Aidan met MacNeil's concerned gaze. It was true. His father had started hunting him when he was ten years old and fostering with the Maclaine family. He'd hunted him lightly then, but he'd hunted him very seriously and ruthlessly from the day he'd been chosen and joined the Brotherhood.

"He'll never forgive ye fer defyin' him, fer servin' the Brotherhood. He'll never forgive ye fer allowin' yer lovers to live. He'll never forgive ye fer hunting down his three deamhan sons, one by one, an' destroyin' their families, their lands. Dinna let him torment ye further, lad." MacNeil's large hand found Aidan's shoulder again.

This time, Aidan did not wrench away. This time, there was so much despair.

A powerful healer like Lady Allie could have saved Ian. A god could have saved Ian.

He forced the hope away. Ian was dead and Moray would have to pay with his life.

"This war must end and there will be one victor. Let us help ye, Aidan. Ye remain a brother, always."

"Do ye ken how Moray can be vanquished?" he asked harshly.

MacNeil shook his head.

"Then I dinna care fer yer help." He started to walk away.

"An' what about Lady Brianna?" MacNeil called to his back.

If you like virgins, my son, it can be arranged.

Aidan faltered. Instantly he reached out for her. She was asleep, but not dreaming. Even though she was not in danger, he did not relax.

His father had known that he'd chosen to go to Brianna in a dream, instead of taking power from the Innocent in the women's camp. Did he also know that Aidan had desire for her, instead of lust? Did he know that Aidan was resolved to protect her? If Moray knew any of those things, Brianna was in jeopardy.

His fear escalated wildly as he met MacNeil's gaze. Clearly the Master knew all of this, too.

"She can come to me at Iona anytime," he said, and he vanished.

If he sent Brianna to MacNeil, she would be safe upon Iona's holy ground. She could look at MacNeil with her huge, trusting eyes; she could annoy him with her unwelcome opinions and she could covet him, body and soul, as she surely would.

He was rigid. He hated the idea of Brianna desiring the other man.

BRIE DREAMED OF THE MEDIEVAL BATTLE, the sound of swords and artillery, shouting men and screaming horses ringing in her ears. She waited frantically for Aidan to appear. She somehow knew he was alive, but she was terrified for him. And when he suddenly slid off his horse and into her arms, he was covered in so much blood that he slipped out of her hands.

He was going to die, she thought, panicked.

But he didn't collapse. Instead, as if she weren't there, he walked of his own accord into his tent.

What had happened? Who had done this to him?

And she felt the huge evil appear behind her. Brie tensed, very uncertain that she was dreaming now.

"Hallo a Bhrianna."

That terrible voice was terrifying and somehow familiar. Brie turned and faced a handsome blond demon, who smiled at her. "It's you, isn't it? You did this to Aidan," she said.

He laughed. "Who else could hurt your lover so badly?"

He reached for her. "My son prefers to amuse himself with virgins, rather than take and destroy Innocence. You yearn to redeem him, but I will never allow it." He pulled her into his embrace. "He will die before there is ever salvation, fair Brianna."

Brie went still, but her heart exploded in terror. "You're not here with me, now! I am dreaming. No one has seen you in sixty-six years!"

Brie tried to struggle free of him. He instantly let her go, laughing. She had to wake up now, before something terrible happened. Panicking, she raced after Aidan into the tent, aware of Moray following, his pace unhurried and unrushed. But the tent was empty.

Crying out, she whirled as the flap fell closed behind Moray. "He left you a virgin. How pleasant for me," he murmured.

Brie felt her clothing vanish. She screamed.

HER SCREAM SHRILLED THROUGH THE NIGHT.

Aidan instantly felt his father's evil. He ran toward

his tent, expecting another scream. It did not come, and fear began. He thrust inside and was greeted with shadows and the dim light cast from one lantern. Brianna lay in bed, thrashing in her sleep.

Moray was not standing over her.

He slipped instantly into her dream and found her naked in the deamhan's arms. Moray laughed. "It's only a dream, my son."

Aidan flung all his power at him.

Moray lifted Brianna and used her as a shield; the energy blazed into her. She went limp and lifeless in his father's arms.

"Tsk, tsk. You destroy Innocence?"

No one could die in a dream! Panicked, he left the dream and sat down beside her, seizing her shoulders. "Wake up!" he roared, terrified that she would never awaken now.

Brianna's eyes flew open.

"Yer nay hurt. 'Twas a dream," he cried, choking on relief.

She threw her arms around him and clung.

He held her hard, as hard and tightly as he could. *Had she died in the dream?*

He was already in her mind. She was reliving the dream, going limp and lifeless in Moray's arms. His father's laughter filled the tent.

He stiffened, glancing warily around. Moray was not present. But Brianna looked up, eyes wide. "Is he here? I thought it was just a nightmare. Aidan?"

"Ye heard him?" Aidan asked carefully.

She nodded.

Aidan breathed hard and reached out, straining. It took a long moment, but he finally felt the black evil filling the confines of his tent. "I'll be seeing' ye in hell very soon," he snarled.

"You'll see me tomorrow," Moray murmured.

And the evil weight vanished. Aidan knew he was gone.

"Aidan? What's going on? What's happening?" Brianna cried.

She was terrified—and in his arms. And it was a soft, warm, caring woman he held. He wanted to soothe her, but not the way he'd so often soothed Ian in his previous lifetime. He wanted to soothe her by moving over her, by kissing her face, her breasts, her hair. All he had to do was take her face in his hands and press her down onto the bed. His body was already hot and inflamed. When his body was in hers, she would not be thinking of this nightmare, his deamhan father and the dream death.

But he made no such efforts.

Moray was hunting her now.

It had become terribly clear. Moray would use her against Aidan, just as he had begun to fear. He must not take her, touch her or soothe her, not in any way. He already cared to protect her, and that made her—and him—terribly vulnerable.

He must send Brianna to Iona immediately.

For one more moment, he held her in the circle of his arms, acutely aware of her warmth and caring, and even of her love. If he did not behave with extreme caution, she would suffer the same fate as Ian—or even a worse one.

"I'll guard ye while ye sleep. I willna allow anyone to step into yer dreams."

Her eyes widened. She glanced down between

them, where he throbbed helplessly against the linen leine. "I can't sleep now," she whispered.

And he realized he hadn't shielded his desire from her—or his anger and fear. Instantly he put a block between them, but that didn't change what he really wanted to do. It didn't ease his body, which clamored for her. He released her and stood up.

Very careful to sound indifferent, he said, "Yer a beautiful woman, Brianna. Ye ken a Highland man will always respond to beauty with virility." He shrugged.

"I'm not beautiful," she said, her green eyes unwavering on his. "Aidan, I just died."

He went still and his heart lurched. *Was this another new power?* "Are ye certain?"

She nodded, looking lost and vulnerable, pulling her covers up to her chin. "No one dies in a dream. I *died.*"

He did not know what this could mean. She had died in Moray's arms, from his own power. He shrugged, forcing indifference. "'Twas only a dream."

"I felt the last moment of my life—I knew it was over. I felt my life *leave,*" she stressed, as pale as his son's ghost. "I even saw the holies—I went to their light."

He met her gaze and saw so much emotion shimmering there. He saw fear and helplessness, which enraged him, and he saw courage and determination, which he admired. But her strained gaze also beckoned him.

He understood the plea and lurked anyway. She wanted him to slip into her bed and make love to her. Of course, she thought about making love to him all the time. He didn't have to lurk to know it. Her eyes gave her away. It was often annoying, sometimes infuriating and always provocative. His body seemed to have a mind and will of its own, for it always responded to her. Now she stared and it only furthered the tension coursing between them.

He swiftly poured her some wine and handed the glass to her. She smiled wanly at him, and he was suddenly sorry that he hadn't taken her to bed previously. Now there would never be that chance.

"I really need Tabby and Sam. Claire said she'd contacted Allie. Maybe she'll show up soon."

He understood why she was so upset, and damn it, he wanted to distract her. "Lady Allie can persuade Royce to come to ye, if anyone can. Brianna…forget about the dream."

"I can't." Then she added, "At least I lived to wake up."

"Drink yer wine. It will comfort you," he said. "A dream isna reality."

She gave him a look. "Yes, it is. I'm a Rose, Aidan. I come from a long line of powerful women and we know all about the other worlds."

He crossed his arms. He had wondered about her empathy for him. "Why do ye have more empathy fer me than others?"

"I don't know, exactly, but it's helped me understand you—and made me even more determined to help you."

"I dinna care fer ye to feel so much of me," he said. "I have to guard myself all the time to block ye."

She slid from the bed, and his eyes widened at the sight of her legs and pink underwear. "You invade my privacy whenever you feel like it. I guess now you know what it feels like."

He stared at her pale, lush thighs and the pink bikini. His pulse was roaring impossibly. Then he raised his eyes. "Ye need to get dressed."

She didn't move. "I felt your desire a moment ago,

too, before you shielded it. It was different. It wasn't about power, not at all. It was the same desire you had in our dream."

He did not like her husky tone and sidelong look. "A Highlander needs sex like his daily bread, while a deamhan needs power. I am a Highlander *and* a deamhan," he said harshly. "I have sex an' take power every single day."

"Demons destroy. You haven't destroyed me. You don't even want to use me. You want good, old-fashioned sex, so I guess that makes you more of a Highlander than half demon."

"I liked ye better," he said softly, "when ye feared me. 'Tis late. Go back to sleep."

She trembled. "I don't think so."

Now she would refuse him?

"I'll sleep when you stop staring at my legs."

He realized he was looking at her pink undergarment again, and what he could see behind the material. He flushed. She was throbbing gently. If he did what he really wished to do, there would be nothing gentle in her body. "Ye want me to stare or ye wouldn't stand naked in the freezin' cold."

"I'm haven't noticed the cold, and I'm not naked."

He went still. A reply escaped him now.

"And you can block whatever you choose, but what you're feeling is really obvious." She glanced at the hem of his leine, which remained tented. She added, her face flushed, "I don't know whether I chose to dream of him or whether he decided to inflict himself on me in my dream, but as I said, I'm a Rose, and I know dreams are another reality." She stared into his eyes, her gaze intense—beseeching, even. "I have never been so afraid, not in my entire life, and I have seen my share of evil. Even though I have woken up alive, I can't go back to sleep. What if he comes back to kill me?"

He was an instant from putting his arm around her and giving her what they both wanted. "Ye need clothes," he repeated. "An' I will keep ye safe, as I promised ye I would do."

She looked right into his eyes. "At first I thought I was mistaken," she said huskily. "I thought you were oversexed, and the desire was because I'm female and anything in a skirt would do."

He was not going to admit anything. He was having trouble speaking, in any case. "Get dressed. Now."

She moved, but not to get dressed. Instead, she dared to touch his cheek. "I think you want me, a lot. And even better, I think you care, at least a little. I think we're becoming friends. And I think that's why you want me. I think you need to make love to me." Her eyes, trained upon his, were as wide as a doe's.

He was aghast.

He picked her jeans up from the foot of the bed and threw them at her chest, where she hugged them. "We will never be friends and we will never be lovers, Brianna," he warned.

"Why not?"

"Because Moray has come back, and not just in dreams," he said harshly. "He was the giant I met on the battlefield."

DEAMHANAIN DID NOT DESIRE, they lusted. They did not protect, they destroyed.

Aidan paced outside his tent, aware that Brianna

was inside, tense with fear and wide awake. Now she needed his protection, from his demonic father. If he wasn't careful, he would slip into Brianna's bed to comfort her, enjoy her every caress and cry and, before he knew it, she would be *healing* him. He would accept MacNeil's offer and become allies with the Brotherhood, and after giving up his vengeance he would be walking with the gods again.

He shook with rage, looking up at a bright, full moon. "I'll never walk in yer light again. Bastards," he hissed.

But Moray was more powerful than ever, and he had to be destroyed, soon. MacNeil did not know how he could be vanquished. If anyone could defeat Moray, it was a mighty god.

But no god would show him compassion, not after all he had done. And he would not beg them for their aid, either, just as he wouldn't beg MacNeil.

But the gods were selfish and greedy, like their children, the Highlanders. Gods liked power and wealth. He could bribe them. And why not? He needed the power and he would enjoy the blackmail.

"Ye hate me as I hate ye," he said harshly, staring at the silent night. "Come face me now an' admit it, so we can begin our bargain."

The night remained blue-black, cool and silent. Only the wolves moved, panting as they lay a short distance from him.

"Let me defeat Moray," Aidan said, thinking of Brianna, "an' I will gladly give ye my life."

The night changed. Stars winked at him; the moon smiled. The wind even sighed.

The wolves sat up.

These were hardly answers. "She has seen the

future." Green eyes came to his mind, at once frightened and determined. "I am to hang soon. No rope can hold me, but give me the power to defeat Moray an' I will accept my fate."

A gust of wind lifted the dead leaves at his feet.

"Cowards," he hissed. "Show yerself an' let us seal our bargain!"

The wind roared, whipping his leine. The wolves growled, hackles raised, and then, abruptly, the autumn night was still and vacant.

That was an answer if he had ever heard one.

AIDAN LAY UNSLEEPING on the bearskin beside her bed, and Brianna was acutely aware of him.

Dying in that nightmare had been terrifying, but when she'd awoken, she'd been in Aidan's powerful embrace. Her fear had vanished instantly. There had been only him and her and the magical pull between them.

Brie smiled grimly to herself, aware that it might be some time before she ever found herself in his arms again.

He wasn't frightening anymore. He had rescued her—twice, if she included his rescuing her from Moray in her nightmare. His bark was really loud and sometimes scary, but he hadn't bitten, not even once. She was coming to believe that a friendship was forming between them.

She had been so terrified for him earlier. The extent of his wounds had convinced her that he was as mortal as she was, but, thank the gods, that he had been healed.

He was no longer such an enigma. His wounds ran soul-deep, and she understood why he had forsaken his gods. He was furious about his son's murder, and his answer to Ian's fate was to turn his back on the Innocent, as if to say, to hell with everyone. That did not make him evil, or even close to evil, no matter what he claimed.

He lay on his back, eyes wide-open, staring up at the tent ceiling. He had stayed with her because she was afraid. He had chosen to comfort her, although not in the way she truly wished. He could be in the women's camp, carousing or worse, but he was not. He was with her to protect her. And it wasn't just because she was his link to Ian's ghost. Something had begun for them, and in spite of the evil facing them, she was thrilled.

She glanced down at him, and he pretended not to see. Two lanterns remained lit—she had asked for the second light—and his beautiful face was illuminated. He had his hands beneath his head, his biceps bulging. One day she was going to be brave enough to entice him to bed.

He thought he was doomed if they made love. How clearly she recalled that now. She couldn't quite figure out why. After all, he had so many lovers.

"Can ye be quiet?"

She hid a smile. "Stop listening to my thoughts."

"Stop thinking so loudly." He turned over, away from her, grunting.

She looked at his back and wished she had the courage to slip onto the fur beside him and snuggle up with him. Of course, cuddling wouldn't last long because her pulse was high and racing, and every fiber of her body throbbed and ached. God, she would settle for touching him all over, and kissing him everywhere….

He turned onto his back and glared at her. "Are ye tryin' to seduce me or infuriate me?"

"I am not going back to sleep."

Their gazes held, and his eventually softened. He knew that she was afraid to go back to sleep. Moray had terrified her as no demon ever had. Moray wanted far more than her death or Aidan's. She had been acutely aware of his sadism when he'd appeared in her sleep. He had delighted in the confrontation.

She sat up. Thinking about Moray made her feel violently ill and really afraid.

Did Aidan have enough power to triumph over his father? Moray had been vanquished once, years ago. How the hell had he come back?

Aidan threw off his covers, standing. "The sun is risin' anyway," he said grimly.

She was pleased to notice he remained as hot and bothered as she was. She was still somewhat amazed that he wanted her, when he had his choice of beautiful women. She had meant her earlier words. He needed lovemaking and love, not sex. She had no doubt, not after all that had happened since her arrival in the past.

Their eyes met.

"Dinna plot to destroy him, Brianna. Ye have no power, and ye'll be the one destroyed," he said.

She sat up. Maybe his constant invasion of her thoughts wasn't that bad. "What will happen next? You won't sleep and I'm afraid to sleep, because your father has returned and he said that the two of you will meet today."

A sick chill swept through her when he didn't answer. She added, "You told me he possessed that giant completely, imbuing it with his will, his words, his voice. He thoroughly disguised his evil, so you didn't even know it was him at first. You could walk out of the tent and speak to Will, only to realize Will is now Moray."

"I dinna have the Sight. Mayhap ye should look into the future, to see what my father will do next." He gave her a dark look, buckling his sword belt and throwing his plaid on.

Brie was still snug under the covers and fur. "I wish I could see at will, but I can't."

He made a harsh sound. "Ye sound like MacNeil."

"Who is MacNeil?"

"A Master who gives too many orders, follows the gods without question and can see—when the gods allow it." His movements had become angry.

His anger brushed and scraped her skin now. "You sound as if he's your enemy."

"Once we were friends. When Ian died, he became my rival."

Brie slid from the bed, shivering as she left its warmth.

He looked at her bare legs.

She hopped into her jeans. "You blame him for Ian's murder, too? Do you blame everyone, or just all your friends, or all the Masters?" She was well aware of her harsh tone.

"He was my friend." Aidan pointed at her, eyes hard. "But he accepted my son's death because the gods wanted it."

"I want to meet him," she said quickly.

Aidan stared.

Brie tried to keep her mind still.

"Ye think he has the key to unlock my secrets an' my heart fer ye?" He laughed at her. "I have many secrets, Brianna, but I lost my heart when my father took my son."

"Bull," she said.

He gave her an exasperated look and left the tent.

Brie jammed on her boots and ran after him. "Aidan, wait. This is important. How *can* he be vanquished? He was already beheaded. In the future, when you kill a deamhan, its evil power is destroyed, too."

"Some say he's immortal," Aidan said, walking over to the first cook fire. Will was stirring what smelled like oatmeal there. "MacNeil told me he's mortal. But he has used the past sixty-six years to increase his powers." He nodded at Will.

Standing there in only her sweatshirt, jeans and boots, Brie was so cold she began jumping up and down. "How does a demon increase its powers?" she chattered.

"The gods gave the Brotherhood three books in the beginning of time. The Book of Wisdom remains on Iona, in its shrine. The Cladich is the Book o' Healing. Before Ian's murder, a powerful deamhan had some of its pages, but they are now enshrined on Iona, too. The Duisean was stolen and no one has seen it in hundreds of years." He paused significantly. "MacNeil told me that Moray has parts of the Duisean, perhaps hidden in yer time."

Brie had a really bad feeling now. "Okay. What kind of power is in that book?"

"Every power known to mankind."

Brie began to tremble, and not from the cold.

"And every power known to the gods," Aidan said.

CHAPTER NINE

THE MISSIVE CAME AT SUNRISE.

The king's lieutenant wished to parlay with him.

The sun was high over the snowy plain as Aidan slowly rode his black charger toward the royal armies, alone. It was a cold winter morning, and his breath and that of his charger's steamed in the air. His men remained behind him, lined up across the muddy road, silent. He could hear the bridles clinking from their mounts, weight being shifted from foot to foot, and Brianna thinking. She was terrified because he rode alone to meet Frasier. She was afraid he'd be arrested, believing he would soon hang.

He thought about his bargain with the gods. Brianna might be right, he realized, but he did not fear his own demise. An eternity in hell would be blissful compared to his life amongst the living.

Ahead, the royal army fanned out across the plain, blocking the road, a seemingly endless sea of armored knights and chargers glinting fantastically in the high winter sun. Another man might have felt a moment of trepidation riding forward toward such might, but Aidan felt nothing but resolve. The march on Inverness was insignificant compared to the war with Moray, and his father had promised him that they would meet on this day.

He looked forward to it, but he feared their confrontation, too, for the first time in his life.

Because Brianna's life was now at stake.

Five knights started forward, detaching themselves from the front lines of the royal army.

Why do you have to be so brave?

He stiffened, having heard Brianna as clear as day, as if she was beside him, speaking naturally. He glanced back at his army of knights and Highlanders and saw her instantly astride her gray mare, in the front ranks. She had expressly defied him; she was supposed to be hidden in his army's midst.

He could not be arrested that day—not that he expected an arrest so soon. At the least, he had to take Brianna to the sanctuary on Iona, where she would be safe.

He faced his adversaries as they paused, the five knights lining up across the road, barring his way. The standard bearer in their midst was carrying Frasier's banner, bearing his lion, crossed swords and fleur-de-lis. Aidan carried his own standard. All visors were lifted, and Aidan was surprised to see that two of the men had black, soulless eyes.

He looked swiftly at Robert Frasier, the man Brianna thought would have him hang.

Frasier smiled coolly in return. He was a big man with dark hair and fair skin, his dark eyes piercing. He spurred his destrier forward. "I have come to ask you to cease from this madness, Aidan of Awe," he said without preamble. "You have long since forfeited all your titles and lands, and only Castle Awe remains. Further aggression will result in the loss of your last stronghold—if not your liberty, and perhaps, your life."

Aidan laughed at him. "Pay me ten thousand pounds, an' perhaps we shall seal a new bargain."

Frasier was angry. "You will not reach Inverness—not without great suffering. We have cut you off from the MacDonald and Maclean armies. There is no hope of victory for you."

Aidan moved his black toward Frasier and felt the man's surprise. He paused only when their horses were shoulder to shoulder and he was knee to knee with the lieutenant. "I like suffering," he said softly. "An' my men lust fer English an' Lowland blood."

And his stallion bit the other charger, causing it to rear back.

Frasier spurred it ruthlessly forward. He looked into Aidan's eyes and said, "Do you not wish to see Ian again…my son?"

His voice hadn't changed, but Aidan froze. Moray had descended anew, taking possession of Frasier this time.

And Frasier's eyes turned blue, then glowed red. He laughed the mocking laughter of Moray, laughter that would haunt Aidan in his dreams—if he ever slept.

"A Ihain!" Aidan roared, drawing his sword in absolute fury. But even enraged, he knew that killing Frasier would solve nothing.

Frasier drew his sword, thrusting viciously, and Aidan met his sword. Metal screamed across the entire plain, imbued with their unnatural powers. Aidan gasped, putting his entire force against their crossed blades, but he could not push Moray back.

"Aye," Frasier murmured, laughter in his tone. "Ye should have taken more lives last night, instead of playin' nursemaid to our sweet Brianna."

In that moment, Aidan's heart stopped. Moray

had spied upon them again. And once more, he distracted Aidan.

They were ringed by the royal knights. Aidan somehow withdrew, wheeling his black backward, and Frasier came at him, striking ruthlessly as if intending a deathblow. Aidan threw all his power at the demon and at the descending sword. The blow should have cut into his shoulder; instead, the great sword hung in the air, quivering just inches from him.

Frasier grunted and began pushing the sword down.

Aidan felt hot metal touch his shoulder. *"A Ihain,"* he roared. He blasted the sword, which flew from Frasier's hand, whirling far across the road.

Aidan thrust his own sword now, but Frasier struck at it with his black energy. Effortlessly, the sword was torn from his hand and hurled far away onto the plain.

The black screamed, rearing in fury, striking at Frasier's charger. The other destrier rose up, striking back, front hooves flailing. Aidan leapt from his horse. "Come down an' fight, *Father,*" he hissed. "If ye have any courage at all!" The body no longer mattered to him; he would fight Moray to the very death in whomever his father chose to use.

Frasier grinned and landed lightly before him. Before Aidan could react, the energy sent him flying backward in a tumbling ball, until he landed hard, not far from the front ranks of his army.

Brianna screamed.

He was on his feet, sending his power up the road at his demonic father. Even as he saw Frasier try to block it, he whirled. Brianna had broken free of his men, and her mare was trotting toward him! "Get her gone from here!" he shouted at Will, who was chasing her.

Frasier's next blow sent Aidan backward through rows and rows of his men, who parted like the Red Sea. He landed on his back, and the sky above spun, stars erupting in the blue skies. Vultures circled there, hungry and waiting for death.

"Aidan!" Brianna screamed.

He got to his feet and saw Frasier coming, his strides long and hard, his eyes glowing with diabolical intent. He was briefly confused. "Do ye think to kill me at last?" he asked, breathing hard.

"Now, why would I do that?" his father asked. "When you have defied me for decades, at every turn, when I had such high hopes for you?"

Comprehension began. Aidan would not die today. But there was no time to dwell on it. Aidan blasted Frasier and sent him backward, but not to the ground. *He did not have enough power to defeat him.*

Frasier leapt up and laughed. "Besides, my dear son, I am hoping to reunite you with little Ian."

Fury exploded within Aidan, blinding him, consuming him. "Ye lie! Ian is dead!" He struck with all the power that he had.

This time, the royal lieutenant was hurled backward through Aidan's army, landing hard on the road before his four knights.

Aidan ran toward him, blasting him repeatedly, but Frasier put his energy forth as a huge shield, and his own power was turned back onto himself and those closest to him. Men screamed, going down, wounded or dead. Aidan halted, not daring to strike again.

Frasier now slowly stood. His expression was ruthless. Aidan tensed in dreadful expectation, uncertain of what he planned.

Then Frasier looked past him, his energy blazing from his eyes, and Aidan knew whom Frasier thought to strike. He cried out, turning.

Brianna was hurled from her gray mare, across the tops of dozens of his men, until she slammed into a huge pine tree. Bones cracked loudly. For one instant she hung there, as if nailed to the wood, and then she slid limply down to the ground, where she lay unmoving.

Aidan froze in horror.

"She is a great weakness," Frasier said softly, his breath against Aidan's ear.

He had murdered Brianna. Aidan whirled to destroy him. Nothing could or would stop him now—and as he roared in rage, he met Frasier's dark, bewildered eyes instead of his father's.

"What happens?" Frasier demanded. "You dare to fight with me?" He was in disbelief. "Where is my horse?"

Aidan ignored him, his heart exploding with fear. He began running to where Brianna lay in a crumpled heap upon the ground, and the short distance felt like thousands of miles. And for the first time in many decades, he prayed to his enemies for her life.

He would do whatever the gods wished, if only they would let her live.

He would die then and there if they would resurrect her.

She lay utterly motionless on her back, as pale as a corpse, a pool of blood spreading from beneath her head.

He knelt, his heart leaping in fresh terror and renewed dread. "Brianna?"

There was no response. Her lashes did not flutter. Her chest did not rise. He knelt over her nostrils, but air did not tease his face. And he pulled her broken body into his arms, fighting a terrible desperation, a gut-wrenching fear.

She did not deserve to die.

He couldn't let her die.

He held her, blinded by sheer panic—the same panic he'd felt the day he'd fought to save Ian's life. It hadn't served him well. He gasped, forcing the raw panic aside, and he focused. He fought to feel her life force.

For one moment he felt nothing at all. The panic tried to leap forth; it wished to flame.

And then he felt her life flickering weakly, bravely—the last gasps of her fading soul.

He held her tightly, fought shocking tears and summoned his white, healing powers.

He did not know how great they were. Long ago, there had been promise. Long ago, he'd begun to experiment with his healing powers, powers no one expected him to have, powers given to him by his grandmother. The last Innocent he'd healed had had but broken bones. It had taken intense effort to mend them, even in 1435.

He cupped the back of her head, where her skull was fractured in many places and bleeding in torrents into his hand. He could envision every broken line. He struggled to find the white power within him, a power he had purposefully walked away from.

Surely it was not lost. But it had been so long, and as he delved deep inside himself, he found only shadows and spaces, empty places. He almost succumbed to despair and frustration. Surely, in one of those great hollows within him, a seed of white power lived!

And suddenly warmth seeped from within him, outward, into his hands.

Relief erupted. He removed his hands from her head and stared at the white, starlike energy in his palm, then he showered the white power over her. A fine white mist began sprinkling over her. Aidan knew he had to direct the healing power to her head. He willed more white power from within into his hands. Clasping her bleeding skull, he somehow willed the mist upward from his palms, into her fractured head.

He did not know how long he sat there, filling her head with healing light. It felt as if he sat with her, her head bleeding in his hands, for hours, but when he realized the bleeding had stopped, the sun remained high and bright. Mere moments had passed.

She had stopped bleeding.

He closed his eyes and felt her carefully with his mind. Her skull was whole. He could not envision a single fractured line.

He gasped in relief and heard her moan. "Dinna move," he said, for she was as white as a ghost and her eyelashes were fluttering. "Let me finish healin' ye, Brianna. Ye will be fine."

Her lashes lifted and her green eyes, filled with pain, met his. "You…survived?"

"Hush," he said. He realized her ribs were broken, as was her right arm, and he sent his healing light now to both places.

Her labored breathing slowed, becoming normal. Realizing he'd healed her body, he glanced at her face. She was staring at him closely, and when their eyes met, a huge warmth filled his chest.

In that singular moment, he *wanted* her to look at him with faith and trust.

She lifted her hand and clasped his cheek. He

became aware that she lay with her shoulders in his lap, and a stunning desire came. It almost hurled him backward into the tree, hollowing his chest completely. It stiffened his body, raised his loins.

His heart thundered.

He wanted to take this beautiful woman to his bed. But he didn't want power.

He wanted pleasure, but not for himself.

He wanted to give it to her.

"Ye should have taken more lives last night, instead of playin' nursemaid to our sweet Brianna."

Aidan froze.

Brianna whispered, "I owe you my life…again."

He looked at her in horror.

AIDAN HAD JUST HEALED HER.

Demons could not heal.

He rose to his feet, his face hard and tight. "Can ye stand?"

Brie closed her eyes, recalling Moray's brutal attack. She had been close to death, and this time it had not been a dream. She would have died if Aidan hadn't healed her.

She trembled, slowly opening her eyes and gazing up at him. They were connected more than ever before. "You can heal. I didn't know."

His expression was grim.

"Demons can't heal, not ever. Was your mother a Healer?"

"Nay, but she was very devout." Clearly he did not wish to discuss this topic any further. He added reluctantly, "My grandmother was a goddess."

Brie sat up, incredulous. *His grandmother was a*

goddess. No wonder he could heal. This new, stunning fact was further proof that there was so much hope. Or was there?

Brie hugged herself now. Moray had taken another man's body again. Aidan didn't have to tell her for her to know. But just to be sure, she said, "Was it Moray?"

His eyes blazed. "Aye."

She exhaled. It was as she had thought. Moray had begun the battle by attacking Aidan, and it had seemed as if they were evenly matched, until he had directed his evil at her.

She hadn't expected it. She was never going to forget being suddenly hurled by his power, so forcefully that it was like becoming a small tennis ball spinning in a cyclone. She had known she would die the moment she'd made impact with the tree.

She would never forget hearing her skull crack; she would never forget the utter comprehension and then the utter terror; and she would never forget the explosion of pain that had followed.

Brie felt sick. She knelt just in case she had to retch.

Aidan knelt beside her, his hand on her back, but whether to steady or comfort her, she didn't know. "Are ye still ill?"

She fought herself and twisted to face him. She was scared to death. As nauseous as she was, every hair on her body now stood on end. She almost felt as if Moray lurked upon them both. "Aidan?" His gaze met hers. "He meant to murder me."

"I'm sending ye to Iona, where he canna find ye."

Brie stared. How could she leave him now? But that demon was after *her.* "He went after me, not you. Why?"

"I mean to keep ye safe, an' he's showin' me he has great power." Aidan's mouth was downturned.

"What does he want? He didn't destroy you in 1436—he destroyed Ian. He didn't destroy you today. Could he have? Does he want to destroy you, or just hurt you?"

"I dinna ken if he can kill me. He has great power now." He hesitated. "I have asked the gods fer help an' they have agreed."

As hope began, he said harshly, "I bargained with them. 'Tis not what ye wish for. I will never worship them. But they couldna refuse my offer."

"What did you offer them?" she demanded, in dread.

He stood, holding out his hand. "Ye need to rest after what ye suffered today."

She took his hand and he pulled her to her feet. Brie did not let go, gripping him tightly. "I still don't understand what he wants. Is this a sick game?"

"He's playin' me." Aidan released her hand. "Aye, 'tis a game for him to toy with me, to torture me, until he breaks me to his will or torments me to death. I dinna think he cares which it is."

Brie stared. How were they going to survive the return of such great evil?

"How do ye feel?"

She wet her lips, focusing on her body just for a moment. "I seem okay." She met his brilliant blue regard again. "What are we going to do now?"

He gave her a chilling look. "Ye'll do naught. I'll hunt him an' finish this."

Dread swept Brie. "And how will you do that? Oh, wait, you've made your deadly bargain with the gods. Don't tell me! I don't want to know!"

"Come to the tent. Ye'll feel better after ye eat an' sleep."

Brie knew she must fight her rising hysteria, but it was really hard to do. "He possessed Frasier—the man who is going to hang you. That cannot be a coincidence!" Her alarm escalated wildly.

He took her elbow and started guiding her toward the camp, which was quite some distance away.

"You know it's no coincidence." She balked, refusing to take another step. "We need help. We need Malcolm and Claire and Allie and Royce and your friend, MacNeil, and all the other white power we can summon."

He jerked his head in the direction of his tent. "I willna ride with the Masters, walk with them or fight beside them."

"Then you are a fool!" she cried, distraught. "Does anyone know how to vanquish him?"

He gave her a cold glance. "'Tis nay clear yet."

"That is exactly what I thought," Brie cried, near tears. She hurried ahead of him, ignoring the knights and Highlanders she passed. As no one crossed themselves, she guessed that displays of superpowers were not all that unusual.

What were they going to do? How were they going to survive? And what kind of deal had he made with the gods, who were probably furious with him?

Aidan fell into step beside her. "Dinna worry so, Brianna. I dinna fear Moray. I can hunt both men at the same time."

Brie inhaled. "Oh, so you will hunt Moray, who happens to posses Frasier at will?"

"Aye."

She felt like slapping him silly. "I have never heard

of a more stupid plan! I think this is some kind of demonic setup for you to hang." She faced him, barring his way, hands on her hips. "But you can't hang. I mean, you can simply leap away, into the future or the past, unless a great power blocks you."

He stared, not answering.

"And Moray has great power now because he has a part of the Duisean. This is getting worse and worse!"

"I shouldna have brought ye to my time. I brought ye into this." His mouth was a hard, tight line. "Yer afraid, an' I dinna blame ye. But ye'll be safe on Iona, Brianna." He paused, then said harshly, "Ye need to stop carin' fer me."

What the hell did that mean? "If you are warning me to prepare myself for your death, like hell I will!" she cried shrilly. It really hit her then. She loved him. Maybe it hadn't ever been a crush; maybe it had been love at first sight. She didn't really know. What she did know was that she loved him now, and she wasn't going to let him hang or go on pretending to be some badass demon. "What did you offer the gods?"

"Doesna matter."

"It matters, damn it."

"Ye'll feel better an' think more clearly when yer on Iona." He tried to force a smile but it vanished as instantly as it formed. "The island's pretty an' peaceful. Ye'll like it there."

"I am not leaving you!" she cried furiously. She realized tears had welled and one had fallen down her cheek. "We're in big trouble, the both of us, *together.*"

"There's nay *we,* Brianna," he said harshly. He took her arm. As his hand closed around her, she tensed, but not because of the contact.

The ground tilted wildly and began to spin. Instantly she knew a vision was coming. Dread began. She knew she did not want to see whatever was about to form. The landscape whirled until she could not see the tents, the men, the cook fires or Aidan. And then the spinning kaleidoscope of color slowed, shadowy images forming.

A huge crowd of men and women in linen tunics and plaids gathered before stone walls. She saw a stately palace, as well, and heard the crowd. There were cheers, jeers, laughter. Brie saw red and gold leaves. Snow dusted the ground.

And she saw Malcolm. He was at the front of the crowd, holding Claire. Those around him were laughing and pleased, but he was crying in anguish.

No, she thought desperately.

She saw Allie, screaming and fighting someone—Royce, her husband.

Brie did not want to see any more. With gut-wrenching horror, she followed Malcolm's gaze and cried out.

Aidan was hanging above the crowd, twirling slowly in the breeze, his neck crooked, his face downturned.

Brie gasped, eyes flying open, clinging to Aidan's arms.

He was staring down at her in concern.

Brie realized she was weeping. He had carried her to the bed in their tent. She had just seen Aidan hanged. Her visions always came true. What was she going to do?

"Ye swooned." His quiet voice interrupted her frantic thoughts.

She moved her hands, seizing his strong shoulders. Power pulsed in his muscles and veins, so much male power. She was not going to let him die. Not now, not when he was changing before her very eyes, not when she loved him so much.

Aidan's mouth tightened.

In that moment, she knew he'd been inside her mind and he'd seen all that she had.

"It's a mistake. It has to be," she breathed, precariously close to more tears.

"Dinna weep for me, Brianna." A false smile came and went. "I am hardly worth yer tears."

"Do not speak that way."

His eyes flickered oddly and his gaze slipped to her mouth, then lifted. "I dinna wish to live to old age." He shifted as if to stand, but did not do so. "Ye must be tired. I will guard ye while ye sleep."

He was sitting on that small bed with her, and she had his huge shoulders in her hands. Her fear was receding, replaced by an acute, painful awareness of him, not just as a sexy, beautiful man, but as a man struggling to make his way back to the light.

She hadn't felt any emotions from him—not since his fury and terror in the battle earlier with Frasier. He was adeptly blocking his feelings from her. But heat was rising in her, replacing the fear. With the slowly incoming tide of desire, there was so much love.

"I almost died today," she whispered. She reached up and touched his cheek in a soft caress and he stiffened, his eyes flying wide with alarm. She dropped her hand and said as softly, "But you healed me. You *healed* me, Aidan, with a white, god-given power. Terrible things lie ahead for us both. I have seen them. I can't sleep. I don't want to sleep. I want you to hold me, make love to me…and chase this all away, just for an hour or so." She lifted her hand.

He pulled away, standing, before she could caress his face again, but his eyes smoldered and his leine fluttered suggestively. "Ye dinna wish to be my lover or my friend, Brianna," he said softly, and as his words washed through her, silken and strong, she knew he was enchanting her. "Ye dislike me now. Ye want nothin' to do with me. Ye want to go to Iona. Ye want to be safe."

Brie cried out, clapping her hands over her ears. *I love him,* she thought. *I want* him *safe! He is my friend and nothing can change that.*

He tore her hands from her ears. "Ye resist me?"

She nodded, even though his words were potent and reverberating through her. *Ye dinna wish to be my friend, Brianna. Ye dislike me now. Ye want nothing to do with me.... Ye want to go to Iona....*

"I am your friend," she whispered. "And we both need one another now."

He leaned over her, holding her wrists, his eyes hard and wide. Brie pressed her mouth in the vee of his leine, against his hot skin.

His heart slammed and then thundered. "Dinna," he warned, but his grasp on her tightened. And as it did, she recalled every single moment of the dream they had shared.

He had been desperate for her touch, and he had kissed her as if he had never kissed a woman before.

She pressed another kiss against his skin and she heard him stifle a moan.

As she looked up and saw that his eyes had closed, his high cheekbones were stained with desire and he'd arched his head back in sheer enjoyment.

Brie slid to her knees and moved her mouth up the column of his strong, vibrating throat. He shuddered.

She lifted her face and pressed her mouth to his lips.

His mouth was tightly closed. He kept her wrists in an iron grasp. She moved her mouth gently against his.

He gasped, and his huge arms encircled her as his mouth opened and their lips fused. His desire exploded between them, unshielded. As it stabbed through Brie, she realized it was even greater than before. Throwing her arms around him, hanging on as if for her life, she kissed him back frantically.

Their tongues sparred.

He suddenly slid his arm around her waist and hiked her up hard against his raging manhood. Brie became faint with urgency and need.

He tore his mouth from hers, panting, blue eyes ablaze.

"Don't stop…don't think!" she begged. But she already knew what he was doing.

He wrenched free of her. "Canna ye see that ye'll be Moray's next victim if I bed ye?"

"I'm not sure I care." In that insane moment, there was only one thing she cared about—the union of their bodies.

"I need power," he cried. "I need lots o' power. Makin' love will not vanquish my father!"

Brie went still.

So did he, staring at her.

He was right. He needed the power to triumph over Moray.

"My father chose to murder ye today because of the dream we shared." Aidan said, finally exhaling. "Think, Brianna. Think about his spyin' on us. Think about how ye make me weak an' vulnerable."

She shuddered. Aidan wouldn't be weak and vulnerable because of her unless he cared. But she did not want to be the one to weaken him. "I guess that means you'll have sex, right? Power and sex, do they always go together?" Her heart thundered now and her cheeks were on fire. But she was uncertain. She wanted him to tell her he'd take power but not during intercourse.

"Does it even matter?" he asked flatly.

She nodded, trembling. "Yes, it matters. It matters to me."

"I am sorry," he finally said. "I am sorry yer here, I am sorry my father hunts ye now, an' mostly, I am sorry ye love me." He started grimly past her, heading for the open tent flap.

She would die if he went to another woman now, after what had just happened, after what seemed to be happening between them. "Take me."

He faltered, turned.

"I understand and I agree. You need power. Lots of it. Take it from me."

CHAPTER TEN

"YE WANT ME TO *USE* YE?"

Brie trembled. In that moment, she could think of nothing she wanted more than to be in Aidan's arms. She knew he wouldn't hurt her. She knew he wouldn't destroy her. She would go out of her mind with jealousy if he went to someone else, and it was damn clear that he needed power. The tension in the tent had become so thick that it seemed airless now. "You can't go to someone else, not after what's happened today."

His gaze was hard, his expression disbelieving. "Yer mad."

He was blocking his emotions, but not doing a great job of it. She felt desire seething from him, a huge, determined pulse trying to reach her. Brie could barely speak. "We both want this, Aidan. Why can't you admit that, as odd as it is, there's this powerful attraction between us, one that began with my empathy through time and you hearing my cries for help across centuries?"

She expected a denial of just about everything she'd said. He denied nothing. "Yer a virgin."

Brie went still. Confused, she managed, "So what?" When he simply stared, as if torn between disgust and dismay, she added, "I'll bet you've had your share of virgins."

"Aye," he snapped.

She almost cringed. She realized she'd hoped for a different answer. "I can't stay this way forever." She flushed. "And you're my friend. Look at it this way—we need each other, even if for different reasons." She realized she was bargaining with him to take her to bed. Apparently she had no shame, but she meant every word. It felt as if their journey had come down to this one moment. "It's time," she added in a soft whisper.

His eyes were hot, smoldering. "I willna use ye," he said harshly, his temples visibly throbbing. "Ye can save yerself for the man ye love." He turned to walk out but the moment he realized what he said, his shoulders stiffened and he faltered.

Brie ran after him and barred his way at the tent flap. They both knew who that man was. "Then this shouldn't be a problem," she whispered breathlessly.

Their gazes locked. "Ye need to save yerself fer yer husband," he corrected harshly. His cheekbones were pink.

"No one saves themselves for their wedding day—not in my time." She touched his biceps and he flinched. "You read my mind all the time, so you know how much I want you. You want me, too, even if I haven't figured out why. You need power and Moray is hot on our trail. God only knows when he'll pop up next and what he'll be capable of. In my time, we call that killing two birds with one stone—or friends helping one another."

He folded his arms, and his biceps and forearms bulged. "I'll be the first to admit I dinna think I have enough power to defeat him. But I willna use ye. My mind is made up. I meant what I said earlier. Find someone else to take as a lover—it willna be me! But I willna leave ye alone tonight, Brianna."

He was going to protect her at all costs, even the cost of his life, but he was still set against them becoming lovers. "Why are you so afraid to go to bed with me?"

He laughed. "I'm hardly afraid!"

"You think you'll make love to me and that it will heal your poor, starving heart and black, withered-up soul!" she accused.

His fury pushed her back against the tent. "I have never made love to any woman, not in my entire life, not even before my fall! Fer the hundredth time, I chose this way an' I like it."

"That's crap," she cried. "You did not choose to have your son murdered before your very eyes and you did not choose to be haunted for sixty-six years. Have you ever considered the kind of life you could have again, if you let go of all your anger and rage? If you dared to heal? If you forgave the gods, who work in mysterious ways? Have you ever considered that you might be a happy man if you let go of your poor, dead son and a nearly impossible quest for vengeance?"

He leaned close, furious with her now. "Ye think if ye spread yer legs fer me, I'll become that happy, good man?"

She knew she flushed. "Not exactly, but you need me. You need my affection, my friendship and my love. And yes, I think our making love could be very healing—for us both."

"I will never forgive the gods, I will never give up my vengeance, an' I will never be a *happy* man. Ian is dead!" he roared at her. "An' the day I have my vengeance, 'tis the day our friendship dies! I am usin' ye to help me with my son."

She knew she'd hit a hundred nerves, but his words really hurt. She felt the ugly truth in them. If she communicated with Ian and set him free, she knew Aidan would send her home.

God, she was going to love him forever, she realized, aghast.

"Yer right," he snarled. "When Ian is at peace, I'll send ye back to yer time."

"I hate that you're reading my mind!" Was she too involved? Grandma's ring was really hurting her now. She had come back in time to save him from hanging and to redeem him. To do the latter, she would have to heal him, and that meant setting Ian free. What she hadn't come back for was a torrid love affair or a life-altering romance. She hadn't gone back in time to fall irrevocably in love.

It was too damned late.

There had been so many moments when intimacy had blossomed between them, but at times like these, it was clear he would be set against her forever, if it was up to him.

She trembled, aware that her feelings were raw. But her heart was decided. "Then go and do what you have to do, Aidan. Go find a few women and take power, so when Moray returns, you can send him to the fires of hell. I'll be okay," she said, turning away from him. It was a lie. She just couldn't understand how he could take another woman in his arms after all that had happened to them.

She reminded herself that she was a Rose, with her

own destiny. He was clearly a part of it, but not exactly the way she'd like him to be.

She felt him staring at her back. He was inside her mind and he knew he'd just hurt her. When he finally spoke, his voice was low and quiet but strained with tension. "The sooner ye go to Iona, the better, so that when I next confront Moray, I dinna have to guard ye, too. Yer a distraction now."

Still turned away from him, Brie rubbed her face. She didn't want to be his Achilles' heel, but she couldn't go to Iona and leave him to face such a horrific and determined evil alone.

Brie didn't know what to do. As Claire had said, women in love could not think straight. But she knew she had better get her head on straight now. His life and future were at stake. Grandma was right. Brie was too involved. If she could, she had to get a grip on her heart and stop loving him. Brie knew that might be impossible. And she'd never stop being his friend.

Brie slowly turned; he was still staring.

"I can't go to Iona like a coward and leave you here to face Moray alone."

"Oh, ye'll go," he said dangerously.

Brie did not like the sound of that, but she didn't want to fight. It was too hurtful. Suddenly he cocked his head, listening to the night.

Brie wondered what had caught his attention, alarm beginning to rise in her. She prayed he hadn't felt Moray. And then a pack of wolves started howling.

She froze, and looked at Aidan, certain the pack had come for him.

Aidan had stiffened, listening acutely to the pack, and she knew he had become unaware of her. His perfect profile was turned to her now, and his expression had changed. It was harder and fiercer than before. His excitement began to change, too.

The wolves' howls grew in fervor, cresting.

His mouth curved, coldly.

Brie hugged herself, alarmed. "They've come for you, haven't they?"

He gave her a sidelong look. "Aye. They want to hunt tonight."

Dread began. "You want to hunt," she accused.

He turned his brilliant blue eyes upon her. He did not speak—he didn't have to. She felt the predatory bloodlust rising up in him, replacing his interest in her—the prelude to a long and savage hunt.

"I'm not leavin' ye," he said softly. "Even if they want me to lead them."

The wolves howled long and fervently again.

Brie started to feel sickened by that bestial bloodlust. "Can you control the Wolf?"

He went to the tent flap, lifting it. Even his stride had changed, becoming looser, yet menacing. Outside, the sky had turned purple. An orange moon was rising, oddly streaked—the way it had been her first night at Awe, when Aidan had shifted into the Wolf to grieve. "Sometimes."

Brie shuddered. The Wolf was vicious and ruthless, more so than Aidan, the man. But animals did not have consciences, and wolves were predators, at the top of the food chain. The Wolf liked to hunt, and it ate its prey.

Aidan remained in his human form, but she felt the beast with them, snarling and hungry, scenting innocent blood.

"I don't like the Wolf," she said tersely.

He glanced briefly at her. "Ye should fear the Wolf. Everyone does." He stared back outside at the fiercely streaked orange moon. "I dinna trust him, either."

Brie sat on the edge of the bed, her stomach upset, pulling her legs up beneath her. Even though the Wolf had destroyed her enemies and spared her, she wouldn't mind never seeing the creature again. "Are you about to shift?"

He glanced at her, his eyes odd now. Still so very blue and so very human, but the stare was somehow inhuman and lingering, direct. "Nay," he said, low and soft.

Brie flinched, because his tone sounded almost like a growl.

His stare did not waver. "Go to sleep. I'll be outside."

Brie could see his tension as well as feel it. He yearned to join the pack.

The wolves had quieted. Brie was certain they were close by, waiting for him. And now she realized that his chest fell rapidly and heavily, the panting of a canine. "Don't go," she whispered.

He didn't answer, slipping from the tent. The moment the flap fell closed behind him, the wolves howled all at once, a huge and savage night cry.

Brie leapt beneath her covers and pulled them up high. She didn't have to strain to feel him now. He wasn't blocking anything from her.

He lusted for the wolves; he lusted for power, blood and death.

She was forgotten.

THE ROYAL LIEUTENANT OF THE NORTH, Robert Frasier, adjusted his clothing carefully. He replaced his codpiece, jerked up his dark hose and tied the drawstring firmly. He tugged down the short skirt of his black velvet surcote, trimmed in gold. His body vibrated with pleasure and power. In another moment or so, he would summon another woman to his bed.

A bottle of fine French wine sat on the table in his tent. He crossed the spacious area, stepping across the dead bodies on the floor—two beautiful women and a beautiful squire. Without a thought for them, he poured a glass. As he sipped, he recalled the events of that afternoon—events that had propelled him to take so many Innocents at once, with most of his army within hearing distance, just outside his tent.

Rage began.

In fury, he tossed the glass aside, receiving no satisfaction as it broke.

Aidan had healed the witch.

Demons did not heal.

He roared in rage and threw the wine bottle at the tent wall. He had known before Aidan was ever birthed that he would have the greatest power of all his sons. A goddess had come to him to taunt him with it.

"This child, your 1,025th son, will be the greatest of your progeny. He will have a power even greater than your own," Faola had whispered. "We have great plans for him."

He had been sleeping and he instantly awoke. He had stared at the beautiful warrior goddess, whom he had never before seen. The goddess had been sent to the ancient kings long ago to mother a race of warriors to defend mankind. He had been certain this was a dream—or a jest. But he had taken one look at her burning eyes and realized she spoke the truth.

"Why tell me this?" he had demanded.

"There will be great travail. There will be great

tragedy. You will covet his powers. You will be his test. Only one of you can prevail. This is written."

Faola began to fade before his very eyes. He had demanded that she wait, but she had laughed at him and disappeared.

Satan had approached him many millennia ago, his offer so tempting. Moray had accepted it instantly and their bargain had been sealed. He could not comprehend why Faola would come to him now. But Satan was more devious than any god, and it crossed his mind that Satan could certainly test him, too. Perhaps Satan had engineered this rivalry with his son and the test was really about him, Moray.

Moray had made certain that Lady Margaret, Aidan's mother, was kept in good health until the child was born. He had quickly put spies amongst the Maclaine foster family, although he soon realized his young son would never die a natural death. He was never sickly. He never fell, never sprained a tendon, never suffered a broken bone. From infancy he could move small objects across tabletops and drop flies with a glance. His foster parents were afraid of him, and only Brogan Mor's will insured that Aidan remained with them.

He had waited twenty-one years for his son to come to manhood, for manhood was always the best time to show a new recruit the pleasure and power of evil. But he had been too late. Aidan had already been chosen by the Brotherhood, and he had taken sacred vows to defend mankind and keep Faith.

Moray had been enraged, but he had calmed soon enough.

Hadn't Faola—or Satan—told him there would be great travail and greater tragedy?

The hunt had begun.

It had taken him another fifteen years to drive Aidan to evil. He had enjoyed every moment of watching Aidan destroy that village of innocent men, women and children, even if he had not lifted his own sword even once. For he had felt Aidan's torment. He had savored every moment of his son's anguish. It had increased his power briefly.

When it was done, Aidan should not have cared about anything or anyone except himself, his power and his next victims. Lust for evil should have ruled him.

But in spite of the crimes he'd committed against God and Innocence that day, he had let the survivors run away to hide. He still loved his son—and demons did not love anything or anyone.

He hadn't been turned completely.

His behavior over the past decades confirmed it. He wasn't a true deamhan. He was only half deamhan, lusting for power as all deamhanain did but leaving his victims *alive.* Like a man with one foot in two disparate worlds, Aidan ignored destruction and death, but did not cause it or relish in it. It was almost incomprehensible. It was not acceptable. It was infuriating.

Only one of you will prevail.

And now Aidan had healed the Rose witch.

Moray had always intended to finish the hunt and finish the turning, but he had been very preoccupied these past sixty-six years, all of them spent in New York City, London and Edinburgh—the triangle of his growing empire. In those cities, death and destruction were on the rise. In fact, anarchy was on the rise in every major city in the world, and he knew his cohorts well. Last night he had leapt to New York in 2008.

Mayor Bloomberg had finally called in the National Guard, which had pleased Moray to no end. He had a plan for the Guard—oh, yes.

Nothing would stop him now. He would be the victor in this trial with his half-demon son. The little witch had power—as did her friends—but he wasn't concerned. He had returned after almost seven decades because he finally had all the power he needed.

And it did not come from the dead on his tent floor.

AIDAN SAT CROSS-LEGGED ON THE ground. The moon was rising above the mountains against a purple sky. A few stars had joined it. He stared up at the flame-colored moon, desperately wishing he were with the pack. The urge to lift his face and howl was bone-deep.

I don't like the Wolf.

Of course she didn't.

The urge intensified. The Wolf had been his salvation ever since the fall. He stared toward the forest, where pairs of glowing eyes met his. The pack continued to wait for him. He could hear them panting softly in the night.

His heart surged. He felt his hackles rise. He felt saliva gather. He was hungry.... When had he last eaten fresh meat?

But he glanced down the rise toward his tent, feeling for Brianna, who was drifting to sleep. He could not go with the pack; he had to stay and guard her from the evil in the night. She had almost died that day because of his war with his father.

But he had healed her.

He hated thinking. The Wolf was thoughtless. He glanced back at the forest and met the steady, intent gazes of the wolves. If he left Brianna now, he had little doubt he would return to find her hurt or dead.

Tired of waiting for him, the wolves turned away one by one, and faded into the forest. Aidan stared after their slinking forms, violently wishing he could go with them.

His head pounded with confusion. Once, long ago, he had been wary of the creature and frightened of it. Then, he had welcomed the Wolf as his best friend. But tonight his heart warred with his body. He could not trust the Wolf to stay sentinel over Brianna that night.

He growled in frustration.

The pack was gone, having sped off into the forest. He stood and started slowly down the ridge. He pushed open the flap and glanced into the night-darkened tent.

One candle burned. The light flickered over Brianna as she slept, curled up on her side, facing him. Her dark hair was loose, a thick mane of waves framing her small, pale face. She was breathing deeply and evenly, and in sleep she looked like a tiny angel of compassion and grace.

She thought herself plain; he thought her beautiful.

A fist seemed to go through his chest. It was the fist of desire, and it chased away the ravenous bloodlust.

Why don't you take me?

He tensed. There had been many virgins, he had no respect for Innocence. But he didn't want to taint her. She deserved far more than a night of passion in his bed.

Why are you so afraid to go to bed with me?

He wasn't afraid. She would not heal him by giving him her lush little body. Sharing a bed wasn't going to miraculously change him into the man he had once been. And even if it could, he would not allow it, just as he wouldn't allow their "friendship" to heal him, either. He would never consider them friends. For the moment, in this war, they were allies. Even if he wished for them to be friends—or lovers—Moray's return had made that impossible.

He had been terrified when she'd lain dying in his arms.

He had not had much time to brood upon the events of the day. He reeled inwardly now to know he still had his great white power. *How was it even possible?*

Had his devout mother been a Healer? If so, he had never been told of it.

So he was not as heartless as a half deamhan should be. He did not regret healing her and giving her back her life. But she was stubbornly fighting for his soul, when he did not care at all about it. She must not be the one to pay the price for his war with Moray. The war with his father had already cost him Ian.

He stared at her pale face, her cheeks slightly flushed from the winter sun, her lashes thick and dark on her cheeks, and his heart turned over, hard.

He must not have feelings for her. He knew that. And he didn't—other than a strange admiration for her tenacity and courage. As for the desire, apparently a part of him had not died along with Ian. But he would ignore his human side, no matter what, until she was gone.

She shifted softly in her sleep.

He tensed, concerned that she was dreaming, but she was not. She remained asleep, but before he could turn away from her, he felt his father's dark power behind him.

Aidan whirled, but the night was silent and empty. Or was it?

Years ago, Moray had brought a great chill with

him, and a huge, foreboding sense that a terrible hammer of evil was about to fall. Aidan strained through the night and shivered. He thought he detected a new chill, just barely drifting into the tent.

He moved to the tent flap and lifted it. Most of the camp was asleep, some in their brats and blankets upon the ground, the rest in tents, with their many fires now barely burning. Even the women's camp was quiet, most of the fires in ashes and embers. He glanced south, where the horses and pack animals were tethered and grazing quietly, unbothered by the shadows and the darkness.

The air murmured around him, brushing up against him, a soft caress that chilled him to the bone.

Moray was there.

He could not see him; he could not feel him. He simply knew. "Reveal yourself," he hissed.

He almost thought he heard his father's mocking laughter, but he felt certain it was in his mind. And then he felt Brianna's dream forming.

He rushed to her bedside to wake her up, but before he reached her, he slipped into her sleep to guard her. He faltered in surprise and dismay.

Brianna wore a pretty blue dress, sleeveless and short, revealing half of her slim legs and all of her shapely arms, and she was breathtakingly beautiful. "I knew you would come to me." She smiled at him, her eyes intent and trained upon him. They were warm with desire, with love.

He knew what she wanted. His entire body stiffened in anticipation.

"We're dreaming," she told him. "Please don't refuse me now."

He wanted to be there with her. He wanted to make love to her. But something was terribly wrong—he sensed impending doom.

"I can't," he said, but he started toward her.

She smiled and stood, holding out her hand.

He faltered. What was he doing in her dream, anyway? He had already realized making love to her in a dream was as dangerous as doing so in the other world.

"Wake up," he ordered her. He had to end this now, before it went further.

Stubborn as always, Brianna shook her head and reached behind her back for the zipper on her dress. Aidan went still.

And then her eyes widened in abject alarm.

Moray materialized between them.

Aidan became rigid with tension.

His demonic father was not using Robert Frasier now. He appeared exactly as he had before Malcolm and Claire had vanquished him; a tall, handsome blond man, oddly ageless. He stood between them, his smile diabolic. "My power is far greater than yours, my son. Dream, Brianna. Dream of your great love, Aidan."

Brianna cried out and Aidan felt her fear. He wanted to rush to her, but he didn't dare. In absolute dread, Aidan stared at his father. "What do ye want of me?"

"What do I want?" Moray asked incredulously. "You want to *make love.*" His blue eyes glowed red with demonic rage.

Aidan shook his head, but he understood. His desire was not demonic. Somehow, his father knew it and would make one of them pay for it.

"You should lust for the pleasure her life can give

you, but you stand there, stricken with *desire,*" he hissed. "Did you think I would fail to remark it?"

"I take power every day," Aidan said harshly. His gaze was on Moray, but he was acutely aware of Brianna standing behind his father, as pale as a ghost. "Brianna, wake up," he ordered.

Brianna seemed near tears.

"She can't wake up," Moray said coldly. "You haven't taken power, not a single time, since you brought her from the future to Awe."

It took Aidan a moment to realize that his father was right. He was stunned. But he met Brianna's frightened gaze. *I willna let anything happen to ye,* he told her silently. *Ye need to wake up now.*

Brianna just looked at him, and he knew she hadn't heard him.

"She can't hear your thoughts. I've made sure of it," Moray laughed.

"Wake up," Aidan cried to her. "Get out of this dream!"

"I'm trying," she cried back. "The sleep is too deep. It's too heavy!"

His alarm escalated as he turned to look at his father. "What have you done to her?"

Ignoring the question, Moray said, "You *healed* her today. I am so disappointed, Aidan." His smile was mocking.

His father knew everything, Aidan thought, and rage began. But he felt a terrible moment of helpless despair. "Tell me what I must do now in order fer ye to leave her alone—in order fer her to awaken."

Moray snarled, "You still protect her, an Innocent. When this day is done, I will own your soul."

"Fine," Aidan cried, meaning it.

"Aidan, whatever he wants, no!" Brianna cried, trembling.

Aidan met her gaze. He was beginning to feel that they were both awake but trapped in the dream world anyway. But she had to be dreaming still, didn't she?

He had to awaken her; he had to get her out of this dream. Moray had come with some terrible, evil intention, and Aidan almost suspected that he had engineered the dream for them.

He was half in and half out of the dream. He started to step completely out of the realm, so he could awaken her, but he was blocked by a great and invisible energy.

Moray laughed.

He met Moray's wide, cruel smile. "I have the power now," his father murmured.

Frantic, Aidan tried to step out of the dream world again. He smashed into another invisible wall.

Brianna cried out, clearly aware that they were both trapped now.

Moray snarled, "I have spent over a hundred years on your fall, and now you embrace a white witch with your heart—and your soul!" He shook with rage. "I own your soul. It belongs to me!"

"Ye took my son. I murdered innocent men, women and children. When will ye be pleased?" Aidan cried. "What more can I give ye?"

Moray whirled and seized Brianna. Then, to his surprise, he shoved her into Aidan's arms. Brianna clung, looking up at him, shivering in fear.

"Is this real?" she whispered.

"Nay," he said, uncertain if he lied. He put his arm

around her and faced his father. "It's me ye want. Let her awaken and go."

Moray smiled—and Aidan saw Ian.

He went still. This was not reality. "Ian?"

His son looked the same—small and dark of hair, with vivid blue eyes. The boy smiled in relief. "Papa."

If Ian was a ghost, he would vanish as he always did. But his son simply stood there.

This was cruel treachery. Aidan reached out and saw his hand trembling.

Moray stepped back, taking Ian with him, out of his reach. "Give me your soul—and I will give you your son."

Aidan felt Brianna choke on despair.

Ian looked desperately at him. "Papa? Please?"

He could hear his son. Was this a different kind of dream? Was it an enchantment? Or was it real?

"Your soul," Moray said softly.

Aidan tensed. He knew his father would have him commit an atrocious crime, and a terrible inkling began.

"Yes," Moray said, lurking. "That is what I want."

Aidan did not move.

Moray wanted him to take Brianna to bed now—and to take pleasure in her death.

"Aidan?" Brianna whispered, looking up uncertainly at him.

"She can't die in a dream, my boy," Moray said. "Go, take her now."

Aidan had his arm around her. She had died in her dream last night, but somehow had awoken alive anyway. His every instinct told him now that she would die in this dream—and she would never awaken from it.

"Do you want your son?"

"Aidan, what does he want?" Brianna cried.

Aidan breathed hard. He ignored her. "'Tis a lie, a trick."

"Give me your soul and I will give you your son," Moray repeated.

Aidan stood there, frozen, aware of Ian staring desperately at him and of Brianna pressed to his side.

Ian was dead. Wasn't he?

He could not destroy Brianna. Could he?

Wouldn't he do anything to get his son back?

"Don't you want to know what your son has been trying to tell you for sixty-six years?" Moray inquired.

"You are disgusting," Brianna shouted. "And you will be vanquished. No demon lives forever!"

Moray laughed at her.

Aidan, shaking and ill, looked at him. There was nothing he wanted more than to know what Ian had been trying to say to him—unless it was to bring his son back from the dead. And as he stared, Ian suddenly vanished.

"Bring him back," Aidan shouted in helpless rage. "Ian!"

But there was no answer. Where Ian had just been standing, the air shimmered and sighed.

"Destroy her," Moray ordered. "Destroy her and the boy will return."

Brianna gasped and became rigid in his embrace.

He didn't dare look at her now, but his grasp on her tightened. It was his duty to Ian to do whatever he had to bring him back.

He looked at Brianna and he heard her thoughts. Her faith hadn't wavered. She didn't believe he would ever hurt her, not even to spare his son's death.

She was fighting tooth and nail for his soul, and she

had been doing so since the day he'd abducted her from her time.

Her white light was a blessing—and the only light in his life.

He could not do it.

His mind was made up. He turned to leave the dream, and he hit that invisible wall again. Furious, he pushed against it, again and again, to no avail.

"No one will ever leave this dream unless I allow it," Moray said in quiet fury.

Aidan's rage knew no bounds and it became savage. He let Brianna go.

"Aidan?" she whispered.

He didn't really hear her. Every hackle raised, he faced Moray and snarled.

Moray's eyes widened in alarm.

Brianna screamed.

CHAPTER ELEVEN

THE WOLF WAS ENRAGED, Brie thought. But Aidan didn't think he had enough power to defeat his father. The Wolf had extraordinary strength, but it was an unthinking beast. She didn't believe it a match for Moray. "Aidan, *don't.*"

But it was too late. The Wolf roared and leapt at Moray. As the beast struck the demon, the layers of sleep crushing her down crumbled. Brie soared upward, opened her eyes and sat up in bed. There was no moment of sudden comprehension, when a person realizes that he has been dreaming. Brie knew she had been in a nightmare just as she now knew she was awake. But that dream had been strange, far different from all others; the dream world was becoming too powerful, too tangible… too real.

Aidan stood by the bed, immobilized. His legs were braced, his body was rigid and he was breathing hard. His eyes were glazed.

He remained in the dream, she thought. She could only imagine what was happening in the dream world—and she had died in a dream last night. She seized his arms. "Wake up!" she screamed at him, jumping to her feet.

He started, glancing into her eyes, his gaze becoming lucid. Relief covered his features.

Brie collapsed back onto the bed, shaking. "Your father trapped us in that dream. I think he was controlling it from start to finish," she cried.

He sat down beside her, clasping her shoulders. "He's gone. He fled the Wolf."

Brie became terribly aware of his large hands on her shoulders and his huge body, inches from hers. She had gone to bed in her T-shirt and sweatshirt, and her legs were bare. She wanted to collapse in his arms, but instead she met his concerned and searching gaze.

"Are ye hurt?"

"You know I wasn't hurt, but I'll admit to being terrified. God, he is toying with us!" All she could think of was what Moray had wanted, and how he had tried to bend Aidan to his will.

Aware of her thoughts, Aidan started to pull away from her.

Brie seized his face in her hands, thinking of his son. "Evil is cruel," she said slowly. "Evil is heartless, without conscience. Still…I'm appalled. Oh, Aidan!" She slipped her arms around him and tried to lay her cheek on his chest.

He jumped to his feet. "Ian is dead," he said, but his tone was uncertain.

"Ian is a ghost," she said as carefully. "And we were dreaming of him."

His gaze flew to hers. "Yer nay certain."

She trembled. "Aidan, he's been dead for sixty-six years. If he were alive, he'd be a grown man."

Aidan cried out.

She leapt to her feet and put her arms around him, but he instantly twisted away.

"Ye'll be safe at Iona. We go by horseback an' galley in the morning," he said tersely. His glance slid down her legs.

He was blocking his emotions for her, but she knew he was filled with pain and anguish. "This is exactly what he wants—to instill fear in us and to torment you even more than he has already," Brie cried. "These demons are worse than terrorists! We can't let them frighten us and we can't let them torment us!"

"An' how should I be, then?" he shouted. "Should I pretend I didn't just see an' hear my dead son?"

"It was a dream," Brie cried.

"Was it?" he demanded. "Because it was the most realistic dream I have had. We were both trapped there by some huge power until the Wolf freed us."

She moved to touch his arm but he jerked away. "I am on your side," she tried. "I can't stand what is happening, either."

He breathed hard. "He's afraid of the Wolf. His power worked on the man, but mayhap the Wolf can escape his spells."

Brie tensed. She didn't want to rely on that beast, not ever. They needed more power—and a few spells of their own. "I'm afraid to ask how much power Moray has."

Their gazes locked. "The next time ye die in a dream, ye won't awaken, ever. I have no doubt of that."

Brie trembled. "I think you may be right."

He suddenly covered his face with his hands, and Brie knew he was thinking about the fact that he had just seen and heard his son. She was desperate to comfort him and she went to him. When he remained unmoving, she laid her hand on his back.

He looked at her, his eyes ablaze. "I could invite him back fer another dream, an' even ask him to bring my son with him. I'd see Ian again."

"Haven't you dreamed of Ian before?"

"I never dream of him. There's only the haunting," he said.

That was as cruel as the rest of his life. She caressed his big shoulder.

He stared down at her. "Ye need to get dressed and stop touchin' me."

She dropped her hand. "I want to comfort you."

His gaze turned cold. "I won't make love to ye," he warned.

Unease began. She turned, found her jeans and slid them on. As she snapped them, she looked up. He was watching her as closely as a hawk. "I really wish I could read your mind. What is it?"

"He told me Ian lives."

Alarm began. "Aidan, it's a lie, a ploy!"

He wet his lips, his stare hard. "Ye ken what he wants now?"

"Yes. He wants you to be pure evil, a demon with no heart, no soul. A demon capable of mayhem, torture, cruelty and murder."

"He wants me to bed ye an' destroy ye, an' enjoy it."

Brie knew Aidan would never be so demonic, but his gaze was hard now.

"If I take pleasure in yer death, he'll give me my son back."

"Ian is dead!" Brie cried.

"Is he?" Aidan roared. "Is he dead or is he alive?"

She felt her insides vanish. She backed up.

He grasped his head as if to wrench it from his neck and let the block on his emotions fall away.

Brie screamed as his confusion, his anguish and rage hit her, blow after blow. She staggered backward as his torment pummeled her, as brutal and random as a hailstorm. As she went to her knees, he just stood there, watching her, his every emotion out of all control, and she became aware of something else woven into the pain.

The knowledge that Ian might be given back to him, if he did as Moray asked.

On her knees, she looked up at him, a hammer banging inside her head.

"Ye'll be safe from us both on Iona." His eyes changed, becoming unwavering and feral.

She felt the beast before she saw it. Anger blazed, consuming every other emotion except for the lust.

There was so much lust.

Carnal lust, bloodlust and the lust for power were all roiling into one huge, explosive force.

Brie crouched, afraid to move. "Don't," she whispered. The man standing before her looked like Aidan, but it wasn't. He was the Wolf and he was beyond rage now. He was beyond all reason.

He glared furiously at her and slammed from the tent, into the night.

BRIE WALKED SLOWLY OUTSIDE AND paused, but saw no sign of Aidan. She was afraid he had shifted already. She prayed he wasn't hunting Moray.

What were they going to do? Moray had all kinds of power. He had seemed in complete control until

Aidan had shifted into the Wolf. Was it even remotely possible that Moray could not triumph over the beast?

Will approached, looking sleepy, and Brie realized it would soon be dawn. He went to the fire, now in embers, and began adding kindling. Brie looked away, dreading the new day. She was pretty certain it wouldn't bring much respite.

Suddenly she felt white power approaching. It was terribly familiar and she turned in confusion, remarking a pair of riders coming up the road from the southwest. The power wafted toward her. Comprehension began, but surely she was wrong. The riders veered through the waking camp toward her and sudden excitement arose.

The riders were a man and a woman. The woman was small and dark, on a jet-black mare, and the man riding beside her on a huge gray charger was a golden Highlander. She had seen him before in her visions and the woman was unmistakable. "Allie!"

Allie leapt from her horse effortlessly and ran toward Brie, arms wide, wearing skinny jeans and a fur jacket. "Brie!"

Brie went into her arms and began to cry. She had never been happier to see anyone.

Allie, who was five feet tall on a really good day and maybe a hundred pounds when wet, held her as if she were a child. "It's all right. Royce and I are here, even if it took me an entire night to convince him to come. We will fix *everything!*"

Brie pulled back to look at her best friend, who was the most optimistic, unsinkable person she knew. Allie remained shockingly beautiful—more so than ever, Brie thought. "I prayed you would come. You heard me!"

Allie grinned. "When Claire told me you were here, I wanted to come right over, but Royce is holding a grudge against Aidan and we had to have it out. He can be the most stubborn, annoying, unreasonable man."

Brie had a bad feeling the moment Allie said the word "grudge" that Aidan had done something pretty unforgivable. She glanced at Royce and her heart actually slammed. The man was a mass of popping muscles, and while gorgeous, he was so obviously a medieval warrior she almost couldn't believe he was Allie's soul mate. He looked as hard and intractable as Allie had claimed. But he was exactly as she had first seen him in her vision, when she had known he was to be crucial to Allie's fate. She smiled and took Allie's hand. "Well, well…well."

Allie laughed, pleased. "Yeah, he's hot." Royce gave his wife an annoyed look. "Hey, Mr. Medieval. Forgive me and come and meet my best friend in the world. You are way too old to sulk."

Royce came over, looking really annoyed now. "Lady Brie." He nodded at her. "I'm pleased t'make yer acquaintance."

Brie decided he wasn't annoyed, he was royally pissed. She hoped he was mad at Allie and not Aidan. "Thank you for coming," she said, meaning it. "We could use your help."

His gaze was assessing, and he gave nothing away. It was impossible to tell if he'd help Aidan or not.

"We will help you, no matter what," Allie said firmly, "or it's separate bedrooms for the next hundred years."

Royce snorted and walked off.

Brie looked at Allie, who smiled saucily at her. "He's very angry with Aidan. I tried to heal him right after his son was murdered and he blew up at me. I know he didn't mean it, but he went berserk with his powers. If Royce hadn't appeared, I guess I could have been really hurt."

Brie started. "Allie, wait a minute. Are you saying that you tried to heal Aidan sixty-six years ago?"

She grinned. "What year did you come from, Brie?"

Brie said slowly, "It's been a year, almost to the day, since you left us for good. Aidan took me back on September 21, 2008."

Allie laughed. "Well, you haven't seen me in a year, but I haven't seen you in 72 years!"

"You look twenty-five," Brie whispered, stunned. "You haven't aged a day!"

"My family tree isn't what we thought it was," Allie said. She hugged Brie impulsively again. "My brother is The Black Macleod—a Master."

Brie felt her brows soar. "Does this mean you're immortal?"

"I have no idea," Allie said happily. Then she sobered, and her dark gaze was scrutinizing. "You look really good, actually. You seem to be in one piece, and you finally ditched those horrible eyeglasses. The pince-nez is sort of cute."

Brie hesitated, thinking about everything that had happened in the past few days. If she looked okay, it was a miracle—or was it?

"Has Aidan hurt you?" Allie demanded, unsmiling. "Because you don't look hurt or feel hurt, not at all, but you *are* distressed."

"No," Brie said, shaking her head emphatically. "He would never hurt me. His bark is really loud, but he has no bite."

"Really?" Allie's eyes were wide.

"And he can deny it, but we're friends." Brie smiled grimly at her.

Allie stared. "Brie, he has no friends."

"He has me. He needs me. Allie, he is in so much pain."

Brie knew she was giving her feelings away and she blushed. But surely Allie would be supportive of her. They'd always been supportive of each other. Allie seized her hand.

"It's really easy to fall for these hunks," she said softly. "And Aidan is one of the most beautiful men on this planet. He has tons of experience, too. He was the most eligible bachelor of medieval times. I mean, he outdid all the modern playboys I ever knew *combined* before he fell. Now, of course, he uses enchantment, not seduction. Has he enchanted you?"

"No. Allie, he isn't evil."

Allie's gaze was searching. "Everyone says he takes power pretty much all the time."

"He leaves his lovers alive."

"Good. I was hoping so."

Brie clasped her hands. "I need you on our side," she whispered. "Desperately."

"You've fallen in love with him." It wasn't quite an accusation.

Brie closed her eyes and nodded. "I didn't mean to. But that day you brought him to Tabby and Sam's loft, I sort of had an instant crush. And since I came back here, it's sort of escalated."

Allie stared. "Are you sleeping with him?"

Brie flushed. "Not exactly."

"What does that mean?"

Brie became uncomfortable. "I'm okay. I can handle this."

"You have no experience with men! You are grist for his mill. The one thing I do know is he uses women all the time. I will kill him if he hurts you. You shouldn't sleep with him."

Brie thought of how wild Allie had been in New York and she started to smile. Allie instantly knew, appearing sheepish. "My sex drive has always been out of control. You're not like that."

If only she knew, Brie thought. "He hasn't used me…he respects me."

Allie choked. "Brie, I beg your pardon?"

"So much has happened," Brie told her. "Since he rescued me from the gang in New York and brought me back here, we have been through hell. He was so angry at first, so dark, so frightening…but he isn't frightening now. Allie, I almost died yesterday. He *healed* me." Allie cried out in surprise. "I believe in him! He has protected me time and again, instead of hurting me. I am going to redeem him."

Allie took her hand, and they both sat down. "You and Aidan," she said. "I would never have thought, not in a million years. I would have paired him with Sam."

"He's not my soul mate," Brie said quickly. "He's just my friend."

"Aidan hasn't protected Innocence since his child was murdered," Allie said. "But he healed you? Are you sure it wasn't a god?"

Brie blinked. "The power was coming from his hands."

Allie began to smile. Tears formed and she swatted at them. "He's my friend, too. He was my knight of swords, remember? I love him. Now, what kind of trouble are you in?"

Brie stiffened. "His father has returned from the vanquished and he has more power than I could have dreamed."

THE WOLF WANTED TO GET OUT OF his body. Aidan wanted nothing more than to let the Wolf free and hunt his archenemy, but he somehow refused it.

He could not leave Brianna alone. He didn't dare go too far from her, in case Moray came back to start another battle or even to finish the war. He kept one sense on her always. As he did, he was acutely aware of what his father wanted him to do.

But Ian was dead.

Alone, he sank onto a boulder, cradling his head. His grief warred with the Wolf's vicious rage.

Papa?

He didn't know what that plaintive tone had meant. He reminded himself for the hundredth time that it was a cruel trick in a cruel dream. Brianna had made an irrefutable point. If Ian were alive, he'd be a grown man. Besides, he'd never dreamed of Ian, not even once. Clearly Moray had the power to foist this dream on him, just as he'd had the power to trap him and Brianna in it.

And then he felt the white power emerging on the plain below.

Aidan leapt to his feet and walked warily to the edge of the ridge. He stared down the snowy slope, instantly identifying the intruders. He was stunned when he realized it was Black Royce and Lady Allie. But of course they would come—Allie loved Brianna, and

Royce would do as his wife wished in the very end. He was torn between dismay, anger and relief.

He crossed his arms, refusing to think about the past. It was impossible.

Did ye summon me to yer bath? Do ye wish fer me to help ye bathe?

He'd stood there at the door to her bedchamber, decades ago, grinning, having heard her thinking his name. She denied it, and he already knew Allie would never do such a thing. She was madly in love with his best friend, Royce. Instead, she had flirted with him, just a little, and he had flirted back and agreed to help her so she could tempt Royce into her bed. He had thought his friend a fool for denying himself such a beautiful woman.

Aidan grimaced. He was not that carefree, light-hearted man now, a man used to laughter and flirtation, a man eager to help a damsel in distress, even if he couldn't have her.

"I can help you, Aidan. Let me help you!" Lady Allie cried.

Ian was dead, lost in the aeons of time. Malcolm had just unearthed him, and Aidan would never forgive his brother for doing so. Lady Allie and Royce, having heard of his son's Fate, had leapt from Carrick to Awe to console him. She was weeping for him. He hated her for her tears.

"Get far from me," he roared.

She shook her head, and showered him with her powerful, healing light.

For one moment, he was incredulous. He would grieve for Ian forever. She had no right!

His grief and rage erupted as one. He roared and

roared and threw his power at her, all of it, wanting her gone, wanting her dead, like his small son, and she was blasted from the bridge. She was small and it was like throwing a ball. She screamed, spinning away across the field toward a stone wall. Royce appeared, catching her. He knelt with his wife in his arms and when he looked up, he was enraged.

Aidan couldn't wait to do battle. He would kill him, too!

"Royce, no," Lady Allie begged.

Royce blasted him with all of his power.

He was trembling now. Lady Allie was very much like Brianna—kind and good. He should not have tried to hurt her, much less kill her. Regret dared to creep over him.

He hadn't felt regret in years.

Royce had walked to stand at the bottom of the ridge, and he stared up at Aidan. Aidan tensed, staring back down at him. Even from this distance, he felt Royce's hostility and wariness. Royce did not trust him. No one trusted him—except for Brianna.

And maybe, considering what Moray wanted, she should not trust him, either.

"Why do ye taunt him? Why do ye act all of twelve years old? He's yer brother an' the two of ye need to make peace."

Aidan did not want to remember how important Black Royce had been to him when he had grown up in a foster home. Although he had not lacked for food or shelter, Aidan had been a burden on the Maclaine family and he had been treated very differently from the Maclaine sons and daughters. Royce had been both a father, friend and uncle to him, even without any blood tie. Royce had visited him as much as possible when he was a very small boy, always bringing a gift. He had taught Aidan how to wield his sword, and how to fight hand to hand. And he had never ceased trying to forge a familial and amicable relationship between him and Malcolm, once the truth of Aidan's parentage had become known to them both. In the end Royce had succeeded, and Aidan and his brother had eventually come to good terms—until the day of Ian's murder.

Aidan felt his heart aching oddly. Determined to ignore it, he reached for the restless, hungry Wolf. It clawed through him, determined to get out.

Royce had started up the hill, his strides long and determined.

Aidan told the Wolf to wait and he composed himself. He would not allow himself any regret, not on any matter. Royce would be a good ally in this war, but Aidan knew Royce would never forgive him for his attack on Lady Allie. They would never be true allies—or friends—again. A Highlander did not forgive and he did not forget. He braced for his onslaught.

Royce paused before him, standing aggressively. "Why did ye take an Innocent hostage?"

Aidan curled his mouth. "To amuse myself."

Royce's gray eyes glittered. "Ye still act like a boy of twelve. 'Tis fortunate that she's nay hurt."

Aidan felt like striking him. "I'm nay a boy of twelve years an' ye willna berate me like ye were wont to do. She's an Innocent, an' ye can protect her now. I'm done."

Royce stared closely. "I dinna believe ye've protected her, Aidan. What game is this?"

Aidan fought the sudden fury of the beast seething in him, and it was very hard to do. "Moray has returned. She needs protection from him until he is vanquished. He is usin' her to destroy me."

Royce went still, his eyes flickering. "I dinna think to ever see the day he'd return," he said softly, after a long pause. "Does Malcolm ken?"

"Nay." Aidan smiled savagely. "Oh, afore I forget. He has powers from the Duisean."

Royce paled.

Aidan shifted. Crouching, he growled long and low at Royce, but Royce did not step back in fear. Annoyed—he'd meant to frighten him, at the least—Aidan searched Royce's mind, which was open. There was no fear, just wariness and anger. His hand, however, had crept to the hilt of his long sword.

He would love it if Royce raised that sword toward him. But he didn't move.

Aidan turned away. It was time to hunt his deamhan father.

"Hunt with care," Royce called after him.

Aidan leapt.

THE PACK STAYED BACK IN THE line of trees, a female whining nervously. The sun was shimmering high in the early morning sky. The wolves would not hunt in the broad light of day.

He did not care. Aidan stood a short distance from the tree line, intently watching Frasier's army breaking camp, still in the Wolf's body. He coursed with power and life; he and the pack had been hunting since dawn.

Frasier's red-and-gold tent was being taken down and bundled up. Aidan's gaze veered past the servants dismantling it, the cart and waiting team of horses. He saw the tall figure preparing to mount a charger and knew it was Frasier, not Moray. Frasier's power was relatively weak compared to that of a deamhan, and it was very human.

Aidan sat down on his haunches, his patience infinite. *Come to me.*

There was no reply.

Behind him, the pack settled, lying down.

Come to me, coward.

The morning shifted ever so slightly—a whisper of leaves, a dancing of dust.

He stared at the army below, aware of his pulse pounding slowly and steadily, rising as he prepared for their final battle. Darkness gathered behind him.

His hackles rising, he turned. The wolves stood, growling. They all stared deeper into the forest. The shadows became longer, darker—emerald turning black, dark clouds forming in the woods.

Dead leaves crunched.

Aidan licked his lips, feeling the black power coming, and he snarled.

Moray appeared in his true form, clad in black robes and hose, carrying only a small dagger and a single ax. "You should fear me, my son," Moray whispered softly.

Aidan growled. *I fear no one.* But he was elated. His father had dared to fight him in his own body, and that meant, possibly, that Aidan could vanquish him at last.

"I trapped you in a dream, and I can trap you anywhere, anytime, as anything."

Aidan tensed. Did he mean that he would trap him in the Wolf's body? It did not matter. He did not care. *Die today.*

Moray threw the ax as he leapt, roaring.

Aidan meant to deflect it, but the ax sliced through

his power. He screamed with pain as the ax pierced through muscle and bone. He landed on Moray, sending him to the ground. Moray's demonic energy was a huge force, and he fought to get past it, to sink his teeth into the jugular vein. It was as if the energy were a coat of armor and he only scraped skin as the black power finally threw him backward.

He tumbled wildly through the forest. Instantly Aidan leapt up, seeing Moray's ax flying back into his hand, summoned with impossible power.

A sliver of fear went through him. This time he deflected the hurled ax, which was aimed at his head. It veered, glancing off his chest instead.

Flesh was ripped open. The pain enraged him, and he tackled Moray, shocked when the dagger stabbed up between his ribs. He tore through the wall of energy with claws and fangs, viciously determined to get to Moray's throat.

From behind, the ax sliced through Aidan's flank. Pain blinded him, but, aware that he must not stop now, Aidan fought to maul his way through the shield of energy. And suddenly he tasted fresh blood as his teeth sank into flesh and tendon.

Moray's eyes widened in alarm.

In another second, he would rip Moray's throat apart, Aidan thought in savage satisfaction.

He sank his teeth deep.

You will never find Ian if you kill me now.

Aidan went still, releasing his jaw, lifting his head.

Moray smiled at him, and his mocking laughter sounded.

It was a lie. Aidan snarled, but before he could rip Moray's throat into shreds, Moray vanished into time.

For one moment, Aidan crouched over the air and the earth, and then the pain blinded him. Whimpering, he sank to the ground.

In that moment, there was shocking clarity, and he became aware of how badly injured he was. He had been wounded in the chest twice, once with the dagger, which had come terribly close to his heart. The ax had knifed into his shoulder, hip and leg and he was bleeding heavily now.

In spite of the daylight and the army not far from them, the wolves had gathered around him, whimpering.

He was going to die.

But he was supposed to hang.

It was the gods, enjoying themselves at his expense. They had never intended the hanging, he thought. Suddenly he was afraid. He wasn't ready to die. He had to vanquish Moray. And what about Brianna?

Her beautiful face came to his mind and settled there, bringing sudden comfort. He softened deep within himself. She needed him. He had to protect her. He could not die, not yet.

He tried to stagger to his paws.

Pain blinded him.

He collapsed. He tried to stand again. He could not bear it. Two of his legs were worthless. Instead, he started crawling to her, inch by painful inch.

CHAPTER TWELVE

"HOW CAN WE VANQUISH MORAY?" Brie asked.

She and Allie sat cross-legged on the bed inside Aidan's tent. The chill from the previous night was finally easing, and Brie guessed that the sun was high in the sky. She had become used to the fact that the only time of day that it wasn't freezing cold was midday, but they had a kettle fire burning and she was wrapped in one of Aidan's black plaids.

She had spent the past hour telling Allie just about everything that had happened since she had first heard Aidan's roars of pain and anguish in New York City. She'd omitted her personal encounters with Aidan, of course. Allie had been wide-eyed and rapt. She had yet to say a word.

Allie bit her lip. "Brie, the gods gave the Brotherhood three books long ago, when they first sent the great goddess, Faola, to mankind to create the Masters. The Cathach is the Book of Wisdom. The Book of Healing, the Cladich, vanished centuries ago, but the Brotherhood has recovered five pages. We're still looking for the rest of the manuscript. But the Duisean is the most important book of all."

Brie's unease escalated. She had told Allie that Moray apparently had a part of the Book. "I would sure like to know which extra powers he has."

"Some of the brethren believe that certain demons are immortal," Allie said grimly.

"Great," Brie said, feeling sick. "If we survive Moray, we can fight him for eternity. Or, at least, Aidan can."

Allie reached out and took her hand. Brie felt her healing warmth seeping into her. She was surprised. "You can heal emotions now?"

"Not to brag or anything, but I am pretty darned powerful." Allie grinned.

Suddenly the tent flap lifted and Royce stepped inside to join them. He was even more grim than his wife. Clearly he had been eavesdropping, because he said, "Every power known to the gods and mankind exists in the Book. Moray could have many different powers, even ones we have not heard of."

Brie felt dread creeping over her. Allie squeezed her hand, and she calmed. "There's one more thing. Moray may have hidden whatever he has of the Duisean in my time."

Royce started. So did Allie.

"This will be right up Nick's alley," Brie said. "I need to get word to him so he can put his agents on this."

"You're still at CDA, working for Forrester?" Allie asked. She slid to her feet, walking over to Royce. She wore sexy boots with high heels along with her jeans. When Brie had first realized Allie was running around the medieval Highlands like a designer sexpot, she had smiled. In some ways, Allie hadn't changed at all. Brie hadn't asked how she'd gotten brand-new-designer boots in 1502, because it was obvious she still liked shopping in the twenty-first century. But that raised a huge question.

"Yes, I am. Allie, why haven't you come to visit us since you left?"

Allie started. "Honey, I don't go back to the future."

Brie blinked. "But the boots? Your clothes."

Allie smiled. "Royce showers me with gifts on my birthday." She sobered. "It's dangerous going into the future, and when we do, it's only to save Innocence. In your time, Royce and I are living at Carrick. We have eleven grandchildren. I was there once, and I'm not sure of the physics of such an encounter, but why take any chances? We fought hard for our love, and one day, I'll be living at Carrick with every modern comfort. I can wait. I will not wreck what we have. And besides, we are awfully busy in medieval Alba."

Brie hadn't had a clue. She glanced at Royce, and for the first time since she'd met him, he was smiling softly, his gray gaze on his wife. Their love was so powerful it washed through her, warm and wonderful, soothing and strong. They were going to love one another like that for an eternity, Brie thought.

"How can we get word to Nick?" Brie asked, suddenly teary-eyed.

"I'll take care of it," Royce said. "This is a matter fer the Brotherhood, Lady Brie. I've summoned a council. I am worried. I dinna think any single man or Master can triumph over Moray now."

Allie plucked his leine. "He has new powers of possession, but I'll tell you about that later," she said softly.

Brie was relieved that Royce had summoned so much white power. Surely a single demon could not defeat the Brotherhood. "Where is Aidan, anyway?" she asked Royce.

His gray gaze held hers. "He has gone hunting."

Brie cried out, standing. "He's gone after Moray so soon? Did he shift? What does he think he can do? Moray almost killed me. He almost killed him. Why couldn't he wait for us to come up with a plan?"

"Royce?" Allie touched his muscular arm. "Did you summon Guy and Tabby?"

Brie turned to her, amazed. "What did you say?"

"Aye," Royce said. He faced Brie. "I dinna like to summon Macleod. He rushes into every war. One day he will lose his head, an' my wife will blame *me.*"

"My brother may be a Master," Allie said, "and a married man, but he is a Highlander first and last—and he thinks himself invincible, which he may or may not be."

"You just asked Royce if he summoned Tabby!" Brie cried. "Surely you didn't mean our Tabby?"

Allie grinned. "Yes, I meant our Tabby, more commonly known as Lady Tabitha."

Tabby was in the past, too. Brie could barely assimilate it. "But I left her at home, teaching first graders by day and using spells to save Innocence by night!"

"Brie, Tabby has become really powerful over the centuries."

Brie started. "Okay, what does that mean? How long has she been here?"

"She's been here since the thirteenth century," Allie said. "We can use her magic against Moray. I am sure of it."

Brie decided not to dwell on the fact that in 2008, Tabby was living in New York without a clue of her fate, but in 1502, she'd been in medieval Scotland for close to three hundred years. "Is she happy? Is she with your brother?"

"She is very happy, and madly in love with another medieval catch. They have kids, lots and lots of them—you know Tabby. They're not all theirs, either."

Brie sat down on the edge of the bed. "Tabby deserves true love. I am so happy for her." But worry began. "I guess Sam is alone in the future?"

Allie sobered and sat down beside her. "Does this mean you're not going back?"

Their gazes locked. "Of course I'm going back. I'm here to save Aidan, period."

Allie looked at Royce. "Brie is going to redeem him."

"Aye, I suspected as much when I spoke to Aidan earlier," he said.

Brie saw them exchange a look and knew they were exchanging thoughts as well. At least she didn't have to worry about Sam being alone, she thought, feeling oddly dismayed. Malcolm and Claire were so deeply in love, and so were Allie and Royce. To yearn for that kind of connection was crazy, but too late, she knew she was secretly harboring just such a fantasy.

Brie sighed. But before she could even finish her thoughts, a savagely murderous rage began.

It hurled Brie backward onto the bed and knocked the wind right out of her.

Aidan was in trouble.

"Brie!" Allie cried, rushing to her.

The Wolf wanted to maim, destroy and murder. "It's Aidan," Brie gasped, the fury consuming her. She had never felt such rage, not ever. Then the pain sliced through her shoulder and she screamed.

A terrific life-and-death struggle began. She needed to sink her teeth into the enemy's throat and rip his artery apart. Then Brie was hurled backward, and before she got up, a sliver of fear went through her.

The flesh of her chest was ripped open. Enraged, she meant to leap again, but a terrible pain went through her chest and she screamed.

Had he been stabbed in the heart?

There were more terrible blows, but the savagery did not diminish. Suddenly she felt her teeth sink into human flesh, and she tasted blood—and it was *good.* A savage, utterly primal, merciless satisfaction overcame her and she barely felt the ax cutting through her leg. *She would kill him now.*

She suddenly envisioned Ian.

And there was only blinding pain, her prey having vanished.

Brie came back to herself, swirling in the thick web of pain, becoming vaguely aware of Allie holding her. *Aidan was hurt…he was going to die.*

"No," she gasped. She fought the pain. She had to swim out of it, no matter how thick the layers, how suffocating, how imprisoning. She became aware of a warmth seeping into her, through her.

Allie was trying to heal her.

"Brie, it's all right! Nothing's happening. It's your empathy, but it's so strong, it's hard for me to get through it."

Nothing was happening? Aidan was in terrible pain, badly wounded. Brie lay breathless in Allie's arms, her heart thundering, struggling to see Allie clearly. Her image wavered, but the warmth intensified. And finally, the pain began to recede.

Allie remained in focus now, holding Brie and stroking her brow.

Brie waited another moment, then slowly sat up. "We have to find him!"

Royce knelt before her. "What happened?"

"He was in a terrible battle. He's been knifed and axed. I am almost certain it was with Moray." She felt tears fall. Her heart surged with panic. Allie stroked her shoulder, but Brie was barely calmed. "He is going to die if we don't find him and heal him."

"Can you feel where he is?" Allie asked. "He must be far away, because I haven't felt his pain yet."

"I don't know. Give me a moment." She gathered her composure as best she could and slipped to her feet, going to the tent flap. She lifted it and ducked outside.

It was midmorning now. The camp had been dismantled, and the foremost ranks of armored knights were already on the march. She closed her eyes, lifting her face to the warm midday sun.

Blinding pain hit her like a tidal wave, driving her into an unmovable wall. Then she realized she'd slammed into Royce's powerful body. *Where are you?* She begged silently, desperately.

There was no response.

But they'd never had telepathy; he had always been the one to read her mind.

Read my mind now, Aidan. Where are you? Let me help you!

A silence shimmered in her mind; there was only his pain and some kind of elaborate struggle. She did not understand it.

Royce had been clasping her shoulders, and he released her. "We'll find him, Lady Brie," he offered, grave and unsmiling. He looked at Allie and then strode off.

Brie saw a young Highlander bring Royce's mount to him. She touched her cheeks, which were wet with tears. *Please come back. Please tell me where you are.*

Allie slid her arm around Brie and did not speak. Brie suddenly felt his pain again, a huge, hard wave that made her double over. Allie sent her more healing light, and as the pain vanished, they shared a grim look.

"I am going to keep my healing power on you, because his pain is too much for you to bear."

Allie was right. God, what had happened to him? "He can't die today, this way," Brie cried, suddenly furious. She swatted at her tears. It crossed her frantic mind that he was supposed to hang, but she was not soothed. Maybe his Fate was death, and it simply didn't matter how he died.

Worse, he'd waited to die once, when he'd been buried alive. What if he was so badly hurt that he would accept his death now?

She looked at Allie, burning with determination. "I won't let him die."

BRIE HAD BEEN SEARCHING FOR him all day on foot. Allie remained a constant shadow, clearly afraid to leave her. Every now and then she doused Brie with white light to keep his pain marginalized. Hours passed. Brie felt at her wit's end. The only positive in the crisis was that he remained in pain, which meant he was alive.

She climbed the ridge for the fifth or sixth time, as it was a good vantage point. Mountains surrounded them. Another huge glen lay to the north, containing a vast, shining loch, and to the south was what was left of their camp. Most of the armies had marched on toward their rendezvous with the MacDonald and the Macleans. Just ahead of her, the air suddenly shimmered and shifted.

Brie tensed, filled with hope, but it was Ian who emerged from the mist.

She went still in surprise.

He pointed at her and began speaking urgently, but she did not hear a word.

"Allie, can you see Ian's ghost?"

Allie hurried to her side. "He's here? I can't see him, Brie."

"Ian, wait. What is it?" The little boy was close to tears, and she knelt. The timing could not have been worse. She needed to search for Aidan, not spend time trying to communicate with his dead son.

The boy trotted ahead of her, then paused and looked at her, clearly waiting.

It was obvious what he wanted. "He wants me to follow him," Brie gasped, and she hurried after the little ghost.

He began to run.

Brie broke into a jog. "I can't keep up with you!" she cried.

But the little boy didn't slow down.

Brie forced herself to keep up, with Allie at her side—Allie had jettisoned her high heels for Nikes earlier. Brie was winded instantly, but Allie breathed easily enough. Knowing Allie, she probably ran miles every day, did a thousand crunches and God only knew what else.

They followed the ghost into the woods that covered the south face of the mountain. "Where is he taking us?" Allie asked.

Brie couldn't answer, but she was praying even harder now to every god she could think of.

"I hope you're right," Allie whispered, "and he's taking us to Aidan."

Suddenly Ian's ghost vanished in the midst of the thick forest. They were on a deer trail, surrounded by nearly impenetrable woods. Brie stopped, so badly out of breath that her lungs burned. And the dark heap of brush blocking their way seemed to move.

She cried out. It wasn't a pile of dirty leaves and deadwood. *It was a wolf.*

Bloody and mangled, it rose up and crawled forward a step, its gaze blue and direct. Then it collapsed.

"Aidan!" Brie screamed, running to him. She knelt in the dirt and leaves, horrified. His left hind leg was almost completely severed from his hip. His chest and shoulder were raw, gaping wounds and his coat was soaked with blood. He was going to die if Allie couldn't save him.

She gathered his large head into her arms and held him tightly to her breasts, overcome with fear. "It's okay. You'll be all right. Allie is here," she choked.

Surprisingly long lashes lifted, and he looked at her with his human blue eyes, which were clouded with pain.

Brie kissed the fur at his temple, suppressing another sob.

Allie knelt beside them, showering him with a thick cloud of white light.

The Wolf's eyes closed and Brie held his head more tightly to her chest, leaning her cheek against his furry neck. *You will not die,* she told him fiercely. *I love you so much.*

The great beast seemed to stir in her arms. She looked up at Allie, knowing better than to interrupt her while she healed. Allie was focused entirely on Aidan, and her body radiated with her white healing power. Brie had never seen so much power coming from her before. In seventy-two years, her healing powers had obviously grown *a lot*.

Brie saw that his hind leg looked whole now and she watched the pink skin knitting and the fur growing back. She stroked the thick fur at his nape, watching his shoulder healing. She couldn't see the rest of his wounds, but she felt his body finally relax in her arms.

Allie sat back, emitting a huge sigh. She was covered in perspiration and she wiped her brow with her sleeve. "He'll live. Wow." She finally looked at Brie very seriously. "He was in a fight for his life."

Brie stroked the Wolf, who lay still now. She and Allie regarded one another, and Brie didn't need telepathy to know that Allie was wondering how they would ever defeat Moray, just as she was. Then she glanced down. Aidan gazed up at her out of his brilliant, human blue eyes, but he remained in the Wolf's body.

He slid back on his haunches and simply sat there, dwarfing her.

Brie tensed. She didn't really like being seated on the ground with the Wolf there, watching her so intently. "Is he healed?" she asked, cautiously standing.

"Yeah," Allie said, wiping her cheek this time. She didn't try to get up.

"Then why isn't he shifting back into a man?" Brie did not take her eyes from the Wolf.

"I don't know." Allie sounded tired.

Brie didn't move and neither did the Wolf. Why hadn't Aidan shifted back? "Aidan? You're making me nervous. Can you come back to us, please?"

He gave her a very human, very direct, extremely male look, and he stood on all fours.

Her tension increased. She reminded herself that he did not look vicious now, but that unwavering stare was unnerving.

The forest shuddered as wolves began slipping out from behind the trees, some gray, some darker, some black. Not one was as pitch-black as he was.

Brie didn't move, frozen, and finally Allie was on her feet, too. "What's going on?" Brie asked Allie.

"I don't know," Allie said, but her hand produced a small, dangerous-looking dagger.

They willna hurt ye.

Brie jerked, for she had just heard Aidan speaking. She looked at Allie, who hadn't reacted. "You didn't hear that, did you?"

"No."

Brie looked at the huge wolf, and it stared back at her. "You almost died. Thank God you're alive." There was no response. "Why won't you shift into a man?"

The blue eyes changed, and she felt a huge and sudden frustration. *I canna shift…he's trapped me.*

Disbelief began. Reason chased it aside. Hadn't Moray trapped them both in the dream for a while?

Ever astute, Allie whispered, "Is he under a spell?"

Brie wet her lips. "Yes, he is."

The Wolf glanced toward the deeper part of the woods and Brie realized he was going to vanish into the forest with the pack. She stepped forward, reaching out, then withdrew her hand, thinking the better of it. She didn't know how much of the beast was a savage, feral wolf and how much was the man she loved. "Please don't go. If you go, how will I find you?"

I ken where ye'll be, Brianna.

His blue eyes held hers. Then the Wolf bounded past her, disappearing into the forest, the other wolves following. Brie just stood there, stricken with dismay.

"Well, at least he's alive," Allie said slowly.

Brie hugged herself. "And a wolf can't hang."

BRIE CROUCHED BY THE TENT FLAP, holding it slightly ajar, her body stiff with tension. She was spying on the Brotherhood.

She'd felt the power, massive and male, emerging from the mists of time, as Master after Master leapt to their camp. Dozens of holy, time-traveling, superpowered medieval Highland warriors were standing outside Aidan's tent. A volatile discussion had begun. Voices were raised, tempers high. Her mouth was so dry she couldn't swallow.

She couldn't focus on their words, although many of them were speaking English. Each and every Master personified masculine perfection in one way or another. Some of the Highlanders were drop-dead gorgeous, like Aidan; others were ruthlessly male, like Royce. Biceps bulged, as did thighs—and the occasional English codpiece. Testosterone thickened the air.

The flap was pulled from her hand, and she straightened, heart slamming, as a Paul Walker look-alike in medieval Highland gear dimpled at her. His eyes were a dazzling shade of green. "Do ye wish to join us?" he asked.

She tried to find her tongue. Why on earth was he undressing her with his eyes? Because of the hour, she was swaddled up in her many layers of modern and medieval clothes, not to mention that she wore the silly pince-nez. She was hardly attractive. "I…er… isn't the council…classified?" she stuttered.

"Why do ye panic so, Brianna Rose?" he asked softly.

"How do you know my name?" she managed in surprise.

"I'm a friend of Lady Allie's. Ye may call me Seoc or MacNeil."

She stared into his eyes and he stared back, his gaze sizzling. The look was impossible to resist. She felt her body warm, responding to his magnetic and sexual pull, a pull she could actually feel. Then she realized what he was doing. "Are you trying to enchant me?"

"I dinna need to enchant any woman," he boasted. "But the nights are long an' very, very cold."

She breathed hard. This man had once been Aidan's friend. She had hoped to meet him. "I will not be seduced. I am with Aidan."

His gaze flickered. "I ken. But he left the Brotherhood long ago. Once, I mourned him. Now I dinna care much for his fate, and I am happy to fight him for a woman."

Brie had to try to make sense of his words. "You're joking, right? You don't intend to fight over me."

He dimpled. "I'd love to fight over ye, lass," he said. "In fact, I'd love nothing more."

Brie gaped at him.

His grin widened.

He must love war, she thought. It was the only rational conclusion she could muster. She was taken aback, but flattered. "Aidan told me about you. But he made you sound like a leader, not a warmonger."

"Aidan hates my brother," Seoc said flatly. "'Tis Neil he spoke of. My brother commands the brethren."

Before Brie could assimilate that, a low, threatening, very angry snarl sounded behind her.

Brie whirled in abject relief. "Aidan!"

But the Wolf seemed as vicious and savage as it had that day in New York. It growled at Seoc and crouched to attack, eyes blazing with murderous fury. *I will kill ye, ye fuckin' bastard.*

Brie jerked in dismay, having heard Aidan as clear as day.

Seoc's saber rang as he lifted it, his eyes blazing.

Brie looked from the Wolf to the Master and she didn't think twice. She stepped between them. "That is Aidan!"

"Aye, the terrible Wolf of Awe, a beast that enjoys rippin' a man to shreds and eatin' from his carcass." Seoc didn't seem affable now. "Get away from the Wolf, Brianna Rose."

"He won't hurt me. You need to leave," Brie cried.

Move away, Brianna. I never liked him very much anyway.

Brie looked at the Wolf, trembling. "Don't you dare attack him," she managed, horrified that they wanted to destroy one another.

Human blue eyes seared hers. *Why? So ye can share his bed tonight?*

Brie breathed hard. Seoc had been pouring it on and she had been affected by him—there was no doubt. But she would never have been seduced. If Aidan didn't know that she was a one-man woman, he didn't know her at all. She gave him a dark look. "You are on the same side!"

I dinna think so.

Seoc said softly, "Yer one of very few who has any faith in him, lass."

She whirled. "I'm asking you to leave us."

He was startled. "Are ye mad? Has he so bedazzled ye in his manly form that ye canna think straight, even now? I willna leave ye with the Wolf. He'll eat ye fer his supper!"

The Wolf growled and stalked past her.

Very recklessly, heart pounding, Brie seized a hank of fur, causing the Wolf to snap at her. She faltered, and the Wolf stared, but did not bite her. Trembling, she tore her gaze to Seoc, not releasing the animal. "Just leave, please!"

Seoc hesitated, his gaze wary and on the Wolf. "Well," he finally murmured. "Maybe it's fond o' ye, too." He sheathed his sword and ducked out of the tent.

Brie released the beast and her knees buckled. She backed up. "I really hope you would never hurt me."

There was no mistaking his anger.

Brie breathed deeply, wanting to defuse his temper. "Thank you for coming back." Her voice caught. "I have been so afraid for you. I was afraid you went after Moray again."

The Wolf stalked to the tent flap and pushed it aside, peering out in a very human manner. Then he faced her, staring.

Already uncomfortable and uncertain, she put a bit more distance between them. "Are you staying?"

She felt a smirk in his silent thoughts. *Aye.*

She hugged herself. She knew he was furious because Seoc had disarmed her. But for God's sake, except for Aidan, she'd never had that kind of man even look at her, much less want her in bed. "I had no intention of sleeping with him. You can't be jealous."

He intended to sleep with ye. The Wolf lay down, his long body barring the path from the tent's doorway.

Brie flushed. He thought she would have given in to Seoc. She could feel it. "Why are you staring?"

There was no answer now, just the Wolf's very human, unwavering cold stare.

Allie pushed her head inside the tent, which did not seem to disturb the Wolf. "I heard he was here." Allie didn't seem frightened at all.

"Is Tabby here yet?"

"No." Allie slipped into the tent, stepping over the Wolf, who refused to budge. She smiled at Brie. "Did you see what's out there?" she asked in a knowing and girly tone.

Brie hesitated, glancing at the Wolf. Better not to open this subject, she thought.

"Brie! Have you ever seen so many gorgeous, hot, supersexed men?" she demanded. "I mean, you do know what sex is like with a Master, don't you?"

Brie felt her eyes pop. "He can hear us!" The Wolf's eyes were blazing.

"I know," Allie said, smiling. "Even though I love Royce, I love being around so many Masters. It just feels so good." She winked.

Brie decided not to answer. She had no idea why Allie was provoking Aidan but she didn't like it. It was bad enough that he was stuck in the Wolf's body.

The Wolf's eyes blazed even brighter.

Allie looked at him. "Is he jealous? Seoc seemed pissed off. Did he come on to you? He's a master at seduction. He probably ran a close second to Aidan—before Aidan fell."

The Wolf finally stood, growling.

"Stop it," Brie said. "You're annoying him. What's happening out there?"

Allie said, "They get their stamina from the gods. I guess a god can make love forever. Royce can go on for *days.* I'll bet Seoc can, too."

"Allie," Brie choked.

"I healed him—he won't hurt me. Not only that, his secret is out. He saved you. The Big Bad Wolf isn't big or bad after all." She gave the Wolf a very big smile. "And he's insanely jealous. I can feel it. I'm empathic, too, remember?"

"Don't torment him," Brie whispered.

"If you decide Aidan isn't the one, I think you should go after Seoc. He's one hundred percent available and I saw the way he looked at you." Allie smiled at the Wolf. "You might want to change your tune the next time you're a man, Aidan. I think you have competition."

"Allie!" Brie protested.

The Wolf snarled menacingly at her.

Allie ignored him. "They're here. C'mon." She seized Brie's hand and dragged her past the Wolf and outside.

Although only a short time had passed, Brie was overwhelmed by so much medieval eye candy. She took a breath. Malcolm and Claire had arrived, and they were speaking with a golden Highlander who looked exactly like Matthew McConaughey. She reminded herself not to drool. Then she saw Seoc standing beside a dark, sinfully handsome Lowlander in a black leather vest, a hip-length padded surcote and indecently fitted hose. The Lowlander was staring at her with open interest. When he caught her eye, he smiled slowly at her. Seoc smiled, too.

Brie refused to smile back. She quickly turned—and fell into Tabby's arms.

She was so relieved, because she was hoping Tabby had a spell that could free Aidan from the Wolf. As she met her friend's warm amber eyes, the changes in her struck Brie, at once.

Tabby was as impossibly elegant as ever, in a long, blue velvet gown, but there was a serenity and peace about her that she hadn't had at home.

"Hi, Brie." Tabby hugged her so hard that it hurt. "I have missed you so much."

When Tabby finally let her go, Brie saw that she was crying. "How long has it been?" she asked carefully.

"I'm not sure. Maybe two hundred and fifty years," Tabby said. "You've changed so much! It must be the glasses. They were so unattractive." But her amber eyes were wide and searching.

"That was my first thought," Allie said from behind them. "But she's in love."

Tabby started, her eyes huge. "Wait a minute. Our Brie, who never dates, who spends most of her life in front of a PC, is in love?" Disbelief changed to excitement as she finished the sentence.

"Brie has found a Master—well, he used to be a Master."

"Who is it?" Tabby asked softly.

Brie tried to smile. She knew Tabby really, really well. She was an earth mother, caring of everybody, beyond protective, especially of her family. She was not going to like this. "He's sort of stuck right now."

Tabby blinked in confusion.

A dark, towering man stepped up from behind her, his expression hard. Tabby softened and smiled at him and Brie instantly knew this was her husband. Like Royce, he emanated a savage and ruthless power. Tabby had always hated alpha men. It was so odd seeing her standing there with a man so medieval and so male. He said grimly, "She dinna choose very well, Tabitha. Ye willna be pleased."

Tabby glanced up at him, her eyes widening. "We don't chose love. Fate chooses it for us."

His mouth softened. "A man must make his own Fate," he said, so softly Brie strained to hear. "An' I chose ye the first moment we met."

Tabby smiled at him and looked at Brie. "He started seducing me about two seconds after rescuing me."

"And ye dinna mind verra much," he said.

Tabby laughed. "This is Guy Macleod, my husband." She spoke with quiet pride. "He, of course, thinks he chose me without any unearthly guidance."

Brie wiped a tear, moved by their obvious affection. "Tabby? Don't flip, please. He's really stuck…in a wolf's body."

Tabby looked at Brie, clearly not understanding. Then she glanced up at Guy Macleod, and Brie was certain a silent communication was sizzling up the airwaves. "Aidan, the Wolf of Awe?" she cried in dismay. "You have fallen in love with a half deamhan? He has taken pleasure in death. He lusts for power. Every lover he has ever had can testify to it. And worst of all, he has allowed innocent children to die!"

"Tabby, he was forced from the light. I am bringing him back, I swear it! And he isn't evil. He has saved me repeatedly. Please help us," Brie cried, seizing her hands.

"Innocent women and children died at Elgin!"

Tabby argued. "Worse, he massacred the inhabitants of his own village at Awe!"

"He was trying to save his son." Malcolm stepped forward.

Brie turned. Too late, she realized the clearing had become silent, and every single Master was listening to them.

Worse, the Wolf stood outside the tent, listening as well.

Tabby shook her head and helplessly began to cry. "No one can come back from that."

CHAPTER THIRTEEN

BRIE STARED AT THE WOLF. "Please," she said to Tabby, glancing at her again.

Tabby nodded, clearly distraught. Brie hurried toward the Wolf. Understanding her, he slipped into the tent, and Brie followed him inside. It felt like a relief to have escaped all those curious and hostile gazes. Tabby entered, but before Guy could follow, she blocked the entrance. "Darling, please wait outside."

A look of sheer mutiny crossed his dark, handsome face. "I beg yer pardon, Tabitha, but when hell freezes over." Guy Macleod stepped past his wife, staring coldly at the Wolf. "I willna leave ye alone with either the beast or the deamhan."

Brie's heart sank even further. She'd assumed she would find more allies in Tabby and her husband, but she had been wrong. No one trusted the Wolf—and she didn't exactly blame them. But no one trusted Aidan, either, except for her and possibly Allie and Malcolm. Everyone kept saying he was feared and despised, and now she had seen that firsthand. Finally she believed it.

They needed help from every possible quarter. She had no confidence that the Masters would rally to his side. However, it was their duty to the gods to vanquish Moray, whether that helped Aidan or not.

Tabby murmured, "He's caught in a powerful binding spell."

Brie started. "Can you release him?"

"I think so," Tabby said. She looked at Guy.

He slipped from the tent. Brie was confused, but Tabby said, "Just wait a moment. I need the Book."

Brie gaped. "You have *our* Book? The Book of Roses?"

"I had to take it with me," Tabby said. "You know that the Rose with the most magic is always the one to keep and guard the Book."

Brie worried about Sam now. "How long will Sam be alone in New York without either one of us?"

"I don't know," Tabby said with a grimace. "It's not a good idea to bounce around the future. The Code says that one must never encounter oneself in another time."

Brie decided not to ask what the Code was. Guy stepped back inside, handing Tabby the massive, worn volume. Over two thousand pages long, it contained spells, magic, myths, legends and the kind of Wisdom a Rose would need in order to save others. Some of the folklore was older than the Bible.

Tabby sat on one of the rugs, cross-legged, glancing at the Wolf. "Come sit with me," she said.

He obeyed.

It only took Tabby a moment to find what she was looking for, which amazed Brie. In the past—as recently as a few days ago—it could take Tabby *weeks* to find what she needed, and half the time she was wrong anyway. Or, her spells were too weak and wound up useless. Now Tabby spoke softly in Gaelic, reading from the page. Brie only understood bits and pieces of the spell. Tabby was calling on different white and holy powers to break the black magic keeping Aidan bound in the Wolf. Then Tabby closed the Book.

Her face had become odd, waxlike. Her eyes seemed glazed. Her body had become rigid. She lifted her hands and murmured words Brie didn't comprehend at all. She wasn't even certain what language Tabby now spoke. The air in the tent swirled, lifting the blankets on the bed, pushing Brie's hair into her eyes, causing the canvas door to flap and then shudder.

And Aidan was sitting beside her.

Instantly Brie felt anger and desire. She bit off a gasp as Aidan stood, starkly naked, his muscles tense and rippling, reaching for a plaid at the foot of the bed. Someone snorted—Guy. Aidan wrapped the plaid around his waist, his gaze moving immediately to Brie.

Their gazes locked and his emotions vanished, carefully shielded from her. Brie inhaled hard. She nodded at him, aware that she was crying with relief.

Dinna cry fer me.

He was still communicating telepathically, she realized, because he hadn't opened his mouth to speak. He turned, his gaze hooded. "Thank ye, Lady Tabitha." His tone was very neutral.

Tabby's expression was utterly normal now. "You're welcome."

Guy helped Tabby to her feet, and he stared at Aidan. "Ye owe my lady a great debt," he said softly. "I'll make certain 'tis repaid."

Brie glanced between the two men. She saw Aidan's tension soar. She saw the same tension on Guy's face. Macleod didn't like or trust Aidan, and Aidan was so easily provoked. That was just great.

She stepped between them. "Thank you for coming to our rescue," she said to Guy, meaning it.

He did not smile at her. "My wife loves ye greatly, but 'tis my duty as her husband to keep her safe. I'll keep her far from this intrigue now." He glanced coolly at Aidan. "I ken ye wish to redeem him, but I dinna think it possible."

Brie looked beseechingly at Tabby, who said, "He's very overprotective. We'll be outside." Tabby squeezed her hand, sending Aidan a worried look. "Brie, if you need us, we'll be in calling distance."

"I'll be fine. I need a moment with Aidan."

Tabby was doubtful. She took her husband's hand and tugged Guy with her. They slipped from the tent.

They were *alone.* Brie didn't hesitate. She whirled, almost colliding into Aidan, who reflexively reached out to steady her. "Thank God you're back!" His strong hands were on her shoulders and his beautiful face was inches from hers.

His blue gaze met hers, blinding in its intensity. His expression was severe. "I owe ye a great debt, Brianna, just as I owe Lady Allie an' Lady Tabitha."

He hadn't released her. He was alive—they were both alive. This last crisis had taken her love to a new, more profound place. Brie was acutely aware of his big, masculine body, and that awareness made her ache desperately to be in his embrace. "You almost died, Aidan. I almost lost you."

His chest rose and fell, hard. He did not speak, but his plaid shifted, tenting thickly. Brie felt his desire the moment he lost control of his emotions. Hot and huge, it pulsed between them, flooding her, drenching her. He wanted her, too. There was no more denying the attraction or, damn it, the friendship. They had been through so much! It was time to be in his arms, his bed. It would be a celebration of life, of hope.

He tensed, shaking his head, his eyes hard and wary. He dropped his hands. "Ye dinna think clearly…ye think only with yer female heat."

Of course, he was reading her mind. She quickly laid her palms on his chest. "Aidan, I am thinking with more than my body and you know it. Don't turn away from me, not now. Not after all of this."

She felt his heart thunder at an impossible rate. "I'm very much alive," he said thickly. "As ye can see—as ye can feel. Ye want more than I can give. Mayhap ye should be with Seoc." He shuddered beneath her hands.

Pleasure—impossible, delighted pleasure—flooded her, coming from him.

It was almost blinding in intensity and in desperation.

She saw that he was fighting his reaction to her, and she couldn't comprehend why. "Aidan?" she whispered. And as she slid her hands up higher, he gasped, his eyes closing, his thick black lashes fanning. He arched backward, causing her hand to press more firmly against his chest and his erection to push more heavily at her, and he moaned again.

It was the most desperate sound she had ever heard. It was also the most sexual.

A sheen of sweat erupted on his face. Brie reached for his waist, gasping as his entire length surged against her belly, and she pressed her mouth to his hot, wet skin, to his rib cage. Excitement exploded in him, in her. But the desperation was even stronger, overwhelming. She could hardly think. She knew he couldn't think clearly now, either.

Instinct prompted her. "I love you, Aidan." She kissed his chest again, then rubbed her mouth there.

"Brianna," he cried, shuddering.

His hard arm went around her. She looked up in time to see his eyes blaze with urgency, and his mouth came down on hers.

Brie cried out; his mouth cut off her cry. She closed her eyes as his lips claimed hers, and exultancy began. *She had wanted his kiss forever!* He bent her backward, but this was better than her dreams. Brie tried to kiss him back. It was almost impossible, and she went still, letting his mouth devour hers. The kiss raged, deep and wet, and Brie began to weep in joy, clinging to him.

He moved her and the back of her thighs hit the bed. She went down on her back and he came down on top of her, his tongue deep in her mouth. Brie moved her hands over his hard, muscular back, arching her hips toward his. He ripped the plaid from his loins and flung it aside.

She stroked past his shoulder blades. He shuddered and gasped. She battled back tears, crying for him, because he was so famished for love and affection.

He broke the kiss. His blue eyes were wide, locking with hers. Brie smiled at him and stroked up to his shoulders, clasping them briefly, and he shuddered again, his eyes closing. When she slid her hand up his neck, he moaned and sank onto the bed beside her, on his back.

The sight of Aidan lying there, arched back into the pillows, the most magnificent man she had ever seen, made her heart slam.

She had to touch him, caress him and give him so much love, as much as she could. Brie raised up and laid her hand on his chest again, and he cried out, seizing it, pressing it hard to the muscles there. *Ye torture me.*

He hadn't spoken aloud. Brie smiled a little at him. "Let me love you, Aidan. Let me heal you." She dropped a kiss on his shoulder and another one on his chest.

"Yer the virgin," he gasped roughly.

Brie was already moving her hand down his tight, cut abdomen. He reared up. As she caressed him, she saw two tears slip free of his lower lashes and track in parallel lines down to his jaw.

He was crying.

She leaned over and kissed his belly, sliding her hand back up to his chest. As she kissed him, she let her love burst forth.

He choked.

She kissed him again, on his throat, and swept her hand down to his navel. She wasn't trying to tease him, but in that instant, she felt a shocking urgency.

He cried out, turning away from her onto his belly. Brie went still, and then the pleasure blinded her.

He was climaxing.

Her own body went wild. It was as if she were having her own release—almost. Instinctively she held him from behind, gasping against her own pleasure, her cheek against his back while he convulsed. He was spinning wildly, euphorically, and she was with him. Then the spinning slowed and he began to float—she began to float. As he went still, she simply held him, loving him so much her chest hurt.

But her body was on fire, throbbing terribly, and she had about five hundred layers of clothes on, which did not help matters.

Trembling, she became aware of the moment he

was coherent. His embarrassment flooded her with its warmth, but only for an instant, because suddenly he shielded his emotions from her.

She bit her lip, flushing. She was the virgin and he had pretty much acted like one. Then, as the disbelief faded, she began to smile. It would be funny if his neediness weren't so tragic. And he was very macho. He wasn't going to be amused at all.

"'Tis nay amusin'." His tone was rough. He rolled over to face her and she glimpsed a still massive erection as he sat up. Desire surged forth. He blocked it partly, but it didn't matter. Her entire body tightened, heated, hollowed. "I am sorry," he said, his face set in hard lines.

"It's okay." She reached for his cheek but he pulled away. He was blushing.

"'Tis nay *okay.*" His stare was direct, even though his cheeks were red. "Yer touch unmans me."

It sure does, she thought, and she smiled. It was sinking in. She was *thrilled.*

"Yer pleased to have taken a boy to yer virginal bed?" he asked softly. But suddenly he seized her belt.

"Very!" she cried, undaunted. And she froze, realizing what he meant to do.

Suddenly he was tugging on her belt. She tensed as he stripped it away fiercely, tossing her plaid aside, as well. "Ye wear too many clothes," he murmured, pulling her sweatshirt off.

Brie lay absolutely still, incapable of speech.

He gripped the tunic and ripped it abruptly from her body.

Brie felt faint, urgency consuming her as he hooked his hands beneath her bra straps, his expression hard.

It crossed her very befuddled mind to ask him not to rip it off, but too late: the straps snapped and her bra vanished. He pressed her shoulders down with one hand, eyes blazing.

There was no point in breathing now. Brie thought she might die soon.

A smile flickered in his hot eyes as he straddled her, his knees were now pushing her jean-clad legs wide.

Brie was whirling in a thick quicksand of desire. She thought she said his name, but she didn't recognize her own voice.

He seemed even more impossibly aroused. He tugged on the snap of her jeans and slid his hand into them, his large palm cupping her beneath her panties. She closed her eyes and gasped, flooded with pleasure and desire, vibrating with the need to soar and peak. But he was very still.

Brie somehow looked up at him.

His expression was strained, his entire body was quivering. His chest rose and fell wildly and sweat dripped off his brow.

He wanted her, she thought, the love surging hard against her chest. "Let me feel it."

"Aye," he said, low and rough. "Aye, I want ye, Brianna." His desire erupted and Brie cried out, shocked by his urgency, his hunger. And then he yanked her boots off, and then her jeans and underwear followed. His desire was pulsating so frantically in her that she raised up, and he caught her face in his hands and kissed her while pushing huge and hot and hard against her soaking flesh. His muscular body shuddered uncontrollably.

Brie lifted her leg to wrap it instinctively around his

hips, kissing him back. He caught her calf to help her. She began to spin as he lifted her other leg. She clawed his back, wanting to scream with the growing urgency, the shocking need, and then she felt him push inside, and she went still.

He slowly filled her. She gasped, shocked by the sensation of their union. She quivered around him, loving him so much it hurt. The pressure he was exerting grew and grew.

He whispered her name.

Brie's eyes flew open. She looked up into his intent, fierce stare, and he smiled at her.

She knew what that smile cost him and her heart leapt in joy.

And watching her, he thrust carefully, deeply, exercising a vast control.

Brie gasped against a brief, slight pain, and then she was full as never before. For one moment she lay utterly still, stunned. She wished to engrave that moment in her memory forever. He also lay still, and as they looked at each other, she knew he was as surprised as she was. Yet somehow, their union was so terribly familiar, like déjà vu.

"Brianna," he whispered again. And she felt him memorizing the feeling of their union, not just of their bodies but the depth of their passion, their caring and connection, their love.

His gaze flickered. He made a harsh sound and began moving inside her, urgently—all control gone. Brie clung and let him take her where he wished. She heard him now, *aye, high above the world,* and the frenzy began. She shattered and sobbed, insane with the indescribable rapture. He cried her name.

Brie wasn't sure how long he swept her through the stars in passion and ecstasy, but it seemed to go on forever—she wanted it to go on forever. She would love him forever, no matter what happened to them. She wept with love and rapture. His mouth moved over her face, her hair. She stroked his hard shoulders. He kissed her softer ones. His rhythm slowed and was even more excruciating. They wept together, this time.

HE OPENED HIS EYES, saw the tent ceiling above and sat bolt upright. *He had fallen asleep.*

Only for a moment, but it hadn't happened in sixty-six years.

He stared down at the woman snuggled against his side, stunned to see her there. Shock turned to horror.

What had he done?

He slid from the bed, throwing on his leine and stepping into his boots, refusing to look at her. He recalled every moment of their time together now. He took his brat and stepped outside into the dark dawn, and then he began to run toward the ridge, past what was left of his camp. Royce and Malcolm stood by a fire near their tent and they turned to stare at him. He didn't care. He ran up the ridge, pounding hard, away from her.

He had not been making love to her. It was impossible.

Deamhanain did not make love.

On the top of the ridge he paused, panting. His mind raced. He saw Brianna as she had been dying on the plain after Moray's attack. He had been terrified she would die, and he had found his healing powers.

He recalled her finding him in the wood. He had

crawled back to her in agony, across miles, so he could die in her arms. He had been so relieved just to look at her again. There had been so much comfort when she had held him.

Last night he had been frantic to soar with her into the light, away from the darkness. He hadn't lusted for power, not once. There had only been a stunning desire. He had sobbed in rapture and relief. There had been *joy.* There had been *delight.*

No! Aidan went still. The wind whipped him, blowing fiercely, indicating that snow was imminent, and he wanted to be chilled thoroughly, so there would be no feeling and never joy.

He could not forget his son!

He could not do this—he could not give her what she wanted. What was happening to him?

Deamhanain did not care about anything other than power, destruction and death. They did not care about anyone except themselves and they did not heal. They did not have friends or lovers; they had objects and victims, whom they used and destroyed. They did not know the meaning of joy. They only knew the meaning of pain, cruelty and death.

He turned and stared down the ridge at his black tent as the gray sky shifted, but didn't lighten. The first snowflakes fell.

There had been so much joy.

In that moment, he knew he had made a colossal mistake, one that threatened his entire existence and his very life.

He breathed hard.

He hated the gods for taking Ian, and he would never forgive them. He would never return to Iona and the Brotherhood. He was the son of a deamhan. He didn't want or need her love or her friendship. She could touch him a thousand times—no, a million—and they could *fuck* again, but he was filled with evil. He needed power, not pleasure, not love and not joy.

He only wanted revenge for Ian.

He must never forget that.

His temples pounded in pain. His heart hurt him.

He had spent sixty-six years in a self-imposed exile. Taking whores and courtesans to bed did not count, as he had not allowed them their humanity. Passing his servants in the hall did not count, as they lived in terror of him. His mercenaries and the villagers also feared him and avoided him. He had lived alone for a reason—it was his vengeance against the gods—and it had kept him inhuman and ruthless.

Yet somehow, in the past few very short days, after long, endless decades of isolation, he had rescued her, healed her and taken her to bed as if he had come to have a concern for her, as if they were lovers, as if they were friends.

But that concern was now over. He would never touch her again, much less bed her. There would be no more long looks and smiles. Last night had been an exception, and it would never happen again. She was his bridge to Ian. That was all.

He roared into the night. He roared again, in frustration and rage and, maybe, in grief. The wolves began coming from the nearby forest. They did not join him; they sat waiting, by the trees.

When his throat was sore, he quieted, but he was not soothed. He was in the midst of a great war, and Moray already knew she was his weakness. Moray might even know she was a vital link to his son. She had almost died because of his war. He had no doubt that Moray would use her again, if he could. And that was all the more reason to take power, as a deamhan should.

Then he would hunt.

The vicious determination arose. The murderous fury crept over him. It was time to end this war, one way or another, and he must do so today. As he moved his mind into the perfect focus of a hunter, the wolves knew, standing one by one. They began to howl.

Their long, lustful cries filled the night.

THE WOLVES AWOKE HER.

For one moment, Brie didn't move, buried under too many covers to count. As her mind awoke, she realized she was deliciously naked—and that Aidan had just spent hours making love to her.

Her heart leapt. She peered through the darkness at his side of the bed, but it was empty.

Slowly she sat up. Tears began, but they were tears of happiness. Her heart was explosive, so much so that she had to cover it with her hand. She had loved him before; she loved him madly now.

Brie prayed that their lovemaking had finally healed him.

The wolves had quieted. Surely Aidan wasn't with them.

She groped the bed, but all of her clothes were on the floor. He had left a single taper burning, so she slipped to the ground, shivering, and found her black plaid, which she wrapped around herself like a blanket. She was hopeful, but she reined herself in. He was a complicated man who had lived with a terrible tragedy for decades. One night might not miraculously redeem him.

But his every touch had been drenched in emotion.

Brianna stepped into her fur-lined boots, went to the tent flap and lifted it. Outside, it had begun to snow heavily. Traveling would be hell. Maybe he'd turn the rest of his men away from Inverness and order them to go home. That would be a huge relief and one problem solved, for now.

Then she saw him approaching, his strides long and hard.

It was a shadowy, gray dawn, and Brie couldn't see his face until he reached her. He wasn't smiling. He glanced from her eyes to her plaid-cocooned body, and she was pretty sure he looked right through the wool. "Aidan?"

"Ye'll freeze," he said brusquely.

She smiled uncertainly and hopefully at him. Couldn't he smile back at her? "Good morning," she whispered.

He nodded shortly. "'Twill snow most of the day."

She bit her lip. Was he going to ignore what they'd spent hours doing? "Are you coming inside?" A snowy day like this cried out for more lovemaking; it would be perfect if the day was spent together in his bed.

"Aye, for a moment." He walked past her.

Brie followed him inside. He put on his sword belt, his back to her. She tensed. He was shielding his emotions, but she was pretty sure she knew what he intended. "You're hunting."

He didn't answer, but he turned and stared at her, his expression hard and set. "Ye should dress."

"Are you hunting as the Wolf, or are you going like that?" she managed, an ice-cold fear consuming her.

"I'll hunt from the tower at Awe," he said tersely. "With Moray in Alba, in this time, I will find him. Unless he shows himself and finds me *first*."

Brie was afraid for him. She didn't want him to go. Worse, she desperately wanted to talk about last night. She wanted him to hug her and smile at her, just once.

His face seemed to tighten.

She was pretty certain he was reading her mind. He had been conscienceless in that regard since meeting her, so why would it change now? "Last night was wonderful," she whispered.

He made a harsh sound. "I'm glad yer pleased." He turned his back to her and removed his shortsword, then began inspecting the blade.

Brie hugged herself. "You don't seem pleased."

He sheathed the sword and poured red wine into a mug. "I was pleased enough."

He was so cold, so distant, so uncaring. "Aidan? Can we talk about last night?"

He whirled. "I dinna wish to hurt ye, but I canna give ye what ye really want. Ye can go to Seoc for that—or another man. Last night was a mistake, Brianna."

She was shocked.

"I need power, not sex," he added flatly.

"Last night was wonderful," she gasped. "Don't do this."

"What do ye think Moray is doin', even now?" he demanded harshly.

Brie sat down hard on the edge of the bed. Was he rejecting her? Or did he mean that their worst enemy had a part of the Duisean, and was probably enhancing all of his evil power with even more life-taking, while they had been making love? Still, that didn't excuse Aidan's cold behavior. She trembled. He seemed entirely unmoved by their affair, and his behavior seemed very much a rejection. "Can you admit that something special began for us last night?"

His gaze was searing. "Last night was an ending—not a beginning."

Brie covered her mouth with her hands. Last night had meant everything for her—but it had been her first time. He was a man of vast experience. He'd had many, many women. She became terribly uncertain. He had seemed as moved as she was, as emotional, but what did she know?

She swallowed. "This friendship we have, this attraction that's between us...I thought it was a big deal, but it's not, is it?"

He slowly set his wineglass down, his back still half turned to her. He glanced at her briefly and looked away. "I dinna ken yer meanin'."

She hugged herself. His brief look up had been enough for their eyes to meet. "I just realized you've had hundreds of women, and what happened last night might be pretty run-of-the-mill."

He stared at the wine bottle and glasses on the small desk.

He wasn't going to respond? "You don't have to be so distant. I know a little about men, through my friends. They can be pretty cold when they're done with a woman." She choked again. This really hurt. She had to get perspective. "It's okay. I really didn't expect anything long-term. I get it. You're done. It was a one-night thing. I won't bug you again."

"Good." He finally lifted his brilliant blue gaze to hers. "Ye shouldna cry. Yer a grown woman an' ye wanted pleasure. Ye'll find yer grand love with another man."

She reminded herself that she had no right to be hurt. Hadn't she known that sleeping with him would be emotionally dangerous? Hadn't she known that while she loved him, he didn't love her, and that the next day she'd want more than he could give?

But she was incapacitated with hurt. A smart, modern woman with an ounce of pride would have held her head high and moved on. Instead, she shook her head. "No," she said very firmly.

She would love him forever, no matter what happened to him, to them.

His eyes widened. "I must go. The Masters can protect ye now. They'll take ye to Iona. When I vanquish Moray, they'll see ye back to yer time."

It was *over?* Just like that?

Brie was disbelieving.

"Dinna look at me and dinna cry," he said harshly.

She didn't move. There was so much tension in the tent, Brie was pretty sure it was the result of his wanting to get away from her, and this very uncomfortable next-morning moment. At last she really understood the pain of rejection.

But she had to rise above her own feelings. He was in danger. His life and his soul were on the line. She had gone back in time to redeem him, not to fall in love with him.

She was a Rose. Rose women never quit.

She wanted to cry. Instead she inhaled. "Is there any way I can convince you to hunt with the other Masters? You've already faced Moray alone—twice—and it didn't work out very well."

His mouth curled dangerously. "I willna hunt with the brethren, Brianna, and they willna hunt with me."

Brie was ready to dispute that when Aidan suddenly stiffened. Brie was briefly stunned by white power before the tent flap lifted. What was this? she wondered, turning to look at the tent's entrance.

The golden Highlander who looked like Matthew McConaughey stepped inside, nodding at them. If he knew he was interrupting a very tense, awkward and private moment, he did not show it.

"I will have a word with Aidan now, Lady Brianna," he said.

Brie was completely distracted. His tone was one of pure authority and she knew he was never disputed. His stature was as commanding, and there was simply no mistaking the holy power that cloaked him. *He was close to the gods, closer than the other Masters.* "Who are you?" she asked. More importantly, what did he want?

His mouth curved. His amazing green eyes were warm and friendly and filled with good humor. "The Abbot of Iona an' yer friend." He added, "Sometimes the Masters accept my suggestions. I manage the Brotherhood fer the gods."

Brie got it. He was commander in chief.

"Ye can call me MacNeil," he said softly, his gaze unwavering.

As overwhelmed as she was by his power, it was really hard not to notice what an incredible hunk he was. Unlike some of the Masters, like Royce and Guy, he didn't have that supermacho, medieval aura. This man was undoubtedly well-traveled, sophisticated and reasonable.

He smiled at her. "My life is nay an easy task."

Brie smiled back. "I'll bet."

And she felt Aidan's anger. She turned. He had crossed his arms across his chest so tightly his biceps bulged. His eyes blazed. Brie now thought about his dispute with the abbot.

MacNeil turned. *"Hallo a Aidan,"* he said softly. "Yer a sight for my sore eyes."

Aidan said harshly, "I dinna care."

Brie tensed in dismay. She had felt MacNeil's love for Aidan, and it had been paternal. "Do you want me to leave?" she asked.

"Ye should stay," MacNeil said, sending her another warm smile. He spoke with authority, but posed a question. "Aidan, will ye come with me to Iona?"

"I will never come with ye to Iona," Aidan said savagely.

MacNeil did not seem disturbed. "Ye healed Brianna with a power only the gods can give. Ye rescued her several times. I believe ye spent last night warmin' her bed in a very mortal way. Ye can deny it, but the facts speak loudly. Lad, ye'll never finish the fall."

"Then I will remain half deamhan, an evil that leaves his victims alive an' a man who enjoys mortal desire. I willna go back to the Brotherhood. Damn ye all to hell!"

Brie gasped. "Aidan, he is your friend, no matter what happened," she tried.

He looked at her, flushing. "Ye think a night in my bed gives ye any rights? It doesna!" He pointed at MacNeil, his hand shaking. "My son was murdered, his body not even in the ground but stolen, lost in time, an' he tells me the Ancients walk in mystery and that my son's Fate was written?"

"I canna change what's written," MacNeil said seriously and softly. "Ye can blame me fer acceptin' Fate, but I dinna write his death—nor did I see it. But I have seen her." He nodded at Brianna, who straightened in surprise.

"'Tis time for ye to clear yer head, Aidan," MacNeil continued. "'Tis more than time fer ye to listen to yer heart, yer soul, lad. Ye have grieved and raged at us all long enough. 'Tis time fer ye to come back."

"I will avenge my son," Aidan said, his eyes blazing. "And I will vanquish my own deamhan father. Then I go to Awe to live out my life, half in and half out of the deamhan world. To hell with yer damned gods." He strode from the tent with so much angry force that the tent walls shuddered even though he did not touch them.

Brie whirled in dismay. "Please don't let him hunt Moray alone! He doesn't have enough power!"

"He has his Fate as well, Lady Brianna," MacNeil said.

"Is his Fate hanging?"

MacNeil hesitated. "They're not lies, Lady Brianna. Yer books speak the truth."

Brie went still. "Are you referring to my history books?"

"Aye." He did not smile now. "Aidan may hate the gods but they dinna hate him, in spite of all he has done. I have seen ye comin' to save our poor Aidan. Dinna give up now."

"You just said my history books are right. If that's the case, he will hang! So how can I save him?"

He touched her and his power flowed through her, at once healing and strengthening, erasing her uncertainty and doubts. “He will only hang if he chooses to die. Lass, yer here fer a great reason.”

Brie cried out, “Is that a riddle? I hate riddles!”

“I dinna have all the answers, lass.” Then he grinned. “Just some of them.”

CHAPTER FOURTEEN

HE WILL ONLY HANG IF HE CHOOSES TO DIE.

Having dressed, Brie stepped outside of the tent. It was snowing heavily now and the day was thick and gray. Why would Aidan choose to die? He had fought his way back to her as the Wolf. Clearly, he had been determined to live. McNeil's words were not helpful and they felt distinctly ominous, as if some new event would make him lose his will to live. Brie had a terrible inkling and she prayed she was wrong. But MacNeil had confirmed what she already believed. She was there to save Aidan, whether he wanted her there or not.

She saw that the remaining Highlanders had departed from the camp, along with all their equipment and pack animals. Only one other tent was left on the plain other than Aidan's. A fire roared before it in spite of the snow, and Brie saw Will tending it, red-faced and looking miserable. She hurried over to him, wishing for gloves and a hat.

"Our master's gone," Will told her. "But I'm to attend yer every need."

Brie nodded, worried to death about Aidan now. Allie stepped out of the adjacent tent, followed by Tabby and Claire, who hung back as Brie's cousin and best friend rushed to her. Allie hugged Brie, and then Tabby took her hand. "Are you all right?" Tabby asked in a low voice.

Obviously they knew what she'd been doing last night. "I'm fine," she said, but it felt like an utter lie and she blushed. Unlike Allie, she was pretty modest when it came to the subject of sex. Tabby was almost as reticent.

Allie slid her arm around her. Her eyes sparked with excitement. "Brie, you spent the night with Aidan and he didn't take power from you! Do you know what this means?"

Brie shook her head to stop Allie's enthusiasm. She knew what Allie was thinking. "Allie, don't. He's not at all happy today. And I'm hurt, because foolishly, in spite of how smart I am, I really thought he cared about me. But we're not friends, and last night will never happen again. He made that really clear." Brie hoped they wouldn't guess how brutally she was hurt.

"He has to care," Allie cried. "Why else bother with you at all? He saved you, protected you, healed you and made love to you." She grinned. "Did I tell you… or what?"

Brie did not want to think about how stunning sex with a superpowered Highlander was. "It just happened and it was meaningless, at least for him. I'm afraid I was the only one who was making love. But it's okay. I can handle it. I still love him and I have to try to save him." She simply had to refocus. "I mean, I am here to redeem him, not to be his soul mate forever."

"You don't know that," Allie said, impossibly upbeat as always.

"I haven't been optimistic about Aidan, and I can't

forgive him for the children at Elgin, but I am almost inclined to agree with Allie." Tabby squeezed her hand. "Last night certainly seems like a monumental turning point. Maybe Aidan can be saved, after all, by you, Brie."

"That's the plan," Brie said, hoping to sound flip.

Tabby didn't release her hand. "I hate seeing you so hurt! I'll tell you a secret. With Guy, there was so much heartache and pain before there was true love."

Brie shook her head. "Don't, Tabby. Don't give me hope. Not now, not today."

"These medieval machos can be total jerks," Allie said. "Royce can still be a royal pain! Aidan is on your hook, Brie, and he's squirming, that's all. He is fighting you tooth and nail, but we all know no one can fight Fate."

The one thing Brie was sure of was that she was not Aidan's Fate. "Speaking of Fate, Aidan has gone to hunt Moray. I am sick with worry for him. I have to ask you both for a huge favor. Please, send Royce and Guy after him to help him. He can't face Moray alone again."

"No problem," Allie said cheerfully. "However, Aidan has gone to Awe. I know, because Royce lurked. He hunts from the tower there."

"We have to go to Awe," Brie said instantly.

Allie took her hand. "Honey, we've been waiting for you."

"Tabby has to come with us, though." Brie looked at her.

"What is it?" her cousin asked softly.

"I was hoping," Brie said, "that you'd help us find Ian and speak with him."

Tabby began to smile. "Yes, Brie, we can have a séance."

"WHERE ARE WE?" SAM ASKED in a hushed whisper. She was in awe as she stared through the swiftly falling snow at the sparkling lake, which was surrounded by the forested Highland mountains. In the distance, a castle seemed to emerge from its gleaming waters. Sam lifted binoculars and saw that she was right. Clad in camouflage, a skullcap and army boots, she was too overcome by where she was to even notice the cold.

Nick was staring at the small LCD screen of the Geographic Locater Device he carried in his palm. The size of a Blackberry, it would tell them exactly where they were. He was dressed exactly as she was, right up to the skullcap and camouflage vest, and they both carried backpacks filled with survival gear and weapons. The rifle he had slung over his arm was loaded with tranquilizing darts,.not bullets. His nose red, he grinned, looking up. "That, kiddo, is Castle Awe."

Sam glanced again through the binoculars. The red castle that seemed to float upon the shimmering silver lake and the falling snow made her feel as though she was looking into a picturesque glass ball. But that castle was real, and they were in the Highlands.

HCU had a huge case file on the Wolf of Awe. She'd had no idea that the Historical Crimes Unit of CDA was as advanced and efficient as it was. It had been gathering data on good and evil for over two centuries, thank God. No, thank Nick Forrester, who had been running HCU for as long as anyone could remember. The Wolf had abducted Brie, and without that file, rescuing her would be like finding a needle in a haystack. "What year did we land in?" she asked cautiously.

"That I don't know. It ain't 2008," Nick said, sounding damned pleased. But on the bridge that spanned the lake, from castle to shore, Sam saw a band of horses and riders. She and Nick had been walking toward the loch for about an hour, and there hadn't been a single road or telephone pole, nor the sound of a car or an overhead airplane. Sam handed Nick the binoculars. "Riders," she said. "It's hard to tell even with the bi's, but I think they're carrying frigging swords."

Nick grinned and lifted the glasses. Sam knew her boss was enjoying himself. He wasn't as bad as she'd first thought. He was certainly fearless, if bossy. She was a control freak herself, so as long as he understood that when push came to shove, she'd make her own decisions, they'd get along just fine. Three days had passed since Brie's abduction. In spite of her having been recruited, hired and trained almost overnight, Nick hadn't explained how he time-traveled. He really didn't have to.

Nick Forrester wasn't what he appeared to be. He was just as different from everybody else as the Rose women were.

Sam didn't mind. The more the merrier. She'd take anything she could get to help destroy the evil that preyed on them all.

He clasped her shoulder, his blue gaze brilliant. "Let's go. There's only one way to find out if we nailed the trip."

Sam nodded. The case file on the Wolf of Awe ended in the fall of 1502. All the sightings of him after the millennium had been traced to years prior to that date. According to the file, he'd been hanged for treason. History confirmed it.

But that made no sense, because he could vanish into the past or the future anytime he chose to. Unless, of course, someone or something had managed to destroy his powers, which seemed to be the case.

Nick had wanted to leap back to 1502, but he hadn't explained why. Logic dictated that the Wolf of Awe could have come from any year after 1436—the year he'd first destroyed Innocence. Her boss was keeping secrets. It was annoying, but she was beginning to trust him. For some reason, he had a clue—or a sixth sense—that told him Aidan had taken Brie to that year.

They began trekking along the shore. In a few hours, as long as the snow didn't get worse, they would be at Castle Awe.

IT ALMOST FELT LIKE COMING HOME, Brie thought, as she followed everyone inside Awe's great hall. Both huge hearths contained blazing fires, and Brie started removing her wet plaid, thrilled to be back at Awe. The great room hadn't changed. It was huge and sparsely furnished, but it felt welcoming, anyway. Servants were covering the trestle table with platters of hot food. She couldn't recall the last time she'd really eaten.

But two men who were dressed like Englishmen were at the table, speaking with Malcolm, Guy and Royce. Everyone was so serious that Brie knew the men had brought trouble.

Malcolm looked across the great room at Claire.

Brie turned. "What do they want?"

Claire hesitated. "They have a summons for Aidan, but Aidan has left orders that he is not to be disturbed."

Brie saw the Englishmen arguing with Malcolm, and then the two men crossed the hall, passing her as they left. Uneasily, she said, "What kind of summons, Claire?" But she already knew.

"He's been summoned to Urquhart."

Urquhart was where Aidan had been hanged. "By Frasier?" Brie asked, her stomach churning.

"It's a royal summons," Claire said, grimacing. "But the king is at Stirling, and someone like Frasier will be there to receive Aidan."

Brie trembled. "He's not going," she said firmly. She would *not* let him go.

Claire's green eyes widened. "Brie, this is 1502. We do not refuse our king. I know you're worried about Aidan hanging, but the refusal of royal will can also be labeled treason."

"But Aidan is already a traitor," Brie said. "He's fought Frasier and the royal armies. He has to stay far from Urquhart!"

Claire took her arm. "I'm the last person to tell you to simply accept this. Do what you feel you have to do. I'll help, and so will Malcolm."

Brie stared at her. In that moment, she had the feeling that Claire really believed that Aidan was meant to hang and that she could not change his fate. She hugged herself uneasily.

Lust for power flooded her.

Brie gasped as the shocking lust swept through her body, swelling it, arousing it impossibly. The power began to course through her veins, giving her impossible strength, and she was savagely elated. She cried out, stunned by the bestial euphoria, the sense of near invincibility.

Someone held her up.

Brie closed her eyes, unable to detach herself from the power roaring in her veins, the urge to use her power to destroy Moray blinding and frenzied. She *could* destroy him now, for nothing and no one could stop her.

"Brie, what is it?" Allie cried.

Aidan was in the throes of taking power, Brie managed to think. She opened her eyes. Royce held her upright, but Allie, Tabby and Claire encircled her, and Allie held her hand tightly.

"It's Aidan," she said, and her stomach lurched, making her feel sick. He had so much power he could easily break down his own castle walls.

"Let me go," she gasped, suddenly enraged.

She staggered through the hall and to the stairway. More power swept through her and she crashed into the wall. The power blinded her this time and she stood still, as wave after wave of power and rapture hit her, stars exploding everywhere. But he still wanted more....

She fought through the thick, sexual waves, the spinning frenzy, the hot, wet euphoria, as if swimming upstream. She reached the landing, breathing hard, and an even greater wave smashed into her, power and rapture becoming one. She fell this time, and wept in ecstasy.

Brie lay on the stone floor, sobbing in pleasure, the power endless now, streaming through her. And then the rapture faded, leaving nothing but the sense of absolute and savage euphoria.

She lay very still. Had Aidan become invincible? Or did he simply think himself invincible?

Booted steps sounded.

Brie looked up and saw Aidan emerging from the chamber. His glittering gaze swept her and he faltered.

Brie pushed to sit up, and their gazes locked.

She reminded herself that he needed power if he

was ever going to survive and defeat Moray. She said softly, "How could you?"

"Ye should be on Iona," he snarled.

Brie shook her head, distraught. "Is anyone alive?" And she knew it was an accusation.

He flushed. "They're all alive," he said, his tone low and dangerous. "I'm half deamhan, remember?"

"I think I hate you," she whispered.

He strode past her.

Brie began to cry. She stumbled to her feet and to the doorway. Shocked, she stared at the three women lying unmoving on the bed. They were fully dressed. No one had a garment askew or hair astray. The bed was perfectly made up.

She opened her mind to the room and the women. The women were alive. The room felt still, clean and oddly chaste.

Brie gasped, shuddered and reached for the door, holding herself upright. She was beyond exhaustion and, unlike Aidan, she wasn't filled with power. Sharing the experience of taking so much life made her feel shaky and weak. She felt sick. She was not certain of what had happened in this room. It almost felt as if he had taken power without touching or using anyone.

But why would he do that?

He saved you, protected you, healed you and made love to you.

Brie reminded herself that Aidan didn't love her—not at all. He could not have rejected her that morning so callously if he did.

"I'll heal them," Allie said.

Brie saw Allie standing on the threshold with Royce, their expressions grim. She crossed her arms, wanting to defend Aidan, as Allie went to the women to heal them. Her hands on one, Allie glanced at Brie. "He didn't have sex." She gave Brie an I-told-you-so look and focused on the blonde she was healing.

Brie found a chair. She had never been more relieved. So much for refocusing and being a pro. She was still in love. And what the hell did Aidan's behavior mean?

"Ah, lass, he's fond of ye," Royce said.

She looked at him.

"I canna lurk on Aidan, he blocks me. But I dinna have to. 'Tis evident."

She was afraid to believe it, especially after being so hurt by him that morning. "Does he have enough power to destroy Moray?"

"I dinna ken."

"Where is he?" But even as she spoke, her senses flew to Aidan's, and she realized he was nearby. She felt his savage, predatory intention.

"He's in the tower, where he hunts."

He was safe for now, she thought. "And when he finds Moray? Can you please go with him? He needs backup. I don't care how powerful he has become."

Royce nodded and walked out. The other women had gotten up and were leaving, looking no worse for wear. Allie came to stand beside Brie. "Are you okay?"

Brie hesitated. "I don't ever want to feel that kind of lust again."

Allie gave her a look. "I can't imagine what the lust for life feels like, but...*La Puissance* is pretty darned amazing."

Brie was pretty sure she knew what Allie referred

to. She felt herself blush. "Do you mean the rapture that comes from so much power?"

She nodded and grinned guiltily. "It's all forbidden. Masters do not take power unless they're in mortal danger, and usually they don't need to—they're so superstrong that they can fight anything. But we dabbled in it. Royce was desperate for my healing power and boy, with sex factored in, what a rush!"

"I was fine with the good, old-fashioned version," Brie said tersely. She did not want to recall last night.

"They say it can be addictive, like a drug. It's why once a Master falls, he usually turns all the way. They start lusting for that power and that rapture…" Allie shrugged.

Brie wondered where that would leave Aidan, if he ever was redeemed.

Allie touched her. "He leaves his victims alive. But he may always fight the urge to take power, the lust for it."

"I'll worry about that later," Brie said tersely.

"Good idea. Tabby's setting up for the séance."

"Right now?" The summons to Urquhart was hanging over their heads, no matter how resolved Brie was to stop Aidan from heeding it.

Allie nodded. "I don't think we should delay. Royce and I have discussed it with Malcolm and Claire. We think you're right. Aidan needs to speak with his son. We think it could set him free and bring him back to us."

He'll die if he chooses to die. Brie hugged her hard, recalling MacNeil's cryptic words. "Let's pray first," she said.

BRIE PUSHED OPEN THE DOOR TO Aidan's bedroom and slipped inside. Tabby had asked for an item of Aidan's for the séance, and Brie had given her the black plaid she'd been wearing. She was tired of being so swaddled up, anyway. Tabby had also asked her to find something of Ian's.

She had never been in Aidan's chamber before. The air within was charged with his testosterone and his authority. She closed the door behind her and glanced carefully around.

The room was barren and cold. Pillar candles were on the mantel, but nothing else. She glanced at the bedroom's only table. A pitcher was there and a single mug. One chair was beside it, without upholstery or even a pillow. It did not look comfortable. She looked at the bed, with only two pillows, blankets and a fur throw. His bedchamber was not a personal retreat; it was neither warm nor welcoming. It was as bleak as the rest of his life.

Why couldn't he let her love him?

Brie turned. The only other piece of furniture inside was a handsome, scarred and iron-bound chest at the foot of the bed. Brie went to it and opened it. She saw a folded black plaid, and she removed it. Her eyes widened.

What on earth?

Brie removed a very expensive, very modern man's black leather jacket with a Gucci label. It was a man's—it was worn—it was Aidan's.

She felt him all over the leather and thought of him as she'd first met him, when he had not been tormented and dark. He'd been in his medieval Highland garb that day, but it didn't matter. He'd been protective of her, kind to and caring of Allie and he'd flirted lightly with Sam. She knew he'd worn this jacket then, before Ian's murder, when he'd walked in the light of the gods, when he'd been carefree and happy, a man with friends, family, a clan.

She realized she was hugging the soft, sensuous leather.

That had been long ago. Even though she was determined to see him in it again, she set the jacket aside. She rummaged through the chest and finally found a pair of very tiny baby shoes. They were pointy and embroidered, and must have been worn by Ian when he was a toddler.

Tabby, Allie and Claire were waiting for her in her bedchamber. All the castle rooms were dark, due to the lack of any kind of modern lighting and the small or glazed glass windows, but it was ablaze with candles and filled with heady, exotic fragrances. Brie thought she smelled vanilla and lilies amongst the brew. Tabby had used chalk or something like it to draw odd symbols on the stone floor, including the large circle where the women were already sitting. She had strewn petals and herbs about the pattern, which Brie didn't recognize. A jagged line went through the circle but it was not connected, although it was obvious it should be.

Each woman sat an equal distance from one another, and it was clear Brie should sit between Tabby and Claire. She handed Tabby the shoes. Aidan's plaid was before Tabby's crossed legs and she set the shoes beside it. Brie sank down and met Allie's excited gaze. "If Sam were here, it would almost be like old times," Allie said, but then she leaned over to take Claire's hand. "I'm so glad you're one of us now."

Claire smiled, but didn't seem as excited. Brie had already decided Claire had a serious nature, which was fine by her. Not everyone could be eternally optimistic and endlessly exuberant like Allie.

Tabby had the Book before her, and she opened it and ran her hand over the adjoining pages. Brie whispered, "It used to take you days to find a spell."

Tabby smiled at her. "My guides are very strong now." She murmured a supplication to the gods for guidance in Gaelic, which Brie was pleased to recognize. Some things could not and would not ever change, and that included the bond between them.

Without having to be told, they reached for each other's hands. Brie thought about the power each woman had brought to the room, and as she did so, Tabby began murmuring her spell. Brie felt the air shift and lift and swell with the power of the Rose women.

She looked at Allie, who was not a Rose, although Brie would bet anything she had holy DNA somewhere in her family tree. How else could she be such a powerful healer? Yet she was sitting there in medieval times in skinny jeans, a leather jacket and Jimmy Choos. And Claire was the daughter of a Master. Just then, she looked like a well-to-do, suburban trophy wife, never mind the long tunic she wore over her modern clothes.

But Tabby looked like a medieval sorceress in her long, velvet gown, her gold girdle and headdress. Her murmurs increased, becoming louder and urgent, and she spoke more swiftly. Brie saw that her eyes were closed and she had gone into a trance, as she had hundreds of times before. Claire's eyes were closed, too. Brie glanced at Allie and they shared a silent look. Brie could almost hear Allie's enthusiastic thoughts. *We'll do this!*

"He's coming," Tabby said suddenly, and she opened her eyes.

Brie saw that Tabby was still in a trance. She sat stiffly, her complexion was waxy and her eyes glowed. Brie glanced at the door and everyone else did, too, except for Tabby, who sat as still as a statue, staring directly ahead.

Then Brie turned and looked across the room, toward the north wall. Ian was standing there. She managed not to cry out in excitement.

He started to speak and she heard him, as clear as day. But he was speaking Gaelic!

"He wants to speak to Aidan," Tabby said softly, her gaze trained on the little boy.

Allie said, "Should we get Aidan?"

Tabby shook her head. "Please don't move. He is upset and he might leave us."

Brie couldn't stop herself. "Ian, can you speak in English?" she asked, her heart thundering.

He looked at her and began speaking in a rush. "Where is my father? I want to come home!" he cried desperately.

For an instant, Brie froze. Heartbroken, she looked at Tabby, but Tabby remained in her trance. She looked desperately at Allie. *What are we going to do? He can't come home!*

Allie shook her head, telling her not to do anything.

Tabby, still in a trance, said, "Do you have a message for your father?"

"Tell him to come and get me! I'm in New York," Ian cried.

His little soul was in New York? What did that mean? Tears fell. Brie would have wiped them, but she was clutching Tabby's and Claire's hands and she was afraid to let go.

"Let me set you free, Ian," Tabby murmured. She began chanting softly again, words Brie didn't completely understand. But she was invoking the great Kaitha, the goddess of mercy, healing and death.

Ian began shaking his head mutinously. "I want Papa! I want to come home. Tell him to rescue me." He was angry and annoyed now. He reminded her so much of his father.

Ian didn't know that he was dead and he thought he could come home. Brie fought not to cry.

Tabby kept murmuring.

Ian began to fade.

Brie couldn't stand it. "Ian, you have a new home now, a wonderful place filled with warmth and light where the gods live, where all your ancestors are!"

He was the barest apparition, and his next words were really hard to hear. Brie was certain she had misheard them. "I'm not dead." And he was gone.

Brie cried out, and looked at Allie and Claire. "What did he just say?"

"He said he wasn't dead," Claire said. "Unless he said, 'I'm dead.'"

"I thought he said he wasn't dead, too," Allie gasped, her brown eyes huge.

Tabby said softly, "He is alive."

Brie saw the color returning to Tabby's waxen face. The odd glow left her eyes and Tabby blinked as her body relaxed. Then her golden eyes widened. "We did it!"

Brie released Claire's and Tabby's hands, standing. "You just said Ian is alive."

Everyone got up, Tabby looking surprised and standing more slowly. “I did?”

“You don’t remember?” Brie cried.

“Brie, I was in a deep trance. I only know that Ian was here. What happened?” She glanced at everyone.

“He seems to think he’s still alive,” Allie said. “And you just confirmed it.”

Tabby was stunned.

Brie confronted her, shaken to the core of her being—the depths of her soul. “I’ve seen you in trances hundreds of times. Sometimes your spells work, sometimes nothing happens or sometimes the opposite happens. Sometimes your guides give you great advice, and sometimes they have sent us into traps and we’ve barely avoided death!”

Allie interjected, “That was then and this is now. Tabby is really powerful, Brie.”

Brie whirled, aware she was becoming hysterical. “So she’s always right? Her spells always work and her guides never screw up?”

Tabby touched her. “I know you’re upset.”

“Upset?” she cried. “Upset doesn’t even come close!”

“I’m usually right,” Tabby whispered. But she was stricken, and Brie knew she was afraid that this time she was wrong.

“How could he be alive? I mean, do the math,” Brie cried.

Claire said, “He should be seventy-five years old, not nine.”

They all exchanged confused glances.

Brie moaned. “What am I going to tell Aidan? Am I going to tell him we had a séance, we spoke with Ian and that maybe his son is alive and wants to come home? No, wait! I'll tell him we think he's alive but we're not sure." She started to cry.

"Ghosts often think they're alive," Tabby finally said tersely.

"Your guides said he's alive!" Brie screamed.

Tabby paled.

Brie covered her face with her hands and gave in to her grief and powerlessness, and now, even rage. Aidan was in enough anguish, and he must never know what had happened.

Her friends gathered and held her close.

CHAPTER FIFTEEN

THE HUNT HAD BEGUN ONLY A FEW hours ago. He was so entirely focused on sifting through time and space and sorting through all the evil he encountered that when he first felt a disturbance in the tower, he ignored it.

In a small village in the far north of Caithness, evil was stalking an entire family. But it was not Moray, and Aidan moved even farther north to Old Wick, scenting another great evil gathering.

The energy in the tower room changed, a ripple moving through the air.

His power shifted in response, his focus torn from Old Wick.

Aidan blinked. The moment his lashes fluttered open, he saw the stone walls surrounding him and was confused. He never lost his way during a hunt. Then he stiffened, sensing an intrusion.

He glanced toward the door and saw his small son standing there.

He cried out, incredulous. As always, there was so much joy and so much pain. But the moment he leapt to his feet, Ian opened his mouth to speak and vanished.

"Ian!" Aidan roared. But the ghost was gone.

Someone began rattling thc barred door, but he

ignored it. Ian had never tried to come to him when Aidan was hunting. What did this mean?

"Aidan! Aidan! Are you all right?"

He somehow heard Brianna, but he did not want her near now. Would he ever learn what Ian wished to say? She was shaking the door latch, but he had bolted the door from within. Very few people would be barred by the bolt, but she was one of them.

Then he realized she was in great distress, as much as he was, and it wasn't because of how he had hurt her that morning. Something else was hurting her now, terribly.

He tore the door off its hinges.

She stood there in her jeans and the dragon sweatshirt, crying. Even more alarmed, he dove deeply into her mind. "Brianna, what happened?"

"I'm fine. Are you okay?" She gazed worriedly up at him.

She had seen Ian—and his child was the cause of her distress. "Ye've seen my son and yer aggrieved because of it!"

"Please don't read my mind now," she begged, clutching his arms. "Just trust me!"

Those words only alarmed him further and he went deeper into her mind. He saw her and the three other women, all holding hands, Lady Tabitha apparently under a spell. Then he saw Ian speaking with them in the candlelit chamber. He cried out, "What is a séance? What did ye do? Did ye speak with Ian?"

She nodded. "A séance is an attempt to bring forth the dead."

She was afraid to tell him something. "What happened?"

She inhaled harshly, pulling away from him. "Let's get out of the hall," she said, glancing away from him now.

She intended to deceive him. He didn't have to lurk in order to know that. He saw it in the way she avoided meeting his gaze. He followed her into his bedchamber, incredulous. Brianna was the most honest person he knew. "Ye'll tell me everything."

She faced him, wringing her hands. "I'm going to protect you," she whispered, her gaze unwavering and strong. "You don't need to know everything, Aidan. I am asking you to have faith in *me*. Trust *me*."

She wished to protect him? Something terrible had happened in that séance, he thought. He stared, searching her agonized eyes. He did trust her—oddly, there was no one he trusted more. But this was not about trust. He had every right to know what had happened at the séance. What was she hiding?

She understood. "Please, don't!"

He lurked ruthlessly now and saw Ian speaking to the women, but he could not hear him. His frustration overcame him. "What did he say?"

Brianna started shaking her head. "It doesn't matter." She reached for him, to comfort him.

He jerked away, and suddenly a succinct thought crystallized in Brie's mind. *He has to be dead...he just doesn't know it.*

Aidan cried out, shocked. "What do ye mean, *he has to be dead?* Ian *is* dead. I just saw his ghost!"

Brianna blanched, and two tears slipped down her cheeks. She took his hand and he let her, too furious to care. She wet her lips and said hoarsely, "Ian doesn't seem to know that he's dead."

He became still.

"It's not that unusual, really, for a soul to be confused. It would explain why he hasn't left this realm and why he keeps haunting you."

Her thoughts echoed terribly in his mind while he tried to comprehend that his son believed he was still alive. "What do ye refuse to tell me?" he asked slowly. "A day ago, ye were certain he was dead. Now, yer nay certain at all. I can feel yer doubt. But he canna be alive!"

Brianna flinched. "I'm not certain of anything anymore."

"Tell me what ye know," he warned, trembling. He had dared to hope that Ian was alive after hearing Moray's claims. But they had been lies, hadn't they?

He read her thoughts again. "He wants me to bring him home?"

Brianna started to cry. "Tabby is figuring out how to send him on, Aidan."

He stared at her in dread. *His son was waiting for him to bring him home.*

He seized her shoulders. "Brianna, I beg ye now, tell me the whole truth."

She choked. "I don't know the truth! Tabby has guides and they're usually right. She said that he's alive, but it's impossible. She must be wrong!"

He cried out.

He had wanted to believe his father when Moray had first taunted him on the battlefield, and he had secretly harbored a terrible hope. But he was being haunted by his son's ghost. His son couldn't be alive. As Brianna had remarked, he'd be a grown man now.

His temples seemed to explode. He clasped his head, crying out. He could not go back and forth between hope and despair this way again!

This had to be another cruel trick.

"Aidan!" Brie cried, reaching for him.

He tore away from Brianna.

He could not stand this!

What if Ian were alive, somehow. What if he was awaiting a genuine rescue?

She laid her hands on his back, standing behind him. "We'll get through this, Aidan."

He flung her off and staggered to the small window, clutching the sill. "Leave me," he somehow managed. "Just leave me." He didn't dare turn to her now.

"I can't," she whispered.

He realized tears were streaming down his face, but he was helpless to stop them.

Don't you want to see Ian, my son?

But that had been a cruel trick. Somehow, Moray was behind this newest trick, as well. Perhaps Lady Tabitha was under his spell now. Perhaps Moray had the power to summon Ian's ghost at will. Or perhaps he could possess the ghost as he had the giant and Lord Frasier.

A sick stabbing went through him. *Ian was dead.*

He was Ian's father; he would know if he were alive.

But for one moment, he had dared to hope.

"WELL, AT LEAST WE HAVE THE right gear and we're not on Mount Hood," Sam said, smiling.

Nick had to hand it to her. She was as tough as he'd thought when he'd hired her.

The snowstorm had turned into a blizzard. They had dug a snow cave and were currently entombed in it. But this was the Highlands. They were at five hundred feet, not fifteen thousand, and outside it was probably an unusual fifteen degrees, not fifteen below. Still, trekking to Awe on foot was impossible now. A chilly wind had kicked up, making it feel like zero and putting visibility at zero, too. Nick had decided they would sit this one out. "Next time, remind me to bring skis," Nick said.

Sam grinned. "Hey, boss, you don't happen to have a toddy stashed somewhere, do you?" Her blue eyes met his.

He began shaking his head, but he reached into his vest and produced a small flask. "Naughty girl," he said softly, handing it to her. "That will bring your body temperature down."

Sam gave him a long look, uncapping the flask and taking a draught. Nick was impressed. He was a whiskey man; that was the best money could buy, and Sam drank like a man. She handed him the flask and said, "I can think of ways to raise it back up. Too bad I work for you. More importantly, I prefer boy toys."

He had to laugh. He wasn't insulted; he could pretty much please a woman all night. He didn't doubt she was really, really good in the sack, but not only did she work for him, she was not his type. She was too smart, too strong and too confident. He liked his blondes helpless—or at least *pretending* to be helpless. But she was beautiful. He'd seen her in shorts and a tank at CDA's gym and she made Angelina Jolie look like the girl next door. And while sex was the best way to pass the time, he didn't sleep with his "kids."

"Hey, Rose? When you grow up, you'll realize some men are like that whiskey you're drinking. Some of us get better with time—lots better."

"You like 'em young…so do I."

She meant it. He approved. "You just might go places, working for me."

She grinned, reaching for the flask. "Hey, boss? I'm going places all right, so prepare yourself. In no time, the nameplate on your door will read Sam Rose."

He laughed, genuinely amused. This one was a keeper. She didn't have a romantic bone in her body. He wasn't going to have to worry about her coming into his office one day to ask him for leave for a honeymoon or, worse, telling him she was planning to have kids. "Thanks for the warning."

"I can play fair."

His smile faded. Good played fair, evil did not. Instantly he worried about Brie again. It had been three and a half days since her abduction.

Sam knew. "Brie is tougher than she looks."

"Crap," he said, his good humor gone. He unzipped his sleeping bag and crawled to the front of the snow cave. It was coming down as heavily as before.

"She'll rise to the occasion," Sam said, but worry was reflected in her tone, too.

He didn't answer. He just hoped his little mouse hadn't been eaten for supper by the Big Bad Wolf.

NO HUMAN BEING SHOULD HAVE TO go through what Aidan was suffering, Brie thought. She trembled, gazing at his tear-streaked profile. He was quiet now, staring out of the window at the falling snow. He hadn't bothered to hide his emotions from her and she had felt all of his pain, grief and confusion. Brie desperately wanted to comfort him.

But after his brutal rejection that morning, she was afraid to go up to him. She had thought they were becoming close. She had been so wrong. But he needed her, more than ever, and she hadn't stopped loving him. She couldn't walk away.

"Aidan?" she whispered uncertainly. "Come sit down with me. We'll have some wine and figure this out."

He slowly looked at her. His gaze remained moist. "Ian is dead, Brianna," he warned. "There's naught to talk of."

He was so beaten down, and it killed her. She started toward him, but he sent her such a chilling look that it stopped her in her tracks. "Dinna even think to offer me comfort. Not now."

She tried to feel him, but he ruthlessly blocked her. "You were brutal this morning. A sane woman would have gone back home or to Iona. But I'm not leaving you to face Moray alone. I'm not leaving you to face your grief alone, either."

She saw him tremble. "I dinna need ye, Brianna. Ye should have gone to Iona."

"You need somebody in your corner," she said tersely. "And I guess that somebody is me."

A long moment passed before he spoke. "'Tis a long ride to Urquhart," he said flatly. "But 'tis a short leap."

Dismay overcame her. Somehow she kept her tone calm. "Please postpone it. I don't think any good can come of your meeting Frasier now. You're really distracted. We can focus on taking care of Ian instead."

"Dinna use Ian to keep me away from Urquhart," he rasped.

"I would never do that. But we summoned Ian in the séance, and we spoke with him. We need to summon him again. Aidan, you should be there."

He cried out.

She had known it would be a painful suggestion. "There has to be a communication between you both."

"Why willna ye leave me be?" he cried. "I have to go to Urquhart. I ken ye think I'll hang there."

"Don't you care?" she cried.

"If I hang, then I will have vanquished Moray and Ian will surely rest in peace then!"

His grief surged, battering her, but she withstood it, overcome with alarm, MacNeil's riddle echoing in her mind. "Oh, God. You will choose to die!"

She suddenly knew that if he went to Urquhart now, he would hang. And it was more than the way he had been speaking. The certainty was so strong it paralyzed her. Brie rushed to bar his way. "I can't let you go."

He halted. "Ye willna stop me," he warned.

She blurted out, "I love you. Don't go."

Their gazes locked.

She touched his face and he flinched. "You hurt me so much, but it doesn't matter. I will always love you. I'm here to save you, body and soul. Don't go."

"Stop," he whispered. "Please stop."

"Stop loving you? Impossible. Stop believing in your redemption? No."

He breathed hard. "If I die, Brianna, all of Alba will rejoice, because that means Moray will be dead. I willna hang otherwise. Brianna, I can find peace in death…and Ian will be free."

She cried out, "*I* will not rejoice! And don't you dare even think you will find peace in death. Aidan, there is peace in salvation."

He stared at her grimly, and she stared back, terrified. "How can ye love me as ye do? I have done nothing but fight ye."

"You didn't fight me last night. You didn't fight me on the plain, when I was dying. You didn't fight me in New York, when those boys were preparing to murder me."

"I am sorry ye care so much," he finally said. "Ye should care for a man like Seoc."

She wiped her tears then caught his rigid shoulders. "We don't get to choose love, Aidan. Just like we don't get to choose Fate. MacNeil saw me coming for you. I know you won't believe it, but I'm your Fate."

His eyes widened.

She felt more tears fall. He hadn't moved. She stood on tiptoe and brushed her mouth over his.

He remained still.

What was she doing, throwing herself at him? She was a dud. She was shy, a techno geek, and no one had ever wanted her. Aidan didn't want her, either.

He had said so.

He had made it very clear that it had been a one-night stand.

Her love wasn't going to delay him or dissuade him. MacNeil was wrong. Aidan was going to hang, and there wasn't going to be any redemption.

Brie broke the one-sided kiss, a product of her hopelessly one-sided love, and sank to stand flat-footed. She smiled sadly at him. "If you have to go, take me with you."

He shook his head and reached out, his hand trembling. With his thumb, he wiped her tears and dropped the shield on his emotions.

Brie went still, her heart thundering, amazed.

"I want ye very much, Brianna Rose. I always have," he said harshly. "I dinna ken the word 'dud,' but I dinna like it very much."

Her eyes widened. "But you said..."

"I lied," he said thickly. "I lied to make ye go away, but yer so stubborn."

Their gazes locked.

He almost smiled, and then he crushed her in his arms, his mouth claiming hers.

In his hard embrace, Brie cried out, kissing him back frantically. *He wanted her!*

And she felt everything from him then, not just the hot desire. She felt the grief, the despair, the hope and something else, something so strong and bright, so profound and deep, so elemental it almost felt like love.

She knew she was wrong—it was something else. It had to be something else.

He groaned, whirling her toward the bed, his manhood raging against her jeans, their lips locked. Brie let him push her onto her back. He lifted her sweat-shirt as she fumbled with his belt. He broke their kiss to drag her sweatshirt over her head. She undid the huge belt and let belt and swords fall to the floor, the weapons clattering loudly. Their eyes collided. He ripped off her T-shirt and she tugged on the leine, lifting it.

He went very still.

His erection appeared between them. Breathing hard, she slid her fingers over his huge, pulsing length.

"Brianna," he said roughly.

She held him so tightly he surged in her hand. His gaze was smoldering and Brie's heart exploded with desire, urgency and love.

He put his knee between her jeans-clad thighs and smiled at her.

There was so much warmth and promise in that smile that Brie simply stared back at him, even more stunned. And then she exulted. *This man cared about her.* She saw it in his shimmering blue eyes, and she could not be mistaken. Somehow, she wet her lips and whispered, "Aidan." She needed him now. She had never needed him more.

"Aye, Brianna," he murmured.

His other knee came down between her thighs and he reached for her jeans, shrugged them down her legs and she kicked them away. Then he paused to rip off his leine and fling it aside. He wore only the gold-capped wolf's fang on the thin chain.

Brie reached up to touch it. He became still, except for the rapid rise and fall of his chest. Her fingers grazed the fang, then slid over his chest. She was ready for pure, hot sex now, and so was he. She was spinning in the cyclone of his desire, and the roar of love made the anticipation blinding.

Aidan went still, gazing down at her. "I have a concern fer ye," he said roughly.

Brie went still.

A flush appeared on his high cheekbones. "A great concern," he added thickly.

Brie looped her arms around his neck. "I love you, too," she said, smiling.

He took her mouth again.

BRIE AWOKE SLOWLY. She was snug and cozy beneath heavy bedcovers. The bedchamber was bright with the light of a new, sunny morning, and she was in a man's embrace. Suddenly Brie was fully awake, blinking against the bright sunlight flooding the room, recalling the time spent in Aidan's arms. *She was still in his arms.* She shifted to look up at him. He lay deeply asleep beside her.

Brie went still, not wanting to awaken him. He had spent an afternoon and evening making love to her. She was certain. If he dared to deny it, she wouldn't listen. A wonderful joy crept over her.

There was nothing evil about this man. There had never been anything evil about him. He had been angry and grief-stricken and he had lost his way. But he was finding it now.

He looked like a teenage-boy angel, no more than twenty or so, his face soft and unlined, carefree. His thick black lashes fanned out against his beautiful face. His mouth was soft and slightly curved, as if he'd fallen asleep smiling. She loved him so much it hurt. She was not looking at a half demon. She was looking at her guardian angel, and by God, he would be the protector of all Innocence soon.

That was his Fate. Not hanging. Not evil.

He had told her once that he hadn't slept since Ian's murder, sixty-six years ago, but he was sleeping now. Of course he was. They'd made love for a long, long time. There had been smiles and conversation, but only at first, because when he wanted to get physical, it was very physical. Her entire body flushed as she thought about his otherworldly stamina and the very unnatural, unbelievably endless climaxes. She'd kept finding him watching her so intently that it was wonderful and unnerving at once.

He had wanted to give pleasure, not take it.

Brie smiled, shivering deliciously.

She was a woman of passion, but it was reserved for one man. She would never be the woman her mother had been. She wondered how she could ever have thought it even remotely possible.

He stirred.

Brie didn't want to awaken him. She wanted him to get his first solid night's sleep in nearly seven decades. She recalled the summons to Urquhart and prayed he would awaken smiling and content. She prayed her love had healed him. If it had, he wasn't going. Or if he did go, he wouldn't allow himself to be hanged.

He was going to wake up and smile at her, and everything was going to be all right.

She realized he was staring at her.

"Good morning," she whispered, and his embrace tightened.

His gaze was soft as she had never seen it before. It moved slowly over her face. Then, to her amazement, she felt his body stiffen against her hip.

"Aidan?"

He smiled at her. "A simple smile an' ye make me want to repeat last night—all of it," he murmured.

"Okay," she said. But she was thrilled to see such a tender smile, and the look in his eyes mirrored it.

His smile widened, and she saw a deep dimple for the very first time. Her heart went still. It was almost too good to be true, she thought.

His smile faded as he continued to gaze at her. "Yer a woman of great passion, Brianna Rose," he said. "Yer nay like yer mother. Yer far more beautiful, kind an' loyal—to the very end."

Brie touched his face. "Down the road you'll have

to stop lurking." Then she froze. What did he mean, exactly?

He threw the covers aside, sliding to his feet.

It was cold, and Brie pulled them back up, alarmed. She watched him cross the room, and it was impossible to take her gaze off his muscular, magnificent body. He knelt to stoke the fire, back rippling, thighs bulging. She stared at his hands, which were large and strong, the harbingers of so much incredible pleasure.

He straightened, glanced at her with a slight smile and then began dressing.

He had said she'd be loyal to the very end. "Is there a rush?" Brie asked carefully.

"Aye. I lingered with ye for an entire day. 'Tis afternoon already." He belted the leine and picked up the black plaid.

Her heart skipped a beat. "You're not going to Urquhart…are you?"

He pinned the plaid to one shoulder. "Aye. I'll ride after I break the fast."

She was disbelieving. MacNeil had been wrong—or had he? She frantically sought Aidan's feelings. He was very calm—too calm! She couldn't find despair, grief or rage. Was that positive? She began to calm down, as well. Had she healed him? "What will you do?"

He folded his arms. "Even I must obey a royal summons."

Brie slid from the bed. His gaze instantly moved down her bare body as she hurried to her pile of clothes. She jerked on the sweatshirt, shivering. "Aidan, it's obvious what will happen. Moray will possess Frasier and you will be accused of treason. He will hope to somehow destroy you in a hanging."

"Yer so clever," he said quietly. "Aye, I believe Moray will use Frasier to try to destroy me. But I'll destroy him first."

"And how will you do that?"

"I took power yesterday, Brianna." He flushed. "I'm nay afraid to fight with Moray."

"But I'm afraid for you! Promise me you won't choose to die!" Her grandmother's ring suddenly hurt her finger.

"I plan to destroy Moray, Brianna," he said, his face hard. "But I have no death wish."

Brie was not relieved or reassured. In fact, she was overcome with dread. "And what if Moray is invincible?" she cried desperately.

"Ye can pray that isna the case."

He wasn't going to change his mind. "What about Ian? What about me?"

His face hardened. "This is fer Ian! Did ye think yer love would make me forget my vengeance? I have spent decades waitin' to kill Moray. I'll do so now—today."

"I can see you will go to Urquhart no matter what I say. Please don't go alone." Brie began to tremble uncontrollably. "Please take Malcolm, Royce and Guy with you. Let me come with you. And Allie—she can heal you—and Tabby, so she can throw her spells at Moray until something works. Please. They love you! I love you."

He reached for her. "Dinna cry fer me. Ye should be pleased. Yer love has healin' power, because I have a care for all ye've mentioned. Malcolm has a son, an' recently a daughter. Royce will wish fer children soon.

The Macleod has many children. There's nay need to bring them into this."

"There's every need," she insisted, throwing her arms around him and burrowing against him. She held him hard, her face to his chest, and he wrapped his powerful arms around her and held her back as tightly. It crossed her treacherous mind that this could be the last moment she ever saw or held him.

"Please, dinna cry," he said quietly, his mouth against her hair. "Yer tears willna change what I must do today."

Fear stabbed through her. Grandma Sarah's image flashed, and she twisted off her grandmother's ring. "Take this."

His eyes widened. "Ye give me a betrothal ring?"

She almost laughed. "No. My grandmother gave me this, and she was the wisest person I have ever known. She fought evil her entire life with spells and magic, like Tabby. I have always believed this ring has kept me safe. Maybe it will keep you safe." She choked. "And it's a token of my feelings for you."

He unclasped his necklace and slipped her ring onto the chain, so it hanged beside the wolf's fang. She decided then that the moment he left, she would follow. He would not face Moray alone.

"Brianna, in truth, I wish to wear yer ring near my heart," he said softly, replacing the necklace around his neck. "Ye have warmed my lost soul."

Brie felt the tears stream. "This is the beginning—our beginning. It is not the end. Remember that."

His blue gaze kept searching hers, and she sensed he was memorizing every detail of her face. "Yer a fine, brave woman, Brianna Rose." He tipped up her face and smiled. Then, although tears covered her face, he kissed her.

When he pulled away, Brie was sobbing.

Finally, she'd read his mind. He believed it was their last kiss.

He gave her a look, then vanished.

CHAPTER SIXTEEN

Urquhart Castle, 1502

HE LANDED IN THE MIDST of Urquhart's inner ward. He leapt forward in time by mere moments. He wished to carry those new, passionate memories of Brianna with him, as he did her ring. He would take them to his grave if she was right about his hanging. He was becoming convinced that her predictions were correct. He knew with his sixth and seventh senses that this was, finally, his last confrontation with Moray, and he intended to be the victor. If he was accused of treason afterward, perhaps he wouldn't dispute the charges. He was so tired of the hopelessness and grief.

He slowly sat up. The bailey was filled with royal troops, their women and servants—the former bloody and muddy, clearly having returned from a battle. It was chaotic within, and he had arrived mostly unnoticed. But two women must have seen him appear like an apparition out of the gray chill, for they stared at him, then rushed away across patches of melting ice, frantically crossing themselves.

He stood and marched to the front doors of the great hall, where the king's favorite lieutenant would be. *I am here. Show yourself.*

Soft, cruel laughter sounded behind him—no, above him. *I am waiting, my son.*

The guards at the great doors stepped aside. Clearly, he was expected. Aidan stepped into a huge, raftered room, filled with English and Lowland noblemen, Highlanders and their servants as well as several beautiful, well-dressed courtesans. Lord Frasier stood before one of the three great hearths, hands clasped behind his back. He slowly turned as Aidan approached.

His dark eyes flamed blue and turned red. "Welcome to Urquhart."

At the sound of that familiar, mocking tone, Aidan fought the profound rage he'd lived with for most of his life. This deamhan had forced him to destroy Innocence. He knew now that he'd live with the regret, the horror, for so long.

Too late, he blocked his thoughts.

"Blood tells," Frasier snarled. "You dare to stand before me, filled with guilt? Then you are more like your mother, the saintly Lady Margaret!"

And now, by God, he hoped so. "Is my son dead or alive?" Aidan demanded. The words had formed themselves without premeditation.

Instantly he knew he had revealed his greatest weakness.

A cruel smile played over Frasier's dark face. "You have defied me since you were a small boy. You defy me still. You defy me when you let Innocence live, you defy me by standing before me, in guilt, in shame. You defy me when you desire the fair Brianna and you defy me when you take her to bed. You belong to me. *You are mine.*"

Chills swept Aidan, the sensation entirely unfamiliar. "I belong to no one," he said harshly, and then he thought he felt Brianna's ring, hot against his chest. Moray knew too much. Because of Aidan, Brianna was in the midst of their war, dangerously so. Once again, he was afraid for her.

He had lost Ian. He couldn't lose her to evil, too.

"Do you really think I'd let young Ian live?" Frasier cried. "And if I did, do you think I would let you take him back?"

More games. Despair rose up and as hope was crushed, fury arose. "Ye played me another time. Ye lied, yet again."

Frasier came close and said softly, "Lady Tabitha was under my spell. I am all powerful now. There is no greater entity in Alba! I chased her guides away," Moray mocked him.

Aidan met Moray's cruel, sadistic gaze. "Good. The truth, at last." Before he could draw his sword, a dozen giants, all possessed with extraordinary strength, seized him. He knew he could fling them off, one by one, but he did not attempt to do so. "What do ye want?" he asked. "Because I willna do yer evil. Ye canna turn me now."

"No son defies his father and no one defies me," Frasier cried, red eyes ablaze. "You will pay for your defiance. Only then will you die."

"I have paid. Ye stole my son. Ye took his life."

"By defying me, you deny me your great powers, which should be mine! Only one of us can triumph—the goddess said so. It will be me." Moray trembled in anger.

Aidan stared, wondering if a goddess had actually promised Moray victory. If so, that would explain his hanging. "Which goddess do ye consort with? Is that how ye survived Malcolm's beheading?"

Moray smiled. "Aye. Faola saved me that day."

"Why would a goddess help ye survive?"

Moray snarled, "I'm her son. Once, I was her favorite."

Aidan went still. He was the son of a deamhan and the grandson of a great goddess. It explained so much. It explained the Choosing and his healing powers. It explained why he had never been entirely turned.

"Long ago, I served the Brotherhood," Moray said. "The fall is not what you fear. The fall frees a man. The fall could have freed you. Faola helped me survive the vanquishing because of the trial between us. 'Tis written."

Aidan tensed. This war was written by the gods?

"She was so hot and lovely last night," Moray whispered in his ear.

Horror began. His heart thundered. "Ye win. I give up."

"Really?" Moray laughed. "I will take your lady love and use her endlessly. I will cause her unimaginable pain, and even greater fear."

Aidan's racing heart slowed. He would never allow Brianna such a Fate. A ruthless calm descended. He would gladly give his life for Brianna Rose. Once he was gone, Moray would have no reason to hunt her, torture her and murder her.

She deserved that much from him.

He looked at his father.

Moray smiled. "Your power is still so fresh, but it doesn't match mine."

Aidan sent all of his power at him, as he had never used it before.

Moray answered in kind.

Their powers met in the short distance between them with explosive force. Chairs fell, the table cracked, lights fell and fires started. Aidan was hurled backward by the explosion, into the wall.

Before he could get up, a blade pierced his throat. He looked up at Moray, who smiled down at him. "Will you die for her?"

"Yes."

"Arrest him."

As he was seized again, Aidan instinctively tried to leap back in time, to the moment he had left Brie at Awe. Nothing happened.

Moray laughed. "You are trapped," he said.

Shocked, Aidan breathed hard and attempted the same leap.

He had been trapped in space and time.

BRIE HOPPED INTO HER JEANS. Barefoot, she ran down the hall and the narrow spiral staircase, stumbling as she did so. As she burst into the great room, she wiped her wet face with her sleeve.

Tabby and Allie sat in two huge chairs before a roaring fire, Claire on a footstool with them. They had their heads together and were in a frantic and hushed conversation. Not one of their husbands was present. The moment Brie barged inside, they leapt to their feet.

Brie ran to them. "Aidan is confronting Moray! He has gone to Urquhart—where he will hang."

Tabby steadied her, her amber eyes filled with worry. "Brie, we think we've figured out what to do about Moray."

"That's great," Brie cried, "but you can tell me all

about it after we leap to Urquhart. Where's Malcolm? Where's Guy? Where's Royce, damn it?"

"Malcolm and Royce went to Urquhart to plead his case before Frasier," Claire said grimly.

"Then where's Guy?" Brie cried. "He can take us!" A glance out of a window as she ran downstairs had her blinded by the whiteness outside. It must have snowed a foot last night. Ordinary travel would be impossible. They would have to leap, as Aidan had done.

Tabby took her hand. "I found a Wisdom," she whispered.

Brie faced her, fighting her panic. Wisdom was dispersed throughout the two thousand pages of the Book. Sometimes the verse was so damned cryptic, it could take days to try to figure out—and even then, they wouldn't know if they were wrong or right until they attempted to carry out whatever Wisdom had been proffered. "Go ahead," she said.

Tabby spoke softly from memory.

"Sleeping evil
The ripest time
To reap protection.
Alas the devil
Bemoans design
Set free the Keepers of the Faith."

"Oh, great," Brie cried. "Another frigging holy riddle. He could be hanged by the time we figure this out!"

Allie showered her with a soothing light. "I guess you're head-over-heels. I have never seen you panicked before, not ever, and we've been in a few big jams."

"I will love him for eternity, and he loves me," Brie

said, and she threw her arms around Allie. "But I have a terrible feeling."

"Has he come back to us?" Claire asked, eyes wide.

"Yes, he has," Brie said without a single doubt. "But this summons is a diabolical setup!"

Tabby said, "We need to find out where Moray's body is when his evil is in another human being."

Brie looked at her quickly. "You have my undivided attention now."

"That Wisdom is not cryptic at all," Tabby said. "When evil sleeps, the devil is in trouble and it's the time for us to reap our triumph. I am certain this refers to Moray leaving his body to possess another being," she continued earnestly. "Where is he when he is Lord Frasier? What is he?" She added seriously, "He is somewhere, and I am guessing he's not walking around. You guys need to figure it out. Meanwhile, I have a spell."

Brie prayed. "What kind of spell?" she asked.

"A spell to block his energy from going back to his body, so we can get rid of the sonuvabitch once and for all," Tabby said. Her golden eyes flashed.

Brie felt relief flood her. There was hope.

Footsteps sounded. They were alone in the great room, but Brie knew guards were at the exterior doors and that no one could enter who should not. The guards opened the doors and Nick Forrester sauntered in, dressed like a commando, carrying a backpack, a machine gun slung over his shoulder.

Brie gasped. It took her a moment to really assimilate that he was in the great hall at Awe in medieval times. *The Masters weren't the only ones who could time-travel.*

Hadn't she always sensed that there was more to Nick than met the eye?

Sam followed him into the hall, also in camouflage, with Guy Macleod escorting them as if their presence was an ordinary, everyday occurrence. Brie thought that maybe it was!

"You okay, kid?" Nick asked, looking Brie up and down quickly. He seemed as unperturbed by where he was as Macleod was to have him there.

Brie was so shocked she could only shake her head. *Nick could fix this.* He was a legend in the agency. They said he never failed a mission objective.

"Oh my God," Sam cried, her eyes huge. She was staring at Allie and Tabby, obviously shocked to find them there, especially as she had left Tabby at home in New York City. Then she ran to Allie and hugged her, hard. "You're obviously no worse for wear," she said, looking across her shoulder at Brie. "Are you okay? Did that bastard hurt you?" She released Allie, her blue eyes narrowing now.

"I'm fine," Brie replied. "Aidan needs our help."

Sam stared for another moment and then turned to Tabby. "Well, this is a surprise, my lady."

Tabby hugged her and said, "I am *very* happy."

"I just left you at home," Sam returned swiftly, "getting ready to go to school and teach your first graders!"

"I don't leave until December of 2008," Tabby said. "I have missed you so much," she said, her tone rough now.

Sam suddenly seemed taken aback, and Brie knew it was hitting her that Tabby was going to find her destiny in the past and she'd miss her sister in the present. Brie turned to look at Guy, who wasn't smiling. He carried one of the largest broadswords Brie had seen, and he looked exactly like what he was—a hard-ass, ruthless medieval warrior.

Sam shook her head. "Never in a million years would I match you with *that.*"

"Guy is my husband," Tabby said reprovingly. "My boy-next-door days are over."

"I'll bet." Sam's eyes narrowed. "You do know that if you ever hurt my sister, I'll make you pay."

"Sam!" Tabby cried.

Guy gave Sam a cool smile. "I'd never hurt Tabitha or ye, no matter yer warring words and manly ways."

Sam looked ready to explode. Allie said, "Sami, you're about two hundred and fifty years too late. If you want to help Tabby out, you need to leap back a few centuries—not that she needs your help."

"Okay, I hate to break this up, but enough of the dysfunctional family reunion," Nick said firmly. He paused before Brie as if he was still her boss, which he was, sort of. "I need a debriefing. Yesterday works for me."

Alarm began. "Aidan could die if we don't help him."

Nick smiled grimly. "He does die, kiddo. I'm sorry, but you read the history books."

"I won't let him hang!" Brie insisted.

Nick was still unperturbed. "Do you know why I'm here? I'm here because you work for *me.* You are my responsibility. *Mine,* not the agency's. And there is no way in hell I'd leave you lost in the past." His glance slid over Macleod. "Not that I wouldn't mind chatting with Mr. Tabitha."

"I am not lost, as you can see! I am here with my

friends." She flushed. "We are vanquishing a terrible demon and redeeming Aidan."

"Since when do you work in the field?" His blue gaze was sharp as he took her arm. "You seem to have survived the Wolf. I'm impressed. But my mind won't change. If *his* power is changing, good for you. But I've got lots of work to do at home and I am *not* leaving you here."

Brie cried out, struggling to get free. "I am not going back to the future," she shouted at him.

"Hey, Nick, wait," Sam began, clearly about to defend Brie's position.

Nick simply smiled. "Get over here," he said to Sam.

Macleod looked at Tabby. "Should I stop them?" he asked.

"Ah, shit," Nick said. He blasted Macleod with energy. As the Master grunted, moving about as much as an oak tree in a summer breeze, Nick's grip on Brie tightened.

"Guy, don't you dare strike back. He's one of us," Tabby cried.

Brie screamed as she was simultaneously pulled into Nick's arms and ripped upward with him, into the ceiling and through it, blasting past stars.

FOR ONE MOMENT, URQUHART'S GREAT room seemed to spin, and then the odd sensation passed. Robert Frasier blinked, standing before Aidan of Awe, who was being restrained by a number of soldiers.

Frasier tensed. He had summoned the treacherous Highlander to Urquhart, but he didn't recall him arriving or having had their interview. "Arrest him," he told the guards uneasily.

Aidan stared unwaveringly at him while his sergeant

seemed puzzled. "Aye, sir," he said. "Shall we put him in the north tower?"

Frasier hesitated, worried about his not recalling whatever had transpired a moment ago. This was exactly what had happened on the battlefield. He had suddenly realized who he was and what he was doing, and he had been in the midst of a dangerous battle with this man. Apparently he had lost his senses for a time.

What did it mean? Was the man a sorcerer? There were rumors that he changed into a black wolf to hunt during the red moon.

"Sit down," he ordered Aidan.

The other man hesitated, his blue eyes showing no fear, before sitting down. But that was to be expected; the Wolf of Awe feared no one, while the world feared him.

Frasier stood before him. "Call off your men, who march toward Inverness even now, having already made their rendezvous with MacDonald."

Aidan stared him in the eye. "My men are sworn to Donald Dubh. *I* am sworn to Donald Dubh."

Frasier began to smile. "Put him in the dungeons," he said. This would please King James. James was furious with the Wolf and had been for years. The Highlander's history was nothing but act after act of defiance of royal authority. James II had been so livid with his destruction of Elgin and his ruthless pursuit of the deceased Earl of Moray's three sons that he had stripped him of all his titles and lands, except for Awe. Frasier felt certain the king had left Aidan with Awe only because he didn't dare try to take it from him.

Of course, the man's young age was inexplicable, but in his forty years, Frasier had seen many strange things, including other men who failed to age—or who could vanish into thin air and reappear the same way. Just thinking about it made him cross himself.

He could withstand phenomena he did not understand. But these lapses into blackness and the return to consciousness, not knowing what he had just done, were something that must cease.

Was he possessed? It was a dark time in Alba, and evil was everywhere. He saw it in his soldiers' black, empty eyes and in their cruelty and lust for death. But they made far better warriors than average men.

He had feared possession for as long as he could recall. He was a very devout man, worshipping every single day, not just to ward off evil but to carry forth God's work and the king's. Now he looked at Aidan of Awe, thinking that his odd behavior was somehow connected to the mercenary. "Under the authority granted in me by King James of Scotland, I hereby charge you with treason against the crown."

Aidan stared at him, his expression hard and tight.

"And under the same authority, I order you hanged." His mouth twisted. A large crowd of spectators was always the best. Execution brought fear into the hearts of everyone, and gave pause to the next lot of conspirators. "Take him away," he said, his hand moving to the hilt of his sword.

But Aidan went forward as docilely as a sheep, as if he did not care that he would soon die.

When he was gone, the hall stood almost empty except for a few courtiers who spoke quietly by the hearth and several guards. The unease returned to Frasier instantly. He tried to shake it off and failed.

A chill swept him.

Frasier turned and saw a handsome blond man in a

courtier's black velvet robes standing by the far wall. He hadn't seen him in the hall earlier, and the man couldn't have walked in without being seen. There was no entrance where he stood, but no man could walk through a wall.

He knew this man, somehow, yet he was certain they had never met. His alarm increased.

And then, before his very eyes, the blond man in the black robes vanished.

Frasier stood stock-still.

First there had been his loss of comprehension and will with Aidan of Awe. Now a stranger who could vanish into thin air had appeared in his hall. In that moment, he knew he'd seen a great evil. He crossed himself and started for the doors.

Two Highlanders strode in, their expressions harsh and set. He recognized the Baron of Dunroch and the Earl of Morvern instantly. Malcolm had received a barony from the king a few years ago. Morvern's title was ancient. The former was half brother to the prisoner, the latter not related by blood.

"We wish a word with ye," Black Royce said, nodding politely in greeting. "We've come to plead for Aidan of Awe's liberty, and his life."

Frasier shook his head. "He has refused to call back his armies. He will hang, and there will be no interference. None."

"You will not give us a word?" Malcolm demanded, his face dark with anger.

"I have great matters to attend."

Malcolm stared in disbelief. "I willna allow ye to hang my brother," he began, but Black Royce seized his arm and he fell silent.

"Your loyalty to the king has been rewarded, but the king has ordered me to end your brother's defiance once and for all," Frasier snapped. "He hangs tomorrow." He started for the great doors.

"Will ye at least let us see him?" Malcolm cried.

Frasier nodded brusquely as he hurried past them. He had meant it when he said he had grave matters on his mind. He would find Father Oliphant and demand he perform an exorcism, immediately.

AIDAN LAY ON HIS BACK ON THE thin blanket that served as a pallet. The floor was frigidly cold beneath the wool, and wet. He didn't care. His Fate was clear now.

The dungeons were as dark as they were dank, and rats blinked at him from the shadows. Lying on the wet blanket, he stared up at the leaking ceiling, droplets of water splattering on his forehead. He was trapped in space and time, but it did not matter. He intended to go on to his death.

He still had his powers. He had tested them on one of the guards, hurling him into a faraway wall. For this he had been hit over the head with the back of a sword and he'd almost lost consciousness. Now his head hurt, but he didn't care. He would not use his powers to break down the door, kill the guards and run away. There was no point.

Nothing mattered now except that he die in order to free Brianna from the devil's grasp. He had meant his words to her earlier. There would be peace in death's embrace. It had been so long; he was so tired. He looked forward to it.

He tried not to think about Ian. It was impossible. He could no longer deny that from the moment his father had become the giant on the battlefield, Aidan had been clinging to a thread of hope. That thread was broken now. But maybe he would meet his son in the next life. And he would trust Brianna to set his son's spirit free when he was gone.

He closed his eyes against a drop of the falling water. He thought about Brianna, who had the sweetest smile he had ever seen, especially when she directed that smile at him, her eyes mirroring her love and her faith. He felt himself smile. His heart hurt him now. Somehow, in spite of all the terrible crimes he'd committed, he had come to care for her deeply. He missed her. He wished to hold her; to make love to her one more time. It was such a foolish yearning, but he could not convince himself to wish otherwise.

Once he was gone, his brother or someone else would send her to her time. She would find someone else to love there, someone ordinary and good. He felt harsh laughter arise. She would never be with an ordinary man. She was far too extraordinary. She deserved someone as holy as a Master. Maybe the man she worked for, Nick, would be the one. He had white powers, even though he tried very hard to hide them.

Bolts began to groan as they were lifted from the dungeon door. Aidan sat up, not terribly surprised. He felt Malcolm and Royce outside, their white power huge and hot. They were very angry, and he knew why. He steeled himself against them.

The dungeon door was pushed slowly open, wood scraping over stone. Malcolm stepped in, his face hard and grim, followed by Royce. Aidan got to his feet. Both men were unarmed.

Malcolm embraced him, bearlike. "Why will ye nay turn yer armies back from Inverness?" he exclaimed.

Aidan met his ragged gaze. His brother was already grieving for him.

In that moment, with his death so close, Aidan was gladdened that Malcolm had come. Royce's face was set differently from Malcolm's. It was saddened, telling Aidan that he still had a care for him, but it was filled with resignation, as well. Aidan knew he understood.

Royce said softly, "He has decided to die."

But Malcolm did not understand; he was not resigned. He cursed. "There's no reason to die! Yer comin' back to us. An' what about Brianna, whom ye love?"

Aidan tensed. "Ye speak like a fool," he said. He would never analyze or identify his deepest feelings for Brianna, and even if he did, he would not confess them to anyone. "I am tired o' this life.' He looked directly at Royce.

Royce stiffened as their gazes locked. A long time ago, Royce had uttered those exact words, and he had meant them. On his deathbed, he had asked Aidan to let him go. Aidan had done just that.

Slowly, Royce nodded in silent comprehension.

"What mad conspiracy is this?" Malcolm cried. "Ye willna die. Ye must leap from this time, this place."

"I canna leap. I have been trapped," Aidan said.

"I'll take ye from here," Malcolm cried.

Aidan seized his arm. "I have my other powers. If I wished, I could flee this place. I dinna wish to do so. I will stay."

Malcolm stared, eyes wide with horror.

"I canna live much longer with my grief," Aidan said, and his tone had turned hoarse. He added, "Ian is gone. He is dead, but nay buried. I canna grieve anymore! What if Moray should use and destroy Brianna? I canna withstand more pain, Malcolm. Moray hunts her only to hurt me. He will have no reason to hunt her after tomorrow."

"So ye think to stay an' die?" Malcolm exclaimed harshly. He had turned white.

"Aye, I think to stay…an' tomorrow ye will let me die."

CHAPTER SEVENTEEN

"HEY, BRIE?" SAM LAID HER HAND on Brie's shoulder.

The pain of the godawful leap and landing was finally receding. Brie's temples still felt as if they'd been split open, and her body felt as if it had been in a really bad, really long game of Twister.

She lay on the floor of Nick's office, curled up in a ball, her face wet from so many tears. Sam knelt beside her, still in her camouflage, smiling reassuringly at her. "You'll be okay. Hey…you're home."

She didn't want to be home! Brie somehow sat up, moaning. And then she saw Nick, standing by the huge window behind his desk, arms folded, stance braced, his back to her as he stared outside. It was raining.

"Damn you!" Brie cried, heaving to her feet. Sam kept her hand on Brie's elbow to steady her. "Send me back! Send me back now!"

Nick turned. "What happened to you?"

"Aidan happened to me. You've even admitted it—he was turning back to us! I cannot let him hang."

Sam put her arm around her.

Nick said, "It's September 26, 2008, Brie. He was executed in 1502." His stare was cold.

Brie's heart stopped. He was telling her that even

though a moment ago Aidan had been very much alive, he was currently very dead. "History is often wrong."

"I don't give a damn about history," Nick snapped, "unless I'm hunting a coincidence. But Fate is Fate." He picked up a folder from his desk and handed it to her. "You've got one hour to eat, shower, whatever. I need a complete debriefing."

Brie was dismayed. "I am going back to save Aidan from execution!"

"If his hanging is meant to be, it will be. You've got one hour, kid. I suggest you look at the file." Nick walked to his door, opened it and waited for them to leave.

Brie shook with rage. "I quit."

His dark brows lifted. "Fine. And when you change your mind, I'll rehire you. You're damn good in the basement."

Brie began shaking her head. Tears battled her eyelids.

"You're still getting debriefed. Thoroughly. Your love life is not going to get in the way of what I do here at CDA."

Brie decided to take the file and walk out of his office, the building, this life. She hoped never to lay eyes on Nick again.

Obviously he could read minds as well as any Master, because his smile was hard. "You're not allowed out of the building, so don't even think it."

Brie cried out and stormed past him, fighting her terror for Aidan. Sam followed, putting her arm around her. "We can use my office," she said, her gaze kind. "You're acting like a thirteen-year-old."

Brie looked at her as they slipped into a small, corner office on the other side of the building. Sam was right. Ranting and raving wasn't going to help. Sam shut the door, removing her vest. She went to a small fridge and took out two bottles of water, handing one to Brie. Brie had never seen her so kind. She was used to Sam being tough and angry, in warrior mode.

"He hired me the moment you vanished with Aidan," Sam said, flopping in her desk chair. "Brie, you know him better than I do. The man can be a royal bastard, but he has loads of integrity."

Brie sat down on the only other chair in Sam's small, very sterile office. She realized she still clutched the file to her chest. She eased her grasp and finally breathed. "How does he go back in time?"

"I have no idea. Probably the way the Masters and demons do—a dash of otherworldly DNA." Sam smiled.

Brie did not smile back. "I have to go back. How can I convince him to let me go?"

"Maybe after the debrief you can talk him into it. Look, Brie, truth is, Nick cares about you. I'm pretty sure that there are a few agents lost in time, and Nick has some personal issues going on here."

Brie's eyes widened.

"Maybe you should read that file. When he said an hour, he meant an hour. Burgers or pizza?"

Brie blinked. "Pizza. If I see red meat again, I'll be sick."

Sam smiled and lifted the phone.

Brie looked at the file and saw Aidan of Awe typed neatly on the index tab. Her heart lurched with dread. She opened it and her disbelief began.

The file was twenty-seven pages long. There were eighteen Sightings, all reported by CDA agents. Brie began to tremble. In 1942 an agent had sighted Aidan in 1428 in London, where he'd destroyed a handful of demons; in 1818 an agent had sighted him in the northwestern Highlands in 1488, during a terrible clan war infested with demons and subs. Aidan's role had been unclear. Brie began to breathe hard. He'd been a Master in the first Sighting, but she was pretty sure he'd been in his dark, angry-at-the-gods mode for the second one. Her heart racing, she found another Sighting prior to 1502, and it was equally ambiguous. There were six more Sightings, and in several, he had reportedly turned his back on the Innocent.

One fact was clear. CDA agents had been traveling through time for the past two hundred years. Nick was hardly the only one who could leap into the past.

She looked up at Sam. "This isn't helpful."

"Keep going."

She had reached the second half of the file. He'd been sighted—and photographed—in Rome in 2007, Madrid in 2005 and London in 2004. There were Sightings in Milan, London, New York and Beverly Hills. Every single one was after the millennium. Photos were clipped to each report. Brie stared at Aidan, clad in the Gucci leather jacket she had found in his chamber and tight, faded Levi's. He had never looked so good. She ignored the fact that there was a woman hanging on his arm in every photo. There were a dozen in all.

She thought she would die from the heartbreak of their separation and her fear for his life. But didn't this mean he'd survived?

She realized Sam was watching her. A box of Kleenex appeared by her right hand. Brie took a tissue and wiped her tearing eyes, then looked up. "He makes it, doesn't he? Look at these photos of him in the twenty-first century!" But she looked again and saw how carefree his face was.

She was looking at Aidan before his fall.

"You didn't read the reports, or you didn't read them carefully," Sam said quietly.

Brie flinched and met her serious gaze.

"All the Highland Sightings end in 1502. After that year, he is never seen in the Highlands again."

Brie was afraid. "What are you trying to tell me?"

Sam was grim. "In those reports, the agents are clear. Aidan is dressed in modern clothes, but he is a medieval man visiting the future, having come from the past. I think in every postmillennium Sighting, he came from a period within several years of his induction into the Brotherhood—which we think was in 1421."

Brie's hands began to shake. Aidan had brought Allie home last year and they'd traveled from 1430. Allie had told them so.

That had been before Ian's murder, before his fall.

Brie threw the files at Sam, standing. "So he is hanged in 1502? That's what you think?"

"It's what I think, Brie. I mean, there's a tomb at Awe with his effigy on it. That's in the case file, too. It's a big deal for the locals. He is a huge local myth—the Wolf of Awe, a man who ruthlessly destroyed his enemies and met an equally ruthless end."

"He isn't ruthless," Brie said.

"If this is his Fate, it is not fair," Sam said. "I can see how much you've changed. I hardly recognize you. But you cannot change the execution, no matter what you want to think or plan, not if it is written."

Brie stared furiously at her.

Sam looked at her watch as a buzzer on her phone

went off. "Pizza's here, and you have twenty-six minutes."

"And what if it's not written? What if I am meant to stop this?"

"Then we need to get our asses in gear."

BRIE STUMBLED OUT OF CDA AFTER dark, with armed escorts that included Sam and two HCU field agents. It was really late, and she was sick with exhaustion. The debriefing had taken eight and a half hours. Not only did Nick know every detail of her time in the past, he knew everything she had learned about the Masters, the Brotherhood and demons in the Middle Ages.

They slid into Sam's car, a black Lexus sedan, and Sam waved the agents off. As she drove the few blocks to Brie's loft, Brie stared out of the window listlessly. She finally said, "I am going to find a way to get back. I intend to go to work tomorrow and start looking for an agent who can time-travel. If Nick won't send me, I'll bribe, extort, threaten or seduce an agent who can."

"Wow," Sam said. "I still can't believe how tough you've become. Hey, if you start working out and get in shape, the leaps will be easier." She flashed a smile. "I learned that during my CDA physical."

"I don't intend to stick around here long enough to get in shape," Brie said, and she thought about the way Aidan had made love to her. He had liked her body just the way it was. Grief ripped at her heart.

"Maybe Tabby can help," Sam said softly, pulling into the underground garage.

"Damn it," Brie gasped, because the car began to tilt and then spin. Filled with dread, Brie seized the dashboard, aware of a vision coming on. For the first time in her life, she wanted to fight her gift. But she gave herself over, slumping in the seat, head back, the car spinning….and then it went still.

Malcolm held Claire, and he was crying.

Aidan twirled from the hangman's noose, head down, lifeless.

It was a gray day, the ground covered with snow.

Vaguely Brie knew she had already seen this and she was confused, until the vision changed.

He hung from a crenellated stone wall, beyond which was a deserted inner ward. Inside the castle, a small, dark chamber was lit by a solitary candle. There was a bed, a small table and nothing else at all.

Brie tensed. The image sharpened. *A man lay on the bed, hands folded, eyes open, but he was as still as a corpse. It was Aidan's demonic father, Moray.*

Brie gasped and sat up, sweat pouring down her face. Had she just seen Moray *dead?*

And in that moment, she somehow knew he hadn't been dead, not at all. He had been in repose, awaiting the return of his black power.

"Sleeping evil," the ripest time to reap protection, or some such thing. Now Brie understood that phrase of the Wisdom. He would be at Aidan's hanging, masquerading as someone else, perhaps Frasier. And Tabby had a spell to prevent his evil from returning to his body. She had to go back now so they could find and finish him.

"Are you okay?" Sam asked.

"I had a vision. If I can get back, I think I'll be able to find Moray, and Tabby has a spell that might end his demonic reign once and for all."

"I'm going back with you," Sam said quietly.

A moment later they were in the elevator and going up to Brie's loft. Tabby had the door open and was waiting for them, both anxious and smiling. Behind her, the loft was filled with the scent of her fantastic cooking.

Sam said in a low voice, "I take it I'm not supposed to mention her Fate is a big, dark medieval brute who looks about as kind and sensitive as a really angry attack dog?"

"I don't think we're allowed to reveal what we know—not unless it's dire," Brie said tersely.

"Are you okay?" Tabby cried, embracing her and dragging her inside so they could safely shut the door and lock it.

"I'm not okay," Brie returned. "I'm so upset my head is going to explode."

Tabby seized her hands. "Sam told me what happened while you were being debriefed. Brie, I'm so sorry."

"Tabby, please find a spell to send me back to him, exactly where I left off."

Tabby's eyes widened.

"I need it immediately." Although she also needed a shower and her own clothes—she'd been given contacts and sweats at the agency—she ran to her computer and powered on.

Tabby and Sam followed her. "You know I never find a spell immediately," Tabby replied. "It could take me days or even weeks."

Brie went to her research files and the last text she'd been reading. She glanced up at Tabby. "Please." Then she opened the page she'd bookmarked.

She desperately wanted the text to have changed. If her love had healed Aidan at all, he would not allow anyone to hang him.

"Brie, when Allie vanished last year, Sam asked me for a time-traveling spell. I couldn't find one," Tabby said worriedly.

"Every day is different," Brie reminded her. "If you can't find a spell, I'll find another way." She hit Enter and text filled her screen.

In December 1436, Aidan the Wolf of Awe, a Highlander with no clan, sacked the stronghold of the Earl of Moray at Elgin, leaving no man, woman or child alive.

She breathed hard and read the rest of the page.

However, Moray escaped the Wolf's wrath intact, to take up his position at court as Defender of the Realm for King James, the same position he had enjoyed ten years earlier. But when James was murdered at Perth the following February, Moray, who was known to be at court, vanished, never to be heard from again. Quite possibly Moray was slain with his king. The Wolf of Awe proceeded to spend the next nineteen years ruthlessly destroying the families and holdings of Moray's three powerful sons, the earls of Feith, Balkirk and Dunveld. Retribution came from Argyll, and in 1458 Castle Awe was burned to the ground. Although the Wolf spent twenty years rebuilding his stronghold, he forfeited his other holdings, his title and earldom (Lismore) to King James II. He remained universally distrusted and feared until his demise. In 1502, after his mercenary role in the MacDonald uprising, he was

> accused of treason by the Royal Lieutenant of the North, the powerful Frasier chief. Badly wounded from an escape attempt, he was publicly hanged at Urquhart.

Brie couldn't see the page now, for her vision was blurred with tears. She wiped them and read on:

> His tomb has been carefully restored at the ruins of Castle Awe on Loch Awe.

Nothing had changed, not one damn thing! Brie laid her head on her arms and let grief and fear wash over her. With it, there was frustration and rage. Tabby laid a hand on her back. "I'll try to find a spell to send you back. Do you want to talk about it…about him?"

"I'm exhausted," Brie muttered, "and thanks to Nick, all talked out." She stood abruptly. "I need to shower and get out of these clothes.

Tabby had never looked more concerned. "I'll fix a tray. You can eat in bed. I am not leaving you!"

Brie smiled slightly. "Thanks."

But as she walked to the bathroom, she thought about her vision of Aidan in effigy and the tomb on Loch Awe. She stopped and went back into the loft's living area. "Sam, has anyone ever been to Aidan's tomb?"

Sam hesitated. "I don't know. I think it's simply a well-known fact that the tomb exists."

"Has anyone seen it? Are there photos?" Brie demanded.

"If there were photos, they'd be in his case file. What are you thinking?"

Just because she had a vision of Aidan in effigy, and

it was common knowledge that Aidan of Awe had a tomb, that didn't mean it was *his* tomb. Historians made mistakes all the time. "I want to see it for myself. I'm going to Scotland."

TWO DAYS LATER, BRIE SAT BESIDE Sam in the front passenger seat of the rental car they'd picked up at Edinburgh International. Loch Awe was a glimmering body of water ahead of them. They'd managed to take a flight over the previous night, had landed in Edinburgh that morning and had spent seven hours driving across the Highlands through spectacular scenery, although it wasn't half as splendid as it had been during medieval times. The signs of modern times had become more dispersed as they left Edinburgh's suburbs behind, urban sprawl giving way to smaller and smaller villages. The towering mountains were stark and bare now. Hundreds of years ago, the forests had been so thick they were impenetrable except by game trails. The landscape was so familiar and so different.

But it didn't matter. Only the truth about Aidan's Fate mattered. Brie gripped the dashboard as they bounced along the rutted dirt road leading to Castle Awe. The sapphire-blue lake with the red stone rising out of its midst was painfully familiar and Brie's heart pounded with hurtful force. She almost expected to see Awe as it had been in 1502, with riders on the bridge and Highlanders in the ward, coming and going. She almost expected to see Aidan, the most magnificent sight of all, striding out of the ward, clad in his leine and plaid and swords.

"Oh my God," she whispered.

Sam braked on a roadside lookout, not speaking.

The red stone rising from the sparkling water was only that—red stone. Castle Awe was in ruins.

All that was left of the spectacular castle, with its many towers, wards and chambers, was two crumbling curtain walls and two collapsing towers. The bridge leading to the ruins was impassable, reduced to three disconnected stone sections. A new suspension bridge had been erected to the north of it. Three cars were parked by it. Tourists were leaving the ruins, making their way across the suspension bridge to their vehicles.

A pair of swans drifted past the ruins of the bridge where Aidan's mighty army had gathered for the march on Inverness. Brie began crying.

"I'm sorry," Sam whispered. "It's awful…such beauty and majesty, coming to this end."

Brie fought her tears and her grief. As if sensing her thoughts, Sam put the little Renault in gear and drove over to the suspension bridge, where she parked. Brie got out of the car, so sick now she thought she might die. With Sam beside her, she started walking slowly toward the ruins.

She didn't know if she could stand the heartbreak.

She missed him so much.

They had only just begun. His tomb could not be ahead.

A husky American man wearing a camera around his neck, dressed in Bermuda shorts and Adidas, was leaving the ruins. He frowned at her. "A waste of time," he said. "The only thing worth seeing is the tomb. The rest is just a pile of rocks."

Sam cupped her elbow. Brie didn't speak as she passed the man, because she couldn't. His ignorance infuriated her.

The gatehouse leading to the inner ward, the great hall and the interior of the castle should have been directly ahead, with its pair of majestic flanking towers. Sentries should have been on those towers and on all the curtain walls. Brie paused, still almost expecting the castle to magically reform itself and for Aidan to step out of the gatehouse passageway, his eyes blazing with interest as he saw her.

"The guidebook said the mausoleum is beneath where the original chapel was," Sam murmured.

Brie wiped her eyes and marched ahead. She was feeling faint—she'd eaten about two bites on the plane and nothing all day. Sam followed as she went into what should have been the inner ward. The great hall should have been to her left; above it, Aidan's bedchamber, where they had so recently made love.

She would give just about anything to be in his arms one more time, she thought. She simply couldn't accept that she would never be with him again. All she had to do was figure out how to get back into the past.

She saw a wood door ahead—a part of the castle wall. Brie hesitated, uncertain if she could really go forward now. But she had to know. Grim, she strode across the rest of the bare ward, the ground rutted with dirt and mud. She began to hear voices of both men and women, all speaking Gaelic, the sounds becoming louder and more vivid. She heard horses whinnying, bridles jangling. Suddenly she smelled game roasting, and she felt the warmth that was always blazing from those massive hearths.

Brie inhaled. If she closed her eyes, would she be in Awe's stronghold when she opened them again? Would Aidan come walking through a hallway or a door with his incredible blue eyes trained upon her? Brie squeezed her eyes tightly closed.

"There's no law that says you have to do this."

Brie blinked. She was not back in medieval times; she had paused before the heavy, splintered wood door leading down into the tomb. "I have to see if it's really him."

Sam glanced at her and pushed it open. "Romantics first," she said softly.

Brie went down centuries-old, worn stone steps, into a small, low-ceilinged stone chamber with two electric lights on the walls. A chill hit her as she saw the stone tomb, set against the far wall. An effigy of a Highlander was carved into the stone atop it.

He lay in repose, hands crossed over his chest, wearing knee-high boots, a leine and a plaid, which was pinned over one shoulder, and a belt with two swords. From this distance, it was identical to the vision she'd had.

Brie stumbled forward, straining to see the effigy's face. She felt so much relief, because although the statue had a strong jaw, a straight nose and wavy hair, it was simply impossible to tell if it was Aidan or another big, striking man.

"Brie," Sam said harshly, tugging on her sleeve.

Brie glanced at her, not liking her expression, and followed her gaze.

The effigy wore a necklace with a wolf's fang.

THEY HAD BOOKED A ROOM in Oban at the Manor House, which was closer than Glasgow. Brie sat in the front parlor waiting for Sam to come down for dinner, trying to keep a grip on her composure. It was impossible.

Aidan had hanged, and that was his tomb, as everyone believed.

She covered her face with her hands. She had to go back in time, just to be with him, even if preventing his execution was hopeless. Maybe everyone was right, and his execution was Fate. Coming to Scotland had been a mistake. It hurt so much.

She dropped her hands, looking at her watch. Sam was showering and changing for dinner, obviously vamping up—she couldn't help herself. Brie didn't care what she herself wore or looked like. She'd stumbled out of the shower, reaching for whatever was in her overnight bag. She was in a pair of jeans, a T-shirt and sandals. She'd managed to change her contacts and brush her teeth. Maybe she should skip dinner, go to bed and cry.

Someone brushed her hand and she looked up, expecting to see Sam.

But no one stood there.

Perturbed, Brie stood. She could have sworn she'd been touched.

And then the air shimmered and shifted on the threshold of the parlor. Suddenly she thought she saw Ian, but it was barely a glimpse. Then the little boy was gone.

"Ian!" Brie gasped. "Come back!"

The reception desk was across the hall, and the pretty clerk there glanced her way.

Brie ran to the hall but Ian wasn't there. Had Ian's ghost found her in modern-day Oban? If so, why couldn't she still see him? What did his failure to materialize now mean? She'd been able to see him so clearly in the past, and even that day in the present when she'd been sedated on Five.

If Ian was reaching out to her, but he could not manage now, Brie was afraid it meant something terrible.

Brie stood in the corridor, trembling. She walked to the front door and glanced out the window, but the little ghost was not standing on the street.

Was she so upset and desperate that she had imagined seeing Ian?

"Please come back," she whispered. He had led her to Aidan once. Maybe he would do so again.

But it was a perfectly quiet afternoon, the air warm and still, and Brie did not feel him, or anything, present.

Breathing hard, Brie stepped outside. It was late afternoon in Scotland and about 10 a.m. New York time. Pedestrians were hurrying to-and-fro, leaving work, on their way home or to a pub. The street was bumper-to-bumper traffic, as well. Directly across the street was a small bookstore displaying the sign, Highland History Our Specialty.

She wasn't sure if she'd seen Ian or not, but if she had, she felt certain he was intent on sending her to the store. Or maybe that was her imagination, too. It didn't matter. Sam was taking her time, and if Highland History was the store's specialty, Brie would buy some books and ship them home. Maybe one day she'd find a historian who disputed the fact of Aidan's death.

Brie jaywalked carefully through the rush-hour traffic. Not a single Scot cursed her or honked their horn; in fact, everyone was excessively polite and waved her on. Brie walked into the bookstore, door chimes ringing. A pleasant woman behind the register smiled at her. "We close in ten minutes, dearie. Can I help you?"

"I just got into town," she said, "and I saw the sign in your window. I'm a history buff."

"You're American," the woman said in delight. "Welcome to the Highlands. I am Mrs. McKay. You must be touring our grand Highland castles. Have you been to Dunstaffnage yet?"

"We were at Loch Awe today."

"Kilchurn is splendid, is it not?"

"We were at Castle Awe," Brie said. "I'm doing research into one of your…" She paused, incapable of continuing. "We were at the tomb there."

"You must have seen the Wolf's tomb, then. I get shivers whenever I go there. What a grand Highlander, eh?"

Brie managed a grim smile.

"You'll want this, then, I think. It's out of print and the last copy we have." The woman went to a crowded bookcase and pulled out a thin pamphlet. "It was written in 1952 by an Oxford scholar." She handed the pamphlet to Brie.

Brie took one look at the title and felt faint. *"The Legacy of Castle Awe, the Wolf and the earls of Argyll."* She was in disbelief. "I'll buy it," she gasped.

The woman smiled, pleased. "He's very difficult to reach, but you should try to interview the Baron of Awe himself. No one knows the history of Castle Awe better than his lordship."

"The Baron of Awe?" Brie asked, chills sweeping through her.

"Aye. He's a descendant of the Wolf's, or so it's claimed. He has a fine home on the eastern shore of the loch, built in the eighteenth century. Of course, he's rarely in residence, as he much prefers city life. I believe he's in Barcelona, but I know he's expected back at any time." Mrs. McKay smiled at her.

Brie wasn't sure that speaking with one of Aidan's descendants would help anything, when the woman exclaimed, "Speak of the devil! There's his lordship now. He's one of our best customers, of course. In spite of his playboy ways, he is very well educated and an avid reader."

Brie felt so much white power that it took her breath away. The Baron of Awe was no ordinary man, she somehow thought, and she glanced out of the storefront window.

Her heart exploded. For one second, she thought it was Aidan stepping out of the black Mercedes convertible.

Her heart raced wildly.

But it wasn't Aidan. He could have been Aidan's twin, but she simply knew it wasn't him.

"Ah, well, all the women look at him that way. He's a handsome fellow, is he not?" She laughed. "I'll get him for you."

Brie couldn't breathe as the proprietress hurried to the front door. "My lord, good afternoon! I hadn't realized you were back in town."

Aidan's double turned and smiled, clad in a navy blue sports coat, a polo T-shirt and tan trousers. He was the epitome of power and old-world elegance, right down to his Cartier watch. "Hello, Mrs. McKay. How is business treatin' ye?" His dimples were identical to Aidan's.

"Very well, sir. Can you step in? I'd like you to meet an American tourist who is researching your family."

The baron glanced past the clerk and saw Brie. His

smile vanished. His blue eyes darkened, a perplexed expression crossing his features.

Brie wet her dry lips. Was this a great-great-great-grandson, perhaps?

"His lordship, Ian Maclean, Baron of Awe," Mrs. McKay said proudly. She stepped back to her register and began taking out the day's receipts.

Brie closed her eyes, becoming faint. This was a coincidence.

He steadied her. "A pleasure to meet ye," he said quietly.

She opened her eyes and looked into his blue ones, and felt a jolt of recognition. She thought of Ian, imploring her to comprehend him, his blue eyes bright, intense, in his small, childish face when she had seen him in Awe's great hall and in Aidan's tent. She breathed hard and whispered, "Ian? Is it you?"

His expression hardened. "Have we met?"

"I'm Brie. I think…I know your father."

The cold look on his face was identical to Aidan's when he was angry. "My father died long ago." He turned abruptly, stepping out of the store.

Brie ran after him, catching his sleeve. "Your father…the Wolf of Awe?" she managed, praying desperately.

His eyes blazed, and they were Aidan's. "Ah, now ye play a *dangerous* game! The Wolf was hanged centuries ago. The truth is right there in that pamphlet ye hold and in the tomb at Castle Awe."

Brie began shaking her head. Her heart was screaming at her that this was Aidan's son. Hadn't Ian begged to go home? Hadn't Tabby's guides told her he was alive? Hadn't Moray said so? She tried to think calmly and rationally—this was probably Aidan's great-great-great-grandson—but she said, "Take me back. We have to stop it. I won't let him hang!"

His eyes widened. He leaned close and said angrily, "Are ye mad?"

"I have to go back! He can't die. And don't tell me it's written!"

He caught her, eyes wide with disbelief, as she began to weep. "I remember ye now. I remember ye from all those years ago when I was a small child being held prisoner, tryin' to tell my father that I was alive so he could rescue me!"

She clung to strong, powerful arms. "Is it you? Ian?" She touched his face.

"But he never came, not for sixty-six endless years," Ian said harshly. *"He never came."*

CHAPTER EIGHTEEN

Urquhart, 1502

HE WAS CAREFUL TO STAY back in the crowd, for it was dangerous to step forth in his own corporeal identity, especially when he was expecting the Brotherhood to appear. A huge crowd had gathered for the Wolf's hanging, mostly Highlanders. He had held and attended hundreds of executions over the centuries. Even in this kind of death, there was so much pleasure and satisfaction to be had. And while hangings were his least favorite form of execution—so little pain was inflicted—the crowd that gathered to cheer and jeer was always festive and bloodthirsty. This crowd was oddly subdued, and he could not understand it. He needed their sadism; he relished it.

Centuries flashed before his eyes. There had been so much power, so much destruction, so much death. But this past century, one single son had defied him. He hated his son with a vengeance.

It was too soon for Aidan to die.

He hadn't suffered enough. Now his son wished for death, in order to protect the woman and find peace. He must change this day, use the woman as he'd intended. There would be little satisfaction in doing so if Aidan were not alive to know of it. He must never allow Aidan peace.

Thoughtful, Moray stared. Aidan had yet to be brought forth from the dungeons. When he appeared, he would be expecting death, but he would be stoic. There would not be any pleasure in those first few moments. His gaze sharpened. Frasier stood with some of his men by the scaffold, grim and severe, intent upon doing his duty. He was merely obeying his king. There was no pleasure to be had in feeling him, either. Then Moray saw the Masters approaching.

He saw Malcolm of Dunroch first—the Master whom he had almost turned, the Master who had almost vanquished him—and Malcolm was near tears.

Moray's anger vanished. His lust thickened. He instantly fed off his fear and grief, swelling with delight.

Then Moray saw the woman by his side, a warrior for whom he had once had great plans. She was pale and in tears, too, clinging to Malcolm's hand. He had considered having his revenge on Malcolm, but he was leery, because the woman made the Master eerily strong. Her power, while not as apparent, ran so deep that he feared it. More importantly, he feared their love.

Other Masters close to Aidan had come, as well. Black Royce and a small, beautiful woman with a shocking white power were with them. The golden Master was resigned and his grief was buried deep, making it far less pleasing, but the woman's helpless rage amused him. She thought to heal Aidan; she had no intention of letting him die. He had heard many stories about the Healer, and he would enjoy bringing her to her knees, too—but not today.

The crowd shifted and murmured. Excitement began.

Moray saw armed soldiers bringing Aidan toward the gallows, his hands manacled behind his back. He began to feel amused. Did Aidan really think to protect Brianna by dying for her? Little did he know his suffering was only just beginning.

Aidan was staring blindly ahead, looking at no one. Then he jerked and looked right at Moray, as if sensing his thoughts. Hatred blazed in his son's eyes.

Moray laughed at him. As Aidan was led up the stairs of the scaffold, Moray left the midward and hurried inside a tower chamber, bolting the door. He lay down on the small bed and willed his power to Frasier, so he could stop the hanging. He would do so only at the last possible moment, when Aidan was a breath away from death.

Nothing happened.

It was impossible. He tried again. *He had been blocked. Someone had shielded Frasier from his power.*

It was too soon for Aidan to die. He hadn't paid for his defiance!

Moray sent his energy into the closest passing human, a husky knight.

Outside, he heard the crowd roar.

"CLAIRE, I CANNA STAY AN' WATCH him die," Malcolm gasped. His heart had been broken since he'd left his brother in the dungeons yesterday, swearing not to intervene. His brother, whom he'd spent the first twenty-five years of his life hating and whom he'd then come to love. He'd spent almost seven decades clinging to faith and hope, refusing to believe the rumors about Aidan. And he knew, in this last hour, that he had been right.

Aidan wasn't evil. He was on his way back to the Brotherhood.

He had to stop this.

Claire clung to his hand. "The history books all say he dies, but I can't stand it, either. Malcolm, do something!"

"Aidan," Malcolm cried.

The noose was around his neck as he stood above the crowd on the scaffold, barefoot and clad only in his leine, shoulders squared, head held high. He had been looking far into the distance, above the crowd, but his blue gaze settled on Malcolm, bleak and worn. He smiled in resignation. *Thank ye fer yer faith.*

"Release me from my vows," Malcolm roared.

Aidan seemed to shake his head. *Take care o' Brianna. Guard her well. Let me go now. I'm done with war.*

Malcolm decided to hell with his vows. But before he could blast the rope into shreds, Royce seized his arm, blocking his power. "Let him go. He wishes to die."

"I canna!" Malcolm shouted at his uncle, well aware that his uncle understood this twist of irony far better than he ever would.

"He is tired o' his grief. He needs peace. Canna ye see it? Canna ye feel it?" Royce asked softly.

"He's my *brother.*"

"Aye, an' he has been grievin' fer his son fer too many years. Now he wishes to protect the woman he loves. He dies blessed, nay in shame or disgrace."

Suddenly Allie left them, and ran through the crowd to halt at Aidan's feet. Tears streaming down her face, she cried up to him, "Let us stop this. Let me heal you!"

"An' can ye save Brianna from Moray?" he asked her softly.

Allie started to weep.

Aidan dragged his gaze away

"Brie loves you...I love you!" Allie sobbed. "Don't do this!"

Soldiers seized her, dragging her back. "Another word and you will be arrested, Lady Morvern," Frasier snapped. "'Tis noon. Hang him."

Allie screamed, fighting the soldiers. Royce rushed to her side. He stepped between the men, taking his wife into his arms. Tabby and Guy Macleod materialized beside them. Those who noticed gasped and crossed themselves, but most eyes were on the man on the platform. The floor dropped. Without support, Aidan swung in the air by the noose around his neck, and finally a loud crack resounded.

Malcolm roared.

"Jesu," Guy whispered, holding his wife upright.

Aidan's head fell forward.

Allie collapsed in Royce's arms. "Let me heal him."

"Let him go, Ailios. Let him go."

A STUNNING FEELING, like a knife sliding deep into her heart, went through her. Brie paled, doubling over.

"Brianna?" Ian slid his arm around her.

She felt dizzy, faint. She blinked up at him. This was Aidan's son. Ian had not been murdered in 1436 after all. Aidan had to know. It might change everything. "What happened?" Brie whispered.

Having steadied her, he released her. He said tersely, "I was released after his execution in 1502. In fact, I later learned I was released that very day." He laughed without mirth. "I had just been returned to Elgin. Evil had no more use for me. It went on to other prey. Because of his black power, I was still nine years old, even though I had been imprisoned in New York City for most of the sixty-six years."

The extent of the abuse he'd suffered hit her. He had been imprisoned for decades *in New York City* and he had been nine years old the entire time. What child could withstand that kind of cruel abuse? "Oh, my god, we have to change this!"

"Ye can't change Fate," he snapped.

She searched his angry eyes. "How did you survive?"

"I spent almost every moment of every day thinking of my father, praying for him to come. I also tried to escape. Every day I had a new plot to trick the guards, and as often, I was beaten soundly for my efforts."

She hugged herself. His suffering had known no bounds. She did not want Aidan to ever know. "What happened after you were released? Malcolm and Royce must have taken you in."

He laughed derisively again. "I made my way home from Elgin myself, on foot mostly. It took me two months, as it was a cold, snowy winter and I was no longer accustomed to the Highlands. In truth, I was neither a modern lad nor a medieval one. And I wasn't nine years old when I reached Awe, Brianna."

"Are you saying that once Moray's spell was broken, you began to age?"

"I was a full-grown man when I reached Awe—only to find it in the hands of Argyll." He nodded at the pamphlet she held, eyes flashing. "There's mention there o' how Argyll seized the opportunity. With my father hanged, he simply marched on Awe and added it to his Campbell holdings. I spent the next fifty years warrin' with him, until I got it back," he added harshly. "It's been mine ever since."

Brie reached for his hand, but he wouldn't let her hold it. "I am sorry. You should know that your father is living with the pain of having lost you and it has been killing him."

"My father is *dead.*"

This time, she seized his sleeve. "He isn't dead. I just left him, very much alive—and grief-stricken over you, Ian. We have to go back in time! What if we can stop his execution?"

"Ye canna fix what is meant to be." His eyes blazed. "Ye love him." It was not a question. "Ye loved him then, an' it must be why ye received my thoughts when I was tryin' so hard to send them to him."

"Yes, I love him. Are you a Master?"

His gaze flickered. "Ye ken a great many secret matters, Brianna."

"I guess I just got my answer." She took his hand. "I'm ready. I'd prefer you hold me really tightly, because I do not want to get lost in space and time."

"He's dead. I have spent my entire life living in the shadow of the legend—and truth—of the Wolf's hangin'. Ye can't change Fate." He jerked free. "I willna try."

"Do you hate your father? Is that why you won't take me back to save him?" she cried furiously.

"What father fails his son?" Ian's eyes flashed.

Brie felt raw despair. "He loves you so much."

Ian made a harsh sound. "I wouldn't know."

"Brie!" Sam shouted from across the street, waving madly at her.

Brie was glad for the interruption. She had never

dreamed, not in a million years, that she'd find Ian this way—a bitter, dark and modern man. Brie saw Sam in her high heels and a slinky jersey dress, hurrying across the street. Every single male pedestrian turned to look at her, and a sedan passing on the street in front of Brie rear-ended a hatchback as its driver rubber-necked her. Ian turned to see what the commotion was about. He stared, his gaze narrowing.

Brie watched Sam weave through the cars. She had stopped all the traffic on the busy thoroughfare.

"Tabby called," Sam said, her smile faltering as she glanced at Ian. "Okay. He's not Aidan, is he? What did I interrupt?"

Brie breathed hard. "Sam, this is Ian—Aidan's son."

Sam was as sharp as they came and she didn't blink. Her gaze had locked with Ian's. "If you can't convince him to take you back, you can give me a shot." But she wasn't smiling, not at all. "Tabby has not found the spell, Brie."

Ian's mouth curved, just barely, and it was a moment before his gaze moved to Brie. "No one can change the past."

Before Brie could respond, Sam said, "Not true. Sometimes mistakes are made. Sometimes Fate is denied, defied—interrupted. And then it can be restored. We happen to know firsthand, because our friend Allie went back in time to change the future, and succeeded."

"Please, Ian," Brie said. "Your father needs you. Take me to Urquhart—take me to the day they hang him in 1502!"

Ian looked back and forth between them. "Fine," he said, looking damned unhappy about it.

"Wait—I'm coming, too!" Sam cried.

But Ian swept Brie close, ignoring Sam, and as they were flung across the slowly moving traffic and whirled upward, she screamed.

BRIE GASPED FROM THE IMPACT of landing, her face against Ian's chest, still in his powerful arms. She was dizzy from the leap and the landing, but she knew she must get up.

Ian said tersely, in horror. *"My God."*

Brie pulled away from him, onto her knees, and she saw Aidan.

He was twirling in the breeze. *He was dead.* The castle walls were behind him, the ground was snow-covered and a crowd had gathered. It was exactly as he had been hanged in her vision.

She staggered frantically to her feet, vaguely aware of Ian's help. "Aidan!" she screamed in horror. She saw that his neck was broken, for his head fell at a grotesque angle. They had arrived too late? Disbelief came. "Aidan, come back to me!" She ran forward and Ian let her go. She loved him too much. This could not, would not, happen. To hell with destiny and the gods! She resolved then and there *never* to let him go. They could go back in time again!

"This is not written," she screamed up at his body, standing below him, the top of her head inches from his bare feet. "We will rewrite this!"

His body seemed to shudder.

She seized his feet to stop him from swinging. "Come back to me, don't leave me. Come back to our future," she begged.

And a visible tremor went through his body. His chest

rose—and fell. Brie stared up at his downturned face and saw his lashes flickering. "Allie!" she screamed.

Brianna.

Brie knew it wasn't telepathy, for she saw his mouth moving. He was coming back from the dead because he was choosing to live.

And she saw Allie's white light raining down on him. As it did, Malcolm, Guy and Royce leapt onto the scaffold, one of them cutting the rope, the other men taking Aidan's body into their arms. A moment later he was laid out on the ground, and Allie was kneeling over him, healing him intently. His lashes moved and lifted, and Brie met his direct blue gaze.

His eyes began to shimmer with relief and love. "Brianna."

She clasped his face, bent over him and kissed him. "You've come back to me," she whispered. Their gazes met and locked.

He sat up, pulling Brie close against his side. Not looking away from her, he said, "Tell Frasier my men will war for the king."

"I'll tell him," Royce said, striding away.

"Do ye ever listen to anyone?" he asked softly.

"I will never forgive Nick for taking me away from you when you needed me the most," she said, seizing his hand. "Why did you choose to die?"

"To protect ye from my father," he said softly. He lifted her chin and feathered her mouth with his. "But Brianna, I felt yer love. And even dead, even with the gods comin', I realized I dinna wish to die. I want to live—I want to live with ye, Brianna."

Tears welled. She stroked his beautiful jaw. "That's a damn good thing, because on top of everything else, there's someone you must meet," she said, and she glanced up.

Ian Maclean was staring at them, his face hard and tight.

Aidan followed her gaze. His eyes widened and he paled. Slowly he stood, in disbelief. "Ian?"

Ian didn't move a muscle, his face filled with tension. "If ye dinna hang—if we rewrite Fate this day—ye need to rescue me. I'm at Elgin," he said, and he vanished in time.

"Ian!" Brie screamed.

Aidan looked at her, incredulous. "Ye found him in the future?"

Brie nodded. She was about to explain everything when she felt Moray's black power. She cried out in warning, but Aidan had whirled.

He was coming fast and furiously. There was no time to scream again. A huge, armor-clad giant rushed them, blazing energy at them, roaring in rage. "Aye, Ian lives! But ye' won't ever see him again!" the knight shouted furiously.

Brie gasped as the force struck her and Aidan, sending her tumbling away from the gallows across the clearing, and into one of Urquhart's walls.

She grunted from the terrible impact of being hurled against stone, but it wasn't as bad as that day on the battlefield, because he had flung his energy at Aidan, catching her only peripherally.

Men roared and swords clashed and rang, louder than she had ever heard them.

Terrified for Aidan, certain that this was the final moment of truth, Brie felt hands on her. Allie's powerful white healing light seeped through her body as she tried to sit. When she could finally do so, she saw Aidan.

He and the giant, who was now Moray, had hewn their swords at one another, the blades blazing with their power, the men in halos. Aidan was cloaked in shining silver, while Moray was clouded in a dark gray light. Damn it, it looked as if they were evenly matched—but Aidan was struggling.

Royce, Malcolm and Guy could not help him, for they were battling dozens of possessed knights.

Tabby knelt beside them and began chanting, her expression instantly becoming waxen as she entered a trance.

For one more moment, Brie did not move. Her gaze was glued to Aidan, and he seemed to slowly be getting the better of the giant. She was acutely aware that Tabby was using the spell she had found to trap Moray's black power so it could not return to his body, wherever it was. She did not want to leave Aidan, but she seized Allie's hand, finally tearing her gaze away from him. "Do you have a weapon?"

Allie nodded. "Of course." She pulled a dagger from her designer boots.

It was so sexy and so *Allie* that, had the circumstances not been dire, she would have laughed. "He's close by, in repose, in a small chamber," Brie said. But Urquhart was a medium-size garrison, with many small rooms. He could be in any one of them.

"Let's go," Allie said, taking her hand.

They ran, leaving Aidan and the other Masters behind, their swords still shrieking eerily with white and black power. Brie and Allie rushed through the first gatehouse, back into the inner ward. They paused, breathing hard, trying to sense where Moray had left his body. Brie cursed in frustration. "How can we find him? Without his evil, there's nothing to sense!"

"I guess we'll do it the good, old-fashioned way," Allie, said, nodding at the closest tower. "A room-by-room search."

And, as Allie started aggressively toward that square tower, Brie suddenly felt a push on her shoulder from behind, directing her to a flanking tower on the opposite side of the gatehouse. It wasn't Allie, who'd left her behind.

Grandma Sarah seemed to give her a hard nod, too.

"Allie!" Brie screamed, rushing toward the tower.

She ran to a narrow door set in the side of the tower as Allie caught up to her. The moment she tried to open it, she realized it was bolted from inside. "Shit," she cried.

Claire ran through the gatehouse, breathing hard, her clothes splattered with blood, a large sword in hand. "Is he in there?" she asked breathlessly, looking exactly as a mythological, avenging Valkyrie might.

Brie nodded and stepped back.

Claire dropped the sword. She grimaced and ran at the door as if it were a punching bag and she was in a kick-boxing match at a gym. The wood groaned but the door did not open. Claire kicked it again, grunting.

Silver blazed, and the door blew in off its hinges.

Brie turned and saw Aidan striding forward, a bloody sword in hand, his expression ruthless. She cringed, incapable of moving. She had never seen him at his medieval worst, and she was seeing his most savage side now.

Then she felt the huge black power coming after them. Brie glanced up and saw the black cloud swirling like a small cyclone from above the gatehouse, into the ward, toward him from behind. "Aidan!"

He saw it and snarled, "Come an' fight me, *Father.*"

Laughter sounded.

Brie glanced into the chamber. Moray lay on the bed, apparently catatonic, exactly as she'd seen him in her vision.

The black energy swirled directly past Aidan into the chamber and to the man lying there.

But it bounced off his body hovering in the air.

A roar of frustration sounded.

"Tabby's spell is working," Brie breathed.

Aidan smiled savagely. "What's amiss, *Father?* Canna ye enter yer own form?"

"Aidan, watch out!" Brie screamed as the black power descended onto him.

But his silver energy blazed, deflecting it. He stepped toward Moray's body, sword raised. Brie turned away and heard the thump of his blade.

A howl of outrage sounded.

Brie tensed as the blade thumped again.

And then the cry suddenly ceased. The chamber was utterly silent except for Aidan's harsh, heavy breathing. Brie didn't dare look inside but she felt the darkness weakening. She looked up. Black, it spun upward into the gray sky, twisting and dwindling, becoming smaller and smaller, vanishing near the pale sun.

She heard the chamber door close. A bloody sword landed on the ground. She turned, trembling, her knees buckling, and Aidan pulled her close.

She went still, her cheek against his chest, his heart thundering there. He held her, hard and tight. It was over.

HE LANDED INSIDE ELGIN'S INNER ward, so determined to find his son that he did not even fall, for he refused to succumb to any pain or weakness now. The black walls of the ward swirled in his vision, and it was a moment before he steadied. He glanced around. Elgin had been in the hands of the chief of the Dunbar clan for several years, although it remained an impressive seat in the earldom of Moray. The current earl bore no relation to Aidan's vanquished, demonic father.

He seized a passing lad of twelve years old, who was leading a cow and her calf to the outer bailey. "I am looking for a boy with dark hair and blue eyes, a bit younger than you. He is prisoner here. He might be in a tower, or even in the dungeons."

The freckled lad blinked and looked away. "I dinna ken."

Aidan lurked. The lad lied. No one was allowed to admit that a boy was being held prisoner in the west tower on its highest floor—if he was really there. Apparently no one had seen him, not really. He had arrived unnoticed, as if on wings.

Aidan released the lad and ran across the ward to the tower. He flung the door open and rushed up its spiral staircase. As he ran up the twisting stairs, he felt the black power above—and he felt his son's thoughts.

I'm on the top floor, Father.

It was Ian. His boy was truly alive!

He reached the landing, blasting the armed guard

there, who crumbled to the floor. "Ian!" he cried, throwing the bolts aside. He flung open the door.

Ian stood there looking exactly as he had that long-ago day when Moray had murdered him, except for the fact that he was wearing modern clothes—a T-shirt, jeans and sneakers. "Father!"

Relief flooded Aidan. Tears streamed, and he rushed to his son. He knelt and wrapped Ian in his arms, barely believing that he held his son, at last. "Are ye hurt?" He didn't dare release him—he was afraid to. Even as he held his small, thin body, he thought of the grown man he had just encountered.

Suddenly Ian pushed away. "I am fine," he said firmly.

Aidan started, having the oddest feeling that he was looking into a boy's eyes and a man's soul. "Let's go home, son."

Ian nodded, his gaze dark and somber now, when a huge presence began to fill the room.

Aidan went still.

The chamber was flooded with white-gold, shimmering light, which rose up around them, flooding the entire room.

The majesty and splendor of absolute justice and power, the nearness of eternity, overcame Aidan. All was right, he somehow thought, dropping to his knees. He bowed his head. He had never felt more humble.

There was no form. Aidan wasn't even sure there was a voice.

"Do you still wish to fight me?"

"Nay," Aidan gasped, stunned. The father of all gods, the greatest god of all, had come to him.

"Your test was designed by the lesser gods, who can be so foolish. But I designed your Fate."

Aidan didn't move, eyes closed, tears falling.

"You recovered your son. Others are not so fortunate, and evil preys on the children in every time, in every place. You will protect them."

Of course he would.

"I leave this memory with you because it will serve you well now. Never forget this day and the days before it."

Aidan slowly looked up.

The god had a form now.

Aidan trembled.

"You are my chosen people," the greatest of gods said softly. "And I have chosen you."

BRIE WALKED INTO AIDAN'S bedchamber at Awe. She'd leapt back with Royce and Allie shortly after Moray's destruction. Aidan had gone to find Ian. Royce had spoken with Frasier, who agreed to take Aidan's offer to King James and recommend that the king accept it. Royce said Frasier was a devout, honest and fair man. He thought a bargain could be arranged; Aidan had a great army to offer the king. This was the least of Brie's worries.

God, MacNeil's cryptic words made so much sense now.

Aidan had chosen to die, but then her love had made him choose to live. And they wouldn't have been able to change his execution if it hadn't been one big, fat mistake to begin with. Brie didn't know how his true Fate had gotten messed up, but if there was an explanation, she'd figure it out. She went to the window and stared out at Loch Awe.

It was a beautiful, sunny winter day, with the snow

coating the shore and hanging thick on the pine trees, the loch gleaming sapphire blue, the mountains capped silver-white against the blue sky. From where she stood she could see the bridge that led to that shore—and it was intact.

She trembled. Aidan had chosen to live, and by now, or shortly, he would be reunited with his son. She did not want to ever visit Loch Awe again and see Castle Awe in ruins.

Brie walked over to the fireplace, where a servant had a huge blaze roaring. She was uncertain. Just where did she fit in, now that she'd saved Aidan's life and redeemed his soul?

He was starting over. He had a new journey to make. Brie knew he'd rejoin the Brotherhood. But Ian had suffered terribly, and father and son were reuniting after a tragically long time. She wanted to stay and help them recover their relationship. It wasn't going to be easy, because Ian was probably going to turn into a grown man in a few days, weeks or months.

She didn't blame Ian for his enmity. Like Aidan, he could and would heal, wouldn't he? She shivered. Someone else would have to take on Ian if he remained as dark and bitter in the past as he'd been in the future. It had been her destiny to heal Aidan.

Brie flushed. Healing Aidan was only a part of why she wanted to stay. She wanted to stay because she loved him so much that it hurt.

She inhaled. He hadn't asked her to stay. Even if he did, she should be sensible and go home. He cared for her—she was certain—but for how long? She had to face that it was going to hurt even more when he one day decided to pursue a really beautiful woman. They'd shared so much, but…

She didn't finish her thought. She felt unbearably saddened when she should have been thrilled.

And then she felt so much hot, blazing male desire and power that she whirled. *Aidan.*

Aidan stood in the doorway, his eyes bright and bold with interest. He still wanted her. Her desire spun, joining his.

"Did you find him?" she whispered. It was hard to speak, because she knew exactly what he had on his mind. He had come to take her to bed and she couldn't wait to be in his powerful embrace. She'd worry about going home in the morning.

For one moment, he simply stared at her, and then she saw his hands move to his sword belt. He unbuckled it as he entered the chamber, leine bulging, laying the swords and belt carefully upon the chest.

Brie took a breath. Her body had fired, everywhere, but her heart wept. She had never thought anyone could be so happy and so sad at once.

"Aye, lass, I found him." He gave her a solemn look.

Brie knew what the sober glance meant. "Is he okay?" she managed carefully.

"He's well enough, considerin' he's been imprisoned for sixty-six years," Aidan said grimly. "He's home now. He's scarred, but he'll mend." He tossed his black plaid on the room's single chair and proceeded to pull off his boots, one by one.

He wasn't hiding his desire from her, but Brie couldn't quite feel the rest of his emotions. He had to be overjoyed—either that, or he was consumed with worry. "Was he happy to see you?"

Aidan met her gaze, about to strip off his leine. "At first." His gaze darkened. "He's been through hell. He blames me. I dinna blame him. I'll always blame myself."

"Don't," Brie begged. "Do not blame yourself. He has a lot to work through. We'll help. Others will help. He has his Fate, too."

"Aye, he has his Fate. I dinna ken what Fate it is."

"What?" Brie gasped.

He hesitated. "Evil preys on the children most of all."

"It's terrible, Aidan, but sometimes it does seem that way."

He smiled slightly at her and tore the tunic over his head. "Will ye help me protect them?"

He was hugely aroused, a mass of bulging muscle. With that face of an Adonis, no man could be more perfect. "You are so beautiful," she whispered. Love made her heart surge, her knees weaken. "It's sort of hard to have a rational conversation now."

His smile flashed. "I need to make love to you, Brianna," he said. He started toward her. "Will ye help me save the children?"

"What does that mean?" He was making it sound like a partnership.

Amusement sparkled briefly in his eyes as he took her in his arms. "I have a really beautiful woman, Brianna Rose. Beautiful an' brave an' very, very clever."

Brie held on to his massive shoulders. "Please don't say anything you might regret tomorrow," she whispered.

He cradled her face. "When will ye realize I love ye deeply?"

She drew in a breath.

"Ye saved my life," he said softly. "Ye gave me back

my son. Ye gave me back my heart. I have hope, and joy." He smiled at her. "I love ye, Brianna. My heart *sings.*"

Brie inhaled again, shaking her head. "You're grateful and you care. It's okay. I never expected love." She touched his beautiful face. "Gratitude and desire aren't love. I don't expect anything, really, not long-term."

"Ye are the most stubborn woman—an' that can be annoyin!" he exclaimed. "I dinna wish fer anyone else. I dinna need a *supermodel.* I need a small, stubborn woman by my side, in my heart and in my bed! I asked ye if ye'd help me protect the children. Willna ye answer?"

"Of course I'll help," she managed. *What did he mean?*

He grinned. "What if I teach ye how to lurk in my mind?"

She stared, motionless, except for her heart, which thundered. "Deal," she whispered.

He dropped the shield guarding his emotions.

His love struck her with the force of an energy blast, but he held her waist, preventing her from reeling backward. Brie cried out, his love for her flooding her, stunning her. She met his mischievous eyes, shocked.

His grasp on her waist tightened. "Will ye swoon?"

How could he love her so much? she somehow wondered. She was whirling in the tidal wave of his powerful feelings. "I might!"

"But I haven't even begun to tease ye yet," he said, and he abruptly jerked on the waistband of her jeans, opening the snap. Brie was instantly, acutely aware of his knuckles pressed into her lower belly, close to the elastic of her bikini underwear. Then his smile vanished. "Listen," he said softly.

Brie searched his gaze.

"Nay, I said *listen.*"

Brie stared into his eyes and he stared back.

I love ye so much. I need ye, Brianna, to sleep with every night an' wake up with every morning. I canna let ye go home, not now, not ever. If I take ye as my wife, to love an' to cherish, until death parts us, will ye stay here with me? I will try to make ye happy, lass....

Brie was stunned. "You want to *marry* me?" she cried. She had never imagined Aidan marrying anyone, ever.

He lifted her into his arms and laid her on the bed, sitting beside her. "Lass, I more than love ye. If ye refuse, I'll marry ye, anyway, usin' my powers of enchantment." His smile faded and his gaze became searching.

Brie somehow nodded. She was going to cry, she thought helplessly, in joy and happiness.

"I may have begun to love ye the day we first met, when I was with Lady Allie." He touched her hair. "Ye were so pretty an' so shy, but I could sense your kindness, Brianna, an' something else…I dinna ken. Ye made me pause."

Brie stroked his rough jaw. "We didn't even speak to one another."

He shrugged. "I dinna have to speak with ye to hear ye well."

Of course he didn't. He was her destiny, and she was his. He'd heard her across centuries—and she'd heard him across time, too.

Her soul mate was a medieval Highlander—with a fondness for Gucci.

"Yes, Aidan, I will marry you."

He grinned, clearly pleased and just a bit smug. He pressed her down onto the bed. "Can we finish this conversation later? I have a great an' pressin' need."

"No kidding," Brie whispered. And a moment later, there was no conversation at all. Brie gave herself over to him—and to their god-given destiny.

* * * * *

She is a schoolteacher by day,
who uses her magic at night to help others.
He is a savage medieval Highlander
whose life is bloody war and mortal revenge.

Turn the page to read an excerpt from
DARK VICTORY
March 2009
Book Two of THE ROSE TRILOGY
Every Rose Woman Has Her Destiny

"SHOW ME WHERE TO BATHE."

They could argue about the intention of the subdemons all day and all night, and never figure it out, she thought. He was clearly determined to stay and protect her...and the police were after him. "All right. You win. But I'll bet you always win—don't you?"

His expression never changed.

Tabby clenched her fists. "You can stay, but only for one night—and you sleep there, on the sofa." She pointed, her hand trembling. "And you will sleep there *alone*."

He murmured, "Then stop thinkin' about me without my clothes."

Tabby didn't reply, because she couldn't think of a suitable response. She marched to the linen closet and returned, placing a pile of towels in his arms. Her mind skidded back and forth between his theory that she was a target and the shower he was about to take. The night promised to be endless. "The bathroom is down the hall."

He walked away and Tabby felt her body explode. It was inexplicable. She prided herself on her intellect. A PhD turned her on more than a six-pack ever could. Her friends had crushes on actors like Brad Pitt and Colin Farrell; she had crushes on intellectuals like

Tony Blair and Tony Snow. She'd rather spend an evening at an exhibit like the Wisdom of the Celts, discussing the various artifacts, than in bed with a boyfriend, pretending to be something she was not.

But this man made her nervous and upset. This man made her shout. Worse, he made her body come alive in ways it never had—in ways she didn't even want to recognize. Medieval or not, Macleod was a walking advertisement for sex. Maybe all women went nuts around him. That was probably it.

Walking into the kitchen, Tabby opened the refrigerator, then closed it. How on earth would he know how to turn on the water faucets or even adjust the water temperature?

What was he doing in there?

She groaned. *Had he taken off his clothes?*

She strained to listen, but did not hear the sound of the shower. All those new pulse points were firing up. She must not go back there to help him!

Her heart was thundering so hard now, she thought it might come out of her breast. Tabby realized she was already halfway to the bathroom. She gave up, suddenly incapable of self-control. But she was only going to help him. She repeated those instructions to herself.

The bathroom door was wide open.

Tabby halted. He stood inside, still fully dressed… and she was incredibly disappointed. His back to her, he was regarding his reflection in the mirror over the sink. Their eyes met in the mirror.

His gaze was lazy and indolent, sensual and hot, promising all kinds of unearthly delight.

She managed, "I came to turn the water on—not for anything else."

From the corner of her eyes she saw his hands moving. He was unpinning the plaid he wore. He smiled knowingly.

She knew she should back away—no, *run* away. No decent woman would stand there while he undressed. She did not move.

The plaid fell from his huge shoulders. He folded it and placed it besides the swords he'd laid on the vanity before she'd gotten there. His hands moved to the heavy leather belt he wore, over the tunic. Tabby couldn't look up. Her eyes were riveted to the reflection of his strong, scarred hands. Heat suffused every inch of her face and body. Beneath his hands, his skirt was tented.... She couldn't really breathe.

He made a soft sound and the leather belt joined the plaid and swords on her vanity.

She stared at the items, then at him. A huge silence fell. Tabby knew it was time to leave. *Now.*

"I never drag women to my bed. They come gladly."

Of course they did.

She lifted her gaze. His eyes were so dark with desire, they were the color of a Highland night sky—purple and black. He slowly turned to face her.

She breathed hard, refusing to take another look at the tented tunic. Her tension had spiraled to an impossible level. She could hardly think.

Why did she have to be so aware of him?

"Men like me because I'm elegant," Tabby said harshly. "I am not elegant now. I just don't get it—this."

His stare intensified. "In my bed, ye willna have to be someone yer not."

She inhaled. She had the awful feeling he might be right. "I'm really not into sex."

He smiled, as if he knew something she did not.

"I'm really hard to please."

"I dinna think so," he said softly, and reached for the V neckline of the tunic.

Tabby's gaze slammed to his hands and her heart stopped. The tunic vanished over his head and fell to the floor.

She looked at his huge, sculpted chest and taut abs—and the hollow below—and went still.

"Do ye still wish to leave?" he murmured.

He was the sexiest man alive—ever.

Maybe he was right. Maybe she wouldn't have to pretend to be the kind of woman she was supposed to be when in bed. Maybe she wouldn't have to fake it to please her partner. Maybe her hormones would take over and she'd have a good time.

She finally looked up. She meant to look into his eyes, but he was reflected in the bathroom's many mirrors. His beautiful face and powerful body were *everywhere*.

She had never felt this way. Her body was a mass of swollen, hurting flesh. She wanted him—but she didn't love him and she never would. She wasn't a liberated woman. If she gave in, it would be the most sordid act of her life. In the morning she would hate herself.

"I dinna think so," he murmured. "In the morn ye'll be verra pleased."

He was reading her mind. "Don't," Tabby whispered, but she had the awful feeling that he might be right.

He suddenly reached out, took her hand and reeled her in.

HQN™
We are romance™
Danger ensues at Draycott Abbey...
CHRISTINA SKYE
NEW YORK TIMES BESTSELLING AUTHOR
CHRISTINA
SKYE
TO CATCH
A THIEF
The last thing rugged navy SEAL Dakota Smith needs on his mission is a tempting woman he doesn't trust. But Nell MacInnes can spot a forgery a mile away, and with a sketch by Leonardo da Vinci missing and a ruthless criminal on the loose, she's the best Dakota's got...even if her family ties to the criminal world aren't as dead as she says they are.
To Catch a Thief
Don't miss this gripping new Draycott Abbey tale!
Available September 2008!
www.HQNBooks.com

PHCS307

HQN™
We are romance™
New York Times bestselling author
SUSAN KRINARD
SUSAN KRINARD
Come the Night
The Great War has ended and Gillian Maitland must marry a pureblood werewolf of her father's choosing–despite the forbidden passion she desires with part-werewolf Ross Kavanaugh. When Ross becomes a murder suspect, Gillian knows she must push him away before the growing hunger they have for each other consumes them both….
Come the Night
In stores October 2008!
www.HQNBooks.com

PHSK315

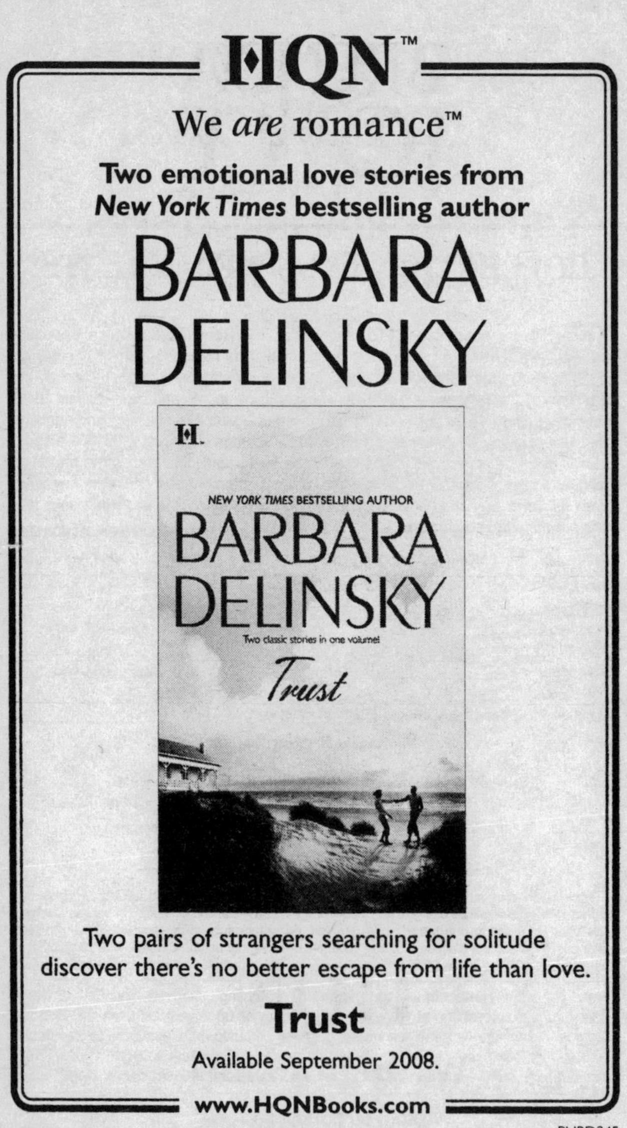
HQN™
We *are* romance™
Two emotional love stories from
New York Times bestselling author
BARBARA
DELINSKY
NEW YORK TIMES BESTSELLING AUTHOR
BARBARA
DELINSKY
Two classic stories in one volume!
Trust
Two pairs of strangers searching for solitude
discover there's no better escape from life than love.
Trust
Available September 2008.
www.HQNBooks.com
PHBD345